Revealed Courage

A Journey Forged Through Fire

Eve M. Harrell

To all the readers who have honored me with their stories.

This one is for you.

The Lord is with you, mighty warrior.

Table of Contents

Prologue

September 1
Wild Rock, Tennessee

Sweat oozed from every pore of her body while a stray hair mercilessly tickled her nose. Maddie stood perfectly still, hoping her body would not embarrass her. *Where is Rachel?* Her eyes darted around the room, looking for her friend. She would know just what to say to this crazy mob.

An uncomfortable silence cut through the chaos, and all eyes turned to her as she let out a loud sneeze.

The maniacal laugh sent a chill down her spine.

"Well, well, Ms. Bennett, looks like the cat released your tongue. The question is, will your Jesus save you now?"

Jolted awake, Maddie looked around the room, sighing with relief as she realized it was all a dream… *But it felt so real.*

A knock on the door broke into her musings.

"Hey, Sis, it's time for breakfast."

A haunted silence followed her brother's declaration leaving Maddie time to ruminate on her dream.

Sun filtered into the room like a beam as she stood and stretched. Thankfully, that was one thing that didn't change— that and Ms. Carolina Wren. After arriving in Wild Rock, the bird visited her every day.

Another good stretch later, she stood before her mirror, her brown eyes focused on one of the things that had changed. Bristling at the gaunt features staring back at her, she placed her hand on her face and traced the line from her cheekbone to her jaw. *Will my life ever be normal again?*

If everything had not turned upside down, she would be visiting colleges in her junior year. Her best friend, Rachel would be a senior planning to leave her fam, and Kate would be alive. Instead, five months after the fire had leveled their community, she was in Wild Rock, walking the halls of a much smaller school, completely devoid of cell phones and social media. Pulling her hair up into a bun, she realized how isolated she had become. *We've all lost a lot,* she thought as she tried to form a smile.

"MADDDIIIIIEEEEE! Grammy said we can't eat until you come to the table!" Matthew yelled from the other side of the door.

"Coming!" She yelled back.

The struggle was real. Fear no longer held her captive, yet anxious thoughts lingered. *Think thoughts that are true; think thoughts that are pure.* The reminder turned over and over in her mind as she tucked a few rebellious locks of hair away. "Yes, God, it is true that life has changed, but you are with me," she said aloud. Looking up, she smiled at the ceiling, picturing Jesus in her mind as she opened the door.

Her mom's anxious tone echoed down the hallway as she went to the kitchen.

"I don't know, David. Are you sure this is a good idea?"

"I trust Mordy, Jacque. Besides, I must finish what I started."

Maddie's ears perked up as she overheard her parents' conversation. After grabbing a plate of eggs and bacon, she sat at the table. *What does he mean by "finish what he started?"* She wondered. As she listened to the heated conversation, she couldn't help but see her mom's reflection in her little brother. The older he got, the more he looked like her—red hair, green eyes, and a passionate heart that loved fiercely. Matthew's deep loyalty reflected their dad's. *The perfect combination,* she thought as he interjected himself into the conversation.

"Dad, does that mean you have to go back to Israel?" Matthew asked defiantly.

Hearing the worry in his son's voice, David's warm brown eyes showed concern, "Yes, Son, but you guys will be safe here."

Sticking her fork under the eggs on her plate, she decided now was a good time to tell her dad what she thought about his announcement. She sat up straight and, with resolute authority, declared, "Dad, we need you here." The confidence in her voice masked the uncertainty of her heart.

Placing his hand on his daughter's, David said, "Ruthie, you'll be okay, I promise. You're surrounded by family and friends who'll keep you safe." His subtle use of her favorite nickname was a slick move. Not to be deterred, she opened her mouth only to be interrupted.

"But I thought we were going to build a shed?"

Maddie's mom, Jacque, patted her son's head in sympathy as she asked, "Is Tom going with you?" Tom was Maddie's best friend's dad. He, his wife Olivia, and their daughters, Rachel, and Hannah, joined them with Maddie's friends Jade and Emma when they moved to Wild Rock after the Atlanta fires. The move had been quite an adjustment for everyone, but they were beginning to settle in.

"Yes. Olivia and the girls are all moved into the cabin. I'll get you guys started, Matthew, and your brother will manage the final barn raising. I expect your Grammy will call in plenty of people from the town to fill in the gaps." David grinned in appreciation at his mom, "Thank you for setting that up for them."

"It was ma pleasure. It's been quite a thang gettin' ever'body situated." Grammy answered.

"I forgot how resourceful Wild Rock can be," David said.

"Community, ma, Boy. We stick together."

David nodded in agreement. "Well, if there is any time that the community is needed, it's now."

CHAPTER 1

A Blessed Companion

Dirt kicked up behind Maddie as she jogged to Rachel's house. Frustration motivated her gait as long brown hair whipped around her face. Stopping to sweep it into a ponytail, she was immediately distracted by the deep green canopy above her. Cicadas and running water created a symphony of sound that soothed her anxious heart.

Continuing the trek to her friend's house, the moment of peace was gone as she ruminated over the conversation at breakfast. *I thought everything in Washington was over. What does Dad need to finish?* She couldn't wait to run it by Rachel.

A bend in the road revealed a green roof covering a bright, cheery porch. As she ran up the steps, Maddie admired the flowery pillows that brightened the dark brown logs. Ms. Olivia had such a way of creating a comfortable space where you just wanted to sit all day. Before she could knock, the door swung open. She smiled as she was greeted by one of her favorite humans, covered in splotches of yellow.

"Hello, Beautiful!" Noticing the direction of her gaze, Rachel touched her blonde curls and laughed as she felt the trail of wet paint left behind. "Painting the bedroom," she explained.

Grabbing her hand, Maddie pulled Rachel outside. "We have to talk," she said, replacing her smile with a more serious look.

"Whoa. That was a shift. Hang on and let me tell my mom where I'm going first."

Maddie sighed impatiently as she leaned over the railing and waited for her friend.

Closing the door, Rachel asked, "What's up?"

The serious expression on her friend's face provided the answer she sought before she even needed to ask. "Did you know?"

"Know what?" Rachel countered.

"Our dads are going to Israel."

"Oh yeah, I heard something about that," Rachel said as she walked ahead of her friend.

"So, what's going on?" Maddie asked as she tried to catch up to her friend. "Is there something that you're keeping from me?"

Rachel stopped in the middle of the gravel road. "Look up."

Stopping short of her friend, she followed her gaze to look at the lush green canopy above them. Once again, creation served to calm her anxious heart.

"What do you see?" A look of peace came over Rachel as she smiled, awaiting an answer.

Maddie sighed at her friend's predictable question, "God's hand."

Turning to look at her friend, Rachel grabbed her hands and looked her in the eye. "Do you trust him?"

As she considered her answer, her friend gasped. A flash of movement caught them both off guard, stopping them in their tracks.

A doe stood in the clearing; her eyes fixed on the humans in her path. The trusting gaze of two fawns standing behind their mom was a gentle reminder of God's hand. The doe looked at them as if to ask, "Are you dangerous?" After which, she turned and ran off in the opposite direction with the fawns close behind.

Maddie giggled as she looked up and asked, "Do you always do that?"

Rachel nudged her friend's shoulder with her own, and they started laughing. "So?" She prompted.

Exhaling slowly, Maddie answered, "Yes, I trust God."

Rachel's blue eyes glinted as she looked at the bright blue sky above them. "What do you trust him for?"

"I trust that God is with us."

Rachel grabbed her friend's hand and led her toward the clearing at the end of the drive. "Alright, let's enjoy this beautiful scenery, shall we?"

Overjoyed as they reached Wild Rock Overlook, the two friends found a smooth section of rock to sit on.

Breaking the peaceful quiet, Maddie blurted out, "Rach, I had another dream." Closing her eyes, she took a deep breath to calm the familiar burning in her stomach.

"What was this one about?"

Placing her shaky hands in her lap, she looked over the valley and focused on a single tree swaying in the breeze. "We were back at the PKO. There was a mob of people surrounding me. They were yelling and cursing at me."

Facing her friend, Rachel asked. "What did you do?"

Maddie looked down as her friend held her scarred hand in her own. "I just stood there. Oh, and then I sneezed."

Rachel laughed, "That'll break the tension."

"Carissa was there."

Shivering, Rachel looked at her friend, "And?"

"She asked me if Jesus would save me now. Then I woke up." Stuck in her thoughts, she curled her legs up and rested her chin on her knees.

"Well, I'm shook. What did you feel?"

"Relieved."

"No, in the dream. What did you feel?"

"At first, I was just trying to hold it together. I was looking for you, hoping you would break me free. When she asked me about Jesus, I felt..."

Leaning in, Rachel encouraged her friend to continue.

"Hmm, I felt emboldened. But then I woke up."

Smiling, Rachel nodded as she turned to lean back on the

rock. "That's good."

"Wait, what do you mean, 'that's good?'" Maddie asked curiously.

"It means you're ready."

Rubbing her temples, she sighed. While she appreciated her friend's logic and encouragement to process things independently, she wished she would tell her straight. "Ready for what exactly?"

"Ready for battle," Rachel answered as if it were obvious.

"Stop beating around the bush," she cried out, "what battle am I ready for?"

"What verse did Sonya challenge you to memorize?"

"The name of the Lord is a strong tower; the righteous run to it and are safe."

Rachel's signature clap rang out over the valley. "Look at you! Sonya would be so proud. So, do you believe it?"

Taken aback, Maddie responded, "Do I believe that God is my Protector?"

"Yeah. Did you feel protected when you stood before those people yelling at you?"

With a shrug, she answered, "I guess. That reminds me; Ms. Lorna said the Holy Spirit can talk to me through my dreams. Do you think he was with me?"

Rachel lifted a brow and asked, "Really?"

"Don't be extra, Rach. I'm trying to learn all this stuff." Maddie sighed as she tried to find the tree she had focused on earlier.

"Girl, the Holy Spirit is always with you, in your dreams and real life. At some point, you need to understand this truth. 'Trust in the Lord with all your heart and LEAN NOT on your own understanding. This isn't an exam we're studying for." Pulling out a small pad and a pencil from her jacket pocket, Rachel sketched the valley before them.

"I just want to figure it all out," Maddie said as she watched the calming sweep of her friend's creative hand.

Rachel shook her head and said, "You might as well give that one up. Just place the dream in his hands. God's Spirit is your companion. Let him lead you."

Sighing, Maddie decided to change the subject. "So, what do you know about Israel?"

Rachel stopped drawing and looked at her friend. "Your dad's friend Mordecai needed help and asked them to come."

"So, no info? Sounds sus to me."

"They'll be fine." Looking down at her pad, blonde curls covered her friend's face as her pencil began to move again.

Frustrated over Rachel's lack of concern, Maddie sighed and rested her head on the rock.

Her friend's lyrical voice encouraged her to join in as she recited an encouraging reminder from Psalm 91. A sense of calm washed over her with each word she spoke.

"'Whoever dwells in the shelter of the Most High will rest in the shadow of the Almighty. I will say of the Lord, he is my refuge and my fortress, my God, in whom I trust.'"

Frustrated over the family's response to his going to Israel, David left the house, slamming the door behind him.

"Son."

The firm voice stopped him even as his foot hit the ground. He turned to see his mom breaking green beans into a bowl as she rocked on the front porch. "Mom, I'm late. Can we talk later?"

"I jes' got one thing ta say, Son. Be careful that yer heart don't ossify."

"Mom, you're speaking gibberish. What are you talking about?"

"In the good book, our Lord Jesus gave a warnin'. Ya see, the people had hardened, calloused hearts. They closed their eyes and ears to the truth. Their hearts could'na understand the great love 'a God, and so they rejected his invitation into a relationship with him. Son, don't harden yer heart to the Lord, else ya take it in yer own hand."

Frustrated over his mom's intuition, David didn't have

time to argue with her. "Mom, I know this is your house and all. . ."

"Yer right, David, this is my house, and that woman in thar, well, I'm the only momma she's got right now. And yer the only husband she's got."

Feeling the sting of his mom's soft rebuke, he retorted, "Thank you, Mom, for reminding me I'm not a good husband."

"Boy, get yer heart off yer sleeve, I ain't sayin' that. All I'm sayin' is don't chase away those that love ya most. Yer duty ain't gonna be with ya on yer deathbed."

He knew his mom was right. *A few minutes won't keep me from catching my flight.* Walking back up the stairs, he kissed his momma on her softly lined cheeks and returned into the house.

Walking into the kitchen, he saw his wife standing at the sink. Guilt washed over him as he saw her shoulders lifting slightly up and down.

David wrapped his arms around his bride and said, "I'm sorry." He could feel the tension immediately leave her body as he squeezed her tightly.

Turning around, Jacque looked into his eyes and asked, "For what?"

"I've been so wrapped up in what's going on in Washington that I haven't been present for you. Are you worried about this trip?" He asked, touching her forehead as he closed his eyes.

Jacque pulled back and nodded as she asked, "David, when will it all end?"

Her honest question tore at his heart. He wished he had a good answer for her.

"I don't know, my Love. But we can't give up."

Standing tall with squared shoulders, Jacque took a deep breath, quickly wiped her eyes, and asked, "What can I do while you're gone?"

Taken aback by her proactive stance, David smiled and said, "Miss me?"

Giggling, she blushed and said, "Well, that's a given. No, I mean, how can I help you?"

He was so used to her words of fear that he wasn't sure how to respond. Thinking about the town hall meeting coming up at the end of October, he had an idea. "I have a stack of papers on my desk. I'm working on a report to give to the mayor for our town hall meeting at the end of the month. Do you mind going through them and writing a synopsis for me? Just write up a document of bullet points from the highlighted items."

Suddenly, Jacque beamed. "Yes, I can do that!"

David could see light in her eyes again. Placing his hand on her cheek, he said, "We make a great pair, Wife. I love you, and I'll be back before you know it.

CHAPTER 2

Raisin' the Roof

After church, Maddie and Matthew went to Rachel's house to help with a barn raising. Excitement bubbled up as she saw the number of cars parked in the gravel drive.

After looking at his sister in surprise, Matthew grabbed his bag, jumped out of the car, and ran toward the house. It only took a few moments before his signature boomerang fell out of his half-zipped backpack. Clueless, he kept on running.

Shaking her head, she picked it up and dusted it off. A notch on the side caught her attention. Stopping to read it, she couldn't help but smile. *Man after God's own heart.* Running her finger over the engraved words, she whispered, "Yes, Brother, you are."

"Hey, you!" Rachel, Emma, and Jade ran up to meet Maddie.

Placing the boomerang in her back pocket, she smiled as she greeted her Fam. Rachel's bright and bubbly countenance was complemented beautifully by Jade's zeal. Jade's long braids bopped up and down as she and Rachel debated the message of the day.

Emma took Maddie's arm as they watched the animated exchange. "And how are you, Friend?" She asked, her dark brown eyes wide with curiosity.

"I'm good. Can you believe this?" Maddie looked around at all the people gathered for the project.

"I know, right? From the first moment we arrived, I've

11

been amazed at how this community works together. It's not like this in Atlanta."

Her friend was so right. Oh, how she loved having her friends here. She still couldn't believe they were all here, safe, from the chaos they left behind.

The sweet, stony smell hit her as she walked on the site. There must have been twenty people in various states of physical labor. Amused, she watched her brother Mike heft shovel-loads of wet concrete between the footings. Looking at Rachel, she pretended to gag as they witnessed a group of girls watching and whispering while Mike worked.

"Hi, ladies. Have y'all come ta help?" Ms. Lorna asked as she wrote something on her clipboard.

"Yes, ma'am, what can we do?"

"Well, it's 'bout time for a break. Do you ladies mind settin' up the snacks and waters on the table over there?"

Always happy to help in whatever capacity, Rachel said, "Sure, we can do that." Looking at her friends, she went into leader mode. "Come on, Girls."

Since arriving in Wild Rock, the community gathered for a project once per month. In June, they worked on a community garden. In July, they added solar panels to the communal lights on Main Street. In August, they installed rainwater barrels throughout the community.

This month, they were building a communal barn on the Monroe property. The property that Rachel and her family moved to was sold to them by Benjamin "the ninny," as Grammy called him. Maddie still couldn't believe how much they bought it for.

"Under one condition," he said, "let us build a barn fer the community ta store their goods."

Mr. Tom and Benjamin shook on it, and Rachel and her family had a home.

A wave of gratitude washed over Maddie as she thought about how the Lord provided for all her friends. Rachel and her family weren't the only ones who were able to join the little community. Emma and her family were given a house on the other side of town. The family who owned the house were happy to have their family take care of it for them in their absence. As Maddie watched Emma and Jade set up the table, she pondered Emma's invitation for Jade to stay with them since her mom stayed behind in Atlanta.

As the world fell into darkness, the little town of Wild Rock seemed filled with Light. She had never seen anything like it. In Atlanta, her neighbors were familiar strangers, but this little town worked selflessly to help their neighbors. "That's the Way, Maddie Ruth," Grammy would say. "Read 'bout it in the book 'a Acts."

"Maddie ta earth, are ya in thar'?"

A hand touched her own, interrupting her thoughts. Jacob Sullivan stood before her with his hand out.

"Can I have some worter?"

"Oh yeah, sure." Bending down, she pulled several bottles from the box underneath the table. Blushing, she handed one to Jacob. "Here you go."

"Thanks. It's mighty hot out here. Don't ya think?" Taking a drink from the bottle, he wiped his mouth with his hand and placed the bottle in his back pocket. As he turned to walk back to the work site, he winked and gave Maddie a smile.

As she watched Jacob leave, she noticed his white t-shirt and jeans were covered in gray dirt. Wavy brown hair sported a baseball cap that was in similar disarray. As he closed his eyes and lifted the water bottle to his face, she couldn't help but think about those eyes that were the stormiest gray…

"Ahem…"

Interrupted once again, she turned to see three pairs of eyes staring at her.

With hands on her hips, Jade mimicked Jacob's walking away as Rachel pretended to gag.

Emma couldn't keep a straight face. When a giggle turned into an unexpected snort, Jade began howling with laughter, which invited Rachel and Maddie to join in the contagious outburst.

"Hey thar, who's in charge here, Young Lady?"

Laughter turned to an eerie silence as the girls looked first at one another and then at the two people standing before their table. The black couple appeared to Maddie to be mother and son. The old woman had a glint in her eye that reminded Maddie of Grammy. The man looked friendly, but he stood tall and remained quiet.

Maddie cleared her throat and peered around the man to find Ms. Lorna, her Grammy's best friend. "The woman with the clipboard? Her name is Lorna."

"Thank ya, kindly." Smiling, the couple left them to walk over to Ms. Lorna.

Elbowing her friend, Jade asked, "Have you ever seen them before?"

Maddie shook her head no.

Watching as the man greeted Ms. Lorna, they were surprised at the expression on her face.

"I don't think she knows them either."

"It's not every day a black man walks into Wild Rock," Jade said as she looked at the couple.

She didn't know what to say. Jade and Emma's dad were the only black people they had seen in the little town of Wild Rock. Looking at her friend as she stared into the distance, she wondered if this bothered her.

Rachel broke the silence as she nudged her friend. "Want to talk about it?" She asked.

Jade shook her head as if to break from a trance. "Naw, I'm fine," she said, flashing a forced smile.

At the night's end, the whole town celebrated the end of the workday with a pick'n grin'n. Banjos and guitars provided a symphony of sound as they danced around a fire as tall as the smallest trees in the clearing. Grammy was adamant that they celebrate everyone's hard work at the end of every town project. Maddie couldn't believe they pulled off building a barn in one day, but having so many hands working together was key.

Sweat dripped from the nape of her neck. Seeking relief from the heat of the fire, she pulled her hair up and left to grab some water.

A tap on her shoulder stopped her in her tracks. As she turned to see who touched her, Jacob tipped his hat. The flip-flop of her heart caused her to feel a bit dizzy, or maybe it was the sudden movement; she couldn't be sure. "Hey, Maddie, it's my turn now," Jacob said, handing Maddie a water bottle.

"I didn't realize how hot it gets up here in September," Maddie said as she fanned her face, hoping to distract him from witnessing her nervousness.

"It's the fire," he said matter-of-factly. "It cain't be more than sixty-five tonight."

And there it was. Embarrassed by his retort, she decided it was time to retreat. "I, um, I'm gonna grab one for my friend. Thank you for the water," she said over her shoulder as she walked away.

Grabbing an extra bottle from the table, she took it to Jade, standing by herself, "Hey, You, what's up?"

"Thanks," Jade said in appreciation. Staring at Rachel and Emma as they danced with Rory and Jared, she asked, "Nothing, why?"

Come on, Jade, Maddie thought to herself. "You're usually the life of the party. Why are you so quiet tonight?" She wasn't going to let her friend get off that easily.

Jade shrugged a shoulder as she said, "Just thinkin'."

Pulling a penny from her jeans pocket, Maddie asked, "Penny for your thoughts?"

Chuckling at her attempt to get her to talk, Jade looked at her friend somberly and said, "You know I can't stay here."

Maddie didn't know how to respond. She knew her friend was considering leaving, but hearing the words made her sad.

Jade touched her heart and said, "There's something in me, Mads. I'm going back to Atlanta."

"Are you worried about your mom?" That was the only reason Maddie could come up with. *Why would she want to leave her friends and run to a place that had been destroyed?*

She shook her head no and said, "No. This is something I need to do." Adding softly, "I think God is calling me."

As her friend stared at the newcomers, Maddie asked, "Do you know them?"

Jade hesitated before saying, "I don't think I've ever seen them, but I feel like I know them."

They stared silently at the newcomers as Grammy approached the woman from behind. When she turned around, they both smiled while giving each other the warmest embrace, one of familiarity and friendship.

Maddie and Jade looked at each other in surprise.

"Wait, does Grammy know them?" Jade asked.

She didn't know how to answer her friend's question. "There's only one way to find out." She took her hesitant friend's hand and led her to her Gram.

"Hey, Grammy!" Maddie said with a little too much excitement.

Grammy lifted an eyebrow. "Maddie, meet ma dear friend, Roseline Walker. This here is 'er son, Charlie.

"Glad 'ta meet ya, Ladies," she said as she firmly shook Maddie's hand.

The Tennessee twang made Maddie smile.

She took Jade's hand as well, but Jade quickly pulled her hand out of the woman's firm grasp as if she had touched a hot poker. Turning away, she walked back to the bonfire.

A little embarrassed by her friend's response, Maddie said, "Hi, Ms. Walker. I'm sorry about my friend. She's not feeling too good today."

"Aw, it's alright Chile. And y'all can call me Momma Roseline."

"Do y'all know each other?" She asked curiously.

"Shore do," Grammy said as she looked at Momma Roseline. "Yer Grandpa George was in the Navy with Roseline's husband, bless his soul."

"Where do y'all live?"

"We're from Nashville, Chile. We came up 'ere on yer Grammy's ask. It 'pears yer town doc needs a little hand, and ma Charlie 'ere is lookin' fer some work."

"You're a doctor?"

"Yes, ma'am," he said, standing tall and reserved.

"Can I ask you a personal question?" Maddie whispered.

Momma Roseline leaned in to listen.

Looking at her friend Jade, she asked, "Do you know Jade?"

Momma Roseline looked at Charlie, who didn't want to return the glance. "Why now, that remains to be seen, don't it?"

A knock on her bedroom door surprised Maddie as she finished her nightly prayer. "Come in," she said as she placed her Bible and journal on the bedside table.

"Yer still 'wake, I see," Grammy said as she entered the room and sat on the edge of Maddie's bed. Maddie picked up her brush to begin her nightly routine as Grammy placed her hand on Maddie's Bible. "Ya still readin' it?" She asked with a smile.

"Yes, ma'am, every morning and every night," Maddie said proudly.

"What'cha readin' on?" Grammy asked.

"I'm reading Acts, like you said."

"Hmm, right interestin' readin', that book is."

As she pulled her hair up to release a nasty knot, she asked, "Grammy, is Wild Rock like the early church?"

"What'cha mean?"

"Well, in Acts, it says the Church cared for everybody. That's kinda like Wild Rock, isn't it?"

"It's how we're all s'pposed to live, Maddie Ruth. It's the Kingdom—the way God intended from the beginnin'."

As she laid the brush on the table, she said, "It wasn't like that in Atlanta."

Grammy laid her hand on her granddaughter's and sighed. "Yeah, I know. Ever'body movin' so fast, livin' fer themselves. They done fergot that we're s'pposed ta take care 'a one another."

"Jade wants to go back," Maddie said sadly.

Grammy nodded, "I figured as much. She's a spitfire, that one. Got a boatload 'a zeal, 'jes like Peter in the good Book."

"Do you mean Jesus' disciple, Peter?"

"That's the one. God's gonna use her to be a mouthpiece, 'jes like he used his disciple. I 'spect he's got some roofs ta raise on her behalf."

Curious over her Gram's response, she asked, "What do you mean?"

Opening her Granddaughter's Bible to the dog-eared page in Acts, she asked, "What did ya notice 'bout Peter in yer readin'?"

A little embarrassed to admit what she had been thinking, she whispered, "Well, I don't know about you, Grammy, but I think he was a bit savage."

A boisterous laugh filled the room as Grammy said, "Well, I'll be. If savage means that ole Peter was feisty and unafraid, then I'd say that's righter'n rain and my point exactly. Yer friend Jade, she ain't 'afraid to tell it like it is. God'll use her to speak his word which'll cause a ruckus 'n those who ain't got ears to hear."

Shocked by her Grammy's declaration, she sat back and considered what she said. *She was worried about her friend, but what if God wanted to use her?*

"What'cha chewin' on?" Grammy asked.

Maddie looked up and said, "I just realized how selfish I was to want to keep her here. If God wants to use her, we've got to let her go, right?"

Grammy patted her granddaughter's hands and breathed in deeply. "Do ya r'member that verse Ms. Sonya taught ya last year?"

"The tower?"

"That's the one. What with ever'thin' y'all been through, God has been with ya. Not by pow'r and not by might but the Spirit a' the Living God that saw y'all through the last years. He's been yer strong tower the whole time."

Maddie laughed. "Ironic, isn't it?"

"What's that?"

"I was so afraid of everything, but he taught me to run to him."

"That's right, and now, it's Jade's turn."

The line for security at the Atlanta Airport wrapped around the room. David looked at his watch for the hundredth time.

"We've got plenty of time," Tom told his friend.

"Why does this take so long?" David asked, a little hot under the collar.

Tom chuckled, "Not used to living like the little guy, are you?"

His laugh sounded a little fake, even to him. Choosing to ignore his friend's subtle jab, he pulled out his passport.

"Did you give Mordecai our flight information?" Tom asked.

With a tilt of his head, he looked at his friend and wondered, *"Is Tom nervous?"* David was accustomed to more secure accommodations but considering he had made the trip dozens of times; he couldn't think of any reason to be concerned. "He'll be waiting for us at Ben-Gurion," he said.

"Will anyone be with him?"

"I expect he'll have guards close by, considering the instability in the area. Tom, are you okay? You're not nervous about this trip, are you?" He asked.

"About that, Olivia has been worried about the unrest. Has it reached Tel Aviv?"

"Not yet. Mordecai said the IDF has a firm hold on the

situation."

"Can we trust him?"

David looked at his friend and said without hesitation, "With my life."

◆ ◆ ◆

The two-hour layover in Dallas gave David and Tom time to go over the specifics of Mordecai's ask and how it might play into the events unfolding around them. The world had gone into a tailspin since the official coming out of Lucien Baldur and his business partner, Helel. The populace did not receive the news of The Kindness Tax well, but world leaders didn't seem to care. For some reason, they believed this crazy idea was a good one. The WTO banded together and named ten leading nations that would lead in ridding the world of food insecurity. It was a coup of the highest proportion. Israel was the only nation that had a lick of sense. They chose to leave the WTO shortly after.

"What is it that you think Mordecai needs?" Tom asked his friend as he took a sip of iced tea.

"I've been thinking about that," David said. "Intelligence is my first guess, but the fact that he invited you leads me to believe he's looking for manpower."

A large group of men dressed in all black marched through the terminal. David watched bitterly as the PeaceKeepers split up to harass weary travelers and force them to show their credentials. He couldn't believe how quickly they took control. After all he and his family had gone through in their own battles against the PKO, he couldn't help but wonder, what would be next?

"That's a first," Tom said as he noticed the men caught in his friend's gaze.

"Hmm," he agreed as he glanced at his watch. "Fifteen minutes to boarding," he said, "let's go."

The flight from Dallas to Tel Aviv was uneventful as David took the time to read through his notes. He couldn't afford surprises on this trip, and the better prepared he was, the quicker this would go.

After exiting security at the Ben-Gurion airport, they spotted a man holding a sign with David's name. Satisfied when the man shared the secret phrase, they followed him to a group of double doors.

A row of black cars with darkened windows lined up next to the curb. The man with the sign opened the back door to one of the cars and motioned for them to enter.

"David, shalom." A dark-skinned Middle Eastern man greeted them as they entered the car.

"Mordecai, good to see you," David said as he climbed into the sleek, black vehicle.

After introductions, Mordecai extended his hand in a firm handshake, "Good to meet you, Tom. Any friend of David's is a friend of mine." His genuine smile, framed by thick, wavy black hair and dark brown eyes, held a warmth that welcomed strangers immediately. While cautious and discerning, Mordy was extremely intuitive. He could soften even the hardest heart, leading them to share their darkest secrets. It was a gift his friend had.

Mordecai made small talk as they drove through the streets. Half-heartedly listening to his friend, David watched as locals filled the thoroughfare. Some rode bicycles, while others walked with friends and family. Israel seemed to be experiencing a peace that Atlanta had lost. If you watched the news, you would believe this was a warzone and Israel the enemy, but obviously, that wasn't the case. His ears perked up as his friend's conversation turned to heavier matters.

"After Helel's famous announcement, Israel announced its own—the raising up of a temple and the re-commencement of animal sacrifice. As you can imagine, this sent our bordering neighbors into a frenzy," Mordecai said.

Tom nodded. His engagement encouraged Mordecai's narrative, "Is Israel expecting a war?" He asked.

"The threat of war is all around us," Mordecai answered, "but this is nothing new." As he pointed up, he added, "Adonai, he will protect us."

David wasn't afraid of war—he had faced much worse. But he was a bit uneasy being away from home. He did not want to be away from his family if war broke out.

"Here we are, Gentlemen." As the back door opened, Mordecai waited for his security detail before exiting the vehicle. "Never can be too careful, eh?"

David watched as Tom stood taken aback by Mordecai Oronoff's opulent yet humble home. "Wait until you see inside," he said as Mordecai solemnly touched the frame of his front door.

"Tell me about that," Tom said as they entered the home. "Why did you touch the doorpost and kiss your fingers?"

"This is a Mezuzah," he said as he pointed to a small container with a rolled parchment inside. "We remember God's commands for our people and show reverence for his presence. We call this the Shema."

"That is beautiful," Tom said as he looked at his friend.

As they walked through the foyer and entered the living space, David was surprised to see that much of the furnishings had been removed. Only a sparse set remained.

"Micah, please place the gentlemen's bags in the guest suite. We will take our leave in my office."

"Yes, Sir."

The low, almost gravelly voice echoed in the foyer as he took their bags.

"Thank you," David said as he nodded to the man.

Nodding in return, it seemed Micah was a man of few words.

As they entered the office, Mordecai grabbed three bottles of water and handed them to David and Tom while keeping one for himself.

"Are you moving, Mordy? The house looks a bit empty from the last time I was here," David said as he sat on one of the few pieces of furniture in the room.

"Noticed that, did you? Yes, it's unfortunate, but it's become necessary to lean up."

"There are rumors of an Israeli war in the states, but everything looked quite normal as we drove through Jerusalem."

"The military stands at the ready on the border, but it won't be long. The reinstating of temple worship has created quite the stir."

"That's a sign directly from Revelation, isn't it?" Tom interjected.

Mordy looked at Tom with an almost jubilant expression and said, "Our King is coming."

David looked at Tom and Mordecai, who seemed to share a secret. "Is there something I should know?"

"We've had this discussion, David, the signs are all there, King Jesus will be here soon."

David shook his head, confused. "Wait, I thought you were worried about the antichrist rising?"

"Yes, if my calculations are correct, we are watching prophecy happen right before our eyes."

"Will someone please explain what you are talking about?" David asked.

"Do you remember our conversation from the car?" Mordecai asked. "After the sacrifice of the red heifer on the Mount of Olives, the temple was raised very quickly. Just as the Word says, now, Jews can observe traditional temple worship."

Looking at David, Tom added, "What comes next is the man of lawlessness ending these sacrifices and taking control of the temple for himself."

"Yes, this is not good for my people," Mordecai said.

"Why?" David asked.

Opening the Bible on the corner of his desk to a marked page, Mordecai read from Revelation thirteen.

"Do you think the man of lawlessness is Lucien Baldur?" Tom asked.

"No, I think it is his business partner, Helel."

David remembered this man as the one who claimed to end poverty in the world. "Isn't he the one who coordinated with Israel to roll out Project Manna so they could manage The Kindness Tax?"

"Let's not forget his overwhelming takeover of the WTO. The only coordination here, David, was outright theft, but based on prophecy, I believe he is the final man of lawlessness, prophesied in Revelation and the book of Daniel."

A bad feeling crept up the back of David's neck. He didn't want to go where his thoughts were taking him. "He stole it?"

"Yes, my friend, his organization hacked into the Mossad and stole the blueprint for Project Manna that I believe may welcome in the beast's mark. It appears you ducked a massive bullet, my friend."

Tom chuckled at Mordecai's humorous misuse of the word "dodged," even as David reflected on the implications of what he could have been involved in. "Duck, dodge, now you know the rest of the story, David. The war has begun, and we must prepare for battle.

"So, what's the plan?" Tom asked as he looked at his friend.

"David, do you still have the blueprint of the PKO locations?"

"I turned them in to my commanding officer," David said.

"Can you get a copy?"

"Why?"

"It's time to go on the offense."

CHAPTER 3

Going into Battle

Kicking off the covers, she turned to place her feet on solid ground. *At least I can count on this*, she pondered as she wiped the sleep out of her eyes. The nightmares were coming with greater intensity. Fear was skulking around again, tightening its grip around Maddie.

She had been reading about Stephen in Acts. If she were honest, the thought of having to die for her faith overwhelmed her. Then there was that part about Stephen seeing Jesus. What was it he said? *'Lord Jesus, receive my spirit. Do not hold this sin against them.' Kinda like what Jesus said on the cross.*

Rachel told her she was facing spiritual warfare. *"God is about to do something, Maddie. Darts coming at you from all directions can signify the enemy trying to distract you because he knows God is on the move. Remember, you are a warrior and must take those thoughts captive."* In these moments, her friend encouraged her to take her eyes off the warfare and place them on the One who called her to battle. She shook her head as if to shake the thought out of her head physically.

The chaos within her was trumped only by the chaos around her. An organization kidnapping innocent people, PeaceKeepers running others out of their homes and businesses, a dark struggle that held her mom in its grip, world governments gone mad, violent mobs killing unknowing victims, and if Rachel was right, they were in the middle of the great tribulation. All of it, out of her control. *How do I take my thoughts captive when they just keep coming?*

As she looked down at her shaking hands, she thought, 'F*ear is relentless.'*

When she thought she had surrendered everything in her past, it would creep up on her like a spider. *I'm in a safe place, right? So, why can't I close the door on this fear?*

Looking up at the canvas she and Emma painted, she yearned to be in the Tower of Trust again. She knew God was with her, but it was easy to forget when intrusive thoughts overwhelmed. *Why won't fear just leave me alone?*

A thought that sounded much like something Sonya would say interrupted her musings: *"Pick up your armor."*

Picking up the Bible from the bedside table, she opened to Ephesians six as she pondered her mentor's words after retreat: *"Our struggle is not against flesh and blood, but against the rulers, against the authorities, against the powers of this dark world and against the spiritual forces of evil in the heavenly realms."*

Shivering at the thought of unseen demons, she asked to an empty room, "But, how do I fight them?"

The familiar voice in her thoughts that always encouraged her said,

Keep reading, Maddie.

"Put on the full armor of God, so that when the day of evil comes, you may be able to stand your ground, and after you have done everything, to stand."

Placing her Bible on her bed, she looked up. She didn't understand why she always looked up. Physically, her gaze saw only the ceiling and a fan, but she knew God was with her, and looking up seemed to show reverence to the greater One.

"So, God, I am to put on this armor and stand?"

That's right, Daughter.

"And then what?" She asked.

Keep your eyes on Jesus. He will go before you.

"Are we going into battle?" She asked a seemingly empty room. The timid question came from a place of uncertainty, but the whispers of God gave her courage she couldn't explain. *"R'member, Maddie Ruth, the Holy Spirit's leadin' will always align with scripture."* This is how she knew God was the one talking to her.

Looking back at her Bible, she noticed 2 Corinthians 10:3-4 scribbled on the edge of the page. Turning to the passage, she read: *"For though we live in the world, we do not wage war as the world does. The weapons we fight with are not the weapons of the world. On the contrary, they have divine power to demolish strongholds."*

"A stronghold," Grammy told her once, *"is like a big castle wall. It keeps ya holed up. If yer holed up by yer Heavenly Father, yer safe. But if the enemy's got ya in his keep, well that ain't no diff'rent than bein' held tight in a spider's web."*

So, the weapons we fight with will demolish the enemy's hold. Boldness began to fill her with courage as she stood.

She froze as a stray thought darted in her mind like an arrow, *"You're not strong enough."*

"No! I can do all things through Christ who strengthens me!" She declared boldly.

"Who do you think you are?" Fear—a relentless voice.

"Not today." Picking up the Bible from her bed, she read from Ephesians six:

> *"I, Maddie Ruth Bennett, will be strong in the Lord and in His mighty power. I put on the full armor of God, so that I can take my stand against the devil's schemes."*

As she prayed on each piece of armor, the intrusive thoughts dwindled, and her faith grew with each declaration.

The words from her mouth projected a boldness she had not felt before. As she stood tall and strong, courage arose within her. Her eyes closed as her head faced upward. A vision of herself in full body armor with a sword and shield crossed her mind. *Perhaps I am a warrior.* God was in the room—she could feel him. She knew he was always with her, but...this was different. It was weird, but she felt a warmth fill her from the top of her head to the bottom of her feet. She remembered having a similar feeling at Wild Rock Overlook. She could go anywhere knowing he was with her.

Opening her eyes, she looked forward and, with resolve, proclaimed,

> *"I am a daughter of the King and will stand on the Name of Jesus. NO WEAPON formed against me will prevail! Do you hear that, Fear? NO WEAPON! So, you can leave right now in Jesus' Name!"*

The drumbeat of her heart was strong, but different from the times her heart beat erratically in anxious fear. Thinking back to the moment she launched herself from the zip line platform, Maddie felt that same rush of exhilaration. Rachel said she was ready—perhaps it was time she agreed.

Wow, Maddie thought as her stomach rumbled. Opening the door to her room, she was immediately captivated by the aroma of Grammy's cooking. Hearing muffled voices as she walked into the room, she was surprised to see Jade and her Grammy deep in conversation over a pot that smelled like oatmeal.

"Jade!"

"Hey Girl! Jade walked over to her friend and hugged her. The hug seemed to last a bit longer than Jade's typical hug.

Hoping she could encourage her friend to stay so that she could share her prayer, she asked, "Do you want to stay for breakfast? Grammy always makes enough for an army."

Jade looked toward the door as if she was ready to bolt. Deciding better of it, she smiled weakly and made her way to the table instead. "Sure, I can stay for a little while."

Maddie had a captive audience as she chatted throughout the meal. Jade was strangely silent as she talked about nothing special.

An awkward silence filled the room as she waited for a response from her friend, who was a million miles away.

Jade turned to Grammy and then Maddie, her mouth full of oatmeal, and asked, "Whaa?"

"Are you okay?" Maddie asked, placing her hand on her friend's.

Attempting to swallow, she wiped her mouth with a napkin and said, "Yeah, I'm fine." Looking at Grammy, she said, "I guess I should tell her now?"

Grammy nodded. "I would say now's as good a' time as any."

Placing her spoon on the table, Jade turned back to her friend. "Hey, Girl, thank you for bringing me here. I'm so grateful for you, and Grammy welcoming me as one of her own."

Anxiety rose in Maddie's chest as she listened to her friend talk. While she knew this moment would come, she had been dreading it. "You're leaving, aren't you?" Maddie asked sadly.

Jade couldn't hold back the tears any longer. "Please don't be mad. I've already heard an earful from Rachel."

"I'm not mad," Maddie responded. Thankful that she wasn't the only one who felt this way about Jade's decision, she said, "The only thing Rachel might be mad about is that she won't have somebody to debate with."

Laughter broke through the tension.

Something had been bothering her for days. She couldn't let her friend leave without getting this off her chest. "Jade, can I ask you a question?" Maddie asked timidly, taking a pretend sip from her empty coffee cup.

As Grammy quietly excused herself, Jade scraped the bottom of her bowl and asked, "What's up?"

Worried over her friend's response, she hesitated, running her fingers around her cup's rim. "What's up with the Walkers? You were kinda rude to them at the barn raising," she said.

Jade's eyes darted as she stood and picked up her dishes, ignoring the question.

Maddie was not going to be dismissed. Walking over to the sink, she leaned over to look at her friend's face. She would think Jade was afraid if she didn't know any better. *Not Jade,* she thought. She had never seen her afraid of anything. "Hey, talk to me." Maddie pleaded, placing her hand on her friend's arm.

Jade turned abruptly and said, "I don't want to talk about it."

"Hey, what is wrong with you?" Maddie asked angrily. "This is not the Jade I know and love."

Jade stopped, completely silent. Her shoulders were slumped slightly as she faced away from her friend.

Maddie immediately felt a wave of guilt cover her. "I'm sorry. I meant to say, if you don't want to talk, that's fine. I just want you to know I'm here, okay?"

Jade nodded silently.

Pouring two cups of tea, she gave one to her friend and asked, "So, when are you leaving?" Thankful to see her friend relax as she smelled the lavender wafting from the hot beverage, she sighed.

Looking into the cup, Jade said, "Mom is picking me up tonight."

Alarmed, Maddie said, "Wait, tonight? So soon?"

Her friend paused as she took a sip of her tea. This appeared to be another conversation she didn't want to have, but thankfully, Jade didn't shut her down this time. "Yeah. We have to travel at night, and she wants to get it over with."

A shiver racked Maddie as she remembered the night they

arrived in Wild Rock. "Why do you have to travel at night?" She couldn't imagine her friend going through that again.

Jade peered intently at her friend. "Maddie, it's not safe to travel anymore. Mom says there are gangs stopping people on the road."

Grammy and Jade both turned to her. Taking a deep breath, she said a quiet prayer to quell the butterflies beginning to flutter. Remembering her prayer from the morning, she knew it was time to stand.

"Can I pray for you?"

Encouraged by her friend's nod, she stood and placed her hand on Jade's shoulder. Taking a deep breath, she began to speak. The prayer was soft and timid at first, but within moments, her voice strengthened as boldness once again took hold. When she said amen, she could feel that same strength from the morning. The weird thing was, she didn't remember what she said.

Jade looked at her friend with tears in her eyes. "Whoa, where did that come from? I've never heard you pray like that, Mads."

Maddie looked at her Grammy, who looked to be warding off tears herself. Shaking her head, she said, "I don't know. God?"

Grammy placed her hand on her granddaughter's shoulder. "Yer ready, ma Girl."

The war begins, and we must prepare for battle. The words ran repeatedly in David's mind as he and Tom walked through the gate entrance for their plane. Walking down the aisle to the back of the plane, he found his seat and secured his belt.

"See ya in Atlanta," Tom called from two rows ahead.

David nodded as a brunette with a laptop bag sat beside him.

"Hi, are you going to Atlanta?" She asked as she settled

into the aisle seat.

Considering they were on a flight to Atlanta, that seemed obvious, but he nodded as he said, "Yes."

"I know, it's a bit obvious, huh? I never know where people are going, but hearing their stories is always fun."

Flying coach was a bit of an adjustment for David. He was used to having the cabin to himself, in quiet, but it appeared he was going to have to share it with a chatty Cathy this round. Opening his laptop, he put in his earbuds, hoping she would get the picture and leave him alone.

"I'm going to Atlanta, too. My family is there. I've missed them," the woman said as she pulled out a Bible.

In an email to Senator Gabriel Hawke summarizing his meeting with Mordecai and Tom, David subtly requested a call on his return to the States. Worried that the email might be intercepted, he decided not to include any marking details. After clicking send, he closed the laptop and put his earbuds away.

Pulling out a book, David read the back, wondering what propaganda Mordy was feeding him this time.

"Oh, you're reading too. What is your book about?" She asked.

The book Mordecai had given him was supposed to be a good mystery. He answered, "Ted Dekker," a new author he had never heard of.

"Oh, I love Ted Dekker! He's one of my favorite CF writers."

"CF?" David asked.

"You know, Christian fiction. Dekker writes Christian mystery, thriller, and fantasy novels."

"Hmm," Mordy always did seem to have the last laugh.

"I'm reading Daniel."

"Daniel?"

"Yeah, you know, the book of Daniel, in the Bible?" David's blank stare encouraged her to continue. "Have you never read the Bible?"

Sunday school memories filled his thoughts: "Does

memorizing John 3:16 count?"

"Of course it does! That is my favorite, 'For God so loved the world, that he gave…,' I will forever be grateful for his gift of grace."

If he didn't know any better, he would think he was sitting next to a slightly younger version of his mom. *Maybe if I open my book, she'll get the idea.*

"I'm loving reading the book of Daniel! I've been studying Daniel as it coincides with history. It's amazing how everything ties out! God is so kind to connect the dots for us."

His interest was piqued. "What do you mean, everything ties out?"

The woman spent the next hour sharing Daniel's five dreams and connecting them to historical events. It had been a while since David's investigative mind had been stretched, and he found this Daniel interesting.

"So, what do you think?" She asked.

"I think that's a lot of history," he said. "I didn't know the Bible was a history book."

Shocked, she smiled at him and said, "Only the greatest history book ever! This is God's history, his love story written to his people. Get it, 'his-story', history? The Bible is the story of God's greatest gift to mankind, his son, Jesus."

Here it goes. He thought as he nodded.

"Hey, can I ask you a question?"

Suddenly wishing the seatbelt light would go off, he sighed and looked at her. "Sure."

After closing her Bible, the woman looked him straight in the eye and asked, "Do you know Jesus?" Her voice was steady and serious.

And there it was. The genuine inflection of the woman's question pierced his apathetic heart. *Did he know Jesus?* He knew his mom's Jesus. Realizing his thoughts left his lips as she lifted a brow, he breathed in frustration.

Placing a bookmark in her Bible, she rested her head against her seat and sighed. "I grew up in the church. When I was twelve, I said yes to Jesus but only because I was afraid of hellfire and brimstone."

Words from his childhood that grated on David's ears.

"When I was eighteen, I walked away from the Church. I decided I knew how to live life better than God." Nodding at him as if he understood, she continued. "It only took three years before I had to file for bankruptcy. Two years later, I was diagnosed with a brain tumor. I had two children; my Navy husband was on the other side of the world, and I felt as if the world weighed heavily on my shoulders. It would be a little orange bible that would open my eyes to the truth."

"The truth?" David asked.

"That I was loved, and I wasn't alone. God knew me, and he saw everything I was going through. Unfortunately, it would take another twelve years before I turned back to him." Smiling, she added, "But he wooed me every step of the way."

"Wooed you? How so?"

"Little touches here and there. The little bible, of course. Invitations to church. A grandmother who prayed for me."

David chuckled, "My mom's a prayer warrior, too."

"See, then you know!" Her serious and gentle tone suddenly turned enthusiastic enough to wake the man in front of them.

"Ma'am, I don't know anything. I know a lot of fearmongers who want to scare you into Heaven. The thing is, I'm not afraid."

"Wow, you've got more faith than I do."

"Excuse me?"

"Oh, that's not meant to be offensive. Truly, I believe that God is with me and that Jesus will return one day to take us home. Not to believe, well, what do you believe in?"

"I believe that life is to be lived a day at a time, and when your time is up, it's up. What's there to be afraid of? Everyone has a hundred percent chance of dying."

"So, you don't believe in eternity?"

"No."

"Like I said, that's a lot of faith. What if you're wrong?"

David wasn't accustomed to strangers questioning his intelligence. "Wrong?"

"Here me out. If eternity is real, wouldn't you want to know Jesus?"

David didn't know how to answer the question. Deciding to change the subject, he nodded to the highlight in her book. "What does that say?"

"Oh, this? This is Daniel 11:21, *He will be succeeded by a contemptible person who has not been given the honor of royalty. He will invade the Kingdom when its people feel secure, and he will seize it through intrigue.*"

"Why did you highlight it?"

"Remember how I told you about Antiochus IV? This is him. He was the antichrist of his day. Daniel tells us that he set up the abomination that causes desolation in the temple and abolished the daily sacrifice."

Alarmed over her words, which sounded much like Mordecai's, he asked, "What was that?"

"The abomination? He sacrificed a pig in the temple and erected an idol, a statue of the Greek god Zeus."

"Why would you highlight this?" He repeated, honestly curious for her answer.

"Well, since you asked, did you hear what happened in Jerusalem?"

He wasn't sure he wanted to hear the rest of her story.

"If you say the heifers..."

"Oh, you know then! Exciting, isn't it? Remember how I told you the Lord wooed me back to him? I believe he does this for all who listen to his voice. Our Savior will return. If you don't know Jesus, I pray that you will soon. Oh, what was your name?"

Stunned as he processed her response, he said, "David."

"David, I will pray for you."

As they exited the plane, David was in a daze. The events of the last three years haunted him. Mordy's words after he cracked the code of the PeaceKeepers came to him like a flood:

> *"David, these messages you have shared with me are evil. It's no coincidence that Lucien Baldur speaks to the world as these messages are being transmitted. Much tactical planning has gone into what appears on paper to be an attack of global proportions. And Lucien Baldur's no order, no peace—well, this certainly sounds like a call an antichrist would make, no?"*

"There you are. How was the flight?" Tom asked as he walked up behind him.

"Huh?" David asked his friend as a familiar voice rose loudly from the front of the line.

"Yes, my passport is valid. It was renewed just a year ago."

"Ma'am, it says here that your passport is invalid. I can only let you into the country if you say the words."

"I will not say the words."

The woman David was sitting next to was being questioned. Stepping forward to help, Tom stopped him, "No, David."

He knew his friend was right, but he was incensed that this Helel thought he was the world's king. *Suddenly, people were supposed to bow down to him?*

David looked at Tom. "She's a nice person; she doesn't deserve this!" He said through his teeth.

"Come on, David, did you hear anything Mordecai told you? The new order is rising, and their god is Helel. He will come after God's people and force them to bow to him, or else."

Helpless frustration filled him as he listened to his friend's wise counsel. For years, he stood up to leaders flexing their totalitarian muscle. It was a slap in the face to see what he thought to be political rhetoric become enforced rule. He couldn't resist asking a question he already knew the answer to: "Or else what?"

CHAPTER 4

A Harvest Moon Hootenanny

The week after Jade left for Atlanta, everyone was in a funk. Rachel wouldn't admit it outright, but Maddie could tell she was worried about Jade's decision to run into danger.

"I don't want to lose another friend!" Her friend yelled angrily as she paced Grammy's kitchen floor.

She didn't know what to say. It had been a year since they lost Kaitlyn, and she knew that Rachel still carried guilt over not being able to save her. She didn't want to lose Jade either, but when Jade had made up her mind, there was no stopping her.

Maddie's dad seemed to be in a similar mood when he and Rachel's dad returned from Israel.

A silver lining in the dark raincloud came on Saturday when Michael brought his fiancée over for dinner.

She loved her new sister-to-be. Melissa Tate was quiet and sweet. With bright blue eyes and strawberry blonde hair, her future sister-in-law was beautiful, yet humble. Over the summer, Melissa had included her in all the plans for their fall wedding.

As they sat around the table, Michael asked if he could say grace. As the family said amen, she watched as her brother kissed his new wife-to-be on the cheek.

A sudden elbow in her ribs broke her sigh and interrupted her ogling. Giving her younger brother the stink eye, she turned red as she realized he was waiting for her to pass the mashed potatoes.

Ignoring the sibling's frustration at the other end of the table, Grammy poured some gravy over the chicken fried steak on her plate and asked, "Melissa, what's left to do fer the weddin'?"

"I think we're all ready," Melissa answered softly. "We're jes' prayin' fer good weather."

"We're prayin' with ya, ma Girl."

"Michael said there's going to be a supermoon," Matthew said with his mouth full of potatoes.

"Matthew," Mom warned.

"Oops, sorry," he said with his hand over his mouth.

"That's right, Boy, we're plannin' fer a harvest moon hootenanny."

"We sure have a lot of hootenannies around here." He said, being careful to swallow before he spoke this time.

Grammy winked at her grandson and said, "Always better than the last."

"I don't have to dress up, do I?" He whined.

"Matthew, we get to dress up. This is your brother's wedding, after all," David answered.

"I'm looking forward to it; this will be my first barn wedding," Jacque said. Smiling at Melissa, she added, "Thank you for allowing me to help with the decorations."

"No, thank you, Ms. Jacque. Mom was so grateful when you offered. She was lost."

"Melissa, you may call me Jacque."

Melissa looked at Michael and blushed. "Thank you, Ms…. I mean, Jacque."

"Wait, so it's in a barn, and I have to dress up?"

"Matthew, that's quite enough, Son."

"The ceremony is under a big oak tree," Michael piped in. "The party will be in the barn afterward."

"Ya know, that's the same oak tree where yer Grandpa George asked me ta marry 'im."

"Wait, I know this one! Wasn't that at a firefly festival?"

"Ya got a good mem'ry, Boy."

Wrinkling his nose, Matthew whispered to his dad, "I don't have to sit by the tree, do I?"

David lifted a brow as he bent down and asked, "Why?"

"I'm too young to get married."

David smiled and gave a low chuckle.

The Bennett house was abuzz with activity on the morning of the wedding.

Maddie wished she had her phone so she could ask her friends how to style her hair.

"Oh, Maddie, you're going to make me cry."

Surprised, she turned to see her BFF standing in the doorway, and exclaimed, "Don't scare me like that, Rach! Hey, how did you know I was just thinking about you?"

"Where did you get that dress?" Rachel asked in awe.

"It was Melissa's prom dress. She let me borrow it." Smiling at her reflection, she did a little spin. The mauve silk gown hung beautifully on her slender frame. The top featured criss-cross straps encircling her neck, leaving her shoulders bare, while the fabric gathered at her waist before flowing into a straight, floor-length skirt. "Do you think I should wear a sweater?" She asked, feeling a bit exposed.

Rachel looked at Maddie's reflection in the mirror and smiled. "No, it's beautiful."

A wave of emotion overwhelmed Maddie as she looked at her reflection.

Grabbing a tissue, Rachel dabbed her eye and then helped her sweep her hair into a twisted updo. "What's wrong?"

"I just realized that I'll probably never go to my own

prom."

"Oh, Girl, you never know what you might get to do. I mean, check this out, you're going to be in a wedding!"

As her friend curled two tendrils on either side of her face, Maddie remembered the moment when Melissa asked her to be in the wedding party, "Me?" She asked.

"Why, a'course you," Melissa answered. "I want my sister to be by my side."

Reminiscing about the moment with Rachel, she said proudly, "She called me her sister."

Resting her head on her best friend's shoulder, Rachel said, "I'm so happy for you, Maddie, and for Mike. He's a different person."

"I know."

"Hey, don't you girls be talking about me behind my back." The low timbral voice surprised both girls out of their moment.

"Check it out, Michael Ryder Bennett all spiffy."

"Can you give us a moment, Rachel?"

Turning to give her friend a sly look, Rachel left the room.

"You really are handsome, Mike," Maddie said as she straightened the pink boutonniere in his lapel.

Tightening his mauve bow tie in the mirror, he asked, "Ya think Melissa will like it?"

"She will love it!" Overwhelmed by a wave of emotion, she asked, "Mike, do you love her?"

"What kind of question is that?" He asked, running his hands through his dark auburn hair.

"A lot has changed. I just don't want you rushing into something because everything is crashing down around us."

The weight of Mike's big hands covered his sister's shoulders. As his green eyes peered into hers, he said, "Maddie, life doesn't stop just because our future is uncertain."

"I know, it's just that sometimes I wonder if things will ever be normal again."

Shaking his head, Mike said, "No, they won't. To be honest, I don't want normal," he replied as he turned to check himself in the mirror.

"Why?"

"Because normal wasn't real. Normal was getting by, trying to be someone I wasn't, trying to find the truth. Now, the truth is so real that I know it's worth fighting for."

"Rachel said we're going into battle."

"Yeah, she's probably right, and do you know what? The best relationships are formed in the fires of battle."

"What do you mean?"

"When you're in a war, you have to trust the guy who has your back. If you can't trust him, you'll die. Relationships that are real reveal themselves in the heat of battle.

Looking at their reflections in the mirror, Michael paused, seeming to choose his next words carefully. "Maddie, I want you to listen to me, a real relationship is worth fighting for— it's worth dying for. Isn't that what Jesus said? 'Blessed is the one who will die for a friend.'"

She didn't want to think about what her brother meant by that, but she had to ask, "Would you die for Melissa?"

Without even skipping a beat, Michael nodded and said, "Yes."

White clouds hovered overhead to provide just enough shade for the wedding party. A gentle breeze teased the dusty rose and white flowers that adorned the chairs and archway. When Jacque prepared the decorations for the day, she proudly shared with her daughter the reason for her new daughter-in-law's color choice. Rose represented elegance and gentleness, while white represented innocence and new beginnings. Maddie thought the choice was perfect as she stood waiting for the march to begin.

In a precious pink dress, little Eva Mae walked down the aisle with her brown hair in curls and a pink ribbon. A chorus of sighs swirled around the crowd as she sprinkled rose petals in everyone's direction.

As Maddie walked toward Jacob, she felt her heart pitter-patter as he smiled at her. The glitter of his gray eyes, highlighted by his royal blue suit, sent her heart into a tailspin. After taking his arm, she immediately turned her head toward the front, hoping to hide her blush from him.

Shifting his weight from foot to foot, Mike stood next to his dad under the big oak tree. Maddie smiled as she noticed him looking around her, hoping to catch a glimpse of the one he had given his heart to.

Rachel and Emma sat towards the front. The knowing looks on each of their faces made her blush once again. *Don't look at them,* she thought as she refocused her gaze on her mom.

Locking eyes on the woman who raised her, she realized she wanted to hug her. She had never seen her mom cry as much as she had in the last week. As she hung the flowers for the processional, her mom admitted, "It's like I'm giving away two babies."

Maddie and Jacob separated at the end of the aisle and stood next to Pastor Ron. As she stepped into her place, she melted under Jacob's gaze, who wouldn't stop looking at her.

The crowd stood when the wedding march began. Everyone gasped as Melissa stood still with her arm locked in her dad's. Maddie sighed in awe at her new sister, who smiled sweetly at everyone before her.

"She looks like a princess," Matthew whispered loudly.

Everyone had eyes on the bride as she walked down the aisle, but she only had eyes for Michael.

Maddie tried not to cry as she watched Melissa and Mike share intense gazes. If she didn't know any better, she would've thought Mike was shedding a few tears of his own.

The ceremony was beautiful. Pastor Ron shared with the crowd how God combined the two into one flesh. He painted a picture of Christ and the Church and shared how we would all participate in a wedding ceremony one day, as we became one with him. "Until then," the Pastor said, "we join in families to fulfill his first command to go forth and multiply while learning what it looks like to serve one another and be one with him."

One big family, she pondered. *Wow, that'll be cool!*

The night was everything Grammy said and more. Matthew's prophetic declaration from two years ago came true as their parents danced around a bonfire.

"I told ya, Maddie. Momma loves it!" He exclaimed.

She never would have thought it to be true, but he was right. Her mom had bloomed out here. She didn't like the idea of being cooped up with her mother-in-law at first, but when Dad left, she and Emma's mom jumped into party mode to put together the reception of the century, as she put it.

Guilt filled Maddie as she recognized her mom's joy over her new life. All these years, her mom was doing everything to provide them with a good life, while her own was squelched.

"Hey, why the long face?" Rachel asked as she brought Maddie a glass of ginger ale.

"I was just thinking about how Mom is finally happy."

"Yeah, looks like it. She's found her calling."

Looking at her friend, she asked, "Does it take everyone such a long time?"

"What do you mean?"

"Mom had to sacrifice herself for us until she realized her calling."

"Orrrr, she had to be prepared for it," Rachel said as she bumped her friend's shoulder.

Maddie looked at her friend with a blank stare.

"There are things God does in us before he can work through us. It's not just about stepping into a vocation—anybody can do that. But if the joy of the Lord is our strength, then he must lead us into our calling. Before he does that, he prepares our heart."

Pondering her friend's answer, Maddie asked, "Do you think Mom knows Jesus?"

"Hmm, I don't know, but I know that he knows her and desires for her to know him." Nudging her elbow, she added, "It's something you can pray for."

Suddenly, Jacob walked over and grabbed her hand. "Come on, let's do a jig."

Looking back at her friend with fake distress, she joyfully allowed Jacob to lead her into a dance.

The harvest moon was low on the horizon as Maddie and Jacob sat on the tailgate of his truck. A sudden shiver caused her to sway her sore feet even harder to keep warm as she listened to Jacob talk.

Taking off his jacket, Jacob asked, "Are ya cold?"

Determined to shake off the chill, she shrugged, digging her fingers into the folds of her dress as he slipped his jacket around her shoulders.

Thankful for the immediate warmth of the jacket, she mumbled her gratitude. As the smell of his cologne wafted up from the jacket, her lips curved into a slight smile as she remembered the first moment they met.

"Ya know, that moon right thar helped the farmers as they worked. That's why it's called a harvest moon, and tonight it's a supermoon," he said.

"Is that why it's so big?"

"Yup. My Pap says it's a reminder ta be grateful."

"Are you?" She asked innocently.

A lock of hair fell over his forehead as he turned to her. "What's that?"

"Are you grateful?"

"I am. Sometimes I feel guilty, though."

Distracted by the hair he seemed to be clueless about, she clasped her hands tightly, fighting the sudden desire to put it in its place. "What do you mean?" She asked.

"Thar are a lot a people sufferin' now, but it's like we're in a bubble here, ya know?"

"Yeah."

"Maddie, I've signed up fer the army."

Alarmed, she turned to Jacob in shock as his jacket slipped from her shoulder.

"With the way the world's goin', I feel a need ta help, ya know?"

A shiver tore through her as he touched her shoulder. "Do

you think God's calling you?"

Looking at her somberly, he nodded, "Yeah, I do."

The joy of the night began to fade as she realized another friend was leaving her behind. "Then you should go," she said as she attempted to keep her disappointment to herself. "When do you leave?"

"The boys and I are scheduled to leave fer Nashville in a month."

"Jared and Rory are going too?"

"Yep, we enlisted on the same day."

She didn't know how to respond. Looking up at the moon, she wondered if Rachel knew.

"Hey, Maddie?"

Moonlight highlighted that pesky lock of hair that he still had not moved. A boldness came over her as she lifted her hand and moved the hair into place. If she didn't know any better, she would think Jacob was getting close to her. *What should I do?* She wondered.

The crunch of shoes on gravel interrupted the moment as she heard her brother yell out, "Hey, Mads, Dad is ready to go."

Groaning over the interruption, she jumped down and straightened her skirt. Watching as Jacob jumped down as well, she took off his jacket and folded it over her arm. Extending his jacket, she cleared her throat to keep from ruining the moment. Her heart raced as she wondered what he was going to say next. "You were going to say something?"

Taking his time, Jacob put his jacket back on.

"Maddie!"

"UGH, coming!" She yelled behind her.

After running his hands through his hair again, Jacob

nodded and blurted out, "I wanted to ask, well, would you like to go out with me tomorrow?"

Clasping her hands together in excitement, she smiled. The thought of going on a real date left behind a warmth that replaced the chill of the night.

"I mean, I was wondering if you'd like to go to the ranch with me. I'm going Saturday mornin' to care fer Mr. Don's horses. Thar's a girl I'm quite sweet on that I'd like ya to meet."

Suddenly embarrassed that she misunderstood the request, she stepped back. *I thought he liked me.* Confused over the look in his eyes, she didn't know what to say. She wanted to say yes, but if he had a girlfriend…

"If you don't wanna, well, I'll understand." Avoiding eye contact, he shuffled his feet as a frown crossed his face.

"I've never been to a ranch before," she said quietly. "What time?"

Smiling from ear to ear, Jacob answered, "I'll pick you up at six?"

Matthew ran up to Maddie and grabbed her arm. "We're gonna get in trouble. Would you come on already?"

"See you then," she said, with a quick smile as she turned to walk with her brother. Looking back over her shoulder, she saw Jacob watching her leave. Keeping pace with Matthew, she suddenly had a deep desire to talk to her best friend.

When David returned from Israel, he wanted to lock himself in an office and study everything he could on this Helel. The book of Daniel was calling him, too. History repeated itself, and he wondered if Helel was like Antiochus, the one the woman on the plane told him about. Hitler, Napoleon, Mussolini, Nero—any of these could have fit the bill of this antichrist. What alarmed David was this "abomination" thing. After watching what happened to her, David wondered if Mordy's warning was coming to fruition. He couldn't worry about the woman now. Hopefully, she received the cryptic message he dropped in her hand and would call Gabriel Hawke, the Senator from Georgia who spoke for him during his senate hearing. He was in a better place to help her anyway. Speaking of the Senator, David picked up his phone and rang his office.

"Senator Hawke here."

Surprised to hear his voice, David asked, "Answering your own calls, now, are we?"

"Well, it's hard to get good help these days." A trace of frustration laced the Senator's attempt at humor. "I got your email, what's up?"

Choosing to get right to the point, David said, "Two things. First, do you remember the plans that were produced after my team found the PKO locations?"

"I briefly remember talk of them in your hearing."

"I need to get my hands on a copy."

"Why?"

David had expected the question, but he wasn't ready to share everything quite yet. With a pause, he considered his response and then said, "I can't tell you. Just know that national security is at stake."

Clearing his throat in obvious agitation, Gabe responded, "David, I am a Senator of the United States Government. That excuse does not work with me."

Lying back in his dad's leather chair, he wondered if he should confide in the man. *It's just too dangerous,* he pondered. With a shake of his head to the empty room, he said, "Gabe, I don't want to implicate you if this goes south. I need you to trust me. Before I do anything, I will tell you."

Refusing to be placated, the Senator raised his voice and said, "Do anything? I don't like where this is going."

David wasn't going to be manipulated into sharing more than he was ready. Rubbing the tension forming in his neck, he took a deep breath and said, "Gabe, you can trust me."

Something in his tone appeared to soften the Senator as he responded, "It will take a while. I will need to subpoena the records as evidence in a case."

Relieved that he didn't have to force the matter, David said, "Okay, just let me know if you need anything from me."

A muffled sound accompanied the Senator's lowered voice as he made one more attempt to coerce David to give more details. "I need you to tell me what's going on."

This conversation was going nowhere. Tapping his fingers on the desk, he thought, *Should I tell him? No, keep to the plan, David.* "Trust me, Gabe. I will let you know once everything is ironed out."

"On your word?"

The question reminded David of similar asks from his dad. "Yes, on my word," he said confidently.

"Okay. What was the second thing you needed?"

Grateful for the change in subject, he stood and walked over to the window. A strange bird flapped its wings on a branch just outside the window. Turning away from the distraction, he said, "There's a woman who will be contacting your office. She is having trouble getting back into the country."

"What's her name?"

Scowling as he realized he never asked, he said, "Here's the thing. I didn't ask her name."

"Well, that narrows things down. David, you are being a bit elusive tonight."

The Senator's sharp tone signaled his impatience. He needed to wrap this up, and quickly. "I'm sure she'll be the only woman traveling from Israel asking for a pardon from Senator Gabriel Hawke."

Relenting with a heavy sigh, Gabe asked, "Okay, okay. What's her story?"

"She was stopped at customs. I think it was a religious

interrogation. She didn't comply."

"Oh, I've been getting quite a few of those calls recently."

"Why is that?"

"Lucien Baldur is forcing people to pledge that they 'will render unconditional obedience to Helel, Worldwide, Czar of Food Insecurity, and the people of the world, duly prepared to fulfill their obligation to the PKO without delay.'" The senator's words were heavy with sarcasm as he mocked the submissive mantra.

David had heard of the pledge, but to the PKO specifically? That was news to him. "Pledge obedience to the PKO? For what?" He asked.

"To submit to the tax authority under Project Manna. It's quite a mess."

The Senator's tone was thick with weariness. This wasn't the time to share his thoughts about the PKO. Feigning ignorance, he asked, "What happens if they deny?"

"Well, apparently, they aren't allowed back into the country. As your friend has learned."

Shaking his head over the unsettling transaction, David wrapped up the conversation and said his goodbye. As the call disconnected, his thoughts returned to Helel. He had to understand everything he could about this man, but he had one more mission to complete before he jumped into research mode. After speaking with his mom upon his return from Israel, it was clear Wild Rock needed some guidance before they made decisions they would regret later.

CHAPTER 5

Practice for Purpose

BZZZZZZ. The obnoxious sound of the alarm clock woke Maddie out of a lovely dream. Turning to mute it, she knocked it to the floor instead.

Grunting, she bent down to pick up the annoying clock. UGH, five a.m. Sitting up, she rubbed her eyes. Grabbing her Bible and journal, she made her way into the kitchen, where the light indicated she wasn't the only early riser. Laying down her books, she went to make a cup of coffee.

"Why good mornin' Maddie Ruth."

"Mornin', Grammy. You're up early."

"I could be sayin' the same 'bout you. Startin' yer chores early today?"

"I finished them yesterday after school so I can help Jacob at Mr. Don's ranch. I wanted to spend some time with God beforehand."

Leaning against the counter, Grammy crossed her arms and said, "Really, now."

"Uh, yes ma'am, that's okay, isn't it?"

"Hmm."

Busying herself with making her coffee, she waited as her Gram sized her up in the quiet.

"Mr. Don's a good man."

"Have I met him?"

"You ain't a horse, so I'd say no."

Confused, Maddie looked at Grammy inquisitively.

"Don had an accident that took his spirit. He's only been hangin' 'round horses since."

"What happened to him?"

"Well now, you'll have to ask him that yerself. Enjoy yer time with Jesus, Love, I'm gonna go out and spend some time with 'im myself."

Sitting down to her reading, she opened to Psalm twenty-three. Ever since Grammy introduced her to this scripture, Maddie took to memorizing a line at a time. She almost had it completely memorized.

Closing her eyes, she breathed in and out slowly. Reading the passage out loud, she invited God into the moment and asked him to speak. Sitting in the quiet, she began to write down what she heard.

Maddie, you are my daughter. When you walk through the valley, put your eyes on me.

She was learning to listen to his voice, always aligning it with scripture. Reading verses four and five of the passage, she recognized the confirmation. She drew a valley with dark clouds and the tower of trust shining a light into the darkness. The tower was her safe place. She knew that God would always meet her there.

These moments of quiet were her favorite. It was such a change from her old life. Before moving to Wild Rock, quiet meant sleeping in or playing on her phone, but now, she enjoyed the quiet of early mornings listening for God's voice.

Father, am I facing a valley? She wrote in response.

Eyes on me, Daughter.

Stuck in her thoughts, she looked at the clock and realized the time. *Fifteen minutes!* With a mix of alarm and excitement, she grabbed her books and ran to her room to get ready.

The cab of the truck was awkwardly quiet as they made their way down the mountain. Since Jacob's invitation on Wednesday night, Maddie was questioning her decision to join him. She couldn't help but harbor anxious thoughts about the mystery person he mentioned. She could hear Rachel's voice, *"Don't overthink it, Maddie, just go and enjoy it."* Nodding to herself, she resolved to do just that.

At the bottom of Wild Rock Mountain, Jacob turned toward the city. She realized it had been a long time since she had left the mountain.

The empty road brought back memories of the night her dad brought them back to Wild Rock. *How is Jade?* She wondered as she looked at the passing farms. *Jade was one of the strongest women she knew, she couldn't imagine anything bad happening to her, yet . . .*

"Here we are," Jacob said as he turned onto a dirt road.

The headlights highlighted a sign that read, "Kalispell." The old Ford pickup hit a dip in the road just as Jacob shifted downward to slow down. The sudden jolt jostled her in his direction, causing her seatbelt to tighten around her hips.

"Oops, sorry. May wanna hold on." He said nervously.

While Jacob appeared proud of his old truck, Maddie wondered if something a little newer would handle the gravel road better.

As they exited the truck, she was surprised to see Jared and Rory on the front porch sitting with an older man wearing coveralls and a cowboy hat.

"Jacob!" A young girl with a head full of red hair in pigtails ran down the front stairs right into Jacob's arms.

"Good mornin' ta you, Holly Polly." Tapping her nose, he smiled as she hugged his neck. "Holly, I have someone ver' special for you to meet. This is Maddie. Maddie meet Holly."

She couldn't help but chuckle as she wondered if this was the girl he wanted her to meet. "Hi, Holly!"

Jumping down from Jacob's arms, Holly quietly grabbed her hand and led her up the stairs. "Papaw, this here is Maddie."

Tipping his hat, Mr. Don said, "Well, hello ta you, Maddie Ruth."

Confused, she looked at Jacob, "You know me?" She asked.

"Why a'course. Ya look a lot like yer Grammy." He said with a smile.

Blushing, she said, "Oh, yeah." She forgot how close the community was, even at the foot of the mountain.

"I'm Mr. Don," he grinned as he extended his hand in a firm handshake. "Ya can call me Don. I understand yer gonna help us 'round here today. We could use another hand."

Suddenly excited over what the day would bring, she nodded. "I've never been on a ranch." Looking around, she asked, "Are there horses?"

Chuckling, Mr. Don grabbed his cane and stood. "Are thar horses? Well, y'all come on now, and we'll introduce ya." Walking down the stairs slowly, he jumped in a truck with Holly, not far behind. Jared, Rory, and Jacob all jumped in the back.

"Come on now, I'll help ya up," Jacob said.

"In the back?" Maddie asked. Momma always told her it was dangerous to ride in the back of a pickup truck.

"It'll be fine. It's only a hop, skip, an' a jump over thar."

Grabbing his hand, she jumped in the back.

The jolt she experienced as they first rode on the property was nothing compared to their ride to the barn. She had to hold on tight to keep from being thrown around.

The truck stopped at a barn longer than Grammy's house. A group of men stopped to wave and say hello as they all jumped out.

A set of double doors opened. Soft white light hanging from the ceiling welcomed them inside. Neighs and clops filled the long room as a ranch hand walked a horse through a set of double doors at the end. Maddie counted ten stalls, five on each side.

Suddenly surprised by the warm hand that had grabbed hers, she looked into Jacob's eyes and followed him to the first stall.

"Hey Charlie, meet ma friend, Maddie."

The long brown face nodded up and down as if to acknowledge her. "Can I touch him?" She asked timidly.

"Yeah, Charlie's a softie."

The pads of her fingers lightly touched his face. Running them over his mane, she was surprised by the coarseness. Charlie nudged her to continue.

"He likes ya, Maddie." Jacob smiled. "Ole Charlie boy here loves the ladies. Charlie, we'll see ya in a bit. I have a few more introductions to make."

Sad that she had to walk away from the affectionate horse, she walked behind Jacob as he introduced her to Ginger, Dakota, Lightning, Jasper, Pippa, Onyx, and Mocha.

A soft whinny toward the end seemed to be beckoning them forward. Jacob grabbed her hand again and said, "And this girl right here is the one I wanted ya ta meet. Maddie, meet Kali."

Surprised once more by the introduction, she couldn't help but laugh under her breath. "This is the girl you're sweet on?" She asked.

"Why a'course, who'd ya think I meant? Holly?"

"Hey!"

Maddie and Jacob turned to see Holly with her hands on her hips and eyes narrowed in a look of feigned anger. Impressed over the little girl's confidence as she stood proudly in her cowboy hat, boots, and pigtails, Maddie started to laugh uncontrollably. Holly and Jacob couldn't help but join in.

An affectionate nuzzle between them turned their attention back to Kali. "Here I am, Girl." Opening the stall door, he walked in and motioned for Maddie to follow.

The earthy smell of dusty woodchips and hay immediately

hit her senses as she walked carefully into the stall. She had never seen a horse up close.

Kali stood taller than Maddie and Jacob. As Jacob gently touched Kali's back, she looked around at him, slowly chewing the hay in her mouth.

"It's all right, Kali. How's ma Girl?" He said softly. "It's okay, Maddie, you can touch her. Jes' don't walk up behind her. Make sure she knows that you know that she sees ya."

Running her hands along the horse's back, she was surprised at how soft it was.

"She's a Chestnut," he said as he brushed her mane.

Her mane was so different from Charlie's. "She's so soft. Why is her mane white?"

"The flaxen trait is inherited. Her pappy had it." Jacob drew near to Maddie, brushing against her arm, "She has a secret."

Chills ran down her spine as goose bumps covered her arms. "What's that?" She asked as she wondered what was wrong with her.

"She's gonna foal in the Spring."

"What does that mean?"

Leading her out of the stall, Jacob said, "She's gonna have a baby. Aren't ya, Girl?"

Surprised to see the horse's enlarged belly, she wondered what it must be like to carry another horse.

"Come on, let's take our girl fer a walk." Handing the lead rope to her, Jacob showed her how to walk her out of the barn.

Kali seemed to like the opportunity to walk down the well-worn trail. Walking slowly, she swayed slightly as she moved. Jacob would stop now and again to allow her to graze.

"So, Kali is your favorite?" She asked.

"Yup, ever since she was a foal herself."

"Wait, how old is she?"

"How old are ya now, Girl?" He asked. "Let's see, I was twelve when she was born, so that'd make her six?"

"Six years old? When do horses begin having babies?"

"Oh, ya can breed 'em 'round eighteen months, but we like ta wait 'til they're 'bout three."

"Three years old? That's crazy."

Maddie focused on the sounds of their footsteps on the soft earth as she and Jacob turned around and made their way back to the barn.

As they led her into her stall, Kali went straight for her five-gallon bucket and began drinking.

They stood quietly for a moment but then caught each other's glance. An awkward tension gripped Maddie just before Jacob interrupted the silence.

"You wanna feed some of the other horses?"

"Oh, I'd love that," Maddie replied with a smile. He smiled back. She followed Jacob as he motioned for her to follow him.

Standing over a bucket filled with carrots, Jacob grabbed a handful, broke one in two, and gave Maddie the other half. Walking to Charlie's stall, he said, "Here ya go." Turning to her, he said, "He loves carrots." Laying the other piece in his hand, he lifted it palm up toward the horse's mouth and allowed him to nibble.

Copying Jacob's soft tone, she held the carrot in her hand and said, "Good horse." And proceeded to allow him to eat from her hand. A sweet nibble signified Charlie's thanks after the carrot was gone.

Jacob gave Maddie half of the carrots, and they each walked to the other stalls to feed the horses. After they fed Kali, she looked at her and seemed to give her a nod of thanks. Grabbing a brush, she began to brush her flaxen mane. Surprised by Jacob's proximity, she found herself in a weird position as he drew very close and held the hand she was using the brush the horse. Short of dancing, she had never been so close to a boy before and wasn't sure what to think about it.

"You're pretty good at this, Maddie," he said softly.

Having trouble focusing on the rhythmic brushing, she said, "Um, thanks."

"Hey, Maddie," Jacob said as he turned her around. The moment reminded her of his penetrating gaze from the wedding. She would think he could peer straight into her soul if she didn't know any better. "I'm gonna miss ya," he said, lifting her chin and kissing her. Everything began to swirl around as his lips left hers. Jacob Sullivan had just given Maddie her first kiss.

The sweet moment was soon interrupted by Kali as she nudged Maddie's arm. "Um, I think she wants more carrots?"

Jacob took Maddie's hand and pulled her out of the stall. As he walked her to the back of the barn, Maddie was suddenly excited and nervous as she realized they were completely alone.

"Hey Jacob? I should probably be getting home soon," she said as he continued to pull her forward. "Jacob?"

The pasture behind the barn seemed to go for miles. With mountains on the right and a forest on the left, Maddie looked around to see if anyone was hanging around. It was so quiet; you could hear a pin drop. In that moment, it was as if they were the only two people at Kalispell.

Suddenly, Jacob stopped and turned around. He placed both hands on her face and asked, "Maddie, can I kiss you?"

Time stopped as both his hands cupped her cheeks. Uncertain what to do next, she worried she would fall as her legs trembled. Nodding slowly, she was suddenly overwhelmed as his lips touched hers. This was a real kiss. The kind that made her blush when her parents dared to kiss in front of her. His arms pulled her close as his hands decided to go on a tour of their own. Lost in the moment, she caught herself surprised as she heard her name. Pulling away, she shook her head. This was too much, too fast. Worrying that someone saw them, she looked around, wondering who called her name.

Jacob's mouth fell open slightly as he looked at her in confusion. "What's wrong?" He asked.

Lifting her hands to warm her suddenly cold arms, she stood wondering how to answer his question.

Relief filled her when she heard the tap tap of Mr. Don's

cane behind them. *Did he call my name?* She wondered. "Maddie, what'cha think of our Kali girl?" He asked from the barn doorway.

Discretely straightening her shirt, she turned and ran to him. Raising her hands to tighten her ponytail, she desperately hoped the voice wasn't his. He didn't look at her weirdly or anything. *Maybe it was in my head,* she thought to herself. As she walked back into the barn, Kali nodded her head again, probably looking for more carrots, she thought guiltily. "She's beautiful." Touching the horse's side as she tried to remove the intrusive thoughts from Jacob's kiss, she took her thoughts captive and chatted on about how soft her coat was.

"Yeah, ya did pretty good with her today. Would ya like to come back and work with her some more?"

Her heart was practically beating out of her chest. While she wanted to return, she wasn't sure being alone with Jacob was a good idea. Determined not to look at him, she stared at Kali's mane as she considered her answer. *He isn't going to be here, Maddie. It'll be okay,* she thought to herself. An anxious relief filled her as she practically shouted, "I would love that!"

If the ride to Kalispell was awkward, the ride back to Grammy's was downright uncomfortable. Embarrassed that she allowed herself to be alone with Jacob, she didn't know what to say. Jacob, on the other hand, drove in stony silence. Maddie felt guilty that she hadn't said anything to him after the kiss.

After parking in the driveway, Jacob parked the truck and sat perfectly still.

What should I do? She wondered. *Does he want me to just get out?* "Um..."

"Maddie, I..." Jacob's hands squeezed the steering wheel tightly, his knuckles white from the tension. After taking a deep breath, he turned to her and said, "I'm sorry, Maddie."

Shaking her head, she whispered, "It's okay." *Not gonna cry, not gonna cry!*

"No, I was wrong. I'm sorry if I embarrassed ya."

"No, it's okay. It's just..." A hundred thoughts filled her mind and there wasn't one that she wanted to say aloud. She was caught between guilt, embarrassment, anger, but then there was something else. Something she wasn't ready to explore. "Jacob, that was my first kiss," she said finally looking down at her hands.

With clenched jaw, Jacob grimaced in obvious irritation. Maddie couldn't tell if he was angry at her or himself.

"It's okay, Jacob," she implored, placing her hand on his. A tear fell silently down her face. She didn't want him to be mad.

Turning to look at her with a sad smile, he said, "I will miss ya, Maddie Ruth Bennett. Will ya write to me?" Willing to say anything to keep him from being mad at her, she said, "Yes, I will write to you."

After several weeks of daily visits to Kalispell, Maddie sat with Mr. Don and Holly on their front porch. Jacob, Rory, and Jared were performing their army workups, so she and her friends decided to come and help in their absence.

The day in the pasture was weighing heavily on her mind. When she and Rachel were walking Kali one day, she told her what happened.

Rachel stopped in her tracks and looked at her friend. "Why were you alone with him?" She asked.

Surprised by her friend's response, she blurted out, "I don't know. I didn't think about it. I mean, the horses were there." She expected teasing but not anger.

Rachel lifted an eyebrow and said, "The horses, really?"

"Well, you know what I mean!" Guilt filled her afresh as she thought about what could have happened. "I know, it was wrong. I just got carried away in the moment."

"Maddie, look at me. This is not condemnation; do you hear me? Your purity is special. God created you for one man—

your husband. Are you willing to marry Jacob?"

"What? No! I mean, I don't know..."

"Exactly."

"It was just kissing," she said, quickly turning away in embarrassment.

Placing her hand on Maddie's shoulder, Rachel looked at her intently and said, "I'm sorry. I know that didn't sound right, I'm just worried about you. Maddie. I know you've known Jacob a long time, but with everything going on around us, you need to be careful, okay? Don't expect anyone to have the same boundaries that you have. We are responsible for protecting ourselves."

Holly's chatting broke into her anxious thoughts. Her sweet voice had a way of bringing joy to any conversation. Even if Maddie's first visit was weird, she loved every visit that followed. There was just one thing that she couldn't shake— Grammy's unwillingness to see or talk about Mr. Don.

A light rain fell as she waited for Aunt Lisa to pick her up. As they rocked, Mr. Don carved a piece of wood while Holly sat at his feet, coloring in a book. Maddie thought this was a good time to ask something weighing heavily on her mind. "Mr. Don, can I ask you a question?"

"Why shore, Maddie Ruth, ask away," he said, turning his ear to hear her over the rain.

"Why do you use a cane?"

"Hmm, that'd take a while to tell, I'm afraid."

Embarrassed, she looked away and said quietly, "Oh, I'm sorry."

"Don't be sorry, Girl. Ain't no law against askin'."

After a long pause, he said, "It was an evenin' jes' like this. I took my Margaret out fer a walk by the barn. She wanted ta see our Trixie, who was set ta foal in the next month. She looked jes' like our Holly here, and ya know, she was a lot like you, my Margaret. She prayed over ever' horse afore they went ta sleep."

Maddie blushed as she realized he knew of her afternoon ritual.

"And she loved to dance." A long sigh escaped his lips. "I've lived here all my life, Maddie Ruth. Bred more fillies than ya can count—two Derby winners, mind ya."

"The Kentucky Derby?"

"Yes, ma'am. I never thought God would let somethin' like that happen on ma land."

"Papaw don't talk like that. Mamaw would not stand fer it," Holly said.

Mr. Don gazed off into the distance. She knew that look. Lying back in the chair, she closed her eyes.

"Yer Grammy tole me 'bout yer friend," Mr. Don said.

Surprised, she turned and looked at him in shock.

"It's okay, Girl. Ya know God was with ya when it happ'ned."

Trying to fight back tears, Maddie whispered, "I know."

"It's okay, Maddie. God is here, too," Holly said as she laid her head on her knee.

She wasn't sure she was ready to share with people who were not in her inner circle.

"My Margaret, she was shot too."

A flash of empathy tore through her heart.

"Like I said, we were walkin' ta the barn, and thar was a fox in the hen house. Ya see, I'd hired a drifter, someone ta take care a my Trixie, but I did'na know he had evil motives fer bein' round."

"What do you mean?"

"Trixie was a broodmare, like Kali. She bred the best of the best. This drifter knew it. When we were walkin', we caught 'im red-handed tryin' to take off with her."

"Wait, he tried to steal the horse?"

"Yes, ma'am. My wranglers were gone fer the night. I thought it strange to see a truck backed up to the barn, but I thought one a the guys left somethin' behind. Did'na think anythin' of it. When I heard Trixie yelp, I knew somethin' was wrong."

Maddie sat quietly as Mr. Don rubbed his beard.

"I did'na have enough time to grab my gun. The thief saw

Margaret and me comin' 'round afore we saw him. Margaret ran toward Trixie, and he, well…"

"He shot her, didn't he?"

The sadness on his face was palpable. "I ran to ma beautiful wife. I heard the other pop and felt a flash a pain in my hip, but I did'na care. My Margaret, she needed me." A tear fell as he paused. The sound of his chair rocking on the old pine boards haunted the spacious porch as he hesitated.

"It's okay, Papaw," Holly comforted.

Growing still to better listen, Maddie placed her hand on his.

"My girls, Janey and Jill, came runnin' out. I could'na' keep her from 'em."

"I'm so sorry, Mr. Don."

He turned and looked at her with a sad smile. "It's okay, Maddie Ruth. Thar's a reason fer our pain, and I've made peace with the Lord." He looked at his granddaughter.

"Ya know, this girl right'chere, she's a gift from the Lord. My daughter Jill's been raisin' her right. She's teachin' me that the best gift we give to our loved ones is our time. It's all we got—that, and Jesus." Waving his hand over the ranch, he said, "This here'll be gone in a flash. But God gave us each other, and we cain't take it fer granted. Ever'thin' ya go through, why, it's practice fer purpose."

David was ready for the Town Hall Meeting scheduled for Monday night. Thankfully, the mayor was impressed with David's report. He could only hope the town would agree with his points.

The town had done a good job of coming together since they decided not to participate in The Kindness Tax. Resources around them were plentiful. Lumberjacks on the edge of town cut down trees for building structures, which the community came together to erect, and an engineer helped them set up water cisterns throughout the town. The old ways became new ways of survival as chickens provided eggs, community gardens provided fruits and vegetables, and hunting groups were sent out for meat. Neighbors helping neighbors—everyone had a purpose in Wild Rock.

For the first time in David's life, he was grateful for this town. When he was a teenager, all he could think about was breaking free, but now this town was providing for and protecting his family. As he and Tom sat down with several of the townsmen, they discussed potential security measures to protect what they were building. He appreciated how the community invited strangers in, but seasoned perspective told him that it was only a matter of time before that would backfire on them. With Tom's experience on the Seal team and his time working for the NSA, he felt they could provide a solid plan to keep the town safe.

One thing he knew beyond any other, keeping his family safe was his purpose.

CHAPTER 6

The Outlanders

Maddie was in a funk the morning after she chatted with Mr. Don. She wished she could talk to Grammy about it, but every time she started to ask, her Gram would divert the conversation. *God, what is wrong with her?* She wrote in her journal.

"Practice for Purpose." She couldn't get this statement out of her mind. *What did Mr. Don mean by that?* After drawing a lightbulb next to the word "purpose," she chewed on the end of her pen as she thought about it. She understood not taking stuff for granted, but how was her pain practice for purpose?

While she wasn't a fan of talking about her pain, she had gotten better at it. Between journaling and prayer, she found talking to God super helpful in letting things go.

A knock on the door broke her out of her thoughts. "Maddie, Grammy wants to talk to us," Matthew said.

I hope everything's okay, she thought as she placed her pen beside her journal. Standing up to stretch, she glanced at her journal, "I wonder if they know about Jacob," she mumbled to herself.

As she walked into the kitchen, her mom and Grammy were deep in conversation. Happy to see her mom laugh at one of Grammy's quips, she breathed a sigh of relief. *Come on, Maddie,* she wondered, *why are you so worried?*

Enamored by a fat orange carrot dangling from the cutting

board, she attempted to slowly grab a piece while they were talking. A quick sting from her Gram's hand stopped her in mid-air.

"That ain't yers, Maddie Ruth."

"It's just one carrot."

"It's one carrot, 'til ya have none. We gotta conserve, Girl, ya know that."

"Yes ma'am," she groaned.

"Maddie, your Grammy and I need to talk to you and Matthew," her mom said. "Let's sit at the table."

Uh-oh. Sitting at the table with her brother, she twiddled her thumbs. Oh, how she missed her phone. *I wonder what the girls are up to.* She pondered.

"Hey Sis, look at what Mr. Tom gave me," Matthew said as he pulled out a knife.

"Whoa. Mom, is he allowed to have that?"

"Yes, Matthew has proven to be very responsible with the knife."

"See, look at what I made." He pulled out a small piece of wood whittled into the shape of a dagger.

"Dude, what're you going to do with that?"

Shrugging his shoulders, he said, "I dunno. Uncle Tom said I would know when the time was right."

Nothing in her demeanor suggested that her mom was concerned about her brother's reckless behavior. As she glared at her mom, she decided a sidebar conversation with her brother was needed.

The concern on Grammy's face, however, was palpable. *What is she thinking?* Maddie wondered.

"Thar's a town hall meetin' tonight. Yer dad's speakin' and yer mom and I are goin'. We want y'all to stay in the house and lock up behind us."

"Lock up, but this is Wild Rock," Matthew said.

"Boy, jes' hear me out. Thar's some outlanders hangin' 'round and we jes' want'cha to be safe."

Relief filled her when she realized the conversation wasn't about her. "Outlanders?" Maddie asked. "Do you mean strangers? What kind?"

"The kind that should'na be in Wild Rock. An that's all I'll say 'bout that," Grammy replied.

"But…"

"No buts, Maddie," her mom interjected. You heard Grammy, lock up behind us when we leave. You'll be fine."

"I'm here, Mads. I'll protect you if anyone tries to break in." Stabbing the air with his dagger, Matthew seemed a little too excited about the idea.

"That's what I'm afraid of," she said.

Darkness came early as Maddie sat at the table with her journal. Yawning, she wanted to go to bed but didn't want to leave her brother alone. With Grammy's lap blanket in hand, she went into the living room and found a comfy spot on the couch. The soft leather reminded her of home. She missed home—Atlanta, that is.

This would have been her Junior year at Marietta High. Football games and coffee dates should have been the norm as she and her friends prepared for homecoming. They would go as a squad, just as they did with everything else, of course. But not this year. *Probably not ever,* she sighed.

The little school in Wild Rock combined all the grades into one little building. The small class was so different from Marietta High, which had thousands of students. When some of their friends arrived from Atlanta, she was so excited for them to meet her Wild Rock friends as she silently hoped things would go back to normal.

When Jade decided to return to Atlanta, Maddie was all in her feels. She couldn't help but be worried, sad, and even a tad jealous as she thought of her friend seeking her calling. Yawning a second time, she knew her dad would never let her go, but she wished…

"Maddie, Maddie, help me!"

Screams called to her from far away. Isn't Jade in Atlanta? She thought as she ran out of the house and made her way through the dark woods. Brambles like the vines at the PKO tore her arms as she pushed her way through. The closer she got to her friend, the more and more resistance she faced.

"Maddie!"

Suddenly, she felt her feet give way as a river of mud carried her down the mountain.

"Maddie, wake up!"

"Huh? Who's there?" Sitting up, she rubbed her eyes, trying to focus on the person before her.

"Are you okay? You were yelling in your sleep again." The concern on Matthew's face touched her as she sat up.

"What was I saying?" She asked.

"I couldn't tell. Sis, are you okay?"

"Well, here we all are. I want ta take a moment an thank ya fer bein' here tonight. I invited Grace's son David ta speak." Pastor Ron waved him to the front. "Dave, come on up 'ere."

"He's an outsider, Pastor Ron, what's he gonna help us with?"

"Benjamin, my David has more experience than you with providin' a safety plan fer the town."

Benjamin stood and yelled, "I don't care 'bout no safety plan, I wanna hear what we're doin' 'bout them outlanders!"

As David stood and walked to the front, Pastor Ron tried to calm the crowd. Relief flooded David as Tom came to stand next to him. The two were a formidable pair when side by side.

Burly ole Clyde stood and said, "Benjamin, don't go gittin' yer gussie up. Sit down an' let these boys talk."

"Thank you, Pastor Ron. Benjamin, I understand your concern. I, too, am concerned about my family and the town's safety and security. That is why we are here. To set your minds at ease, we would like to share our backgrounds. Tom and I both served in the Navy and have experience in preparedness."

"Navy, hmph, jes' a bunch a' sissy squids. What do you know 'bout safety?"

"Benjamin, you Ninny, don't make me come over thar'," Grammy shouted in frustration as she stood facing Benjamin's direction.

Tom placed his hand on David's shoulder as he prepared to stop his mother from doing whatever she was thinking.

Pastor Ron stepped forward as he said, "Benjamin, Grace, have a seat. Benjamin, can we agree to listen and save our questions 'til the end?"

Benjamin sat back down and crossed his arms.

"As I was saying," David continued. "Tom and I have extensive experience in safety preparedness. We served together for fourteen years. We had teams on the ground in Sudar, Africa, when they experienced an economic collapse. Tom is currently providing safety training for special operations armed forces. Tom, would you like to share a little of your resume with the town?"

"It was in Sudar that David saved my life."

David looked at Tom curiously as if to say: *That wasn't in the script.*

"Sudar had just experienced an earthquake. We were called in to provide humanitarian aid and maintain peace, in conjunction with the established local assistance center that was set up by our government. Unbeknownst to the local government, a coup from a neighboring country was planned, and a group of guerrillas staged an attack. David rooted out the coup and prepared our teams for a counterattack. When the guerrillas rushed in, we were caught in the crossfire. David used his body as a human shield to protect me; otherwise, I would not be here tonight." Tom looked at David with gratitude. "David's team was integral in setting up a safety plan to drive out the guerrillas and help the Sudar people create their own community policing program."

The room was pregnant with anticipation for the next part of the story.

David had never shared this story with his mom. Giving him a look of disapproval, David added, "You didn't have to share that little bit of information, Tom. However, while we're sharing war stories, Tom's team physically trained the local police force in Sudar, and that leads me to why we are here. Wild Rock has chosen to withdraw from the TKT, so you have experienced a loss of social services from the federal government. While you have done a tremendous job coming together as a community to help one another, one thing is lacking. That is security."

"Pardon me, David, but this ain't Africa. The people a' Wild Rock look after their own," Clyde interjected as he looked around the room for affirmation.

"Yes, and you do an excellent job, Clyde. But if something catastrophic were to happen, where would you turn? Doc Walker is the only doctor in town, and he's on loan from Nashville."

"What 'bout them outlanders?" Benjamin added.

David nodded to Benjamin. "We don't know that these strangers are dangerous, Benjamin, but there may come a time when we, too, must face an external force that threatens our safety. We need to have a plan. So, we have devised a comprehensive plan to submit to the town today for approval."

Uncle Tom and Pastor Ron joined David and Tom at the front as Jacque passed out informational packets to everyone in the crowd.

The rest of the night was spent discussing the area's environmental and infrastructure hazards. An emergency management team and neighborhood watch program were set up, with Uncle Tom, the mayor of the town, as the primary communication lead. At the end of the night, David pulled out a map, and they charted an evacuation route in addition to shelter locations in case of an emergency. David chose not to share his concern about the strangers who seemed to be casing the town, but he knew this was something that would need to be addressed—sooner rather than later.

As the room cleared, only David, Tom, Olivia, Jacque, Pastor Ron, Uncle Tom, and Grace remained. "Ya did a good thing tonight, David ma Boy."

"Thanks, Mom, but this is only the beginning."

"Benjamin has a point, Dave. What do you think 'bout these outlanders?" Uncle Tom asked. "They've been creating quite a ruckus with their cameras, pens, and clipboards. I sense a coup of our own brewin'."

"I think we should watch and wait. Do we know where they're staying?"

"As I understand it, down in the valley, near Don's place, Kalispell."

David's mom looked at him with alarm.

"What's wrong, Mom?"

"Maddie and her friends have been goin' to Kalispell ta help with the horses."

Pastor Ron placed his hand on her shoulder. "Grace, they're safe with ole Don. Kalispell is a fortress, prob'ly safer than Wild Rock."

"It ain't Kalispell I'm worried 'bout."

"Don would never do anything to put your granddaughter or Wild Rock at risk."

"Hmph," she snorted as she crossed her arms and looked away.

Surprised at the exchange, David decided to pay a visit to Kalispell and see what his mom was worried about.

As they walked into his childhood home, David felt a rush of nostalgia. He wished his dad were here. When he was a boy, they experienced a storm that came close to destroying this house. For months, they were without power and transportation. It was in that season that his dad's mantra, "Do it afraid," was sealed on David's adolescent heart as he watched his dad lead their community into recovery. From then on, he determined to follow in his dad's footsteps and do the same for everyone in his purview.

David's heart softened when he saw his two youngest children at the table working on a puzzle. He was proud of them both as they showed courage through the chaos they'd experienced. He knew they were both sacrificing to be here, but rarely did he hear a peep out of them.

Placing one hand on each of their shoulders, he said, "What are we building?"

Maddie jumped in surprise as she glanced at him. "Dad, don't scare me like that!"

David laughed at the annoyed look his daughter threw him. Her sensitivity was endearing. As he peered closely at the design, he saw something that he was certain they had missed.

"It's a barn, can't you see?" Matthew answered."

"What I see," David said as he focused on the board, "is one piece out of place."

"NO! Where?!?" They cried out in unison.

"I don't know. Looks like you've got to figure that out," he laughed as he walked away.

CHAPTER 7

Eyes to See

"Will the rain ever stop?" A loud groan accompanied a heavy stomp as Matthew attempted to get all the mud and water off his rain boots.

As she shook raindrops from her soaking wet coat, Maddie couldn't help but wonder the same as she watched her brother yank his rain jacket off in a dramatic display of aggravation.

"Boy, what're you goin' on 'bout?" Grammy asked as she walked up behind them.

"I was just wondering when it would stop raining. All this rain is cutting into my boomeranging."

Maddie raised an eyebrow and asked, "Is that even a word, Matthew?"

Aghast that his sister would even ask the question, he shouted, "Of course it is! Uncle Tom said so."

"Well, if Uncle Tom said, then it must be so," Grammy chuckled. "Hang yer jackets up and let's start a fire. I'll get some hot tea to warm our bones."

"Grammy, can we have some hot chocolate—with little marshmallows?" Matthew asked as he pinched his fingers in front of his face.

"Now, ya know, Matthew, we don't have all them fancy fixin's you'ns are 'customed to." As she walked into the kitchen, she pointed toward the front door and added, "Go grab us some logs from the porch and I'll see what I've got stashed fer a rainy day."

Grammy, Maddie, and Matthew had spent the morning covering spinach and arugula plants in the garden. They couldn't risk losing the plants, so they covered them with tarps and buckets to shield them from the heavy rain and wind.

As Matthew grabbed an armful of extra logs from the porch, Maddie swept the fireplace hearth and added wood to start a fire. She loved sitting in front of the fireplace. There was just something about a roaring fire that calmed her heart. As challenges continued to hit them from every side, she was learning to enjoy the little things.

"Here ya go, Love." The cup of piping hot tea was a welcome distraction from the cold, wet weather. "Matthew, I had jes' a smidge of cocoa in the pantry. I'm 'fraid this is gonna be the last of it for a while. Enjoy it while it lasts."

"Oh man," he groaned as he took the cocoa from his Gram.

As Maddie stared into the flames, a knock at the door broke into her musings.

A breeze threatened the intense fire as Grammy opened the door. "Well, hey thar', Girls! Yer jes' in time for some tea and a fire. Hand me yer coats thar'. Can I get ya anythin'?"

Shaking off the rain from their slickers, Emma and Rachel shed their coats and shoes to join their friend by the fire.

"I would love some tea, Grammy," Emma said with a smile.

"Yes, me too, please. I was hoping you'd have a fire," Rachel added. Turning to Maddie, she said, "We missed you at school. Everything okay?"

"I'm good," Maddie said as she looked at her friend. "Grammy needed help, so we stayed home. I'm all caught up on classwork, so I figured it wouldn't be a big deal. Did I miss anything?"

"Only Jacob being Jacob. He decided to give a dissertation on the artistry of banjo-plucking." Emma said with a laugh.

"He looked disappointed not to have a full audience. I think he missed you, too," she added was a wink.

"Here ya go, Ladies," Grammy said as she handed them both a cup. Warm yerselves a'fore ya catch a cold."

Fighting a shiver, Emma was relieved at the promise of a hot beverage. "Oh, this is so good. Thank you, Grammy."

"Yer welcome. I'll be in the back room if ya need me."

"The house is awfully quiet. Where is everybody?" Rachel asked.

"Mom and Dad went to visit Mr. Don, and I'm sure Matthew is around here somewhere, probably building some kind of doomsday weapon."

"That's a bit dramatic."

Rolling her eyes, Maddie said, "He's been carrying a knife and a dagger everywhere he goes."

"Why?"

"I don't know. Uncle Tom is teaching him how to build weapons from trees."

"Dad says we must learn to protect ourselves. It's okay, Maddie. Remember what Laura said? Our dads won't always be here to help us, so it's up to us to learn to defend ourselves," Rachel encouraged.

"I know, but weapons? I don't think I can use a weapon to hurt someone," Maddie countered. "To be honest, I don't even remember much of what she taught us," she added sarcastically. Laura was the expert in Korean martial arts whom Maddie and Rachel's dads had hired last summer to teach them all self-defense.

"I'm with you, Girl," Emma agreed.

"I remember she told us to look around and be aware of our surroundings. If I had known that two years ago, maybe none of the stuff would have happened to us."

Emma placed her hand on Rachel's shoulder. "Oh, Rach..."

Conflicted over the reality of it all, Maddie wondered, *why did they go through all that training, anyway? How do weapons and self-defense help anybody when people still die?* She didn't want her friend to get mad or anything, but she couldn't just ignore these thoughts. "Hey, not to sound salty or anything, but after everything we learned from Laura, Kate still died." She said softly.

"Do you think I don't know that?" Rachel's raised voice caught her friends off guard. Grabbing the fireplace poker to stoke the flames, she stared into the embers as she moved her lips in prayer. Crackle and pop sounds from the wood broke through the heaviness in the room as if it were a thick, invisible blanket. Her lips quivered as the elephant in the room stood before them. "Every night I fight the urge to blame myself for Kate's death," she whispered as she raised her hand. "Before you argue, I'm the oldest. I knew what to do and I just didn't..."

Anger arose in Maddie at the thought that her friend was stuck in this cycle of blame. "What?" She asked.

Confused over her friend's question, Rachel responded, "What do you mean?"

Maddie stood with hands on hips, pacing the floor in front of them. "What could you have done?" Stopping to point, she said, "She was in the back seat. Somebody broke through the glass and grabbed her." Waving her hand around the room, she added, "What could any of us have done, even if we had weapons?"

Rachel hugged her knees to her chest and responded weakly, "Maybe, if I had been in the back."

Emma leaned forward and locked eyes with her friend, daring her to look away. "Come on, that could have been any of us, but God chose to bring our friend home that day. Have you ever thought about that?" She asked. Grabbing both of her friend's hands, Emma encouraged Maddie to sit back down as she said, "Girls, I know you're hurting. I hurt too! The one thing I learned from Laura was to be prepared. I think it's what God wants for us, too. He is our Protector, but he gives us eyes to see and wisdom to know the right thing to do. It's up to us to use what he's given us when we face danger, right?"

Rachel and Maddie nodded at their friend's wisdom. The fire that had fought Rachel's poking suddenly roared in the big brick fireplace. Each of them sat staring in awe at the power of the fire before them.

After a few moments, Rachel looked at Maddie and asked, "Hey, not to change the subject or anything, but why did your parents go to visit Mr. Don?"

Shrugging, Maddie said, "I don't know. I overheard Grammy talking about some strangers staying near Mr. Don's. I think Dad's afraid they're going to do something."

"I don't remember any strangers hanging around Kalispell."

"Yeah, me neither. I think he just wants to be safe."

Grabbing the fire poker again, Rachel turned the log over. "My dad said they put together a safety plan for the town. He's worried the people here are naïve to what's happening."

Quiet filled the room as each girl sat in her thoughts. Maddie was tired of worrying over the next shoe dropping. If her dreams were any indication, it was going to happen regardless of how she felt about it. Her friends were right, she needed to be aware of what was happening around her and seek wisdom. God didn't give her all these friends so she could do it alone.

A determined look on her face, she turned to look at her friends and said, "Okay, Girls, it's time that we prepare for battle. Rach, I've been praying on my armor every day. What else do we need to do? How can we pray for the town and Jade?"

Rachel smiled and said, "I thought you'd never ask."

The girls put together a safety plan of their own—a spiritual safety plan. Rachel drew a crude map of the town and gave them each what she called "territory." They were to walk over their territory and pray over it. "We're taking territory for the Lord," she said as they wrote the names of those they knew and decided to pray for them and their families.

"Even Benjamin?" Maddie felt a little guilty after she uttered the words.

Rachel chuckled, "Even Benjamin."

So, on that rainy day in Wild Rock, Tennessee, a plan was born to take territory for God's Kingdom.

She would never forget the moment her Grammy walked in, got on her knees, and joined them in intercession. She opened Isaiah sixty-two, and just as they did at Wild Rock Overlook, she prayed that they would not remain quiet, but that all would see God's glory.

As they finished their prayer, Emma asked if they could include Jade and Atlanta.

"A'course, Girl!" After which, they went into intercession for their friend.

Maddie didn't know what Jade was facing in Atlanta, but she trusted that God had her in his hands.

Later that night, a knock on the door interrupted her prayer journaling.

"Come in," she said as she set her pen down.

"Maddie Ruth, it was a mighty fine thing ya girls did today."

"Yeah, I don't know where it came from, but I just felt like we had to do something."

"Prayer is and always should always be yer first response. That's Holy Spirit stirrin' in ya."

"I seem to always pray when bad things happen. So, if I pray before something bad happens, will it keep it from happening?"

Sighing, Grammy responded, "No ma'am, but yer invitin' the Almighty into it so he can give ya wisdom and discernment as ya walk through it. God's Spirit helps ya not only walk with him, but pray with him, even when ya don't know what ta say."

Revelation filled her as she asked, "Hey, Grammy?"

"Hmm?"

"Remember when you said that God provides peace in the storm?"

"Yes ma'am."

"I think I'm finally beginning to understand, but I have to seek it, don't I?"

"Well now, ya gotta seek him. Jesus said, "Seek first his Kingdom and his righteousness and all these things will be given to ya. That includes his peace, cause he is our peace. Goodnight now, Maddie Ruth.""

As raindrops fell on the metal roof above them, she said a prayer of protection over their house. If she were honest, 'your will be done' were scary words to say, but Grammy was teaching her that it was God they needed, not just his protective hand. "Thank you for your peace, God. Whatever happens, I know you are with us. But if you could keep the house and our family safe? Well, that would be great."

A panicked knock on the door the next morning would test her newfound resilience.

The door was violently thrown open as Uncle Tom and Michael rushed in.

"Grammy, Maddie, Matthew, grab your things, we have to go now!"

"What're ya talkin' 'bout, Boy? Tell me straight!" Grammy yelled.

"I don't have time. Grab your jacket and your rain boots, we need to get to the safehouse, now."

Stuffing her socked feet into her boots, Maddie grabbed her jacket and called her brother.

"What is it, Mads?" Matthew yelled down the hallway with a loud yawn.

Repeating Uncle Tom's instruction, she said, "Get your jacket and your boots, we have to go now!"

Matthew jumped into action and obediently grabbed his things.

As they descended the stairs, she couldn't help but notice a torrent of water flowing down the hill. "Where's mom and dad?" She asked.

"They're in town," Michael responded. "Don't worry, Rachel and Emma are safe too."

Michael knew her all too well. She gave a small sigh of relief knowing they were safe, but the scene around them was indicative of the real danger they were in. Uncle Tom navigated his 4x4 through pools of water deep enough to take her mom's little car out. As they ascended the mountain into town, Maddie knew that whatever was happening was putting their lives at risk.

The safehouse was a big warehouse made of blocks that had been built to store their supplies as they collected them. Over the past six months, the townspeople filled the huge building with every item they could find. Dad said they couldn't buy anything, so they had to share everything they could find. A cold room held cured meats, non-perishable foods, and personal items. She had only been in this building once and was amazed at how much the town had pulled together in such a short time.

"Mom, Dad!" Matthew ran to his parents with his sister not far behind.

"What's happening?" She didn't like the look of worry on her dad's face.

David placed each hand on his children's shoulders as he said, "The rain has caused a bit of flooding, so we have decided to bring everyone to high ground for safety."

"Flooding?

"Yes, we'll be fine, Ruthie, just stay with your brother, okay? I'll be back in a bit."

Looking at her brother, Maddie wondered what, if anything, they should do.

"Maddie!" As she turned around, she saw Emma run toward her with Rachel in tow.

"I'm so glad to see you! Do you know what's going on?" She asked.

"Yeah, there's been a mudslide on the other side of the mountain," Rachel said.

"Mom said houses have been completely wiped out," Emma added, obviously worried.

Suddenly alarmed, Maddie asked, "Have you seen Amy Jayne?" Everyone looked at her with empty stares. *I just can't lose another friend,* she worried. "Father, please let me see her," she prayed quietly as she scanned the room. She didn't want to admit to her friends that her stomach was in knots, but she knew God would understand.

There were so many people in the safehouse, yet so many were still missing. "Where are Aunt Lisa and Eva Mae?" She asked anxiously.

"Ricky went ta grab 'em. Don't ya worry, Girl," Grammy said from behind.

The building that once seemed so large suddenly felt claustrophobic. As the room closed in on her, a hand grabbed hers. In slow motion, she looked down and then up at the face of her best friend. She could feel her heart beating a hundred miles a minute even as her friend looked her in the eye and encouraged her to breathe slowly. Listening to her friend's encouraging voice, she took a deep breath in and exhaled. Closing her eyes, she followed with four more breaths and felt her heartbeat begin to normalize.

"Are you okay?" Rachel asked as she squeezed her friend's hand.

With a nod and a weak smile, Maddie answered, "Yeah, thanks. Just when I think I've got it beat…"

"It's okay, you did well. Let's pray for those who are missing."

A commotion from the double doors at the front of the safehouse turned everyone's attention forward. "Make a path, y'all. Over here, Doc Walker!" Someone yelled.

Maddie watched as an unconscious man was carried to a make-shift bed and laid flat on his back. The doctor tore off his right pant leg and used it to apply pressure to a wound in his thigh that was oozing blood. Leaning down, he listened for breath sounds and took his pulse. Pulling a cuff out of his pocket, he formed it around the man's arm loosely and then applied a tourniquet above the wound. "You, grab me towels, and a basin of warm water."

Placing her hand on her chest, she looked around with surprise as she asked the doctor whom she met at the barn raising, "Me?"

Doc Walker placed the stethoscope earpieces into his ears as he took the man's blood pressure. "Yes, you! Hurry, Girl!" He shouted impatiently.

Maddie ran to do what the doctor instructed. She was thankful to see her friends right behind her. As she filled a bowl with warm water, Rachel and Emma grabbed towels from a shelf. Running back to the doctor, they laid everything down and waited for the next instruction.

"Are you a praying woman?" Doc Walker asked.

Surprised at the question, she answered, "Yes, Sir."

"Then I suggest you start prayin'."

Maddie looked down and touched the man's hand. God, what should I pray? She asked silently as she recognized Benjamin. Looking up at Rachel, she suddenly wanted to cry. "Even Benjamin," her friend had said the day prior. Words bubbled up from deep inside her. She began by asking her Father in Heaven to meet them there and to touch Benjamin's body. As she asked for wisdom for Doc Walker, he exposed the wound and looked around for other injuries. A vision of her dad working on her friend immediately brought tears to her eyes. Placing the memory aside, she heard her Grammy say, "Ask fer what ya want the Father ta do, Maddie Ruth." Courage rose up within her as she began asking God to heal as only he could. "You are Jehovah Rapha," she heard herself say, "nothing is impossible for you." After a few moments of praying, she was spent. There was nothing else to do, she was at peace. "In the strong and mighty Name of Jesus, amen." The voices of those who joined her in prayer agreed with their own amen.

Benjamin moaned.

"Doc, has he been impaled?" Someone asked from behind.

"Whatever caused this wound appears to have exited his body and there do not appear to be any broken bones, thankfully. At this point, we need to control the bleeding and give him a few stitches." Looking at Maddie, he asked, "Can you find a first aid kit?"

"What happened? What're you doing here?" Benjamin asked belligerently as he began to gain consciousness.

Looking at Benjamin calmly, Doc Walker answered, "You gave us quite a scare, Benjamin."

"He's savin' yer life, Benjamin!" Grammy yelled from behind. "Don't you be sassin' nobody, now."

Benjamin's eyes softened as he peered at the doctor through eyes filled with pain.

Realizing she was still holding his hand; she placed it on his shoulder. Just as she turned to follow the doctor's instructions, someone placed a first aid kit in her hand. Turning to give it to the doctor, she sat back down and attempted to distract Benjamin from the pain. "Are you okay?" She asked.

Crinkling his eyes together as if to give her a smart retort, he thought better of it and mumbled, "I guess I'm feelin' a bit better." His brows raised humbly as he turned to Doc Walker, "Thank ya kindly fer savin' my life." His eyes filled with tears as he added, "I'm indebted to ya, Doc."

Doc Walker smiled as he looked at Benjamin and said, "It's my pleasure, Sir. We can't have you goin' down with the ship, now, can we?" Moving his finger in front of Benjamin's face, he asked him some questions to confirm he wasn't confused or in shock.

"Now, Benjamin, I'm going to elevate your legs just above your heart. This may hurt a bit."

"Yassir," Looking at Maddie, he squeezed his eyes shut tight as the doctor propped his legs on a small round pail wrapped in a blanket. Looking at her intently, Benjamin asked, "I'm all alone now, ain't I?" He asked. "Ma house is gone, I ain't got nothin' no more."

Choosing her words carefully, she said, "Mr. Benjamin, you know that God is with you, I mean, he just performed a miracle right here by saving your life and blessing you with all these people who prayed for you. You're not alone, Sir, not at all."

After Benjamin was stabilized, a group of men moved him into Uncle Tom's truck. They had to get him to a hospital to confirm there were no internal injuries. She and her friends prayed they would get to the hospital safely.

Later that night, she and her Aunt Lisa worked to get Eva Mae to sleep. The heaviness of the day was overwhelming to everyone, but to Maddie, her bubble of safety had burst. *I'm not safe anywhere,* she worried.

"Aunt Lisa?"

"Yes ma'am?"

"You told me once that God gives you hope in a fallen world."

"Yes ma'am, he shore does."

"How do you stay calm when things like this happen?"

"Well, I reckon I have a choice. I can choose to focus on the light or allow fear to drag me into darkness." Shrugging her shoulders, she looked at her niece as she added, "I choose light."

"How do you focus on the light when everything is so dark?"

Aunt Lisa laughed, "Nothin' good comes easy, Maddie, and that's the beauty of it. The more hardship we face, the more dependent we become on our heav'nly Father. It's then we see his light all 'round. Thar ain't no place I'd rather be.

"Thar's a story in the Bible 'bout King David. He was overwhelmed by darkness too. He prayed a prayer askin' God to light up his eyes so he wouldna' be overcome by his enemy in death."

That sounds a bit extreme, she thought. "Why did he ask for that?" She asked.

Leaning down to kiss Eva Mae, Aunt Lisa pulled the blanket up to her daughter's chest and smiled. Turning to Maddie, she whispered, "David was bein' chased by King Saul and he thought God had forgotten 'im."

"But what did he mean when he asked God to light up his eyes?"

"Shhh," Aunt Lisa motioned for her to quietly follow her. Grabbing a Bible and a lamp, she led her niece into an unoccupied corner. Opening to Psalm thirteen, she said, "After he asked God to light up his eyes, he prayed that he could trust in God's unfailin' love. David asked him to give 'im eyes to see so he's not stuck in the weeds of his problem."

Maddie couldn't hold the tears back any longer. Looking at her aunt, she asked, "Can I ask for that? I'm so tired of being in the dark. I want to see what God sees so I can do what he wants me to do."

Aunt Lisa smiled at her niece as she lifted her chin, "Ya shore can, but know that it's a dangerous prayer."

"Why?"

"When ya see through God's eyes, ya see all the sufferin', the pain, an the sorrow, but ya also see all the joy. Ya gotta know what to do with the both of 'em."

"Do? What can I do with someone's suffering?"

"Well, ya lay it down first and then ya 'tend to the hurtin'. Jes' like ya did with Doc Walker. What'd ya do when he needed a hand ta help Benjamin?"

"I prayed and then gave him my hand?"

Aunt Lisa chuckled as she closed her bible. "That's right. When the Lord calls, you'll know. Then, ya jes' give 'im yer hand."

CHAPTER 8

Miracles in the Mud

The following day brought a solemn atmosphere to the safehouse. As people wandered in, Mom would check them off while offering a blanket, a towel, and a warm meal. While shocked that they had to use the safety plan so soon, the people making their way to the safe house were grateful.

Maddie, Rachel, and Emma worked with Doc Walker to patch people up as they came in. Matthew took charge of the children by giving them little projects to keep them busy. This gave the adults time to debrief and strategize their plans for the day.

Grammy was holding prayer vigils for those missing loved ones. Worried over Amy Jayne and her brother James, Maddie took a break from helping the doctor to pray with her Gram. *Father, please tell me how to pray for my friend. Please help the searchers find them.*

After praying, she had a strong desire to talk to her dad, who was deep in conversation. Tapping his shoulder, she said timidly, "Hey, Dad." Shifting her weight from foot to foot, she tried to be patient, but the longer she waited, the more worried she became. "Dad," she said a little louder.

Turning to look at his daughter in frustration, David answered, "What!"

Mortified when the room went quiet, she swallowed as she remembered her friend. Her dad's gruffness wasn't going to intimidate her. "Amy Jayne, has she been found?" She asked forcefully.

David's face softened when he saw angry tears threatening to fall on his daughter's face. Offering her the chair beside him, he squeezed her hand. "Let me look." Glancing through the list of names, he couldn't find Amy Jayne. "What is her last name?"

"Don't forget about James, too," Matthew piped in.

"Amy Jayne and James Wright. Oh, and I think her dad's name is Patrick?"

Grammy walked up behind them. "Who're we lookin' fer?"

"Amy Jayne and James. Have you seen them, Grammy?"

Grammy searched the room and shook her head sadly, "No, no, I haven't seen 'em." Her eyes went blank as she zoned out. Pulling out of the trance, she looked at her son and said, "We gotta find 'em, David." Grabbing Pastor Ron's hand, she looked him in the eye and said, "Don, we gotta get Don. Can somebody reach 'im?"

Confused over Grammy's sudden change in demeanor, she wondered *why Mr. Don?* She and her friends pulled away from the table as they listened to a man having a two-way conversation over the radio.

"What should we do?" Emma asked.

"I'm going to go with them," Maddie said.

Rachel looked at her friend and said, "I'll help Doc Walker. Emma, can you help me? Maddie, can you radio in once you find her?"

"Thank you, Rach." Maddie could never express with words the gratitude she felt for her friends. Suddenly nervous over what they would find, she began to wring her hands.

Placing her hand on her friend's shoulder, Rachel looked her in the eye and said, "She's okay, Maddie, I just know that God has her in his hand."

David was in soldier mode. Shaking off his guilt over yelling at his daughter, he focused on the rescue at hand.

The list of missing people was long. Cut off as they were, he highly doubted they would receive any help from the outside. Since he and Tom had the greatest experience with search and rescue, they were in charge. They would focus on finding survivors for at least the next ten days. Recovery would begin once there was little chance of finding survivors.

He was familiar with destruction, but the trip to take Benjamin to the hospital in the valley had been difficult. Thankfully, the road was still intact, despite the numerous trees that had fallen. They had to cut and move two trees out of the way as they descended the mountain. He couldn't believe the change in the valley's landscape. Everything to the left was destroyed, whereas everything to the right, while waterlogged, was mainly intact. It was as if the river had cut a line straight down the middle and taken everything to the left with it.

As they prepared the team to find survivors, David asked his daughter to describe her friend and brother.

"It's okay, Dad; I'm going with you."

"I don't know if that's a good idea."

Maddie looked up with resolve, "Dad, you can't shield me forever. Do it afraid, right?" The pleading in her eyes was mixed with firm determination. "Please, let me help."

David snickered. *She was his daughter through and through. She was right, he couldn't shield her forever.* "You need your coat, boots, and heavy-duty gloves. We don't want you getting hurt."

"Yes, Sir!" Excited over the opportunity to help, she looked at Rachel and received the pair of heavy-duty work gloves she handed her.

"David, ya gotta get Don, ya hear me?" His mom looked at him imploringly before they walked out the door.

David remembered the aloof man from his visit to Kalispell the week prior. Pastor Ron and Clyde thought he might be harboring the strangers who seemed to be taking inventory of the town. When he and Jacque visited him, the man didn't seem to have much to say other than he was grateful for their "raisin' up Maddie right." While David didn't see any evidence of strangers hanging around the ranch, he figured he would check in occasionally to see if anything unusual was taking place.

After their safety meeting, Uncle Tom rounded up a box of radios that had been in storage. They were surely coming in handy this week. Grabbing a radio to take with them, he called out to someone who worked on Don's ranch. David couldn't understand the person on the other end of the static.

"Don, we need Don. Is he 'round?" Uncle Tom asked again.

Chhhh, "We don't…" Chhhh, "Whose askin'?"

"This is Pastor Ron. We need to talk to Don, please."

Quiet filled the truck's cab as they made their way to the Wright place. Then suddenly, static caught them all off guard as they heard, "Don here."

Grabbing the radio from Uncle Tom, Pastor Ron blurted out, "Don, we have an emergency. Can you meet us in Wild Rock?"

"That would be a big negatory, Pastor. I ain't been up that mountain in years and I ain't gonna do it now."

"I hear ya, Don, but yer kin are in trouble. Time fer ya to get off yer duff and get up here."

"She stopped bein' ma kin the minute she left. Ain't nothin' changed."

Pastor Ron took a deep breath. He looked at David and said, "He's a hard man since his wife's death."

Turning back to the radio, the Pastor said, "Don, it ain't yer daughter Janey."

The silence on the other end of the radio was deafening. After a few moments, static filled the cab again, after which they heard the words, "Give me the address."

After Pastor Ron shared the Wright address, David asked, "Mind telling me what's going on here?"

"Well, I ain't been a bettin' man in a lotta years, but if I had a dollar, I'd say God's 'bout ta perform a miracle right chere."

David had a bad feeling as they drew closer to the Wright property. The sight before them was worse than Sudar. Piles of rubble created in the flood's aftermath seemed to take on a life of their own as creaks and groans filled the eerie quiet. Turning to ask Tom a question, he noticed the shadow of grief on his daughter's face. Tom shook his head as he grabbed Maddie's hand.

"Is this it?" Uncle Tom asked as they drove up to the lot.

The river flowed directly in front of what was once a house. David couldn't believe his eyes. The road in front of the house was now part of the river's bed. His heart sank even as Maddie sobbed. "Ruthie, you can stay in the truck if you need to."

She took a deep breath and said, "No, I'm going, too." Pride filled his heart as his daughter resolved to lay down her grief.

As they exited the truck, David had to look where he was going. Debris littered the property like a bomb had gone off. As Uncle Tom pulled out a map, a dark blue Dodge drove up behind them. The man named Don hobbled out of the truck in horror at the sight before him. "Where are they?" He yelled. "Where are my grandbabies?"

Pastor Ron ran up to the man to calm him down.

Maddie looked at her dad in shock. "Grandbabies?" She whispered.

After a few moments, Don recovered and hobbled over to the truck. "What do we know?" He asked with authority.

Uncle Tom signaled to David to take the ball.

Pointing to the map, he said, "This is where the house used to sit. The river that used to be here is now here. Considering the river's flow is southeast, we need a group to head in that direction. Tom, can you and Don search around the house? I'll take Maddie, Pastor Ron, and Uncle Tom downstream along with Don's crew."

"You've got it," Tom said.

"Can we pray?" She asked.

We're wasting precious minutes, he thought as he listened to his daughter pray for a miracle. David didn't know what kind of miracle was possible twenty-four hours after a flood wiped out a community. *God, if you're up there, we need you now.* He added silently.

He wouldn't dare leave his daughter behind. If her friends were buried under the house, the last thing he wanted was for his daughter to be the one to find them. David had seen great darkness in his life, and while he was proud of his daughter's courage, he didn't want her ever to have to lift a broken body from the rubble. Taking a deep breath, he looked up. They needed a miracle—*God, if these kids are alive and down this river, I will believe in your miracles.*

After an hour of tromping through debris and calling their names, they heard a faint voice echoing across the river, "Here! We're here!"

Peering through a pair of binoculars handed to him by one of Don's men, David couldn't believe it, but there sat two people covered in mud on the other side of the river. One waved to them as the other sat perfectly still, holding their arm.

"Dad, is that…" Maddie said excitedly, even as she looked for a way to cross.

"Maddie, wait, we can't cross here."

Chhhh, "Bud…" Chhhh, "Hey, Bud, are ya thar?"

David watched as Bud lifted his radio to answer, "10-4, watcha' got, Don?"

"We found Patrick; he's gone."

His daughter's face fell as she listened to the somber announcement.

"I'm sorry, Don. Hey, but I think we got yer youngin's. Thar two babies sittin' on the east side of the riverbank."

"Alive or dead?"

Bud smiled, "Well, if thar's any indication, the one jumpin' up and down, well, I 'spect that's yer granddaughter. Covered in a little mud, but she's a little Janey, through and through."

Grateful to have found them, David had no idea how they would pull them out. The river was too broad and deep to cross, and there was no road to travel to the other side. Looking at Pastor Ron, he asked, "Any idea how we can rescue them?"

"I've got an idea. You two stay here. I'll be back."

Waving to the kids to sit tight, David, Maddie, and Bud waited for Pastor Ron and Uncle Tom to return. Thirty minutes later, he began to get antsy. He didn't like where this was going. Suddenly, a loud sound hovered overhead as the wind whipped around them. Amazed, he watched a helicopter fly over the river and hover over the scene.

The sound of footsteps over gravel signified the quick return of the pastor as he yelled, "One of us needs to cross to the other side and take the kids about a half-mile east. Thar's a clearing over thar where Jerry's gonna land."

"Jerry? That was fast. You sure do have friends in high places," David laughed.

Pastor Ron's face lit up with a wide grin as he declared, "The highest."

After a great deal of argument, it was decided that Bud would swim to the other side. He knew the terrain, and he was the most fit. David watched as the man successfully made it to the other side and made contact with Amy Jayne and James. After receiving the signal to move on, he and the others returned to the truck to wait.

As they reached the truck, he saw Tom and Don standing on the edge of the property.

"You found them?" Don asked.

"We did. A helicopter is picking them up now."

A humble look crossed Don's face as he looked at Pastor Ron. "I owe you my life, Pastor."

Placing his hand on Don's shoulder, Pastor Ron answered, "No sirree, you don't owe me nothin'; however, these kids need to know their grandad."

Looking toward what was left of the house, Don agreed, "Their dad is dead. They'll be comin' back with me."

David watched his daughter approach Don, who was fighting his own emotions. "Mr. Don, it's okay. Hey, God gave you a miracle today. He may have taken your wife to be with him, but now you have her grandchildren to care for. I'm certain Ms. Margaret is very pleased right now."

A tear rolled down the man's cheek when Maddie spoke his dead wife's name. Leaning on his cane, he stared off into the distance, seemingly lost.

David was speechless. Unfortunately, his work had led him into a few conversations with people who had lost loved ones. This wasn't a conversation he was comfortable with at all. Yet, his daughter seemed to know just what to say. He was moved by her heart for the man, even if he didn't know what to say himself.

Chhhh, "David…" Chhhh, "Bud ta David."

The moment was interrupted by the static of the radio. Taking the radio from the Pastor, he responded, "David here."

"We gotta take James to the hospital. He's got a nasty break. Tell Don to meet us."

Don looked toward his men and said, "Come on, let's go."

"Dad, can I go, too?" She asked.

Uncertain whether the drive down the mountain would be safe for his daughter, he looked at Don.

"She'll be safe," Don said, "I'll stake ma life on it."

David didn't realize he was holding his breath until he released it. Looking at his daughter, he said, "Okay, Ruthie, but you listen to Don, okay? And wear your seatbelt. The ride down is a bumpy one."

"Yes, Sir." Excited, she grabbed Don's arm and walked him to the truck.

"Hey, Don. Can we borrow two of your men to help us with Patrick?" Pastor Ron asked.

"Of course. I'll send Bud back fer 'em in the evenin'."

CHAPTER 9

Death Doesn't Have the Last Word

When the flood began, Amy Jayne and her brother were in the living room, their dad asleep in the back bedroom. A loud rumble shook the house, so they walked outside to see what was happening. Amy Jayne knew something was wrong immediately and grabbed her brother's hand while grabbing hold of the door frame. The moment her brother was yanked from her hands was the most excruciating moment of her life. There was no way she would let him go without her, so she let go of the door frame and allowed the river to carry her away.

Maddie held her friend's hand as she told the harrowing story.

Looking at her friend, Amy Jayne said, "We were goners, but I ain't never gone down without a fight, and I wasn't gonna start now. The house, it went down like matchsticks. I ain't never seen nothin' like it. Daddy always did say it was a sigogglin mess of a house. Anyway, I grabbed holt to a piece a wood even as I fought to stay up. When I saw James, I coulda' sworn thar was an angel above him. I swam with all ma might to get to him, and then thar he was, right in front of me. The river jes' spit us out onto the bank. It was a miracle, Maddie."

She couldn't help but hug Amy Jayne tightly. Pulling back, she asked, "What did he look like?"

"Who, James?"

"No, the angel."

Amy Jayne laughed, "He was big—I don't remember nothin' more'n that. I jes' know he was holdin' on to ma brother." Looking at James lying on the hospital bed, she smiled. Tears welled up in her eyes as her voice broke. "God is real, Maddie. He saved us today." She sobbed as she grabbed hold of her friend.

As Maddie hugged her, she wondered how to share the bad news. Letting her go, she grabbed a tissue and handed it to her friend. "Amy Jayne, about your dad..."

Her friend's countenance fell as she continued to cry. Maddie had learned a long time ago that words were not always necessary. Recognizing this as a moment to be with and listen, Maddie decided to leave the announcement for another time as she sat quietly holding her friend's hand.

On day three of their confinement, the sun came out. Grieved over the stories of ruination left behind, Maddie was somehow encouraged by the resilience of those suffering. Landslides from the rain rushed over the landscape, taking trees and homes with them—a hodgepodge of devastation had turned her beloved Wild Rock into a war zone. She couldn't believe the destruction. Century-old homes were turned into rubble.

When one of the search parties asked for additional help, Maddie and her friends jumped at the chance. While she loved helping Doc Walker patch people up, she wanted to help more people like Amy Jayne. As they set out to aid in the search and rescue, she and her friends were overcome with emotion as they witnessed so much destruction in their community.

"Give me eyes to see," Maddie prayed quietly.

Look for the blessings.

The word in her heart was clear. She knew it was God. She had to focus on the light, not the darkness.

"Hey, is that Duke?" Uncle Tom asked.

Seeing the Great Dane sniffing on the side of what used to be a house, she wondered what or who he was looking for.

"I thought Clyde was out of town visiting his family."

"Oh no, please not ole Clyde," Emma cried.

Pulling on gloves, they began picking up wood and brick pieces.

Duke walked over to Maddie and looked up at her expectantly.

"What is it, Boy?"

Turning around, he led her through the yard to the back of the house.

"Maddie, where are you going?" David asked.

She pointed toward the dog, who was leading her somewhere. Suddenly, she could hear a weak voice calling from underneath the rubble. "He's here!" She cried out. "Help! Clyde is here!" Bending to her knees, she began to pick up the broken wood pieces surrounding the man. *There's so much,* she thought as she dug.

"Help…"

"It's okay, Mr. Clyde. We're here. We'll get you out."

As her dad and Michael ran over to help her, she heard Clyde say, "Hazel, please help Hazel."

Maddie's heart dropped. She knew exactly who Clyde was referring to. "Where? Duke, show me, Hazel," she said.

Duke suddenly went sniffing at the other corner of the house. Bending down, he immediately began digging at the ground. Rachel and Emma ran over to help.

"It's Hazel," Maddie said. "Remember the woman at The Refuge? We must help her!"

Her heart was pounding as she joined Duke in digging furiously for her friend. She had to get to her.

"Maddie…" Rachel's dad bent down to look her in the eye. "Let us, okay?"

"No, please, no." As she tried to stay strong, she was having a difficult time holding her emotions together.

"It's okay, Maddie. Dad will take good care of her." Rachel grabbed her friend's hand, who turned and hugged her tightly. Echoes of their sobs reached the hills behind them. It was all just too much.

Walking back to Clyde, she forced a smile as she checked his pulse. Looking at her watch, she followed Doc Walker's routine and said, "Ninety," sounds good. Michael brought a makeshift stretcher made of a sheet, and he and Uncle Tom picked up Clyde as Maddie's and Rachel's dads cared for Hazel.

"She's dead, ain't she?" Clyde asked.

What do I say in a moment like this, God? She wondered.

"Ya know, you girls brought her back ta me."

"We did?"

"Shore did. Ma Hazel and I separated years ago—a misunderstandin', mind ya. But she tole me that she met y'all at a shelter in Atlanta and had a mind ta make things right. We were jes' makin' amends when…" Clyde's voice broke.

"It's okay, Mr. Clyde."

Clyde mumbled as they began to carry him off. Suddenly, he looked at Maddie intently and grabbed her sleeve as he said, "We woulda been married fifty years…" Dropping her arm, he gazed into the distance as they carried him to the truck.

Surprised, Emma whispered, "They were married."

A sad smile reached Maddie's eyes when she realized the weight of his revelation. As she grabbed the hands of her friends, Rachel said, "Remember, death doesn't have the last word; only Jesus does."

In the weeks that followed, the town of Wild Rock

experienced tragedy and loss like never before. But in the face of such heartbreak, they served one another to rebuild what they had lost. After finding Clyde and Hazel, Rachel and Amy Jayne decided to work with the search teams, Emma helped the women prepare meals, and Maddie chose to help Doc Walker. She just didn't know if she could handle more loss. Besides, with Doc Walker, she felt like she was making a difference.

In addition to Hazel and Patrick, four lost their lives. A family lost their mom. Rachel was on the team who found an older couple still in their bedclothes. A couple who had followed Maddie and her friends from their church in Atlanta lost their two-month-old son when the river raged through their home. Maddie held the woman as she sobbed in grief over the loss.

People from neighboring towns joined in the search efforts. The man who owned the helicopter returned daily to take the wounded who needed more care to the hospital.

When it was time to leave the safehouse and go home, she found herself in a state of confusion. Watching her Grammy fall to her knees in gratitude was beautiful, yet there was grief in her eyes. The house was miraculously untouched, so why did she grieve?

Maddie, her friends, and family would venture up to the safehouse to help in the search efforts. They would all come home exhausted, but her dad would come in looking as if he had aged ten years. The search was taking a significant toll on him. He would come home each night to hold his wife who didn't seem to mind his dirty state. *God, I've never seen my dad like this. Please help him.* Feeling helpless herself, Maddie didn't know what else to ask for.

Unable to contain her worry one night after dinner, she asked, "Dad, are you okay?"

"Hmm?" He asked, distracted.

"Are you okay?"

"Yeah."

Pausing as she considered her next words, she said, "No,

you're not. It's okay to talk about it, Dad. Talking about our trauma helps us move past it."

"Straight from Mr. C, huh?"

She winced at her dad's sarcastic quip.

"I've experienced a lot of trauma, Ruthie. I wouldn't even know where to begin." He had, but this time was so much different and too close to home.

Maddie grabbed her dad's hand. "How about finding God in your pain?"

Finding God in his pain. *Where was God when he had to tell Ms. Nellie that the home her dad built with his bare hands was gone? Where was God when he had to pick up a two-month-old and tell his parents that he was dead? Where was God when his wife…* He didn't want to go there. Filled with an anger he didn't want to show his family, he promptly left the table.

As he walked through the house, he was stopped short by a painting hanging on the hallway wall. David placed his hand next to the painting, searching the expression of peace mixed with gentleness in the man's brown eyes. "You know who that is, don't ya, Son?" His mom asked.

"Mom, where do you get these?" He asked sarcastically.

"I surround myself with Jesus. He's ma hope in ever' circumstance."

"It's only a painting."

Touching the frame, she said, "This, ma David, is a reminder that Jesus has all of us in His hand. It's days like this that I need remindin' too." Touching his arm, she said, "Tell me what yer thinkin'."

David turned to look at his mom and pointed to the painting. "Where was he when I had to pick up a two-month-old from the river?!" Years of pent-up anger brewed just under the surface as he pondered those he knew.

"Come with me, Son."

David followed his mom to her room, where she sat in a chair and grabbed a photo of her and his dad.

"When ma George caught pneumonia, I wondered where God was." Looking up at David with a pained look, she said,

"I watched yer daddy become a shell of a man a'fore ma ver' eyes. After we buried 'im and y'all went back to Atlanta, I was lost. It was jes' me an' Max, and Lisa a'course."

Guilt stabbed David in his gut as he looked out the window above her. "Why didn't you call me?" He whispered.

"And say what? You had yer own life, David." Nodding, she placed the photograph back on the table and added, "Bein' lost was the best thing that ever happened to me."

Confused, David sat on the edge of her bed and asked, "What do you mean?"

She met his gaze with serious, unwavering eyes. "It was when I was lost that I was found."

"Mom, I don't…"

Ignoring his interruption, she continued, "Thar's only one other time I felt like that. Yer dad had jes' gone off to the Navy. I held ya in this room and cried. I did'na know how I could raise ya with yer dad gone. But God met me right here and showed me a strength I never knew. I found that same strength when I had to say goodbye to ma love. It was this book that did it." Grace picked up her Bible and placed it in her lap. Opening to the book of Isaiah, she read, "When ya pass through the waters, I will be with ya; and when ya pass through the rivers, they will not sweep over ya. When ya walk through the fire, ya will not be burned; the flames will not set ya ablaze."

"I don't mean to be disrespectful, Mom, but tell that to the people who lost their lives in *your* river."

Tilting her head, she looked at her son, "David, yer friend said that you used yer body as a human shield to save him in Sudar." Standing, she walked over and sat down next to him on the edge of the bed. "Where was God in that moment?"

Shocked at the question, David looked at the photograph on the table, "Do it afraid," he said softly. He could hear his dad's voice even now.

"Yer dad always said that whenever you faced somethin' hard. Remember when y'all had ta fight a bobcat fer a deer?"

David snickered, "We didn't fight it, Mom. As I recall, the

bobcat was distracted when the deer ran off."

"Well now, the way I heard it tole, you and yer dad gave the bobcat what fer' and then saved that sweet little deer from annihilation."

Shaking his head, David said, "What's your point, Mom?"

"You have a choice, ma Boy, ya can face yer fear or tuck tail and run. When ya face yer fear, you ain't alone. God was with ya when you faced the Bobcat. He was with ya when you saved yer friend. He was with me when ma George died. He was with you and the town when y'all came up with a plan that saved much more than we lost, and he's here now." Grabbing both of his hands, she squeezed them tight as she added, "And Davie, ma Boy, thar ain't nothin' that surprises ma God. When ya found that sweet little boy, he a'ready had him in his perfect hand, jes' as he has us right now. God, not death, has the final word."

David didn't know how to respond as his mom looked straight into his soul. One thing was certain; however, a little piece of the armor that guarded his heart for so long had been chipped away that day.

CHAPTER 10

Little Blessings

The holidays were a blur in the aftermath of the flood. As Matthew put it, the town of Wild Rock was flipped upside down.

Grammy reminded them that life would be like that, and they had to learn to find the little blessings no matter their circumstances.

That reminded Maddie of the words she heard when she prayed for eyes to see, "Look for the blessings." After Grammy's pronouncement, she asked what it meant.

"Well now, I'd say the Lord was givin' ya a word, Maddie Ruth."

"Yes, but how do I find blessings in the middle of all this? Aunt Lisa said to find the light, which I get, but blessings?"

"Ya find 'em by lookin' a'course. Ya got eyes, don't ya?"

"I prayed for God to give me eyes to see just before I heard those words."

"Sounds ta me like the Lord answered that prayer. So, did ya?"

"All I see is destruction."

"No, Girl, did ya see the blessin's?"

She wasn't sure how to answer her Gram's question. It was easy to see little blessings when things were good, but when things were bad...

Grammy huffed impatiently, "What miracles have ya

103

witnessed this year?"

"Benjamin, Clyde, Amy Jayne—oh, and Michael."

"That's good, mighty good. Did ya read the book of Acts? The early church knew a little somethin' 'bout findin' blessin's when life was hard. What did ya read thar?" She asked.

"Well, I kinda stopped reading. Grammy, did you know that Stephen died because of Jesus?"

"Yes, ma'am. We all gotta die sometime."

"But to be stoned? I don't see a blessing in that."

"Girl, grab my Bible and open it up to that passage."

Maddie opened to Acts seven.

"Alright, now I want ya to read startin' with verse fifty-four."

As she read to the end of the chapter, she was a little frustrated, "They stoned him, but why?"

Taking a deep breath, Grammy closed the book and looked at her granddaughter. "Maddie Ruth, thar have been many who have died fer Jesus and the good Book says thar are more to come. The truth is, it's an honor to die fer him. R'member, Jesus said 'Greater love has no one than this: to lay down one's life fer one's friends.'" Standing, she straightened up her back and walked to the kitchen window.

Worry filled Maddie as she watched her Gram move so slowly. "Are you okay, Grammy?"

"Maddie Ruth, the way I see it. Ya got a choice," she said as she ignored her question. "Thar's a gem in that book that'll help ya on yer journey, but you gotta find it. Now, I want'cha to write down those miracles and find the truth 'bout bein' blessed in the challenge. Go on now."

On Christmas Eve, she and the girls visited Kalispell for the first time after the flood.

"Hey y'all!" Amy Jayne lit up when she opened the door. "Papaw, Maddie, and the girls are here!"

Mr. Don hobbled into the living room to welcome them.

"Well, hello, Maddie Ruth! Kali and Charlie'll be happy to see you. They've missed ya. You'ns come on in and grab some hot chocolate."

Little white lights covered the room in a soft glow. Since they had to conserve energy, Maddie, and her family only decorated Grammy's house sparsely. That didn't seem to be an issue here as she looked around. Even Mr. Don's piano was aglow in light, with a little Christmas tree sporting bright and cheery colors. *Oh, how I miss this,* she thought to herself.

"It's so warm in here," Rachel said as she removed her coat and gloves. "I've missed having central heat," she added.

"Is Matthew with ya?" James asked Maddie as he and Holly walked into the room.

"No, not this time, James. Hey, look at you. How's the arm?" She asked.

He swung it low, like a pendulum, as he said, "Oh, I can raise it halfway now. Go 'head, push it down."

Uncertain if she should, she responded, "I don't want to hurt you."

"You won't hurt me. Doc Walker says it's all patched up; I jes' need to strengthen the shoulder. Go 'head, push it."

Maddie pushed James' arm down and smiled as he raised it halfway.

Proud of his accomplishment, he grabbed Holly's hand and ran off to the kitchen.

Amy Jayne brought out a tray carrying a hot chocolate with marshmallows for each of them.

Grabbing a cup with three marshmallows, Maddie winked at Rachel when she gave her a dirty look.

"How are you doing?" Rachel asked as they sat on the couch.

With a sad smile, Amy Jayne took a sip and answered, "I miss ma daddy, but I'm so happy ta see James happy."

"Do you like it here?" Maddie asked.

Amy Jayne squirmed uncomfortably. "It's differ'nt," she admitted. "I'm tryin' to figure out why we did'na know 'bout Papaw before."

She wondered how much her friend knew about her grandmother's death. She didn't want to share something with her friend that Mr. Don hadn't shared. Deciding that changing the subject might be better, she pulled out her journal from her bag to get their help in her little project.

"Grammy challenged me to write down our blessings this year." Maddie looked at each of her friends individually and added, "I know this has been a hard year for all of us, but I wanted to take some time and hear what you guys have seen."

Mr. Don hobbled into the quiet room as everyone sat with their thoughts. Sitting in his armchair, he pulled out his knife and began to whittle.

"Well, mine's obvious," Amy Jayne said. "Without the Lord and y'all a'course, me and ma brother'd likely be dead."

"For me, I would say Grammy sharing Wild Rock Overlook with us and calling us Watchmen," Rachel said.

Joy brightened Emma's face as she looked at her friend. "I was so excited to write that song with you, Maddie. Remember, Peace?"

Noting the expectant look on her friend's face, there was no way Maddie could share what she was thinking, *I miss my little keyboard.* She immediately rebuked herself for thinking something so selfish. *This is a time for blessings, not negativity,* she thought to herself.

Emma looked as if she had a secret, adding quietly, "When we moved to Wild Rock and started building gardens, I could hear melodies in my head. I've been humming a few, and I think I might have a song from one."

"No way! Will you sing it for us?" Maddie asked.

"Oh, I don't know, it's kinda a song between me and God."

"Well, you don't have to share if you don't want to, but if you do…"

"Oh, okay! Mr. Don, do ya mind?" She asked as she walked over to the piano.

"Not at all, ma Girl. Aside from Holly, that piano never gets any lovin'."

Emma practiced for a moment and then began to play a beautiful ballad.

She loved to hear her friend play. Emma had a way of helping her feel God's peace when she worshiped.

> *"Good morning, Father, thank you for this day.*
> *You've given me eyes to see your hand in all*
> *you've made. Lead me into your everlasting*
> *faith. Good morning, Father, thank you for this*
> *day."*

Maddie listened as Emma thanked God through her song for giving her eyes to see his love and peace. It was simple, yet powerful.

Closing her eyes, she considered how God poured out his peace over the year—Grammy welcoming them to live in Wild Rock, the town coming together to build the community garden, her prayer over Benjamin, and the Lord saving Amy Jayne and her brother. Despite their hardships, God was always there, just as he showed her in the tower of trust.

"What about you, Maddie?"

Lost in her thoughts, she didn't hear the question, "Hmm?"

"What are your blessings?"

"A year ago, I never would have thought we'd be here on Christmas Eve." Flipping through the pages of her journal, she attempted to translate her thoughts into words. "Grammy said when life got hard, the town always came together and worked it out. And now…" She couldn't help but wonder what Grammy was like at her age. "And now, it's our turn. Y'all, seven months ago, we were in Atlanta having coffee dates and planning prom, and now we're working alongside people who've lost everything, yet have something that most people spend their whole lives searching for."

"What's that, Maddie?"

"They have courage. Come on, you've seen it, haven't

you? Clyde just lost his wife, and there he was, right next to Benjamin in his wheelchair, building his new house, laughing as if nothing had happened! What is that?"

"I know, that'd be God." Amy Jayne shouted.

"Yeah… Matthew says we're living in an upside-down world, and he's not wrong. What was important a year ago just isn't anymore."

Leaning forward, Rachel asked, "Would you go back? To Atlanta, I mean?"

Stunned, Maddie played with the corner of a page in her journal. Would I go back? She pondered. "It's nothing like Wild Rock."

"What if we could bring what we have here to Atlanta?"

Butterflies in her stomach began to flutter as she thought about going back. "I don't know."

"Hear me out." Rachel stood and began to pace the room. "Maddie, the people here in Wild Rock are resilient. They have courage because they've trusted God to get them through every hard time, right? This has built their resilience and their courage. They trust each other because they've had to. We didn't have that in Atlanta because we had it easy. Now, we're learning that God is with us, too."

Rachel's zeal was beginning to rub off on her. "So, you're saying that what we've done here, we can do there?"

"Exactly! Maddie, if the PeaceKeepers have had anything to do with those men who burned down our homes, can you imagine what Atlanta is like now? Wouldn't you want to bring hope to our hometown by shining God's light into that darkness?"

If she were honest, she did not want to think about Atlanta. But her friend was right. The blessings they had experienced this year revealed one thing: God was in Wild Rock and with them.

On New Year's Eve, Maddie, Matthew, and Grammy sat

before the fire. Grateful for some warmth on this cold day, she pulled out her long list of blessings and added "fire" in big letters.

"What'cha got thar'?" Grammy asked.

"This is the list you asked me to make," she said.

"Ahh, yer praise list, huh?"

"Praise? Oh, I thought we were writing blessings."

Grammy laughed, "Yer givin' praise fer his blessin's, ain't ya?"

The revelation brought joy to her heart, "Oh, I guess I am," she exclaimed.

"That looks like a long list. So, what'd ya learn?" Grammy asked.

"Well, it was more of an epiphany, I guess. When God told me to look for the blessings, he was telling me to look for him, wasn't he?"

Grammy smiled as she patted her granddaughter's hand. "You've come a long way, ma Girl," she said proudly. "So, what're some of the blessin's ya wrote down?"

Maddie proceeded to share the list with her Gram and her brother. Including her friend's blessings, she realized the picture of God's presence was even more significant than she thought.

"How about you, Grammy?" Matthew asked.

"What's that?"

"What blessings did you see this year?"

Grammy smiled as she stood up and walked toward the back hall.

"Hey, where are you going?" Maddie and Matthew looked at each other, confused.

After a few moments, Grammy walked back into the living room carrying what appeared to be a long sword.

"Whoa, Grammy. Is that yours?" Matthew asked. His face lit up in amazement.

"Yassir, it is." Pulling the sword out of the sheath, she laid it flat on her hands and showed it to her grandchildren.

"Dude, this is so cool!"

"I don't understand. What is this for?" Maddie was not sure what to think.

Grammy knelt slowly, placing the sword tip on the floor with her hands firmly grasping the hilt.

Encouraging her grands to follow suit, she closed her eyes and began to pray,

> *"Father, it's the end of a hard year. We come before yer throne a grace, and we jes' wanna say thank ya fer always bein' with us and fer us, jes' as ya promised. Lord, we lay these blessin's a'fore ya an we give you praise fer without you, we can do nothin', but through Christ, we can do all you've called us to.*

> *These blessin's are livin' proof of that. Lord, I thank ya fer' my family. I thank ya fer blessin' me with a son who is loyal and kind. Thank ya fer my daughter-in-law who loves ma son and cares fer him well. I thank ya fer my grands here who are learnin' to be men and women after yer own heart. Father God, I ask that you bless 'em and keep 'em. Make yer face ta shine upon 'em and be gracious ta 'em. Turn yer face to 'em and give 'em yer perfect peace. And Lord, protect 'em. Encamp yer angels around 'em.*

> *May they always know yer presence and yer peace. Anoint them by the power of yer Spirit to go in the strength and the courage you've given 'em to fulfill the purpose for which they've been sent. May you, God, be glorified in ever'thin' they do. In the strong and mighty name of Jesus Christ, we pray these things, amen, and amen."*

When she finished praying, Grammy held her hand up for help. Maddie and Matthew both grabbed an arm and helped their beloved grandmother up. Laying the sword flat on her hand, she offered it to her granddaughter and said, "Maddie Ruth, this ain't nothin' new to ya, but I fight ma battles on ma knees. This sword here is jes' a symbol of ma surrender. The true sword is the sword of the Spirit—the Word of God. Today, I want to give you this sword to encourage ya in yer own battles. Ma mission is comin' to an end, ma Love. No, no, don't ya be cryin' now." Wiping a tear from her granddaughter's face, Grammy continued, "It's yer turn now. You an yer brother got an excitin' mission ahead of ya, and it's Jesus who's gonna see ya through, the sword a truth that'll cut through the nonsense, and his Spirit who'll lead ya through the fire."

Looking at her Grammy through a veil of tears, she said, "I don't know what to say."

"Well, I 'spect ya can say yes or no."

"Will you be here to help me?"

"Fer as long as the Lord allows." She placed her hand on her granddaughter's shoulder and said, "Maddie Ruth, yer the little blessed one who'll be a companion ta many. God has called you to this time and place fer his purpose. Keep seekin' him, and you'll see his blessin's. Ya don't need me when ya got him."

Maddie had no words, but immediately hugged her Grammy, letting her silent tears fall freely. Matthew followed suit, and in that quiet moment, the world stood still. The mantle had been passed.

CHAPTER 11

Birthing a Miracle

Maddie lowered her hand and said with confidence, "Be healed in the strong and mighty Name of Jesus." The girl, completely transformed from scraggly hair and hollow cheekbones to translucent skin and bright, shiny hair, looked up at her and smiled. The pure joy on her face was unmistakable. In awe of the transformation, she joined in the girl's joy.

Suddenly, a man grabbed her and yelled, "What are you doing?"

Surprised by the jolt from behind, she tried to hold on even as the girl's warm fingers slipped out of her hand. This wasn't the time to fight. As he dragged her into a holding cell, she began to sing. Suddenly, she knelt as Grammy's sword fell into her hand. A bright light filled the room with warmth. Looking up, she knew she was free…

Digging deep into three layers of blankets, Maddie tried to ward off a chill as she sought the warmth of her dream. Her heart was beating a hundred miles a minute. *What was that?* She wondered as she tried to remember.

Grabbing her journal and a flashlight, she attempted to write the details of what she knew about the unsettling dream before she lost them, and then she prayed for wisdom.

Going back to sleep was a challenge as thoughts plagued her. It was cold and, frankly, too early to arise from the warm blankets. Deciding to open her bible instead, she turned on her flashlight and picked up where she left off in her reading from Acts sixteen.

"That's it!" She said as she popped up from the covers. *I was dreaming that I was the one in prison. That's the blessing Grammy wanted me to see! But what is that stuff about being healed?* She wondered. Returning to the beginning of chapter sixteen, she read Paul's prayer for a woman with a spirit. *At that moment, the spirit left her,* she read.

She wished she could talk to her Grammy or Rachel, even. She needed to know what this meant! *How could Paul pray a spirit out of a person?* Deciding that three a.m. wasn't the best time to talk to anyone, she snuggled under the covers and prayed Psalm 91.

As she drifted back to sleep, the sunflower crowns from her dreams the year before came into view.

> *She knew this garden, but this time she wasn't alone. Someone was walking beside her. The same light that Maddie felt in her first dream surrounded her as they walked. She suddenly recognized people lying in the grass. They all had the same deathly pallor as the young girl in her first dream. She knew just what to do, "Be healed in the strong and mighty Name of Jesus," she said. The prayer became a song as she and the person beside her touched each person. Joy filled her heart again as she watched them come alive before her.*

"Maddie, breakfast!"

Attempting to grasp the disappearing images from her

subconscious, she yelled, "Not today, I'm dreaming."

"Come on, Mads, you know the drill. If you want coffee, you've gotta get up."

Realizing there was no going back to the lovely dream, she sat up to a beautiful ray of sunshine beaming through the bedroom window. Excited to talk to Grammy about her dreams, she quickly grabbed her journal and threw on a sweatshirt and a pair of sweatpants.

"Good mornin', Maddie Ruth. How'd ya sleep?"

With a yawn, she grabbed a cup and said, "Morning, Grammy. Crazy. I had some weird dreams that woke me at three a.m."

"Really? Three a.m., eh? That's a might early."

"I know, right? I was hoping I could share them with you this morning."

"Not this mornin', Love. I've got some business to tend to."

"Business?"

"Yes, ma'am. I'm goin' with y'all to Kalispell."

Shocked, Maddie asked, "Really? You're going to talk to Mr. Don?"

"It's time," she replied. "Eat yer breakfast and get dressed. I'll be talkin' with Jesus."

"Yay! I get to see James. Do you think I can ride Charlie?" Matthew asked.

As she swallowed a warm spoonful of oatmeal, she said, "I don't know, but we should be able to take him out."

As Aunt Lisa drove them to Kalispell, she wondered what Grammy wanted to talk to Mr. Don about. Something told her it was about Amy Jayne and James, but she couldn't be sure.

"Hey, y'all, come on in. Grammy! Oh, it's so good to see you. It's been a long time."

"Too long, Jill, too long." Grasping the hands of Don's

youngest daughter in a firm shake, she said, "Thank ya fer havin' me, and thank ya fer takin' care of ma youngin's. I hope they've been good."

"The best! Your Maddie here is a horse whisperer."

Looking at her blushing Granddaughter, she smiled, "She has a way, doesn't she?"

"Yes, ma'am, she does. How are you, Matthew? James'll shore be happy to see you."

"Can I go to his room?"

"A'course! You go on now, ya hear? Maddie, Amy Jayne's in the kitchen with Holly if ya wanna say hello."

"Thank you, Ma'am," he said as he made his way to the back of the house.

"How's Kali? Has she had her baby?" Maddie asked.

Jill smiled, "Not yet. Any day now. Would you like to be here? I know Doc Walker would appreciate yer prayin' hand."

Wow, what an opportunity! Excited at the thought of watching a horse being born, she wondered how soon it would be. "When's she expected to foal?" She asked.

After filling two cups with hot coffee, she handed one to Grammy and motioned for her to sit at the table. Turning to Maddie, she responded, "Doc Walker thinks this weekend. She shore is ready."

Maddie sensed she and her friend were being excused, but first, she had to make sure she understood her limits with the horse. It would hurt her heart to do anything that could hurt Kali or her baby. "Can we walk her today?" She asked nervously.

"No, ma'am, we want to let her rest. She's got a big day ahead of her. But I know she'd appreciate yer brushin' her. We want her to be good and clean a'fore she foals. You can bunk with Amy Jayne. She's been sleepin' in the apartment waitin' fer Kali to deliver."

Nodding in agreement, she walked with Amy Jayne into the living room so the adults could talk. As they made plans for the night, she couldn't help but listen in to the conversation in the kitchen. If she didn't know any better, she'd think Grammy was crying. *I wonder what's wrong?* She worried. She'd ask her Gram later.

Maddie was so happy to see Kali. When they first met, Jacob showed her how to approach her—never from the back, always from the front. Maddie would knock on the stall door and speak softly to the mare. She would walk in, ensuring the fourteen-hundred-pound horse could see her, and then softly touch the side of her face.

It was obvious that something exciting was unfolding. Amy Jayne told Maddie that Kali was holding her tail up and constantly looking at her abdomen, which meant they had to ensure that her stall was clean and well-bedded with clean straw in preparation.

If truth be told, Maddie was a bit nervous. She had never attended a delivery before.

Ms. Jill walked in with a brush, towels, a wrap, a bag, gloves, and cleaning supplies. "Evenin' Ladies. How's our girl?"

Amy Jayne hung the pitchfork they had been using back on the wall as she said, "She's been lookin' at her abdomen, Jill, jes' as ya said. She knows somethin's 'bout to happen, doesn't she?"

"Oh yes. This'd be her third, so she's got some experience. I want'cha to let me know if you see her start sweatin' or havin' any discomfort, hear? We'll need to call Doc Walker in when that happens."

"Yes, ma'am."

"Here's a wrap fer her tail. Brush her down real good. We'll want to wrap her tail and warsh her hindquarters when she goes into labor. I'll take care a that once it comes time."

"What do we need to watch for?" Maddie asked.

"She'll get real restless. Call me on the house phone here if she's walkin' 'round agitated and raisin' her tail a lot. I'll be out ta check her calcium levels." Ms. Jill walked toward the barn door. "Oh, and Girls, give her space. Find somethin' to keep yer mind's active. If she thinks yer watchin' her, she might jes' be stubborn enough to delay delivery."

Maddie loved caring for the horses. She knew they were powerful enough to hurt her, but she wasn't afraid. "You're God's creation, aren't you, Kali?" After brushing her mane, she touched her forehead to the horse's and prayed for protection over the mare. Kali whinnied as she seemed to nod an amen to the prayer.

The stall had openings that allowed the girls to watch Kali without being overbearing. Pulling out a deck of cards, Amy Jayne teased that she was the queen of the card game.

"Well, let's find out!" Maddie returned with a laugh.

"Rummy!" Amy Jayne blurted out.

Maddie playfully threw her cards down in feigned frustration.

Suddenly, they could hear Kali getting restless in her stall. Picking up the house phone, Maddie called Jill, who joined them with Mr. Don hobbling not far behind.

"Are ya ready?" Jill asked the two as she texted Doc Walker.

"I cain't believe we're 'bout to see a horse bein' born!" Amy Jayne bopped up and down in anticipation.

Maddie breathed in deeply. The cold night air was intermixed with the smell of hay and manure. The other horses neighed in what sounded to her like encouragement for the mare who was about to give birth. This reminded Maddie of the story of Jesus' birth in Luke 2. *The anticipation of new life was exhilarating!*

After washing her hindquarters, Jill wrapped her tail with a clean wrap and said, "Okay, Girls, we want to stand back and give Kali space. Yer gonna see her restless and looking behind her often. This is normal."

The horse swished her tail and turned to look at her flank

just as Jill explained the early signs of labor.

Around one a.m., Doc Walker walked into the barn and asked, "What'd I miss?" just as Kali began to lie down and get back up.

Maddie felt helpless as she watched the horse in discomfort. She wished she could help her, but all she knew to do was to pray.

Maddie and Amy Jayne played cards for the next hour as Ms. Jill and the Doc watched the mare.

"Doc, we've got a problem," Ms. Jill said.

The girls laid their cards down and jumped up with Doc Walker.

"We've got a red bag. Girls, we need ya to pray. We don't want to lose this foal."

Doc Walker pulled out a pair of sharp scissors and disinfected them. Maddie looked on in horror as he cut a red sac under the horse's tail. A whoosh of blood fell as they slowly and carefully pulled a pair of legs out of the horse.

Taking Amy Jayne's hands, Maddie began to pray. Shortly after, a song of healing rose from her belly. She didn't understand what was happening but trusted that Doc Walker and Jill knew what to do. Singing seemed like the right thing to do.

What seemed like moments later, Maddie watched in awe as the baby horse worked to get its bearings. Kali alternated between cleaning her new baby and lying back to finish the birthing process.

"It's a miracle. Look at this sweet foal! Come 'ere, Maddie, Amy Jayne. Yer prayers are answered. Look at 'er, isn't she precious?"

They didn't want to crowd the mare and her new foal, so Jill allowed them each to come in one at a time and say hello. Maddie laid her forehead on Kali's and whispered a prayer of thanks for God's hand in the birth. "You did good, Kali," Jacob would be proud. Moving to pet the new foal, she began to weep quietly at the opportunity to watch life enter the world.

As Doc Walker turned to leave, Maddie asked, "Is Kali, is she okay, Doc?"

"She should be fine, Maddie. We need to monitor her for the next 72 hours. If she looks lethargic or doesn't want to nurse, we'll need to take further action, but otherwise, she should be fine. Tomorrow night, we'll take some tests to confirm the foal's colostrum is normal and there is no infection."

"Amy Jayne, what would ya like to name our sweet filly?" Ms. Jill asked.

Caught off guard, she looked at Maddie with a questioning gaze. "What do you think, Maddie?"

With everything their community had gone through this year, one name stood out over any other: "Hope."

Amy Jayne nodded even as tears filled her eyes. Looking at Ms. Jill, she agreed, "Hope, we'll name 'er Hope."

"Hope is a good name and something our community needs a lot of right now." Doc Walker said. "Maddie, thank you for praying. Your prayers encourage me in my faith."

"What do you mean? I didn't do anything."

He touched her shoulder and said, "Yes, you did. You obeyed the Father and connected those who needed healing to the Healer."

Suddenly, Maddie remembered her reading from Acts. She did that in her dream; she connected those who needed healing to the Father. "So, he healed through … me?"

"Well, to be clear, Jesus is the Healer, but his healing power is applied through your faith-filled intercession."

Maddie's eyes widened as Doc Walker used the term Rachel had used. "So, I'm an intercessor?"

The doctor laughed at her innocent question, "I'd say so. I challenge you to read about Hannah in the Bible. Her prayers birthed a miracle, too. Your travailing heart reminds me a lot of hers. And remember, with this gift comes great responsibility. Stay close to the Father, my friend, and he will lead you to those he wants to heal." Yawning, he zipped up his bag and gave a salute. "I'll come by tomorrow afternoon.

Jill, call me if there is any change."

Jill shook the doctor's hand, "Thank you, Doc. We owe you for tonight. You are a great blessin' to our community."

She couldn't stop thinking about what Doc Walker said. When she returned to Grammy's, she immediately looked up Hannah in the Bible and read First Samuel 1. Sad when she read of the many years of anguish Hannah experienced over her inability to have a child, she wondered if she could be so faithful in prayer.

As Grammy made dinner, Maddie told her all about the birth. She shared how the doctor challenged her to read about Hannah. "Did you know that she prayed for years for a son?"

"A faithful prayer warrior, that one." With a furrowed brow revealing her curiosity, Grammy turned and asked, "What'cha chewin' on?"

Insecurity filled her as she thought about her answer. She loved hearing what the doctor had to say, but there wasn't anything special about what she did, was there? Her gram knew her well enough to help her separate fact from fiction. "Doc Walker said I was an intercessor like her."

As she added spice to the soup she was stirring, Grammy asked, "So, what'cha think 'bout that?"

Leaning against the counter, she looked out the back window and asked, "Remember the dream I told you about?"

"I shore do."

"In the dream, there was a girl who looked almost dead. I prayed for her and she..." She tailed off as she tried to collect her thoughts.

Leaning over as if to share a secret, Grammy asked, "She came alive, did'na she?"

Stunned that she could read her thoughts, Maddie exclaimed, "Yes! But how did you know?"

Turning the stove off, she picked up the pot to move it to

a back burner. Motioning for Maddie to move, she bent down and said matter-of-factly, "Well, that'd be the Spirit a God workin'."

The question she had been dying to ask was on the tip of her tongue, but Maddie just couldn't believe it could be true. *What will Grammy think?* She wondered as her foot began tapping nervously. Conflicted, she decided the only way to know for sure was to ask. "Did the Holy Spirit heal her through me?" Anxiety threatened to steal her peace as she waited for the answer.

After fumbling through the lower cabinet, she yelped excitedly as she found the hidden lid, "That sucker thought he could hide from me!" She exclaimed, holding it up like a prize. After placing the lid on the pot, she asked, "What do ya think intercession is, Girl?"

Frustration over her ignorance filled her as she blurted out, "I mean, I just prayed like I prayed for Kali. Doc Walker said we birthed a miracle. What does that mean?"

Grammy lifted her hand to move a lock of hair behind her ear. Her eyes crinkled at the corners, revealing the love she had for her granddaughter. "When yer obedient in prayer, yer a vessel God uses to heal, love, encourage. Yer prayers meet Heaven an' stir God's heart. Thar's an ole fashioned word fer intercession called Paga, which means 'to meet.' Yer meetin' with Almighty God and His Spirit is movin' as ya connect the person to him. He can do whatever he wills through someone obedient and willin'."

Perhaps my question wasn't so crazy, but how does it all work? She wondered as she asked, "I'm not gonna lie, that's wild. How do I pray for a miracle like that?"

Walking over to the breadbox to grab the homemade rolls inside, Grammy said, "Ya listen."

"Wait, I'm confused." Grabbing the rolls so she could help, she couldn't help but admit to being a bit disappointed there wasn't more to it than that.

Placing her hands on her hips, Grammy huffed and looked intently at her granddaughter. "How did ya know what to pray fer Benjamin?" She asked loudly.

Her eyes widened as she stammered over her answer, "I don't know, it just came to me."

"That's right!" Pausing to grab Maddie's hands, Grammy lowered her voice and smiled, "Ya listen, Girl. The Holy Spirit's gonna tell ya what to pray. Jes' as he tole ya fer Benjamin, jes' as he tole ya fer Kali and her Hope. He'll tell ya ever' time ya listen. That's how ya birth a miracle, ya listen, and ya release what ya hear."

The nondescript envelope on the table caught David off guard. "From the office of Senator Gabriel Hawke" was stamped inside. Wondering what the Senator from Atlanta would want with him, he took the letter to the back room to read it privately.

Dear David,

The colleague you sent to me has received a pardon and will be allowed back into the country. Thought you should know.

Gabe

Colleague. Who was the Senator talking about? The only person he "referred" to the Senator was—oh, that's right, the woman from the plane. David smiled, something going his way for once. She was allowed back into the country. Well, that was good news. *What did he mean by "received a pardon?"* He wondered. Digging into the envelope, he pulled out a securely folded set of plans in a plastic bag. Mordecai would be thrilled when he learned that phase one of Project Shutdown was complete. Tapping the letter on his knee, he decided it was time to return to his research to prepare for his next. Wild Rock had enough help to rebuild. It was go-time.

CHAPTER 12

Shaking the Foundations

A week after Kali's foal arrived, Maddie was still thinking about intercession. As she watched God heal Benjamin and little Hope, she felt part of something but didn't know what. She didn't want to lose that feeling.

As she and her friends pruned and mulched in Grammy's garden, she asked them about it.

"You are part of something," Rachel said, "God is writing his story and inviting you to partner with him in his kingdom."

Emma lifted her hand as a caterpillar marched down her thumb. "Just like he partners with us in gardening," she said as the caterpillar looked up from her hand.

Pulling a dead plant from the ground, Maddie asked, "What exactly is his kingdom?"

"When Jesus came to earth, he established his kingdom through those who followed him, and then he sent the Holy Spirit to live in their hearts. Those who follow him are walking in his kingdom."

"But why can't we see it?"

Exasperated, Rachel's eyes widened as she stared at her friend, "Have you learned nothing? Open your eyes."

"Look, don't get salty. I just want to understand," Maddie retorted.

"Maddie, when Benjamin was injured, what did you do?"

Throwing a frustrated glance at her friend, she said, "I prayed for him."

"That's right. When Kali was delivering Hope, and y'all were worried she would die, what did you do?"

"We prayed."

"Yes. That's kingdom work. And you watched as God moved in both situations."

"Yeah, but he didn't do that for Kaitlyn."

"How do you know?"

Emma and Maddie looked at their friend in shock.

"How do we know that Kaitlyn was not saved right there? Maddie, you said it yourself; you dreamed of her in that tower. How do we know that God wasn't doing everything we prayed for? We don't know God's thoughts, and we don't know his ways. We have to trust him."

"You're right. I just don't want to say the wrong words, ya know. I'm afraid that I could say something to make God mad." Feeling roots break free as she dug through the dirt with her gloved hand, she remembered when she learned to plant at the PKO. Life continued to grow around her even though she was surrounded by so much darkness.

"Emma, why do you like gardening so much?" Rachel asked her friend.

Setting the caterpillar back on the ground, she looked up and said, "You know me, it's my therapy. No, but really, how can I not? Think about it: we plant a seed and watch it grow. Then, we harvest the plant, pick the seeds to plant again, and eat them. It's the circle of life."

"But then something like a flood damages everything you worked so hard for," Maddie interjected.

Shrugging, Emma said, "So, we plant again. That's the beauty of life: even when it dies, it lives."

"Wait, what did you say?" She asked.

"That's the beauty of life."

"No, after that."

"Even when it dies, it lives?"

"After Kaitlyn died, I talked to Sonya. She told me about a

baby that she lost."

Rachel gasped as she said, "No, I didn't know that!"

"Yeah. She told me that she prayed for him to live, but God let him die."

"I can't imagine," Emma said.

"It's something she said that I didn't understand until now. She said God saved her through her baby because he taught her to trust him. That's life, right? Is that what the kingdom is, Rach? All of God's people coming together as they trust him?"

On cloud nine, Maddie hummed a song as she brushed Kali. After talking with her friends, intercession made so much sense. After they prayed over the town, Rachel encouraged her to read John seventeen.

"Kali, did you know that Jesus prayed for us? When Paul prayed in prison, the Holy Spirit was with him, praying too. When we prayed for the town, the Holy Spirit was with us. When Wild Rock prayed after the flood, the Holy Spirit was praying with them, too. They weren't alone because God's Spirit was in them and with them interceding on their behalf. That "thing" we're part of? It's God's kingdom, Kali! Imagine that. God chose me," she said happily to the horse.

Kali, munching on her nightly straw, turned toward her when she heard her name.

Looking down at the new foal sleeping in the straw, she said, "You know, Kali, God gave you a miracle. Pausing to lay her forehead on the horse's neck, she added, "Can I tell you a secret, Kali? I'm glad Jacob brought me here, really, I am, but I'm worried I did a bad thing. Do you think God will forgive me?"

The contrast of the horse's flaxen mane and chestnut coat distracted her from her worried thoughts. Fascinated over God's creative hand, she ran the brush through her mane one last time as she said, "He gave you a miracle when he gave you Hope." Sighing, she looked at her watch and realized the time. "Well, Girl, I've gotta go. Aunt Lisa will be here any minute." Laying the brush down, she placed her forehead on the horse to pray. "Father..." Suddenly, a male voice interrupted her prayer.

"Rocco, good to see ya, Man. Are we alone?"

"As alone as we'll ever be. Don's granddaughter went up fifteen minutes ago. What'cha got?"

Maddie bent down so she wouldn't be seen.

The plan is moving. Be ready on Friday at nine p.m.

"I don't know, Marty. Don's done made peace with 'em. We need to lay low and let this one go."

"What's wrong with you, Man. Thar ain't no letting go. You know the rule: NO ORDER, NO PEACE. If this town doesn't want to comply with the new order, it must be taught a lesson. Them high and mighties won't know what hit 'em."

Kali neighed as she picked that moment to nod her goodbye.

Panicking, Maddie covered her mouth and sank into the straw next to the foal, trying to cover herself as much as possible.

"What was that? I thought you said we were alone?"

"It's that spoiled horse. She's wantin' more dinner I 'spect. Come on up to the house; I'll get ya a plate a'fore ya have to leave."

Maddie didn't know what to do. As the lights went down in the barn, she rested her head against the stall and closed her eyes. NO ORDER, NO PEACE. The PeaceKeepers were here. She had to tell her dad.

Quietly standing and brushing the straw from her pants, she whispered, "Hey, Girl, I love you. Take care of baby Hope, okay? I'll be back." She placed her forehead on Kali's again to finish her prayer and quietly made her way to the man door on the side of the barn. Her heart beat wildly as she opened the door, looking right and left. "God, I need you," she whispered.

The ride to Grammy's was awkward. Maddie's silence deterred Aunt Lisa's attempts at small talk. All she could think about was the PKO.

"Hey, are you okay?" Aunt Lisa asked. Pulling the car to the side of the road, she turned to her niece and said, "Girl, look at me."

Shallow breathing betrayed her. Pausing to take another deep breath, she said, "I was praying over Kali before coming to meet you, and I heard…" Her words were lost in the hum of the engine.

"What'd ya hear?"

A wave of fearful thoughts crossed her mind. *The PeaceKeepers are coming. We'll never be able to fight them. They're too strong.*

A strange courage arose within her. A new fight was brewing in her desperate heart. *Nope, I am not going back!* She thought. *The PeaceKeepers may be strong, but God is stronger. He is our Refuge and Strength. Jesus has overcome, and so shall we overcome.*

"Maddie?"

The entrance to the mountain distracted her from looking directly at her aunt as she decided how much to share. "Do you know the Outlanders everyone keeps talking about? I think I know who they are." Turning her focus back to the tree in front of the car, she allowed the engine's song to soothe her shaken heart. "Can we go home?" Resting her head against the window, she closed her eyes and whispered a prayer.

"Okay, let's get ya home. Will ya be alright?"

Nodding, she replayed the conversation from the barn in her head. *Dad will know what to do,* she thought, resolving to trust in God as she placed her fear in his hands.

Aunt Lisa put the car into gear and began the ascent to Grammy's.

As they exited the car, Grammy joined them on the front porch. Her big smile immediately changed to one of concern as she noticed Lisa's worried glance. Maddie didn't want to say anything to her Gram just yet. After walking over the threshold, relief filled her as she saw her dad sitting at the table with her mom. She immediately ran to him.

Seeing her worried expression, he stood to face her. Lifting her chin, he asked, "What's wrong, Ruthie?"

"Dad, they're here."

"What do you mean, who's here?"

Determined to be strong, she squared her shoulders and looked up into her dad's eyes. The concerned furrow between his brows gave her courage. "Two guys were at the barn. They're planning something, Friday night, nine p.m." She tripped over her words as she attempted to tell him the whole story. Her lips were moving faster than her brain.

Placing his hand on her shoulder, he looked at her intently and said, "Whoa, slow down, Ruthie. Tell me again from the beginning."

Slow, Maddie, she encouraged her racing heart. Starting from the moment she began to pray over Kali, she shared everything she could remember.

Disappointment filled her as she watched her dad's jaw clench and eyes squint. The blank look on his face shook her as he gazed at something behind her. Did I say something wrong? She worried.

"How do you know these men were from the PKO?" He asked.

"NO ORDER, NO PEACE. That's what they said, Dad. No order, no…" She looked at her Grammy imploringly as he turned and walked away.

"David, no, it's too dangerous."

"Jacque, I don't have time for this." Turning to his wife, he threw up his hands as he said, "Do you want this? Because I've been in places where this is not possible." David paced their bedroom floor as he tried to get a grip on his emotions.

"I've seen girls like Maddie sold for a dime." His voice broke as he asked, "Do you want that? I've watched young men like Michael and Matthew influenced by men so evil that it makes me want to throw up. DO YOU UNDERSTAND?! If we don't fight for what is ours, it will be taken. Is that what you want?"

Helpless, his wife stood still, tears streaming down her face. David didn't want to make his wife cry, but he had to make her understand what was at stake.

A soft knock on the door grabbed his attention.

"Can I come in?" His mom opened the door and immediately walked to his wife. Looking at her son with darts in her eyes, she said, "Cain't ya have a little mercy, David?"

"Mom, not now."

"David, I know yer angry. I'm angry, too. But takin' it out on yer family ain't gonna help nobody."

Sitting down on the bed, he collapsed under the weight of the world. "What would you like me to do, Mom? Open the door and let them in?"

"No, Son. I would like you to first lay down ever'thin' yer holdin' on to so tightly. Ask the good Lord fer help. He's helped us before, and he'll help us agin."

"I appreciate your faith, Mom, truly. But evil men are making their way up here. I don't know how your God is going to stop them."

"David Allen Bennett, what was it ya tole me ya prayed after ya found the youngin's by the river?"

A heavy sigh left him as he remembered the promise he made. "Not fair, Mom."

"What was it? Come on, Boy, spit it out."

"If the kids were alive, I would believe in his miracles."

David shook his head and laughed as he watched his 5'1" mom stand tall and smile. "Come on, Mom. No, 'I told you so.'"

Putting her hands up in surrender, she said, "Hmph, thar ain't no gloatin' here, Son. I'm jes' happy to know that ya see him." Placing her hands on his cheeks, she whispered,

"That's it. Ask him right now, where is he? Ask him to show ya what he's doin' and how he wants you to act." Stepping back, she added, "David, it's his plan, not yers, not mine, not Jacque's or Maddie's. It's the Lord's that will be victorious. And those who know him and foller him, well, they'll be victorious, too. NO MATTER WHAT they face!"

David stood and walked over to the window. He knew this season wouldn't last. When he saw the home that had been his safe place left in ashes, he knew his foundation was shaken. But somehow, he had hoped they would be safe here. *Is there anywhere that is safe?* His thoughts betrayed him as they left his mouth.

"Only in the arms a' Jesus, Son. Jesus tole his disciples in John 16:33 that a time was comin' when they'd be scattered. He tole 'em this so that in him they'd have peace. He said, 'In this world, we'd have trouble. But'" pointing up to the ceiling, she exclaimed, "'TAKE HEART! I have overcome the world!' That promise is fer us jes' as much as it was fer them."

CHAPTER 13

Do Not be Afraid

Shame covered Maddie as she sat in the middle of her bed. "God, I am so sorry," she cried, "You made a mistake; I don't think I can be an intercessor."

Who told you this lie?

The familiar gentle whisper stopped her in her tracks. A message her pastor gave at Woodlands filled her mind.

> *"It's possible that right now, you are overwhelmed by the mountains in your life that lead you to thoughts of hopelessness. Perhaps you even feel guilt and shame over those thoughts. May I encourage you with this? Galatians 5:1 says, 'It is for freedom that Christ has set us free. Stand firm, then, and do not let yourselves be burdened again by a yoke of slavery.'"*

Stand firm. Two words her Grammy repeated throughout her life. *"Who are you going to believe, Maddie? You get to choose."*

Her bible and journal sat open to Acts 18:9: "Do not be afraid; keep on speaking, do not be silent. For I am with you, and no one is going to attack and harm you, for I have many

131

people in this city."

I am with you.

Maddie's gaze fell on the tower painting hanging on her wall. God had revealed himself to her through her Grammy, her friends, Ms. Carolina Wren, and the Tower of Trust. She knew she was never alone, but who was she listening to?

She wrote "STAND FIRM" in her journal and prayed, "God, you've been with me before; you will be with me again. I choose to listen to you."

When she opened the door to her room, she heard the low timbre of her dad's voice coming from his bedroom. She couldn't make out every word, but she would think he was praying if she didn't know any better. After his frustrated response to her telling him about the PeaceKeepers, she didn't know what to think.

The sound of her brother's humming lured her into the kitchen. Intrigued over his intense focus, she looked over his shoulder to see his latest carving. "What'cha doing?" She asked.

"Making an arrow," he said as he carved the wood along a marked line.

Curious, she sat down and placed her chin in her hands. After a moment, she asked, "Matthew, what are you making all these weapons for?"

"Hunting, Self-defense…"

"Have you hunted with these weapons?"

"Sure. Uncle Tom and I nabbed a rabbit just the other day."

Her eyes widened with alarm as she exclaimed, "Not a rabbit!"

Rolling his eyes at his sister, Matthew said, "Come on, Mads, I'm not a little kid anymore, I'm thirteen. Besides, what do you think Grammy cooked last night?"

Cringing over the use of her hated nickname, she shook her head and then realized that he was referring to what they ate...for dinner! Totally grossed out at the thought, she tried not to think about it and decided it would be best to just change the subject.

The gentle rhythm of the whittle caught her attention. As she narrowed her eyes to see the detail he was carving, she asked, "Hey Matthew?"

"Yeah?"

"Do you remember when you almost drowned last year?"

"Yep," he said.

"Were you scared?"

Matthew shrugged his shoulders, "Not really."

Surprised, she asked, "Why not?"

"I knew you would save me," he answered matter-of-factly, without even looking up.

Surprise turned to concern as she saw the nonchalant look on her brother's face. "How did you know that?"

"Maddie, do you know what I remember when I was sick in the hospital?"

"What's that?"

Tilting his head, he looked at his sister solemnly and said, "I remember you promised that you wouldn't let me die. You've never backed out of a promise yet."

"Yeah, but Matthew, we were babies then."

"So? You're my angel sister. God gave us each other. Besides, he's got too much for us to do to let us go yet."

"What do you mean?" She asked.

"Well, you're a prayer warrior like Daniel, and I'm a warrior like King David."

Her brother was so smart, but he too often spoke over her head. "Who's Daniel?" She asked.

Rolling his eyes again, Matthew got a bit snarky when he retorted, "Come on Mads, you know, Daniel and the Lion's den?"

"King David, Daniel and the Lion's den—getting a bit deep in here." David interrupted as he walked into the kitchen.

Embarrassed, Matthew lowered down into his chair and

went back to carving.

"Are you okay, Ruthie?" David asked his daughter.

Distracted over her confusion about this Daniel, she turned to straddle the backside of the chair, and said, "Yes, Dad, I'm good. Are you okay?"

David looked at his mom and said, "Yes, we're Bennett's. We've got warrior blood."

Matthew couldn't help but smile as he sharpened the end of his dagger.

"Dad, what do we do now?" Maddie asked.

"I'm meeting with the town tomorrow night to come up with a game plan."

"Do you think we should talk to Mr. Don?"

"We, Daughter, shouldn't do anything. I will talk to him in the morning."

"But…"

"No buts, Ruthie."

"Dad, I know you want to protect me, but at some point, you have to trust me."

"I trust you, Maddie. It's the PeaceKeepers, I don't trust."

"Okay but hear me out. Everything I've gone through has been for a reason, right? I can't be afraid; no, I won't be afraid. Please, Dad, let me help."

"Okay, how would you like to help?"

Stunned at his sudden change of heart, she was short on words. Watching as her dad crossed his arms impatiently, she blurted out, "I can ride the horses!"

Laughing incredulously, her dad said, "Horses, what are we going to do with horses?"

She didn't know where the answer came from, and if she were honest, she didn't know what to say next. But somehow, she knew the horses could help them.

"David, horses can go where cars cain't." Grammy said, "And Don's got the best of 'em in the county. I'm sure he'd let us use 'em."

Thinking back to Sudar, David remembered how the Sudar police force preferred horses over the US preferred jeeps and desert patrol vehicles. The horses were great on reconnaissance missions. Looking at his daughter, he thought, Perhaps Maddie could provide surveillance without being seen. He'd have to pair her with someone. There was no way his little girl was going out alone.

Emboldened by her dad's silence, she said, "I'm a Bennett, right? I've got warrior blood!"

The chaos in the church fellowship room was giving David a headache.

Pastor Ron gave him a sympathetic nod as he stood. "Alright, now, let's all settle down. This ain't the first time we've faced a challenge."

"Pastor, what are we gonna do?" Benjamin asked. "We jes' finished rebuildin' after the flood. If these rabble-rousers come and destroy what we done, well thar ain't gon' be nothin' left!"

Tom leaned over and whispered to David, "We need to get a handle on this meeting."

"I know." Standing to meet Ron at the front of the room, David said, "You've all been through a lot. It's taken a great deal of courage to get to this place. Mom reminds me that Wild Rock has resilience and grit. I admire that.

"What are some of the things you have learned in the past year? I'd like to hear some of the challenges you've faced and how you've managed to overcome them."

The room was quiet. As everyone pondered the question, a door in the back opened and everyone could hear the clomp of a cane. David nodded to Don as his mom went to greet him.

"What's he doin' here?" Clyde yelled from the front.

A shrill whistle from the back quieted the roar that began from Clyde's question. Everyone turned around to see Grace Bennett standing with her hands on her hips. "I invited him if ya must know. If ya got somethin' to say, well now, ya can say it to me."

Apparently, there wasn't a person in the town willing to face Grace Bennett. Nodding to her son to continue, she took Don's arm and led him to the front. His daughter, Jill, followed behind him.

"There has been talk of strangers who have been asking questions of Mayor Tom and others in the town. Benjamin, I told you and the town here, that we didn't know if these strangers were dangerous. Well, now that we know who they are, I can confirm that they are very dangerous."

"I told you!" Benjamin exclaimed as others began to talk amongst themselves.

"Okay, so what are we going to do 'bout it?" Clyde asked.

Pulling out a roll of drawings, David gave one to Uncle Tom, the town's mayor, to hang on the wall.

"It's our understanding that they will come in here." Pointing to an old road on the backside of the town, he looked at Don who nodded.

"That road ain't been traveled fer years. Can they even get through it?"

"Actually, we noticed fresh tracks just this morning," David answered. "Thanks to Don here, we have a pretty good idea of who and how many."

"How do we know that Don ain't the one leadin' 'em?" Benjamin asked.

Don stood and leaned on his cane. "If I were to lead 'em, do ya think I'd be here tonight?"

"Dad, no," Jill whispered as he made his way to the front.

Shooing her hands away, he said, "It's time, Dorter."

David moved out of the way to grab a chair for Don.

"I'm fine but thank ya kindly." Looking around the room, he said, "It's been a long time since I been in this room." The quiet was thick as he considered his next words. "My Margaret loved it here. Y'all know, she 'bout helped with all yer youngin's, bringin' 'em into the world and all." Lost in the moment, Don let out a heavy sigh. "I loved my Margaret with all ma heart. When she went to be with the good Lord, I thought my life was over. And I wasn't kind to any of ya. Least of all, my own kin." Fighting back tears, he said, "But I'm here to make amends. I'm sorry to you Grace fer the way I treated ya and yer family. Clyde, I'm sorry fer the words I said to you when ya tried to console me." A tear fell down his face as he almost lost his balance.

"Dad," Jill cried out with concern.

Using his cane to center his body, he yelled, "No! It must be done!"

"Don, would you like to sit down?" David asked as he moved the extra chair forward.

"A real man stands when he's got words, David. So, I'll stand 'til I'm done."

David sat close behind Don just in case he needed help.

"When Janey left, I was bitter. I did'na want anythin' to do with her or them babies ever' a'gin." Putting his hand up over his mouth, he wept bitterly. "I cain't believe the way I acted and what they had to go through. I was wrong and I jes' want you all to know that I'm makin' it right. Amy Jayne and James are with me now. I told 'em what I did and I tole 'em they'd never have to worry a'gin, but their Papaw would care for 'em. Now, I'm comin' to make amends with the town. I'm so sorry fer the way I treated all of ya. I wanna help if you'll let me."

Grace and her best friend Lorna walked to the front of the room to hug Don. "A'course we forgive ya, Don. Don't we, y'all?" Everyone nodded as Jill walked up behind and helped him back to his seat.

"Thank you, Don," David said. "I want the town to know that Don and I have had a great deal of conversation about these men. He's given us critical intel that will help us in the coming days."

"So, who are these outlanders?" Clyde asked.

David didn't want to answer this question but figured he had no choice. "I was on a mission that uncovered a plot planned by a group called the PeaceKeepers."

"Wait, ain't that the same group that's burnin' down

churches and food plants?" Benjamin asked.

"Yes, they are the same, Benjamin, and they're all run by Lucien Baldur."

"He's the Antichrist!" Someone yelled from the back.

Concerned over the direction the meeting was taking; he looked at Pastor Ron who stood. "Come on now, y'all. We done talked 'bout this. Are ya gonna be 'fraid or are ya gonna stand?"

"Thank you, Ron. He and this Helel, are the ones who are pushing the Kindness Tax. They are the same ones who have brought nations together in a one world government and have attempted to destroy towns like Atlanta, and now they appear to have their sights on Wild Rock. But, Ladies and Gentlemen, I'm going to take a quote from my mother's favorite book, if you will bear with me." Opening his mom's Bible, David read from Joshua 1:9: "'Have I not commanded you? Be strong and courageous. Do not be afraid; do not be discouraged, for the Lord your God will be with you wherever you go.' Now, the way I see it, the people of God faced war at every side, yet they trusted in their God. I see each of you on Sunday nodding and singing praise, but do you believe what you're singing? I'm still trying to figure your God out, but I made a promise to seek him, and seek him I shall. If God's people could trust him, then I figure so can I.

"Now, there are four role-players in a war. There are the perpetrators, the victims, the bystanders, and the protectors. We've all got a choice in the role that we play. I personally am not going to stand by and watch the PeaceKeepers take what everyone here has built. If you believe in this God of yours, then you'll stand with me."

After a few moments, the townspeople began to stand. Benjamin, being the last to stand said, "The Lord saved me when yer Dorter prayed over me, David Bennett. So, I guess he has need of me fer some reason, so I'm with ya, too."

CHAPTER 14

A Deadly Snare

Clouds covered Wild Rock Mountain as Maddie and David descended toward Kalispell. She wasn't interested in participating in the conversation between her dad and Mr. Don. She wanted to talk to Amy Jayne.

As they drove along the fence, she smiled at her friend, who was riding Mr. Don's horse, Onyx. She had to admit to being a little jealous of her friend's red hair, contrasting starkly against the brilliant white of the Camarillo horse.

"I'll get out here, Dad," she said as she jumped out of the Tahoe. Kali's whinny greeted her as she walked through the barn doors.

"Hey Girl, how was your night?" Grabbing the lead rope, she led Kali and baby Hope to her bale of hay in the corral.

"Maddie!" Amy Jayne dismounted Onyx and led her to the water trough.

As she hugged her friend, she couldn't help but share in her friend's joy. This was the Amy Jayne she first met two years ago.

"Guess what!" Amy Jayne couldn't contain her excitement.

"What?"

"Jacob and Rory are coming home tomorrow."

"Jacob?" She asked weakly, her heart skipping a beat.

"Yes! I overheard Jill telling Don last night."

139

Confused, she asked, "Do you think they're coming because of the PeaceKeepers?"

"PeaceKeepers? Who are they?" Amy Jayne asked.

She looked away and replied, "Oh, nobody."

Amy Jayne pushed her friend on the matter, "No, not nobody, who are they?"

"I-I'm not sure I should say."

"Come on, Maddie, what's goin' on?"

"Well, I heard one of the guys talking to a stranger the other day outside the barn. They're planning to come into town tomorrow night and do something."

"Do what?"

Shaking her head, she suddenly didn't want to think about what they were planning. "Honestly, I don't know, Amy Jayne, but they're not good people. They're the reason we're here."

"Wait, so these PeaceKeepers are the same ones that burnt down yer home?"

Nodding, she answered, "Yes."

"Well, that ain't good. So, what's the plan?"

"My dad met with the town last night, and they've come up with something. He's here to talk to Mr. Don about it this morning."

"Well, come on then. Let's put the horses up and go listen."

"No, Amy Jayne. We can't."

"Why cain't we? This is our town, too."

Amy Jayne was right; this is our town. "Okay, come on."

As they walked up to the back of the house, Maddie suddenly had a bad feeling. "I don't know if this is such a good idea," she said.

"Come on, we'll go in the back door. They'll never see us." Amy Jayne opened the back door softly and tiptoed into the kitchen. Maddie followed close behind.

"Don, where did you hire this guy?" David asked.

"He jes' showed up. We got hands always comin' in and out. That's the way it is, Son."

"You don't do background checks?" David asked sarcastically.

Don laughed. "Boy, where do ya think ya are? New York or somethin'? We live by our word out here."

That's weird. Maddie thought. *After what happened to Margaret, wouldn't he be more careful when hiring new employees?*

"Okay, so we think we're looking at twenty, right? Is that what he said?"

"That's what he told me. Expect twenty to help with the wranglin'."

"What's wranglin'?" Amy Jayne whispered as Maddie shrugged.

"We'll have a group here and here," She heard her dad say. "I think we need to leave the girls here. Do you have something to keep them busy?"

Busy? Disappointment set in as she realized he had no intention of letting her help.

Amy Jayne gestured toward the door and led her back outside. "We cain't let them do this alone," she said.

She shook her head as the sting of rejection set in. "You heard them, they don't want us to help," she said bitterly.

"Maddie, look at me. Thar's one thing this life has taught me: 'If it's meant to be, it's up to me.' Thar ain't no way I'm gonna sit back and let somebody take Wild Rock. NO WAY! The boys'll be here tomorrow. Let's ask yer dad if you can spend the night, and we'll come up with a plan. Between the four of us, we should be able to make some noise that'll send these PeaceKeepers packin'."

She nodded even as guilt set in. Disobedience was not a thing in the Bennett household. Short of a few white lies, she couldn't remember the last time she went against her dad's wishes. But Amy Jayne was right, she couldn't stay behind and wait for someone else to fight this battle. There was too much at stake.

The rest of the day was spent caring for the horses. Maddie walked Kali while Jill helped Little Hope ease into her halter. Enchanted with the way Jill patiently spoke to the foal, she wondered what it would be like to care for horses for a living. "What do you think, Kali?" She asked her charge. "Do you think I should become a breeder or a vet?" Laughing when the horse nodded in agreement, she said, "Well, it's settled then!" She couldn't wait; in a month, she would be able to ride the mare. Excitement filled her as she thought about all she had to tell Jacob. The guilt from earlier faded away as she rehearsed their conversation.

When Maddie's dad came to pick her up, Amy Jayne asked Mr. Don if she could stay the night. Incensed when her dad agreed too quickly, she turned and made her way back to the barn.

Maddie, lay this anger down.

Stopped in her tracks at the still, small voice, she sighed. She didn't want to have this conversation right now. *I'll pray later,* she decided as she went to help Amy Jayne prepare the horses for the night.

Friday morning, she awoke with a sour stomach. She couldn't shake the guilt she was feeling over the thought of deceiving her dad. *Too many secrets,* she thought to herself. *I wish I could talk to Rachel.* She sure did miss her phone in moments like this.

I'm right here.

"Maddie, come on, horses gotta eat!" Amy Jayne called from downstairs.

Throwing on a t-shirt and a pair of sweats, she hurried to meet her friend. Glancing at the desk in the corner, she realized it had been a hot minute since she had written in her journal and prayed. "God, can we talk later? A lot is going on right now."

After grabbing a Tums from the medicine cabinet, she ran after her friend.

Surprised by the male voice talking to Kali, she walked to her stall and found Jacob talking softly to the horse. He's here. A mixture of fear and excitement filled her as she thought about seeing him again. Wiping her sweaty hands on her pants, she said, "Oh, hi Jacob."

Turning, he stood tall and with his quirky one-sided smile, he said, "Hey, Maddie. Good to see ya." He was close enough that she could smell his cologne mixed with the scent of hay and manure.

An overwhelming feeling came over her as she noticed how his shirt strained across his shoulders. His wavy hair had been replaced by a buzz cut that highlighted his widow's peak. Afraid that he might touch her, she stepped back as she realized she couldn't trust herself. "Um, hey," she repeated.

"Ya already said that," he bantered with a smile.

Raising her hand toward his head, she said, "You cut your hair." Embarrassed, she pulled away quickly.

"We had to—army orders."

"How was it?"

"Boot camp? Aw, it was hard, Maddie. Thar's a lot of bad stuff happenin' right now."

"Yeah," she agreed.

The sadness on Jacob's face was replaced with a lift of his brow as he turned toward Kali. "I see you've been takin' good care a' my girl."

Half expecting him to touch her, she held her breath, disappointed when he turned away. Pushing the thought away, she realized she was happy to introduce him to Kali's new foal. "This is Hope. Hope, meet Jacob."

Jacob crouched down and touched the foal. Hope had become used to the attention and sniffed at this new human. Kali paid no mind as she continued to eat away at her hay.

"When was she born?" Jacob asked.

"A month ago. Oh, Jacob, it was the most amazing thing!

She was a red sac? I think that's what it's called."

"And she's alive? Wow."

"Yeah, the doc said the placenta detached from the uterus?"

"Mr. Don lost another foal a year ago from a red bag delivery. Ya gotta catch 'em right when they're born, else they die. Looks like Kali had an angel by her side that night." Looking at Maddie, he said, "Thank ya kindly fer bein' thar fer her."

Blushing, she said, "All I did was pray. Doc Walker and Ms. Jill did all the work."

"Well, yer prayers are powerful, Maddie. The day after ya prayed fer me at boot camp, well let's jes' say I was havin' a bad time of it. I wanted to quit. When I got yer letter, I felt like the Almighty breathed new life into me. Thank ya, by the way."

She wasn't sure how to respond. *Why didn't you write me?* She wondered. *Did the kiss mean anything?* "I'm sorry I only wrote you twice. Things were so crazy around here after the flood that I didn't have much time."

Jacob tilted his head and said, "I'm sorry I wasn't here fer the flood. It looks like it was bad." A look of disappointment crossed his face.

I wish I could tell what he is thinking. She wasn't used to this serious side of Jacob. "Yeah, we lost some good people. How's your mom's place? When I saw her at church, she said there was some pretty bad water damage."

"It's lookin' good. Some neighbors came by and patched it right up. No mold or nothin'."

"Oh, good."

Turning to brush Kali, he said, "Ya know, me and Rory are only here fer a week and then we get shipped out."

His soft words struck her with a sinking feeling. Fear gripped her as she realized she may never see him again. "Where are you going?"

"My orders are to Atlanta," he said matter-of-factly, without even looking up at her.

Caught between alarm and excitement over the thought that she might see him if she decided to visit Jade, she said, "Atlanta's in a pretty rough state. Are you okay with that?"

"I signed up fer four years, thar ain't no turnin' back now," he said with a grimace.

Maddie wondered what the next four years would look like without his quirky smile to cheer her up.

"Hey, Jacob!" Amy Jayne ran up to them, stopping short at the sight of their long faces. "Whoa, am I interruptin' somethin'?" she asked with her hands up.

Cleaning horsehair off his hands, he said, "No, we're all good, ain't we, Maddie?" Jacob turned to look at Amy Jayne. "Are ya helpin' out here?"

"I live here now," Amy Jayne said with a smile that didn't quite reach her eyes.

Confused, he looked at Maddie as Amy Jayne grabbed them both by the arm and said, "Let's take a walk and I'll tell you'ns all 'bout it."

As Amy Jayne told the story, everything began to fall into place. Margaret's tragic death, Amy Jayne's mother leaving, and her dad falling into alcoholism. Moved by the emotion in her friend's voice as she shared Mr. Don's apology to her and her brother, Maddie thought, *Amy Jayne has finally found her home.* "Do you miss your dad?" Maddie asked.

Stopping to look at her friend, a tear fell as Amy Jayne said, "More than I could ever tell," she said. "If I'm honest, I feel a lil' guilty."

"Why?" Maddie asked.

"So many years I took care 'a James. I almost hated him, my dad. How could he jes' let go like that! Ya know?" Surprised by the loud shout that left her mouth, she walked over to the fence separating the pasture and leaned over as if she were inspecting it.

Placing her hand on her friend's shoulder, Maddie nodded. "He loved you and your brother. The last year has been great. He's been there for both of you."

"I know, that's why I feel guilty." Looking at her friend,

she said. "Maddie, you don't know how many times I prayed my daddy would go home to be with Jesus so he would'na suffer any more."

"But he stopped drinking, didn't he?" Maddie asked.

"Yeah, but he still loved her." Tears fell unapologetically down her cheeks as she turned back to the pasture.

Jacob stood watching the exchange silently. Turning with his back to the fence, he said, "I'm not gonna' lie, I never woulda thought ya'd be livin' with the likes a' Mr. Don. He ain't exactly been good to this town."

"Jacob, he loves us, he truly loves us!" Wiping the tears from her face, she stood ready to fight for the man who took her and her brother in. "Fer the first time, I don't have to be checkin' in on James ever' second of the day." Laughing at the thought, she added, "I think he likes the freedom from his big sister. He's been hangin' out with yer Matthew." Turning to look at Maddie, she laughed, "They've been makin' all kinds of weapons."

The change of subject shed light on the heaviness she was feeling. "Matthew told me he caught a rabbit for Grammy to cook!" She said, pretending to be offended by her brother's actions.

Jacob bent over laughing as Maddie stood with her hands on her hips. "And what's so funny, Mr. Sullivan?"

The laughter was gone as he placed his hands on either side of her face. Looking at her intently, he said, "I think yer delightful, Ms. Bennett."

Rocking back, wondering what she should do, Maddie swallowed hard and averted her eyes, feigning a smile.

The moment was gone as quickly as it came. Stepping back, Jacob shook his head as he turned away.

"Whoo, you guys." Amy Jayne pretended to fan her face as Maddie gave her friend a light shove.

Jacob turned around and started walking back toward the house. "Speakin' of makin' weapons, what's this I hear 'bout tonight?" His quick pace left the girls with no choice but to catch up.

After the pounding of her heart subsided, she proceeded to tell him what she heard in the barn.

Jacob's whole body stiffened as he made a fist. A myriad of emotions crossed his face as he stood still. Dropping his arms, he bolted forward—a man on a mission.

Fear filled Maddie's heart as she watched her friend's face turn red. This angry side of Jacob wasn't one she was accustomed to. Maybe I shouldn't have said anything and just let dad handle it, she worried.

"It looks like we came home at jes' the right time." Turning around to face them both, he looked at Amy Jayne and asked, "So what's the plan?"

Around three p.m., her dad came by to give her a story about staying at the ranch so she could alert him to the arrival of the PeaceKeepers. As he handed her a radio and a pair of binoculars, he said, "This is very important, Maddie, can you do this?"

With a nod, she said, "Where will you be?"

"Tom and I will be at the entrance on the backside of the mountain."

"What about Rachel and Emma?"

"They're at the safehouse with Grammy and Aunt Lisa." Placing his hand on her shoulder, he said, "They'll be fine."

Guilt once again filled her as a thought crossed her mind:

You need to tell him, Maddie.

A fresh surge of anger covered her as she looked at his stern features. She so wanted to tell him what they were planning but knew he would shoot it down. "Okay, Dad." Placing the radio in her back pocket and the binoculars around her neck, she hugged him and said, "Please be careful."

Kissing her forehead, he said, "I love you, Ruthie." And

with that, he was gone.

A surge of adrenaline filled David as he and Tom worked out the final details for the night. After a year of feeling powerless, David was finally in control. The map he and Tom reviewed was old and outdated. They had spent the last forty-eight hours going over the topography and updating it so they could share it with the team.

The icing on the cake came when Pastor Joe from the Warriors of the Way called and told him they would be joining them. David was on top of the world.

He would never forget Joe and his mighty men—a group of old men who chose to go after the PeaceKeepers and expose the PKO for what it truly was. Working with them to rescue his daughter and her friends two years ago reminded him of missions in the Navy when he worked alongside some of the smartest and most dangerous men in the world.

As they were drawing out the back road, the door to the church fellowship hall suddenly burst open as Joe and his hodgepodge group of burly men tromped in.

"Hi ho thar, David Bennett!" Pastor Joe said as he grabbed David's hand in a firm handshake.

As they greeted one another, Joe said, "David, I shore am sorry we could'na make yer hearin' in DC."

"It's okay, Joe. What's meant to be will be. Were you successful in the rescue?"

Joe looked at his crew with great pride as he said, "Shore was! A whole posse a youngin's rescued and taken to their families. These boys are the best a' the best!"

Pastor Ron walked into the room to see what the commotion was about. "Joe, Marty! I did'na think I'd be seein' you guys!"

"Well, I'll be. Is that Ronald Tucker?"

"Shore is! Look at you, Joe, you've put on a couple a pounds since I seen ya last."

Rubbing his belly, he smiled mischievously and said, "It's that southern cookin'. My Peggy is the best!"

"Peggy ain't left you yet?" Pastor Ron teased.

"Naw, she's got too much of God's love in her. She's an angel, she is. God gifted me with that woman to keep me alive, I'm sure of it."

Confused, yet intrigued by the exchange, David stood quietly as he listened to the men reminisce.

"Oh, David, I did'na see ya standin' thar. Here we are reminiscin' and all," Ron said.

The suspense was killing him, he had to know. "I was wondering how you two knew each other."

Pastor Joe elbowed Ron in the ribs, "Well, back in the day, we were in a motorcycle gang together."

In disbelief, David couldn't help but join his friend, who burst out laughing.

"Two pastors in a motorcycle gang. Well, if that doesn't beat all," Tom said.

"Wait, didn't you know my dad?" David asked Joe.

Pastor Joe looked at Pastor Ron with a side glance, "Shore did."

"Wait, don't tell me."

"Should we tell 'em, Ronald?"

David shook his head as he exclaimed, "No way, there is no way George Allen Bennett was in a motorcycle gang. There is no way my mom would allow it!"

Suddenly, everyone started laughing as David stood there in disbelief.

"You know what? I just don't even want to know," David said as he turned back to the map.

As the laughter died down, Pastor Joe grabbed his belt straps, "Well, I guess it's 'bout time to get down to business.

CHAPTER 15

Timber!

An ominous silence filled the truck cab as Maddie and her friends made their way to the back trail entrance. Even as she walked boldly into the night, her courage disappeared with the sun. *I'm glad I didn't mention the horses,* she thought as a wave of fear and guilt overwhelmed her. *What if Dad finds out? Or worse, what if something happened and he wasn't there?* Looking out the window, she prayed, *Oh God, please don't let anything bad happen.*

The silence was deafening. *God? Where are you?*

A feeling of unease deepened as Jacob parked at an unfamiliar house. "Whose house is this?"

Jacob turned the keys, looked at her, and said, "Awe, it's okay—the owner is on vacation.

"We'll be out of sight here," he added. "It'll be okay, Maddie, I promise."

A shiver ran down her spine as he gently moved a lock of hair behind her ear.

"Are ya okay?" he asked.

"Jacob, I don't know if this is a good idea."

"We'll be fine. I've parked here before."

"No, I mean, maybe we should just let Dad and the others handle things tonight."

Amy Jayne leaned forward from the back. "This is our town, too. We cain't be 'fraid to protect it."

150

Maddie turned and looked at Amy Jayne. Rory sat in the back, completely quiet. She didn't think he liked the plan, either. "I'm not afraid, I just…"

"Yer 'fraid, admit it. Ya heard Jacob, we'll be fine." Bristling at the finality of Amy Jayne's response, she realized how much her friend sounded like her mom.

Taking a deep breath, she resolved to move forward with the plan. *Do it, afraid,* she mumbled to herself.

David, Tom, and Pastor Ron took their places at the back entrance to Wild Rock. David couldn't wait to see their surprise when the PeaceKeepers met with the roadblocks set in place. Pulling his radio out, he checked in with the other team. "Come in, Joe."

"Joe, here, go ahead." Radio static filled the night air.

Turning the volume down, David asked, "Everyone in place?"

"That's affirmative."

"Good, that's good. Send the code word when the shipment arrives."

"Roger that. Joe out."

"I sure am glad Grammy's mighty men showed up," Tom said as David placed the radio in his back pocket.

Buttoning his coat, David said, "Me, too." The spring night smelled of snow. Looking up at the clouds covering the usually starry night, he hoped it would hold off. A glance at his watch confirmed another forty-five minutes before the action was set to begin. That is if this wasn't all a ruse. Experience taught him never to expect a plan to go as expected.

The sound of rustling leaves caught them off guard. Placing his finger to his lips, David stood and walked toward the sound to see what was there. A deer ran off before him with a fawn not far behind. Shaking his head, he returned to the temporary fort.

An hour became two when the shrill sound of an alarm sent them into high alert.

"Oops, sorry," Pastor Ron said quietly, silencing his watch.

Tom threw a kind glance David's way. *The man has the patience of a saint.* David pondered.

Suddenly, the sound of static once again interrupted the quiet with its obnoxious sound.

"The package is delivered; the package is delivered!" David stood as the anxious tone came across garbled over the radio. Grabbing a pair of binoculars, he scanned the area until he caught sight of the second team. A bright red glow began to take shape in the distance. The sound of a gunshot sent them running toward their ATV.

"David, one of us needs to stay here," Tom said.

"Okay, you two go ahead and radio back if you need help."

"Are you sure?" Tom asked.

He placed his hand inside his jacket pocket and said, "Yes, I'm sure. I have backup right here."

As they drove away, David raised the binoculars again and scrutinized the area. As the lights of the ATV disappeared into the forest, he found himself frustrated by the dense trees encumbering his view. "Come on!" He muttered angrily as he tried to discern what was happening. If David hated one thing, it was being away from the action.

After another hour, he decided to take matters into his own hands. It was time for plan B. It wasn't his favorite option, but one that would buy them some time. Grabbing the chainsaw, he put on a pair of goggles, walked over to the marked tree, and began cutting. The tree was notched and roped to control the direction of the fall. After setting a solar-powered light behind him, he worked from the left side of the trunk and made efficient work of the fall. The deep thud moved the ground as the tree made for a safe deterrent from anyone wanting to pass. Another tree down, he felt safe enough to make his way to the other side of town.

The sound of his radio going off broke his concentration. "David."

Stopping to grab his radio, he lifted it and said, "Go."

"We've got a problem."

Silence followed the sound of static. "Delta on point," he answered again, using his NATO codeword.

Nothing. It looked like he was going to have to run.

As he settled into a rhythm, David heard footsteps behind him. Finding the nearest tree, he stopped and hid to wait for whoever was following behind. As the steps drew closer and closer, he realized these were no human footsteps. Placing his hand inside his pocket, he hoped he wouldn't have to lay out an animal.

Quieting his breath, he waited for the footsteps to reach him. Just as he noticed the bobcat, his radio went off again. The abnormal sound alerted the animal to the presence of his human adversary, but he didn't seem to know David's exact location. *Perhaps I can keep him from seeing me,* he thought as he slowly made his way around the tree.

The deep growl from the other side of the tree was not a good sign. Deciding it was time to make himself known, David removed his jacket and raised it above his head to appear larger. As the animal moved before him, David backed away slowly while facing the animal. Once the animal locked eyes with David, he stopped growling. David continued to walk away slowly. He knew the bobcat would leave him alone if he kept his eyes fixed on the cat and didn't run.

David's heart was racing. He needed to get to the other side of town, but having a bobcat tracking him wouldn't help matters. It was time to make some noise. Pulling out his car keys, David began to jingle the keys while making loud grunting noises toward the cat. He didn't want any humans to be alerted to his location, so he tried to be as guttural as possible. Before he knew it, the bobcat grew tired and ran off. *Finally,* he thought. After a few moments, he put his coat back on and made his way towards town.

Grateful that another life was saved on his watch, he pulled out his radio and attempted to get someone to answer. "Delta on point," he said. Giving it a few moments, he repeated the codeword.

The static interrupted David's shuffle through the leaves again, "Delta, Whiskey, Golf, Alfa, Papa. Tango. Bravo. Foxtrot." David stopped to analyze the code: D-W-G-A-P-T-B-F. Years of deciphering the code words of others helped him decipher the message quickly. "David, we've got a problem. They brought fire."

"No," he said as he picked up the pace again. It didn't take long for him to see the result of their message. He watched in horror as not just one, but two structures went up in flames. "No, no, no…" he muttered as he began to run again. *Where is the cavalry when you need it?*

The utility company in the valley had turned off the streetlights months ago. It was David and Tom's idea to install solar LED streetlamps, which, on sunny days, gained enough power to light the streets brightly. For once, David was thankful for the change. Since they had been under cloud cover for several days, the lights were not as bright as normal. This would work to David's advantage by not drawing attention to his arrival.

His early morning runs prepared him for the mountain topography. While the town was small, horizontally, the hills created quite a challenge. As he ran up Main Street, he turned left toward the safehouse. Confirming that the building was safe, he ran through the courthouse lawn to view the entrance to Wild Rock. Climbing up the stairs, he found a dark spot where he could overlook the entrance. His binoculars gave him precisely the view he needed to see what he was up against.

Eighteen men, dressed all in black, surrounded Joe, Tom, Pastor Ron, and the handful of townsfolk standing guard. *Where are the other men?* He wondered. Relieved to see that the burning structures were only utility barns, he thought, *we can replace food.*

A strange light caught David's attention from the tree line of the entrance. Focusing on the light, he began to see a pattern. *Well, I'll be, Morse code,* he thought with a laugh. He had found the rest of Pastor Joe's men—The Warriors of the Way. The varying durations of light flashes reminded David of his early days of code. This was one of the first languages he had to learn working in Navy Intelligence. He was a little rusty but thought he could translate. Pulling out a pen and the map he was carrying, he proceeded to write out the flashes:

A long flash, pause, two quick flashes, pause, two long flashes, pause, a long flash followed by three quick flashes, pause, one quick flash, pause, one quick flash followed by a long flash and another quick flash, and then nothing.

- / .. / -- / -... / . / .-.

TIMBER

Before he knew it, a tree came tumbling down behind the PeaceKeepers. Not just one tree, but three! "Yes!" David said as he pumped his fist in the air.

As the trees descended, they spooked the PeaceKeepers while giving Joe and the men he was with time to turn the tables on them. David watched in awe as old Pastor Joe laid out the men and took their weapons. Figuring this would be a good time to be of assistance, David jumped the railing and ran around to the backside of the semi-circle of men, surprising one of them from behind. "You can put your weapon down now," he whispered menacingly. The man placed his weapon down and his hands up.

Watching over five of the attackers, Tom said, "Well, it's about time you showed up. Brought the cavalry with you, did you?"

David looked behind him as the Warriors of the Way made their way to the group, looking mighty proud of themselves.

"What're we gonna do with these Outlanders?" Pastor Joe asked.

As Uncle Tom, the mayor, watched over another two, he said, "I've called the sheriff; he's on his way with a paddy wagon."

Elbowing his friend, Tom whispered, "I thought there were twenty?"

Nudging the group leader, David asked, "Where's the rest of your crew?"

"Hmph, wouldn't you like to know?" He said with a colorful expression added.

"Don't be smart; we've got eyes everywhere. We will find them. When we do, it will be much harder for you. So, where are they?" David asked impatiently.

The man turned his head.

A group of Joe's men left the circle at David's nod. Once the attackers were captured, the plan was for a group to go and stand guard around the safehouse. This was where most of the town was hidden, including his wife, mom, and younger son.

Looking around the circle, he took inventory of the men standing guard. Seeing his oldest, Mike, standing guard made him smile. He was proud of his son and the about-face he had taken since leaving the PeaceKeepers. It looked like everyone on both teams was accounted for. He needed to check on Maddie and her friends but decided to wait until the Sheriff made his way up the mountain.

"You realize we're going to have to cut some logs for the sheriff to make his way in here," David said to the mayor.

"Already got it handled."

Even as Uncle Tom spoke, a group of men with chainsaws cut up the trees lying across the main entrance. Impressed by their quick work, David said, "Efficient."

"Invite a passel a' lumberjacks to the party, and you'll have enough wood fer a house in no time."

"Oh, good. Then we can get these gentlemen to rebuild

our barns," David said sarcastically as he nudged the leader.

David could hear the siren in the distance. *Won't be long now,* he thought. Just as the blue lights crested the entrance to the town, the crackle of his radio went off in his back pocket. Looking at Tom with a questioning gaze, he pulled it out and said, "David, here."

"Dad." Looking down at the radio, he waited as the crackle of the static garbled the words.

"Was that?" Tom said as the radio sat disturbingly silent.

David shook the radio, hoping to hear the rest of Maddie's message.

"Mr. Bennett, if you want to see your daughter again, you will let my men go."

CHAPTER 16

Courage Revealed

Feelings of déjà vu overwhelmed Maddie as she stared down the barrel of a gun. She was afraid but more so angry that she allowed herself to get into this predicament. *I wish I had listened to my gut,* she thought irritably.

"*The Holy Spirit will lead ya, Girl, but ya gotta learn to listen to 'im.*" She could hear her Grammy's voice even now. Guilt flooded her as she realized he had warned her, but she ignored him, allowing feelings of fear to lead her instead. She knew her dad would be angry, too. He trusted her, and she let him down.

There were only two men to their four, but they were men with guns. The shock on her friend's faces revealed their fear over this fact.

Father, forgive me for not listening to you and disobeying my dad. Please give us the wisdom to get out of this mess. The silent prayer was all she knew to do in the moment.

As she was forced to say something over the radio, she tried to think of a witty codeword to alert her dad that she was okay, but the leader of the two snatched the radio away before she could say anything more than his name.

As they sat in the quiet, a light snow began to fall. Thankfully, she and her friends decided to wear heavy coats. Their captors, on the other hand, were not as lucky. Their signature black hoodie, jeans, and mask did nothing to ward

158

off the wet Tennessee cold.

Suddenly, an idea popped into her head. Pretending to shiver, she pointedly looked at the one marching in place and said, "Pretty cold, isn't it?"

The man just stared at her.

Does he even speak English? she wondered.

Turning to the other man, she said, "So, you're a BAGMAN?" Maddie asked in her snarkiest voice. She couldn't see his face for the mask, but his eyes widened in shock at her knowledge of the tattoo on his arm.

"Yeah, I know all about you," she added. "Oh, you didn't know? My brother has one that looks just like it." The pretend shiver turned into a real one as she tried to stay calm. Looking at her friends, she nodded for them to follow her lead.

"Bagman, what is that anyway?" Amy Jayne asked with a sudden boldness. "Do ya have to wear a real bag? Ya know, 'round these parts, we call our grocery bag a paper poke. Is that what ya are? A poke?"

Maddie shook her head as the man seemed confused by the picture painted by her friend.

"Naw, more like a pig in a poke," Jacob said as he suddenly kicked the knee of the one marching in place and knocked him down.

The next few moments passed in a blur. Before she knew it, Jacob and Rory had the men on the ground.

"What's a pig in a poke?" She whispered to Amy Jayne as they kicked the guns into the brush.

"It means ya don't have all the info 'bout what's gonna happen."

Maddie's nerves began to calm as she let out a laugh.

"Well, I'll be, now, what we got goin' on here?" A tall figure walked into the clearing just as the girls approached their captors.

A flood of relief filled her as she recognized Mr. Don's partner, Bud.

Bud snatched the masks off the two PeaceKeepers. "Why,

fancy meetin' you here, Rocco. I don't think Don's gonna like you and yer new friend's shenanigans. Marty, is it?"

Maddie nodded at Amy Jayne as she realized these were the two whom she had heard outside the barn.

"Bud, is my dad, okay?"

"He's jes' fine, Maddie. But yer gonna have to 'splain this one to 'im."

"I know."

Headlights illuminated the clearing as two officers stepped out of their car and walked toward them. "Are these the boys makin' a ruckus?"

"Yassir, I think all the foxes are accounted fer. The hen house can sleep safely tonight."

"Hey, Mr. Bud, can I say something to Rocco and Marty?"

"I don't know. Yer dad would have my head if I let somethin' happen to ya."

"It'll be okay. I trust you guys."

"Alright, but you stay where I can see ya."

Maddie walked over to the police car where the officers were putting the men in the car.

"Officer, can I say something to them?"

"Make it short, Lil Lady, we've gotta get ta bookin'."

She was trembling, but she had to say what was burning in her heart. "Rocco, Marty, I want you to know that I'm not afraid of you anymore. The PeaceKeepers may have tried to take my peace, but God gave it back. I want you to know that I forgive you and I'm praying that you'll find Jesus and the peace he has for you, too. He loves you very much."

Before she knew it, the man named Rocco spit at her feet. "That'll be the day," he mumbled while Marty completely ignored the exchange.

"Now that's no way to talk to a lady!" The officer slammed the door and said, "Don't take no offense, Ma'am. A night in the lock-up will cool his heels."

◆ ◆ ◆

The ride to the top of the mountain was excruciating. The courage Maddie felt standing before the PeaceKeepers left as quickly as it arrived. She was sad over the response she received from Rocco and worried over the one to come from her dad. She laid her head against the window and noticed the light dusting of snow as it transformed the landscape around them. The mantle of shame that overwhelmed her felt too much like that layer of snow. It would be so easy to wrap up in the cocoon of shame, but experience taught her that wasn't going to help her.

The bluegrass song in the background seemed a good distraction from her thoughts. "Hey, Bud, can I ask you a question?" She asked.

"Yes, ma'am, ask away."

"How did you know where we were?"

"Yer friend here's truck," he said. "I been watchin' you, Boy." Bud looked at Jacob in the rearview mirror. "You think you've been hidin' that truck, but ya ain't."

"Um, I thought the owner was out of town." He said uncertainly.

Bud laughed, "That don't give you the right to park thar. Now, does it?"

"No, Sir."

"Now, this time, it worked in yer favor, but I don't wanna see you parkin' thar agin, got me?"

"Yes, Sir, I gotchu."

"Now I got a question for you'ns. What 'xactly did ya think you'd gain by hangin' out at the bottom of the mountain?"

"We were going to alert my dad when the PeaceKeepers drove by," Maddie replied nervously.

Bud paused before letting out a loud guffaw. "You woulda been down thar a long time. Ya know those boys've been up thar all day." He said, looking at her under his hat.

"So, you knew where they were all along?"

"Shore did! Thar ain't nothin' that passes by ole Bud."

"Why didn't you tell my dad?"

"Sometimes, ya jes' gotta let things happen. A man's courage is revealed when he steps into it."

As she pondered Bud's words, a familiar anxious feeling arose in her belly when she recognized her dad's outline hovering under the roof overhang.

Amy Jayne touched her friend's shoulder as she said, "It's okay, Maddie, we're all in this together."

"Thanks," she said absently.

The leader of the eighteen PeaceKeepers who were lying on the ground decided to get cocky when he heard his comrade's voice. If David were to get his daughter back and serve up justice to this ragtag bunch of miscreants, he had to stay calm. He wasn't going to let him get under his skin.

"I think I know where they are," Bud whispered as he tried to decide what to do next. "Want me to go get 'em?"

The more he worked with the people of Wild Rock, the more he loved their resilience and courage.

When Bud's voice came over the radio, the leader of the PeaceKeepers groaned. He knew it was game over.

David nodded to the sheriff to take the PeaceKeepers to jail.

Guilt stabbed him in the chest when he watched his daughter step out of the truck. *He promised to protect her from the world, but could he protect her from herself?*

He didn't know whether to hug her or yell as she stood before him. His training told him that yelling wouldn't solve anything, but his father's heart wanted to lash out at the men who tried to take his little girl. The problem was that she was standing in the way.

"Dad, I…"

"Not now, Ruthie." Seeing the sadness on her face, he knew he had to do something, so he grabbed her in a big bear hug and said, "You're safe."

Relief filled Maddie as her dad's arms wrapped around her. She was so worried she would get into trouble, but instead, she only felt the love of a father who loved his daughter.

"But Dad."

"There are some people in the safehouse who want to see you; go on in. You two boys hang out here with me."

As she opened the door, she threw a nervous glance to Jacob and Rory and made her way inside.

"Maddie! Amy Jayne!"

Emma and Rachel ran to their friends as soon as they entered the room.

"What were you thinking?" Rachel asked.

"What do you mean?" Maddie countered.

Emma touched her friend's arm and whispered, "Do you want to go back?"

"I wasn't going back," she said with certainty.

Rachel raised a brow and asked, "How do you know?"

Hugging her red-headed friend, she said, "Amy Jayne would've eaten them for lunch."

Later that night, as she sat in Grammy's living room, she had to get something off her chest.

"Hey, Grammy?"

Her gram's eyes popped open at the sound of her name. "What's that, Maddie Ruth?" she asked sleepily.

"Oh, I'm sorry, I didn't know you were asleep."

"Jes' restin' my eyes," she said as she sat up straight in her chair.

Suddenly nervous to ask her question, she asked, "Have you ever lied to someone?"

"As a matter of fact, yes, I have."

Surprised over the answer, she asked, "How did it turn out?"

"I almost lost a good friend."

"Was God mad at you?"

Grammy smiled as she looked at her granddaughter, "I think God was sad more 'n like it. He hates sin even more when his children get caught up in it. But I don't think he was mad at me. Naw, I know he weren't, cause he's the one that helped me make it right."

"If you don't mind me asking, who was the relationship with?" Maddie asked.

"That'd be Ms. Lorna. When she decided to go and be Ms. Nashville, I was jealous. I could'na 'magine bein' without my best friend. Yer Grandpa George and I had jes' gotten married, ya see, and I told her if she wanted to leave me fer Nashville, well that'd be jes' fine with me; I had a man now, and I did'na need her. That was a lie a'course, I needed her more 'n ever when George took off fer the Navy."

"Did you reach out to her after he left?"

"No, ma'am. I had a stronghold a' pride 'round my heart."

"How did you reconcile?" She wondered.

Tears clouded Grammy's eyes as she answered, "I never knew how hard she had it. I was so jealous and angry that I could'na see the forest fer the trees. When I found out she was sick, I was covered in shame and knew I had to make it right."

She remembered this story. "Was that when she overdosed?" She asked.

"Yes, ma'am. That girl saved me jes' as much as I saved her. God was in the middle of all of it."

"He does turn the things the enemy meant for evil good, doesn't he?" She asked. *But will he forgive me?* She wondered as she pondered just how much she should tell Grammy about all that had happened.

"That he does." Grammy turned her head and squinted one eye as she asked, "Hey, what's this all 'bout anyway?"

Averting her eyes in shame, she blurted out, "I lied to Dad. He told me to stay at Mr. Don's, and I told him I would. We had a plan to hang out at the foot of the mountain and wait for the PeaceKeepers to show." A sudden need to justify her actions arose as she cried out, "We just wanted to help!" Dropping her chin to her chest, she realized she couldn't tell Grammy about what she did with Jacob.

While watching her granddaughter fight her inner battle, Grammy sang a song lightly under her breath as she rocked in her chair. After a long pause, she asked, "Did ya?"

Maddie's hands were shaking. *Why couldn't I have just left well enough alone?* She wondered. Confused over the question, she asked, "Did I, what?"

Leaning forward, she asked, "Did ya help?"

Clasping her hands to ground herself, she whispered, "No ma'am, I think I just made things worse."

Sensing her granddaughter's anxiousness, she grabbed her hand and said, "It can be like that. What'd God say 'bout it?"

Trembling as guilt tore through her over her lack of prayer, she said, "I haven't heard anything."

Lifting her eyebrows in a questioning gaze, Grammy asked, "Did ya ask him?"

Maddie paused as she realized she hadn't prayed as she should. *Maybe once,* she thought. "I did, but he's been silent." The little white lie ate at her as she realized she hadn't prayed about Jacob at all.

"Hmm, silent, huh? Tell me what yer readin' in the Bible."

Maddie turned to her in surprise, "Reading?"

"Yeah, if ya wanna hear his voice, ya gotta talk to him. How do ya talk to him?"

"By praying and reading his word," she mumbled.

"You got it, Girl. So, have ya been prayin' and readin' his word?"

Guilt covered her again as she realized how long it had been since she sat with the Lord. She had been so worried about Jacob and the PeaceKeepers that she forgot to go to the One who would give her peace. "No, ma'am, not like I should."

"What'd ya do when ya knew you were in trouble?" Grammy asked.

Thinking back to the moment when the PeaceKeepers held them at gunpoint, she remembered her short prayer. "I prayed for wisdom," Maddie answered.

"Well, sounds to me like God turned somethin' the enemy meant for evil into good," she said.

Maddie smiled when her Gram repeated her revelation. "Yeah, I guess he did."

Grammy's eyebrows drew together as she asked, "Maddie Ruth, do ya trust him?"

"God?"

"That's who we're talkin' 'bout, ain't it?"

"I do trust him, but…"

"But, what, Girl? Spit it out."

Feeling the need to defend herself again, she blurted out, "Everybody had their own plan, Grammy. Dad told me I could help, but then told me to stay behind. Amy Jayne and Jacob both said we needed to protect our community."

"And what did yer voice say?" Grammy asked.

The pointed question was telling. To be honest, she was confused over whose voice to listen to. "I knew what the PeaceKeepers were capable of," she said, "I guess I just wanted to keep Wild Rock safe."

"I get it, but ya gotta do it God's way."

What is God's way? She wondered. "If I had stayed behind like Dad said, how could I have helped?"

Grammy smiled as she sat back in her chair and crossed her hands over her belly. "Well, I'd say you've got the answer to that one. How could you have helped if ya weren't thar?"

"I could've prayed."

"That's right. R'member, God's ways are not our ways. When the world is tellin' ya you've gotta fix it, God is waitin' fer you to trust him. Ya gotta decide who yer listenin' to."

Grimacing as she realized she had messed everything up. "Mr. Bud said that a man's courage is revealed when he steps into it. Would it have been more courageous for me to stay behind?"

Turning to look at her with a questioning glance, Grammy asked, "Now, what do you think?"

"I don't know, it sounds kinda weak to me."

Grammy's response was interrupted by a big yawn. Pausing, she covered her mouth after which she said, "I want ya to read the book of Daniel." She shook her head as a second yawn threatened. "Thar's a boy who had courage, even in captivity. What yer gonna find, Maddie Ruth, is that courage is being willin' to be obedient to God, even when afraid. He'll lead ya to do what's needed when you follow 'im." Lying her head back against the chair, she closed her eyes and added, "Maddie Ruth, I'm jes' gonna close my eyes for a sec." A gentle snore rounded off the last word as her head slumped forward.

After laying her Gram's favorite blanket over her sleeping figure, she wrote Daniel in her journal and decided now was as good a time as any to start.

David was in a dark place. *It was time to act!* After the adrenaline wore down and everyone was safely home, David stewed with anger. The thought of his daughter staring down the barrel of a gun infuriated him, even if this group of PeaceKeepers were terrible hostage-takers.

Picking up his phone, he texted Mordecai. "Package received." He couldn't risk sharing more info in case his calls were being monitored. Mordy would know what to do with the information.

CHAPTER 17

The Invitation

The aroma of coffee was the only thing keeping Maddie awake. After a long night reading the book of Daniel, she was trying all she could to keep her eyes open. She just could not put the book down. Obedient—she had been anything but! As she breathed deeply from the steam rising from her cup, she realized that intercession was finally beginning to make sense, and she had some things to do. "I have so many questions for you, Rachel!" She shouted into the confines of Grammy's backyard, but they would have to wait for another day.

Standing on the back porch, she breathed in the cool morning air and sighed as the sun began to rise between the trees. She was thankful for the peace of the morning. As a heavy layer of fog lifted from the grass, a symphony swirled around her from the three-part whistled notes of the Carolina Wren and his partner, who chattered in reply.

Maddie and Mr. Carolina Wren had become good friends. She had to rename him "Mr." when she found out the male was the one responsible for the beautiful song she had grown to love. She couldn't help but wonder what they talked about. *Was the male looking for food and telling the female where to find it? Was the female fussing over the mess left behind?*

She was grateful to Ms. Lorna for sharing her love of birding with her. Earlier in the month, she walked her through her beautiful garden sharing the sounds of morning with her as she pointed out all the beautiful flowers she cultivated.

"It's a cacophony straight from the Father's heart," Ms. Lorna said as she placed a cluster of daffodils in her basket. "This here garden is jes' on loan to me. While God cultivates the garden of my heart, I am cultivating the garden he has given me to steward."

"Grammy called the heart a garden, too. What does that mean exactly?" Maddie asked.

"Well, the good Book says that the heart is deceitful. God tells us to guard it fer ever'thin' you do flows from it. When we say yes to Jesus, we are givin' him permission to tend and transform it. Then, we are protectin' it by fillin' it with God's word. Paul said in Ephesians that we are to take up the Sword of the Spirit, the Word of God. The Word of God is powerful and sharper than any two-edged sword, piercing to divide our soul and spirit." Picking up a hoe, Ms. Lorna began to pierce the ground. "See how the dirt divides?" Bending down to pick up a handful of dirt, she separated it. "So soft," she said with a faraway look. "If I don't cultivate this here dirt, the flowers won't grow. The dirt must be soft and easy to work." Ms. Lorna took her hand and placed the handful of dirt in the middle of her palm. "Do ya feel it?"

Surprised at how easy it was to roll around in her hand, she said, "It falls apart! We have clay in Georgia, but it's not like this."

"Ya know, the clay doesn't have to stay that way. Georgia has some beautiful gardens, which must be cultivated, too."

Remembering a field trip to Atlanta, she

asked, "Like the Botanical Gardens?"

"Yes! Jes' like 'em. Your heart is jes' like the soil, Maddie. When you allow Jesus in, he tends to the soil of yer heart and cultivates it from hard red clay to something soft and supple, ready fer plantin'."

"So, what does all that have to do with the Sword of the Spirit?" She asked.

"Awe, r'member how I said that we're called to guard our hearts? The Lord gave us his armor to do that very thing. The breastplate covers our heart with the righteousness of Christ. The shield extinguishes all the flaming arrows before they can hit our heart. The Sword guards our heart and is the only offensive weapon, next to prayer, mind ya, in our arsenal of armor."

Maddie pretended to wield a sword in response. "But how does it guard our heart?"

"The Sword is the Word of God. First, our God uses it as a mirror to reveal the places he wants to transform; then he writes his Word on our hearts. This serves as a deposit for that next time you need to pull the word out in offense. Kinda like this." Laying her basket on the ground, Ms. Lorna moved before her and said, "Raise your arms."

Following her instructions, she raised both arms in front of her.

"Okay, here we go." Ms. Lorna crouched in a battle position as she said, "In yer right hand is the shield of faith. I want you to see it in your mind's eye. In yer left hand is the Sword of the Spirit. Again, I want you to see it. Do you see it?"

Determined to understand what Ms. Lorna was teaching, she nodded.

"Maddie, yer stupid. Thar ain't nothin' you

can do right," Ms. Lorna said as she pummeled a fist into her other hand.

Her heart fell as her mentor's words cut her to the quick.

"Now, hang on a minute, don't take it personal, Girl, jes' follow along. Take that shield and say, 'No, I am wise as a serpent and gentle as a dove. Go 'head, say it."

She felt silly, but she repeated Ms. Lorna's words.

"Alright, now, 'Maddie, God doesn't love you. Who are you to think otherwise?'" Ms. Lorna paused and said, "What's yer response?"

She thought quietly. Suddenly, the scripture from John chapter three popped into her head, "God so loved the world that he gave his son?"

"That's right. Jesus said, 'As the Father has loved me, so I have loved you. Now remain in my love.'" Pointing to her mentee's heart, she added, "You have a choice to believe this truth and to wield it when the enemy tells you otherwise."

Laughing as she watched Ms. Lorna pretend to fight a sword battle, she said, "Grammy gave me her sword and told me she fights her battles on her knees. Is that what you mean when you say prayer is an offensive weapon like the sword?"

Smiling, Ms. Lorna placed her hands on her shoulders and said, "Yes." A somber look crossed her face as she added, "Thar's a spiritual battle wagin' right now." Waving her hand around the garden, she said, "Ya feel it, don't ya?"

"Yes, ma'am."

"God gave us Jesus and his armor that is

designed to protect us in the battle. Unfortunately, many don't know how to use their authority in Christ. But God is training you up. You're an intercessor, you know that, right?"

"Like Hannah in the Bible?"

"Yes, ma'am. Perhaps even like Ezekiel."

"Who was he?"

"A prophet—God anointed him a Watchman. His job was to pronounce God's Word to the people. God wanted his people to turn back to him, and Ezekiel was sent to sound the alarm and warn them of danger."

Making a mental note to learn about Ezekiel, Maddie asked, "Is an intercessor a Watchman?"

Ms. Lorna picked up her basket and began walking through a row of future flowers. "Not always. A Watchman is always an intercessor, but an intercessor may only be called to stand in the gap and pray while a Watchman is called to watch, pray, and share God's Word with the people when called."

"How do I know if I am a Watchman?"

"You'll know. If God calls you to intercede, you intercede. If he calls you to sound the alarm, he'll prepare ya. But first," she laid her hand on her heart as she said, "you've got to let his Word in."

That morning, everything became clear. Perhaps that was where her courage came from when she heard of the PeaceKeepers plan to attack Wild Rock. She just wished she hadn't messed it all up.

"Good morning, Ruthie."

Surprised, she jumped as the subject of her thoughts came to stand beside her. Maddie crinkled her nose as she smelled his steaming black coffee.

"Good morning. That's a strong cup you've got," she said as she lifted an eyebrow and plugged her nose for effect.

Peering into her cup, her dad teased, "Hmm, have a little coffee mixed with your creamer this morning?"

Giggling over the banter, she figured now was a good time to apologize. "Hey, Dad?"

His smile turned intense as he interjected, "It's okay, Ruthie. I understand why you did what you did. I'm sorry I didn't trust you."

She felt a weight lift off her shoulders. It was as if the mantle of shame from disobeying her dad had been lifted just like Grammy said. "Thank you. But I shouldn't have disobeyed you. I'm sorry." She placed her head on her dad's shoulder as he pulled her into a side hug.

"Why are you up so early?" He asked.

"I spent the night reading."

Leaning against the railing, he said, "Oh yeah? What are you reading?"

"Oh, you wouldn't be interested," she said nervously.

"Try me."

Maddie took a deep breath and decided to lay all her cards on the table. Turning to look at her dad, she said, "Okay, last night, Grammy and I were talking, and she challenged me to read the book of Daniel. I couldn't sleep, so I stayed up late reading. Everything was so crazy last night, and all I could do was go over everything that happened."

"And?"

"And, what?" She asked.

Raising a brow as if he had a secret, he asked, "What did you learn in the Book of Daniel?"

"Daniel was an intercessor. He had dreams, Dad! Oh, and there was this furnace where three men were put inside, and the king saw four. Do you think the other man was Jesus? Not only that, but there was a lion's den that Daniel was thrown in, and the lion didn't touch him! Can you believe it?" She was so excited to share everything she had read. She couldn't help herself when she had a captive audience.

Smiling, David watched his animated daughter as she excitedly shared her story. *Who knew she would love this Jesus thing so much?*

"What are you laughing at?" She asked when she came up for air.

"I'm proud of you," he said.

"What do you mean?"

"Ruthie, you gave us a scare two years ago. I couldn't understand your anxiety, and if I'm honest, I felt responsible. I didn't know what to do. But you found a way to work through it, didn't you?"

"Dad, you know what it was, don't you?"

"What's that?" He asked as he sipped his coffee.

Taking a deep breath, she blurted out, "It's Jesus. He's given me so much peace. I didn't understand my anxiety either, but Rachel and Grammy showed me how to seek him and find the hope he has for me. It's like the hope I was looking for was him." Maddie felt a bolt of confidence surge through her. "Dad, can I ask you a question?"

"Sure."

"Do you know Jesus?"

David turned and leaned over the railing, looking out over the horizon. "Know him? I don't know, Ruthie. I'm still trying to figure out if I even believe."

"I get it. I had to decide too." Emotion welled up inside of her as she tried to communicate the love she had received. "Grammy says there's no greater love than that of the one who gives his life for a friend. That's what he did. He gave his life for me and... and for you."

As her dad sipped on his coffee, she felt vulnerable. She was shaking inside as she wondered what he would say. Remembering how Kaitlyn responded in the beginning, she didn't want to push him away. This was probably a good place to stop.

"Hey, Maddie, you've got a visitor," Matthew yelled from inside the house.

"Go on, Ruthie. I've got some thinking to do," her dad

said.

Wondering who could be visiting at this hour, she went inside and immediately screamed at the top of her lungs, "Jade!"

The two girls grabbed hold of one another and jumped up and down as they both yelled their excitement.

"What's all this ruckus?" Grammy asked as she ran into the kitchen.

Happy to see her, Jade exclaimed, "Oh, Grammy, I have missed you so much!"

"Well, lookee at ya, Girl! All grown up ya are!"

Gently touching her hair, Maddie said, "I love your hair, Jade! When did you cut it?"

"I had to get rid of the braids. This is so much easier. Do you like it?" Jade asked as she primped for her friend.

"I love it! Oh, wait until Rachel and Emma see you!"

Taking a deep breath, her friend said, "I'm not ready to see them yet. I wanted to talk to you and your dad first."

Her dad took that moment to walk into the kitchen. Silently imploring her dad to stay in the room, she responded, "Well, here we are. What's up?"

As they sat down at the table, Grammy brought each of them a plate.

"Oh, my goodness. Grammy, I have missed your cooking so much! This looks amazing."

Watching as her friend began to eat like it was her last meal, Maddie began to worry over what might come next.

"This is so good," Jade said with a mouth full.

Not wanting to place too much attention on her friend, she began to eat the oatmeal in front of her. Grammy really did make the best oatmeal.

Sitting back in her chair, Jade placed her hand on her stomach and sighed. "Sorry, it's taken me a while to get here, and I haven't been able to eat since I left Atlanta."

"How is Atlanta?" Her dad asked.

Jade's eyes glazed over as she stared at the painting behind them. Her lips were moving, but no sound emerged.

Placing her hand on her friend's, Maddie asked, "Is everything okay?"

Jade shook her head as if to shake out of a trance. Looking at her friend, she folded her hands together as she leaned forward over the table. A sorrowful look crossed her features as she breathed deeply.

"What is it?" Maddie asked.

"Girl, it's bad in Atlanta. So much darkness." Lifting her eyebrows, she sat straight up and shook her head, "Yet so much light! It's crazy, Mads, but God is doing something in that city. I've been working with these people from the WTL who are evangelizing in Atlanta."

"WTL? Who are they?" Her dad asked suspiciously.

"Oh, sorry Mr. Bennett, Way, Truth, and Life. You know, Jesus said, 'He is the way, the truth and the life, no one can come to the Father except through him.'"

"How exactly are they evangelizing?" He asked.

"It is incredible. Pastor Chris will stand up and share about Jesus. We serve food to the people who come to hear the message and next thing you know there will be ten people wanting to get baptized! Some of the men bring these big silver tubs and fill them with ice that melts. They get baptized in ice! Can you believe it?" She asked, shaking her head. "I've never seen anything like it!"

Confused over her friend's enthusiasm, Maddie asked, "Wait, but I thought you said it was bad in Atlanta?"

"No, but that's the thing. It is terrible! Every day there are riots, people breaking into buildings, graffiti everywhere, people dying. You wouldn't recognize it." Pausing, she looked through the glass door into the back yard and then turned her attention back into the conversation. "But then there are these pockets of light that are exploding all over the place. Maddie, I had the opportunity to lead someone to Jesus and then baptize them! ME!"

Excited for her friend, she grabbed her hand and squeezed. She always knew Jade had a fire in her.

David looked on at the interaction between his daughter

and her friend. "You said that it took you a while to get here. How did you get here?" He asked.

Looking down at her lap, she mumbled, "I hitched a ride."

"Wait, what?" Maddie asked. "I can't believe…"

"Hang on," Jade said, putting her hands up. "Before you read me the riot act. It was a friend of a friend. But the car broke down halfway here and we had to get it up and running. He dropped me off and went on his way."

Concerned where this story was going, she asked her friend, "He?"

Rolling her eyes, she said, "Yeah, he's harmless."

"Why didn't your mom bring you?" Her dad asked.

That faraway look came over Jade's face as she responded, "She wouldn't have let me come."

"So, why did you come?"

Maddie looked at her dad, wondering why he was acting so suspicious. He seemed to be worried about something.

"Mr. Bennett, I know you brought us all here to protect us, and I understand why you did. Please know I am so very grateful to you for it. But, Sir, we need the girls in Atlanta." Jade lifted her hand again as Maddie's dad tried to interrupt. "Before you say anything, I just want you to hear me out. If the book of Revelation is true," turning to look at her friend directly, she said, "and I believe it is. If Revelation is true, we are in the very last days, which means that Jesus is coming soon. Maddie, the darkness is so thick in Atlanta. I'm not gonna lie. But the Light is so bright! Remember when Sonya said that we were made for such a time as this? This is that time! I think everything we went through was for a purpose so we could help as many as possible come to know Jesus."

She could see the weariness her friend carried as she slumped in her chair. *I'll bet she hasn't slept in days,* she worried as her dad remained silent.

"Jade, why don't you go to my room. You can grab a hot shower and a nap. Feel free to borrow some of my clothes, and we can see the girls this afternoon if you want."

Jade got up from the table, hugged Maddie, and took her

up on her offer. As she made her way back to the bathroom, Maddie made eye contact with her dad.

She could tell he was about to speak, but she beat him to it.

"Dad, please don't say anything yet. Let's just think about what she said and chat in the morning. Please?"

After a curt nod from her dad, she turned to help her friend settle in.

As Maddie helped her friend, David decided to take a walk to Tom's. The brisk walk allowed him to think through the events of the morning. He wondered what his daughter would say if he told her that he, too, was reading the book of Daniel.

Her question earlier caught him off guard. *Do I know Jesus?* He pondered. The events of the last few months had certainly piqued his interest in his mom and daughter's so-called Savior, but he still didn't know if he could believe in someone who let so many bad things happen. Not to mention the fact that he had to give everything over to a God he couldn't see. *I just don't know how to do that,* he mused.

It was the announcement of his daughter's friend that threw him over the edge. He believed she was sincere but was not sure he could let his daughter go back to Atlanta, especially if it was as bad as Jade said it was.

Thankfully, Tom opened the door to his knock. David didn't want to share the ideas he was harboring with anyone else in earshot.

"David, good morning. It's a little early for a visit, isn't it?"

Looking around his friend, he asked quietly, "Are you busy? I need a word with you."

"Sure, want to take a walk?" Leaning in the doorway, Tom said, "Hey, Liv, David's here. We're going out for a bit. I'll be back."

Silence enfolded them as they walked toward the road that would lead them to town. After half a mile, David said,

"Gabe sent the plans."

"You received them?"

"Yesterday."

Tom took a deep breath and nodded. "Okay, what's the next step?"

"I have a guy at Magnum Lock who will find the ISPs used by the PKO."

"That sounds like a monumental task."

"Eh, we've got connections," David said with a shrug. "There's another matter I wanted to discuss." After they had passed the next house, David shared Jade's story with Tom. "What do you think?" He asked.

"I think she risked a lot to hitchhike from Atlanta, Georgia, to Wild Rock, Tennessee."

"The question is, why? She wants her friends to join her. Something's fishy here."

"I agree that something's off. I assume she doesn't have transportation to return?" Tom asked.

"None that I could see. She said the man who dropped her off went on his way."

"You don't think. No, surely not…" Tom trailed off as his eyes glazed over.

"What are you thinking?" David asked.

"I'm finding it a bit strange that Jade happens to show up the morning after an attack on the town by the PeaceKeepers."

David stopped in the middle of the road. He could not believe that he hadn't thought of this first. "My instincts may be a bit rusty."

Tom's eyes widened as he tried to take back his words. "Hang on, Dave, let's not think the worst here. This is their best friend we're talking about. I don't think she would…"

"Would what? She was at the PKO, too, Tom. Remember how their friend was lured into that place?"

"But not Jade. She's too strong."

"Is she?" David narrowed his eyes, squinting at the sun that had made its way over the trees. Shaking his head, he said, "It can't happen again, Tom." Clenching his jaw, he looked at his friend and added, "I won't let it."

CHAPTER 18

The Harbinger

"Oh no!" A glance at the kitchen calendar reminded Maddie of a commitment with her girls. While she wished to nap as Grammy and Jade did, a certain community garden was calling her name. After putting on her work boots, she grabbed her gloves and slipped out of the house quietly.

"Where have you been?" Emma asked.

Out of breath, she said, "Sorry, I forgot today was our scheduled day to work. I had an unexpected visitor."

"Wait, who?" Rachel asked as she leaned on the pitchfork she was holding.

"Dad and I were hanging on the back deck, and suddenly, Jade showed up in my living room."

"No way! Jade?"

"Yeah. She hitched a ride here."

"No, she did not!" Rachel exclaimed.

"She did. She's asleep at the house now." Pulling on her gloves, she asked, "What can I do?"

"Can you tackle those weeds?" Emma asked.

"UGH, not the weeds! Don't you have some seeds to plant somewhere?"

Placing her hands on her hips, little Emma in her big floppy hat was a force to be reckoned with. She didn't have to say a word.

Maddie immediately got on her knees and began the dirty

181

chore. "Hey, by the way, Jade invited us to go back with her."

Looking at her friend as if she had gone insane, Rachel asked, "To Atlanta? What did you say?"

Maddie shrugged as she pulled a big clump of crabgrass. "It sounds like some cool stuff is going on down there."

"And you're okay with this?" Emma asked. "I thought the whole city was destroyed by the... You know who."

"I don't know," she countered, beginning to wonder if it was such a good idea, after all. "She sounded like she needs us. Can y'all hang out tonight? It'd be better if she explained."

"I need a shower," Rachel said with a frown.

"Me, too." Emma agreed. "Can we meet at your place at six?"

"Sure." After another two hours of work, the girls put their tools away in the shed and made their way home.

After saying goodbye to her friends, she made her way to Grammy's. Worry over her friend overwhelmed her. Something wasn't right, but she couldn't put her finger on why she felt that way. Turning right before the house, she walked through the woods to the familiar path that led to Wild Rock Overlook.

She settled on her favorite rock and pulled her knees to her chest. The awe of the valley still took her breath away. Breathing deeply of the cool mountain air, she decided it was time to lay everything down.

"God," she prayed. "I'm worried about my friend. Is everything okay with her? Jade said that she thinks we are in the very last days and that Jesus is coming soon. Is it true?" A gentle breeze swirled around her. She didn't expect a real voice to answer her, but maybe, just maybe...

Suddenly, a familiar tune caught her attention. Looking up, she noticed Mr. Carolina Wren perched on a branch above. Smiling at her old friend, she began to sing the song she and Emma wrote from the bird's tune.

Ms. Lorna was right; worship did help her to let everything go. *What was it she said? Something about angels encamping around her when she praised God.* Looking around, she didn't see any angels, but then that's how it always was with God.

Looking up, she said, "Jesus, it's all about trust, isn't it? I have to say, I can't wait to see you face to face and hear you talk back to me."

As Mr. Carolina Wren flew away, the leaves on the tree he was perched on began to sway in the wind. If she didn't know any better, she'd think they were giving his performance a round of applause.

As Maddie walked up the stairs to the house, she heard footsteps from behind. Turning around, she was relieved to see her friend running up the drive.

"Hello, Beautiful!" Rachel said with a smile.

"Well, hello to you. Got a shower, huh?" Taking a whiff of her dirty t-shirt, she said, "I think I need one."

"You're fine. How's Jade?"

Stopping short of walking into the house, Maddie answered, "I'm a little worried if I'm honest. She was so hungry when she arrived. I haven't seen her since this morning. Hopefully, she got some rest."

"You said she hitchhiked here?" Rachel paused and then asked, "I wonder why her mom didn't bring her?"

"Jade said her mom never would have let her come."

The door suddenly opened with their friend, full of life, jumping on the porch to surprise them.

"Jade!" Rachel screamed as she grabbed her friend.

A voice from behind surprised them as they were chatting. As Emma crested the landing, her signature bear hug made their reunion complete.

"Oh, you girls don't know how happy I am to see you!" Jade said.

As they made their way into the house and through the kitchen, Grammy gave them a bowl of fruit.

Grabbing a handful of blueberries, Jade said, "Thank you, Grammy!"

Rachel threw Maddie a concerned friend look.

The girls sat on the back porch and caught up. Rachel told Jade about the flood, and Emma shared how they were rebuilding the gardens that were destroyed.

Jade shook her head slowly as she said, "Gosh, y'all have been through a lot in the last year."

"Tell us about Atlanta," Emma said. "Have you seen Marvin, by chance?"

"As a matter of fact, I have," Jade said with a smile, popping a strawberry into her mouth. "He asked about you just last week."

"He did?" Emma blushed, suddenly self-conscious. Lowering her voice to a whisper, she repeated, "Um, he did?"

Jade laughed. "Girl, I have missed you."

Impatient to hear her friend's news, Rachel said, "Spill the tea! What's going on?"

"The PeaceKeepers didn't just burn down our neighborhood. They tore through the city and the suburbs. Churches, restaurants, police stations, all gone. The only thing they "kept" were the hospitals. Atlanta itself is a ghost town—graffiti and shells of buildings are all that's left." Jade paused as a shiver ran down her spine. "Only one "church" was left, and now it's a PKO."

"Speaking of hospitals, where's your mom?" Rachel asked.

"She's working, as always." Jade said bitterly. "Anyway, the people who could leave Atlanta, left, but there is a small group that moved underground. That's where we're staying."

"Underground? What do you mean?" Emma asked.

"Years ago, an underground area of retail shops was built. It was closed a while ago, but a small group of people remaining in the city have moved in. Some big hunky guys are keeping watch." She arched her eyebrows as she flexed an arm muscle. "Kinda like your Warriors of the Way, Maddie."

"Are y'all able to build gardens?" Emma asked.

"We have a couple, but unfortunately, it isn't enough to feed everybody. Pastor Chris has worked out a deal with some local farmers to barter."

"Barter?"

"Yeah, trade labor for food. It works out most of the time. Well, until the PeaceKeepers find our meeting places and take the food."

"Wait, what? They're taking the food from you?"

"Yeah, it's stupid. They threaten to take the Kindness Tax from us one way or another."

"I'm sorry, Jade."

"Don't be sorry. You guys won't believe what God is doing! It's crazy! I was telling Maddie that we feed people and baptize them daily. Since I arrived, I know we've baptized at least a hundred people."

"Wow, a hundred?"

"Yeah. Most people are hateful—they want nothing to do with us. But then there are those so hungry that they come for the food but leave with Jesus."

"Wow, that's awesome. I wish…" Rachel trailed off.

An expectant look crossed Jade's face as she asked, "Wish what, Rach?"

The girls all laughed as animated Rachel got into her storytelling stance.

"I've been thinking about this, and I think I'm supposed to be there. In fact, I know I am!" Rachel exclaimed. "The Bible tells us this is going to happen, and the Lord is going to pour out his Spirit on his people." Looking at Maddie, she added, "I've been having dreams too—dreams of baptizing people."

"Come with me, Rach. All of you, come back to Atlanta with me. We need you!"

"I don't know. My dad, he's…" Rachel looked longingly off into the woods. "After last night, I don't think he'll ever let me go anywhere."

Surprised, Jade asked, "What happened last night?"

Concerned, Maddie said, "The PeaceKeepers tried to attack Wild Rock."

"No way! Last night, but that's…" Jade trailed off, visibly alarmed.

"It's okay, Jade." Emma looked at her friend proudly, "Thankfully, our girl here heard about the whole thing and alerted the town so we could be prepared."

"I just wish I had been there."

"Honestly, it was nothing. I expected worse. They gave up a little too easily if you ask me," Maddie said.

"What do you mean?"

"There were twenty men with guns. Most of the townspeople didn't have a gun. I think our dads and the guys from The Way were the only ones who were armed. So how were they able to outsmart twenty men with guns?"

"I never considered," Rachel said, "Do you think they'll come back?"

"Either they're really dumb or it's not over," Maddie admitted. She hated thinking like this, but she was feeling a bit sus after hearing her dad talk to Mr. Tom.

"What should we do?" Emma asked.

She blurted the first thing that came to mind. "I think we should start by praying."

After the girls prayed, they spent the night playing a board game. The laughter around the table was contagious. *Oh, Kaitlyn, if only you were here,* Maddie thought as she looked around the table. The animated looks on her friend's faces reminded her how very much she missed having everyone she loved around the same table.

Gazing at Grammy's painting of Jeremiah 29:11, she remembered when Emma asked if she missed their home in Atlanta. To be honest, that place reminded her of pain and fear, but now she knew God had more for her. What if Jade was right? She said that everything they went through was for a purpose. *Maybe I'm supposed to go back.*

As the girls settled in for the night, she pulled out her journal. The routine was so helpful, even if she did have to write by candlelight. She started by doing a brain dump of all she had been thinking about. This helped her to put her thoughts down so she could form a prayer.

Father God,

I'll be eighteen in a few months. The last three years have been crazy. You helped me overcome anxiety and fear. My mom and dad found each other again. My mom is happy and has decided never to drink again (thank you for that.) You saved my brother Mike and gave him an amazing wife who loves him so much. You saved me and Jade and even though Kaitlyn is not with us, I still believe that you saved her too. You've given me songs that come out of nowhere. NOWHERE, GOD! How do you do that?!? I'm just so thankful that all my Fam is here in one place. I know that no matter what we face, we can face it together. And so, I thank you. And God? Please show me what you want me to do. Do you want me to go back to Atlanta?

If you ask me to go, I will go.

Maddie

Sunday morning was Easter Sunday. Last year's Easter was haunted by the fires in Atlanta, but this year Maddie desired to be intentional in her celebration of the day. Early that morning, Grammy took all the girls to Wild Rock Overlook. They were surprised when Matthew snuck up behind them. The early morning was spent with Grammy reading the Easter story to them. As they watched the sunrise, Grammy reminded each of them that the days would be shortened before Jesus' return. She reminded them to be patient and endure, not to be afraid but to remember that the Lord their God would be with them.

Afterward, it was time for church. As they walked into the sanctuary, she was surprised to see Jacob and Rory. The look on Rachel's face made her think that she was surprised, too.

"Look at that, my two girls are in looooove," Jade said, as she placed an arm around each of them.

Aghast, Rachel blurted out, "No way!"

The bench where they chose to sit was filled with Doc Walker and his family. "Hey, Momma Roseline," Maddie said as she scooted to her end of the bench.

"Well, Good mornin' to you, Chile. How y'all doin' this fine mornin'?"

"We're fine, my friend Jade came back from Atlanta," she said with a wave to Jade, who did not want to join her.

"Who ya got thar?" Momma Roseline asked.

"This is my friend. You met her last fall when y'all moved into town."

"That's right, yer Jade, ain't ya?"

A red flush moved up her neck to her face as Jade answered, "Yes, ma'am."

"Well, now, it's good to see ya a'gin. I don't r'member seein' ya 'round lately."

"No ma'am, I've been in Atlanta with my mom."

"Hmm, yer mom, huh? How is she?"

Surprised by the strange question, Jade said, "She's fine, I guess? She's a doctor, so she works a lot."

"I r'emember." A strange look crossed Momma Roseline's face as she looked at her son. "You used to put in a lot of hours too, did'na ya?"

"Now, Momma, you know that Doctorin' is a callin'."

"I know, I know. Well, Jade, it's good ta see ya. Maybe we'll see y'all at the picnic later?"

Jade's eyes widened as she looked at Maddie. "Sure," she answered.

The Easter message was all about Jesus' death and resurrection. Maddie thought she had heard it all before, but at the end, Pastor Ron spoke about Jesus' return.

"Jesus will return, my friends. He tells us in Matthew twenty-four that the Son of Man will appear in heaven. Revelation nineteen shows us what his second coming will look like."

A picture of Jesus on a white horse with an army behind him crossed Maddie's mind as the pastor read from the passage. The idea was exciting yet terrifying at the same time.

"Are ya ready?" He asked. The pulpit became a foundation for the pastor to lean on as he began to weep.

The room was so quiet, you could hear a pin drop. Maddie, unsure of what he meant, leaned in so she wouldn't miss a thing.

His voice shook with emotion as he quietly added, "Jesus will return for his bride, and he will defeat sin and death once and fer all. Never you doubt it! Revelation twenty-one promises that our God will dwell with us forever, but first, he will remove the enemy's snare. Now, I have one more question fer each of ya: If our God is a consumin' fire and his glory covers all the earth, jes' as this Book says—if that's true, well, when ya stand a'fore Jesus and the glory of the Lord shines all 'round, purifyin' everythin' in his path, what will be left?"

The pastor sat down and placed his forehead in his hands. His words were quiet but powerful. As Maddie looked around, she noticed each person leaning in to listen. There was a heaviness that she could not explain. *What will be left?* She wondered.

As he looked up at his congregation, you could see the weariness of a pastor who prayed for his flock. "I cain't answer these two questions fer ya, but one thing I can do. Jesus came to set captives free from the sin that entangles. And Friend, he is right here, ready to receive all who will come to him. Will you come?"

A loud clap broke the silence as a voice from the back of the room shouted, "Well, well, well, what will be left?" A group of men, all in black, stood in the open doorway. The one in front suddenly burst forth with his eyes on the pastor. Maddie's stomach began to churn. *Why were the PeaceKeepers back?*

"A moving message, to be sure, but where is your Jesus?" Looking around, the man mocked the Pastor as he stared him down.

Pastor Ron stood tall, "He's right here," patting his chest. "Fer anyone who says yes to him."

Poking Pastor Ron's chest, the man asked, "Here? Oh, Ronald, your heart is deceitful; it deceives you to think that Jesus would come in here. You said it yourself, nothing impure will enter God's Holy City. Why would God let *you* in, knowing how you've lived your life?"

David stood quietly. He waited for the right moment to interject. "How can we help you?" A group of men, including Rachel's dad and Uncle Tom, the Mayor, stood with him.

"Ah, David Allen Bennett. Now this, my friends, is your real savior. Oh yes, the man with a plan. Only one problem, he chose the wrong side."

"How can we help you?" Maddie's dad repeated forcefully.

"Oh, David, this is a friendly visit, of course. We at the PKO are here to serve you, the community, but where there is no order, there is NO PEACE. So, consider this a friendly warning. We've been patient, but Mr. Baldur's patience has run out. The time has come to declare your allegiance."

"As you said, I have chosen. Now what?"

"To the people of Wild Rock, there is a new Sheriff in town. Jesus, he is old news; it is Helel who will save you from the rebellious disorder that has infected this world. Project Manna is non-negotiable. If you want to live peaceably, then you will bow down to the new world order."

"Or what?"

Ignoring David's interruption, the man said, "Where is your mayor?"

"I am Mayor Tom."

Looking down at the mayor, the man asked, "Mayor Tom, where does your allegiance lie?"

"Excuse me?"

"Do you want peace for your town?"

"Yes, of course!" Uncle Tom exclaimed.

"Then you will say the words."

"No, Tom, don't," David whispered to his friend.

A shuffle from beside Maddie took everyone's attention from the front. She watched in horror as her Grammy made her way out of the pew. "No, Grammy!" She whispered. "You don't know them!"

Grammy ignored her granddaughter and hobbled her way to the front. The room suddenly became charged with electricity. Even David could feel the authority his mom carried, as every man moved out of the way so she could walk through.

The man standing next to Pastor Ron was speechless. If Maddie didn't know any better, she would think a wave of fear crossed his face.

As Grammy reached the stairs, she looked up and nodded briefly as she said, "Sir, what's yer name?"

"What?"

Placing her hand on her hips, she squinted her eyes and asked, "Did I mumble? What's yer name?"

"Mom…"

Grammy ignored her son's interruption.

"My name is Kayn."

"Well, Kayn, my name is Grace Bennett, and I want you to look at me. I am a servant of El Shaddai, Almighty God. My Lord and King is Jesus Christ, and thar ain't nobody on this earth who will change that. My allegiance is to him," she shouted as she pointed up. "Now that we have that out of the way, you are in my town, the town my Lord blessed. This is holy ground and Jesus is here, you make no mistake 'bout it." Wagging her finger toward the man, she leaned forward and said, "You can come in here and spout yer lies, but you will not change this truth. I don't know who this Helel thinks he is, but I do not need to defend myself before him or you. You and yer boys are gommin' ever'thin' up in the wake of this order you spout. Do you think yer bringin' order outa chaos? The only thing yer doin' is destroyin' good people's hard work. In my town, that's lower'n a snake's belly in a wagon rut. Now, my Jesus died fer even you, but if you reject the word a God, then you will be judged fer it. But fer me, if I am thrown into a blazin' fire, the God I serve is able to save me from it, and he will rescue me from yer hand. But even if he does not, I want you and yer Helel to know, *Kayn,* that I will not serve yer god or worship the image of the beast you've set up. My eternity is secure in him."

The electricity Maddie felt when Grammy walked to the front seemed to fill the room as person after person stood and said, "Me too. Jesus is my King!"

Standing with her Gram, she repeated the words, "Jesus is my King!" Grammy's stand left her with a wave of emotion and desire for her own. *Father, fill me with this same courage,* she prayed silently.

Kayn breathed deeply. The nervous darting of his eyes scanned a room full of people who were not going to go quietly. Looking down at his men, he said, "Come on. It's obvious we're not wanted here." Looking at Pastor Ron, he said, "It ain't over."

As the pastor watched the men walk out of the church, he said proudly, "Well, I should say not. Jesus ain't returned yet."

David was shaken. He was incensed over the potential danger to his family and friends, while at the same time moved by the response of the townspeople. Something was happening that he couldn't explain. *He felt like he was losing control, but was it such a bad thing?*

After they arrived home, he made the call he had been

dreading. Calling in a favor to a friend at Magnum Lock Security, he worked out a deal to get the information he needed for the US PKO locations. Next, he needed to work on the international locations. He felt a foreboding as he thought of the consequences of being exposed. This was espionage, pure and simple. No different than what the PeaceKeepers had attempted.

But this was personal—this was war.

CHAPTER 19

It's Only See Ya Later

Maddie couldn't wait to journal everything that happened that day. After the PeaceKeepers left, the whole church came to the front to pray. Pastor Ron was high-key emotional as he watched his church repent before God. She had never seen anything like it.

Grammy was the first to pray. She knelt and asked God to forgive her for allowing fear, pride, and unforgiveness to control her. She then asked for protection over the town as they waited for Jesus' return.

A chorus of prayer lifted as others followed suit.

When Maddie knelt, everything she had been holding on to played like a movie reel: her anger over Kaitlyn's death, the guilt she felt over allowing herself to be alone with Jacob, the PeaceKeepers, and the fear she harbored over an uncertain future. The more she faced, the more she realized that the only thing she could control was her response. As she listened to her Gram's prayer, she knew that it was time to lay it all down. "Father, I'm so tired of being afraid. I give it all to you and ask that you forgive me for following others. Help me to keep my eyes on Jesus," she prayed. "Help me to stand on Your Name as I stand with You." An arm draped over her shoulders as she wiped the tears from her face. Opening her eyes, she watched her dad close his and pray silently.

Suddenly, the heaviness was gone. All the guilt and fear she had been carrying disappeared as she prayed. Her friends sat in awe over their own breakthroughs. Rachel ugly cried as she too laid everything down. Emma held on to Jade, who had a big smile on her face.

The service went on for hours. When Pastor Ron released everyone for the Easter picnic, his voice was hoarse.

Afterward, Maddie couldn't help but ask Jade why she smiled.

"This is exactly what is happening in Atlanta!" She exclaimed. "God did this, Mads! He truly does make good what the enemy means for evil!"

Everything looked brighter that day. The golden color of yellow daffodils surrounding the church yard reflected the sun's light as they fluttered in the breeze. The big oak stood proudly as an array of vibrant tulips bordered her trunk. Even the bees looked happy as they flitted in and out of the violet petals.

"I'm beginning to see like you, Rach."

"What do you mean?"

"I don't know, everything looks so beautiful today."

Rachel laughed as she bumped her friend. "When God gives you his eyes to see, everything looks brighter."

Surprised at her friend's words, she looked up and wondered if it was true. *Is this what it looks like to see through your eyes, God?* She thought.

Suddenly, her gaze was distracted as Jacob walked up to their table.

"Hey Maddie, can I borrow you for a sec?"

Looking at Rachel, who raised a brow discreetly, she said, "Sure."

"I promise I'll be good," he said as he looked at everyone at the table. "I want to show ya somethin'," he added as he handed her a flower.

She could feel the warmth of a blush making its way to her face. "Thank you, it's beautiful." The sweet scent from the daffodil reminded her of the honeysuckle from her

Grammy's garden.

As Jacob led her down the path behind the church, an anxious knot grew in her stomach. "Where are we going?" She asked.

Jacob stopped and took her hands. "Maddie, I promise I won't do anythin' that makes ya uncomfortable. You have my word." His eyes lit up as he increased his stride. "Besides, I have a surprise fer ya."

"Okay," she said, relieved at his promise.

Jacob turned right at a fork in the trail and said, "Okay, close yer eyes," leading her forward.

Her heart fluttered as she obediently followed her handsome friend.

"Okay, ya can open 'em."

A gasp escaped as she looked up at a big wooden cross. "Whoa, how did…." She was at a loss for words.

"Rory, Jared, and I erected it. What do ya think? We worked on it yesterday. Uncle Tom gave us the wood. Yer brother helped us put it in the ground."

"Wait, Matthew? He didn't say anything," she blurted out, a little disappointed.

"We told 'im it was a surprise." Chuckling, he added, "He was lookin' at me all mornin' at church."

On the left sat a simple bench freshly varnished. "Can I sit?"

Touching the bench, he smiled and nodded. They both sat down and looked at the cross.

"How tall is it?" She asked.

"Fifteen feet and heavier'n an icebox." Jacob paused as he gazed at the work of his hands. "What do ya think?" He asked again expectantly.

Looking on in awe, she said, "It's amazing." Turning to look at him, she asked, "But why?"

"I been watchin' you. God's doin' somethin' in ya—in all of us. It's kinda weird, ain't it?"

Looking at the cross, she asked, "What's that?"

"He chose our time. Ya know when they say that we we

were chosen fer such a time as this? He chose us to face all of this," he added, waving around them.

"Yeah, but what does that mean?" She asked.

The usual light in Jacob's gray eyes turned dark. His joking demeanor was replaced by a melancholy strength. Turning to place an errant curl behind her ear, he said, "Maddie, I have to leave tomorrow."

"Tomorrow?"

"Yeah, we've got school and then we leave fer Atlanta."

Remembering what Jade said about the state of her city, she asked, "What will you be doing?"

"We'll get our orders when we get thar."

Should I tell him that I'm thinking about going back? She pondered nervously. Deciding against it, she placed her hands in her lap and sat quietly beside him.

"I don't want you to be 'fraid."

Alarmed, she turned to look at him. "Afraid of what?"

"No matter what happens, I want you to r'member the cross. R'member what Jesus did. When he died on that cross, he had us on his mind. What yer Grammy did this mornin' was one 'a most courageous things I ever did see. When it's my turn to stand, I want to have courage like that."

"Yeah, me too," she agreed.

"Maddie, since the first moment I laid eyes on ya, I felt somethin' I never felt a'fore. Watchin' ya dance 'round the fire makes me want to spin ya 'round ferever. When I see ya with Kali, my heart gets all warm inside. I want to kiss ya, but I know I cain't. Maddie, I'm so sorry I messed up. I know I went too far that night behind the barn. I was jes' stupid and I promise it ain't gonna happen again. I didn't want to leave with that between us."

If she were honest, she wanted him to kiss her, too. Confused over the feelings fighting for room in her own heart, she looked at her folded hands. "Thank you, Jacob." Looking up at the cross, she said, "This means more to me than you know." Grabbing his hand, she looked up at him and smiled. "I like you, too."

As if he had momentarily forgotten to breathe, he suddenly let out a loud whoosh and smiled that quirky smile she was beginning to love.

"Is this goodbye?" She asked quietly.

Stepping back to ensure plenty of distance stood between them, Jacob lifted her hand and kissed it lightly, "No, it's only see ya later."

The candle in front of her flickered as she wrote Jacob's last words in her journal. Drawing a daffodil beside them, she looked out the dark window and pondered Jacob's reference to her Grammy's courage. *I want to have courage like that, too.*

Maddie sketched a furnace with a blazing fire. Remembering the story of Daniel's friends Shadrach, Meshach, and Abednigo, she knew that her Grammy was referencing their bold declaration to the king when he tried to kill them. Could I stand like that? She wondered as she prayed.

> *God,*
>
> *Jacob was right. Watching Grammy stand in front of the PeaceKeepers today was one of the most courageous things I've ever seen. I know it was you. Rachel said that you've blessed us by allowing us to see and read stories of people who stand in the face of persecution. Lord, how can I be courageous when it's my turn?*

Opening Ephesians six, she read starting in verse ten. This had become one of her favorite passages. After reading, she remembered Grammy walking down the aisle to confront the PeaceKeepers. *Was she afraid? She didn't look it. I'll bet she was wearing her armor.* She thought. Rachel said she carried the authority of Christ as she walked. *"There was nothing those men could say because they are under his authority, too."*

> Help me, Lord, to be strong in you and in
> your mighty power. Help me to put on my
> armor and to stand firm, just like your word tells
> us. Wherever I go, please go with me. Like
> Grammy says, I can't do anything without your
> power. In Jesus' Name, amen.

Monday brought rain with it. Not the soothing type that made for good napping weather, but sledgehammer punching weather. Since it was spring break, Maddie and Matthew were stuck in the house with Grammy as their mom and dad ventured out for supplies.

The kitchen, normally a place buzzing under Grammy's command, was clean and quiet. *Where is she?* She wondered as she turned back to the living room. A glimpse of a moving rocking chair through the front window captured her attention as she opened the front door and stepped out.

"Hey, Love, ya found me, did'na ya?"

"Is everything okay, Grammy?"

"Shore 'nough. Have a sit, it's mighty quiet out here."

Giving her Gram the side eye, Maddie laughed as she said, "Have you heard the rain?"

Chuckling, she closed her eyes as she rested her head on the back of the chair. "The rain reminds me that everythin' returns to him."

The familiar saying brought her back to the night she came to Grammy's—the summer after the PKO.

"Grammy, where is that passage again?"

"Why, that'd be Isaiah fifty-five." With her eyes closed, she rocked slowly in her chair as she recited the scripture.

"Can we talk about yesterday?" She asked her Gram.

"Why shore, what'cha want to talk 'bout?"

"Why did you confront them?"

The rhythmic sound of the rocking chair on creaky wood stopped as Grammy turned to look at her granddaughter. "Maddie Ruth, I want ya to listen to me. When God's people came out of the wilderness and prepared to walk into the promised land, they had to take it by force. Moses sent twelve spies into the land to check it out. Do ya wanna know how many came back trustin' in the plan?"

"How many?"

"Two—Joshua and Caleb."

Confused, she looked at her Grammy and asked, "What happened to the other ten?"

With a curled lip to show her disgust, Grammy said, "They were skeered of the giants."

"What happened?"

"Well, the Lord called Joshua to lead his people and told him to be strong and courageous, to not be 'fraid nor discouraged, fer the Lord his God would be with him wherever he went."

"Don't you have a painting of that in your kitchen?"

Grammy smiled, "Yes, ma'am. I need a daily reminder."

"So, why did you confront the PeaceKeepers?"

"I ain't skeered 'a no giants." She looked at her granddaughter keenly and added, "And I did'na raise anyone to be skeered of 'em either."

Boldness shot through Maddie like an arrow. The rain seemed to double down as puddles formed in the front yard. *Father, please, not another flood.* She prayed silently.

"Yer gonna face the storm, my beautiful Granddaughter. Yer gonna face persecution louder'n June bugs in a jar. Thar's gonna be hate thrown at ya like the flamin' darts the bible talks 'bout. Listen to me, Girl," Grammy leaned in when she regained her granddaughter's attention. "You carry that shield of faith like it's an appendage on yer body." Shaking her head, she added, "Don't you let it fall. You carry that sword of the Spirit knowin' that it's yers to carry. Almighty God gave it to you to use in the battle. And r'member when you face that flamin' furnace, Jesus will be with you, jes' like he was with Shadrach, Meshach, and Abednigo." Her eyes watered even as her voice broke.

"Grammy, you're scaring me."

"No!" Grammy yelled as she hit the arm of her rocking chair. "Ain't you been listenin' to me? Thar ain't no room fer fear! You got me? The enemy uses fear as a snare to distract you. You've got to be ready!"

Maddie's breathing became shallow. She could feel a panic attack coming on, but this time she knew what to do. Breathing deeply, she focused on a birdhouse hanging from the rafter of the porch and prayed. "The Lord is my Shepherd…"

"That's right, keep prayin'."

"I shall not want. He makes me to lie down in green pastures…"

"See 'em, Girl. See the green pastures."

Rocking to the cadence of the passage, she said, "He leads me beside quiet waters. He restores my soul."

"Yep, you got it, Girl, keep goin'."

"He leads me down paths of righteousness, for his name's sake."

"That's Jesus' righteousness, don't you forget it."

"Even though I walk through the darkest valley, I will not be afraid, for you are with me, your rod and your staff they comfort me." The panic subsided even as her voice grew louder. *What is it about prayer?* She wondered. A sob interrupted her wonder as her Gram wept beside her.

Thinking that Grammy was worried about her anxiety, she consoled, "I'm okay, Grammy. It's over."

Nodding, she smiled at her granddaughter as she closed her eyes.

The next hour passed peacefully. Maddie's eyes grew so heavy as she listened to the soft snores of her Gram.

The sounds of boots on the stairs suddenly jerked her awake. A man whom she had never seen before stood before her.

"Maddie do not be afraid," he said. "You can go back to sleep." He added with a loving smile.

Closing her eyes, she could have sworn that she smelled the scent of honeysuckle and daffodils. And was that the sound of Mr. Carolina Wren—in the rain? "Okay," she whispered as she curled up in the chair.

It seemed only a few minutes passed when she was suddenly jerked awake a second time.

"Maddie, wake up! Maddie!" Her brother was shaking her violently.

"What, what is it?" She asked, annoyed that the peaceful moment was interrupted.

"It's Grammy, something's wrong. I can't get her to wake up. I don't think she's breathing." Matthew cried.

Suddenly awake, she turned to her Gram. "We were just talking," she said. "Grammy? Grammy, wake up!"

David smiled as he heard his wife's gentle laugh. It was a gentle balm after driving through the pouring rain. Closing the door to the Tahoe, he lifted his rain jacket over his head and made his way to the back.

"Dad! Dad, come quick!" He heard from the front porch.

Suddenly, in dad mode, he ran around the truck and up the front stairs.

"It's Grammy, she won't wake up!" Maddie yelled.

David looked at his mom, sitting there so peacefully. He knew right away. Bending on his knees, he placed two fingers on her throat—no pulse. She was gone. He stared at her quietly for a moment, as his family stood waiting for a reply.

"Dad, is she okay? Mom? Please, tell me she's okay!" She yelled; her voice strained.

The emotion threatened to expose him as a lump formed in his throat. *Get a hold of yourself, David,* he thought. The quiet was deafening. Taking a deep breath, he stood and looked at Maddie, who was fighting tears as she waited for him to give her even a glimmer of hope. As his heart pounded in rhythm to the rain above, he wondered how he could tell his daughter the woman she loved so much was gone. Shaking his head in pain, he did the only thing he knew; he grabbed her and hugged her tight as he said, "Maddie, I'm so sorry."

"Noooooooooo!" Maddie broke. It was all just too much. "I was just talking to her," she cried into her dad's chest. There was still so much she wanted to say. How could she make it even one day without the woman who was like a second mom? *Please, God, please bring her back.*

CHAPTER 20

A Life Well Lived

"Be strong and courageous. Do not be afraid, I am with you, Maddie."

The man looked familiar—tall, long brown hair, beard, and loving brown eyes.

"Where have I seen him before?" She wondered as she stepped into the room.

Suddenly the room became very hot. Fire surrounded her on all sides.

"What do I do?" She yelled.

All the doors were shut tight. There were no windows.

Then the man was right beside her. "Do not be afraid, Maddie. I am here."

"Hey, Sis, Mom said you need to get your shower before we go," Matthew called through the door.

"I don't want to go." She mumbled as she rolled over.

"Maddie, it's Grammy," Matthew whispered sadly, "you have to go."

Red, puffy eyes opened as her brother knocked and then quietly entered the room. Walking over to lay a cup on the nightstand, he said, "Here, Sis, it'll be okay." Walking to the bedroom door, he looked over his shoulder and with a sad glance, added, "We'll be together today."

Last week was a blur. Struggling between high levels of joy that Grammy was with Jesus and low levels of grief when she realized she wouldn't see her in the kitchen anymore, Maddie found herself in a dark place. No more walks in the garden, no more talks in the kitchen. It was all…over.

"No, please God, I don't want to cry anymore," she said as she forced herself to walk to the bathroom.

The coffee was hot and tasteless. She was thankful for the hot liquid to warm her from the chilly room, but it didn't give her much joy.

After turning the shower on, she stepped in and let the water run over her. Maybe it would keep her from thinking. The cold porcelain tub contrasted with the hot water pouring through the faucet like a mad hatter. Perhaps she could just disappear into the drain like the drops that swirled around her feet.

"No! Thar ain't no room fer fear!" Grammy's voice echoed in her mind like the echoes resounding off the bathroom walls.

There was a war going on in her head. Sad thoughts would overwhelm her until she just didn't know what to do anymore. It seemed so much easier just to give in to them. But she couldn't, "I won't!" she shouted into the air. "I will be strong and courageous!" She cried as she allowed the tears to fall down her face.

After Kaitlyn died, she felt empowered to bring herself back from the darkness, but this time, she just felt weary. Everyone was suffering in some way. Her dad was back to his brooding self. Her mom was trying to keep the house under control. Mike was working his fingers to the bone, and Matthew was trying to hold everyone together. Even her friends walked on eggshells around her. They didn't know what to say, and she didn't either.

Oh, how much she loved Matthew. Three years ago, when she turned fifteen, he was just a little kid, running around her to share the latest thing he was into. Now, he was taller than she was, building houses, weapons, and now crosses. She had no idea how much that cross would mean to her until this week. It was too hard to go to Wild Rock Overlook, so the cross became her special place to talk to God. She could talk to him anywhere, but there was something about being in nature. And at the cross, she could almost see Jesus…

A beam of sun shone through the window, gleaming off the silver of the shower head. Maddie focused on the light, "Help me, Jesus." She prayed.

Wise words from her mentor encouraged her in that moment: *"Give yourself permission to feel the anger and sadness, then surrender them at the Lord's feet."* She opened her hands and placed the grief in her hand. "I need you, Jesus. I don't know how to get through this day without you."

As they drove into the church parking lot, awe filled the family as they noticed the number license plates from other states.

"Wow," Matthew said. "Where will we park?" He asked worriedly as his dad pulled up to the front of the church.

"Maddie, Matthew, there will be a lot of people here today. If it gets overwhelming for you, it's okay to step away, okay?" Dad said in the rearview mirror.

Nodding, she stared out of the window and rested her forehead on the cool glass. She felt numb and empty. The sunny day did not match how she was feeling on the inside.

As they walked up the stairs to the church, the doors opened. As Pastor Ron quickly ushered them into a living room, a dull ache filled Maddie. She noticed a similar pain in the pastor's eyes. It seemed everyone was grieving today.

Placing his hand on her dad's shoulder, he said, "I want ya to know how much we loved Grace."

"Thank you, Ron. It means a lot," David said.

"As you can 'magine, thar are a lot of people here. Even people from yer part of the woods. I ain't seen so many

Georgia license plates in one place."

Maddie looked up in surprise. "Georgia? But how do they know?"

"We made some calls," Mom said.

"I thought we couldn't use the phone," she said.

David looked at her and said, "For emergencies only."

The two hours that followed were so encouraging to her grieving heart. Person after person walked up to share a testimony from Grammy's life. She had no idea how much her grandmother served the community. Even a soldier flew in to give testimony of her praying over him when he was in the hospital. *How does that even happen?* She wondered.

After the service, Ms. Lorna shared her testimony of how Grammy saved her life. "If it weren't for my dear friend," she said, "I wouldn't be here today." Afterward, she sang her new song, "Life Well Lived." "This is for you, Grace," she whispered, her voice trembling with emotion.

The song gave Maddie memories of Grammy's soft hands, her smile, and how she encouraged everyone to enjoy each day. Afterward, Ms. Lorna reminded that Grammy was in Heaven. "This is her homecomin' and her mission is complete," she said. "One day, we will be united, but until then, we're still on mission."

We're on mission, Maddie thought. "That's it, isn't it, God?" Opening her bible to Isaiah fifty-five, she read the scripture that Grammy recited so many times. The word that goes out from your mouth will accomplish what you desire and achieve the purpose for which you sent. *Grammy finished her mission, now it's my turn.* Suddenly, she felt lighter. The grief she had been holding on to seemed to lift as she realized *I have a purpose—pain leads to purpose.*

She felt as if that message had been told to her by so many: Grammy, Rachel, Sonya, Aunt Lisa, Ms. Lorna, and Mr. Don. But she didn't understand until she heard the testimonies of so many touched by Grammy completing hers. *She truly did live her life well, didn't she?*

Maddie spent the afternoon encouraging those who said

they would miss her Gram. When Rachel, Jade, and Emma came up to give their condolences, she hugged each of them individually and said, "She loved you all so much. Thank you for being here to honor her today."

Rachel immediately beamed at her friend. "I will miss her."

Smoothing Maddie's unruly hair, which for some inexplicable reason seemed to be grieving with her, Jade smiled sadly as she said, "Yes, me too."

"Me three!" Emma said as she pulled them all into a group hug.

"Hey, can we go to Wild Rock Overlook tomorrow?" Jade asked. "We can have our own service for Grammy there. A going away party."

The idea of going to her Gram's favorite place filled Maddie's heart with joy. "Yes, I would love that," she said.

A soft hand on her arm interrupted her laugh as Momma Roseline said, "Maddie Ruth, we want you to know that yer Grammy was the most genuine person on the planet. She will be missed."

"Thank you, Momma Roseline. Wasn't your husband in the Navy with Grandpa George?"

"Yes, ma'am."

"I would love to hear about it sometime."

"Why, that would be nice. Why don't you girls come up tomorrow? We can have tea."

Suddenly excited for the date, she looked at her friends, who shared in her excitement, all except for Jade, who looked uncomfortable. After making the needed arrangements, she said goodbye to Momma Roseline and Doc Walker and finished greeting those in line.

After everyone left the sanctuary, Maddie walked around the church. This was another place she would never see her Gram. Shaking off the sad thoughts, she thought back to Jade's deadpan expression when Momma Roseline asked them to tea. Come to think of it, every time they had spoken with the Walkers—The Monroe barn raising, the bonfire, and now, Grammy's funeral—she was so disconnected. *Why was Jade so cold toward them? She could have at least pretended to be happy. This is not like her at all,* she thought. Making a note to talk to her friend later, she joined her family as they sat down to a private meal with the church.

David knew the day would come when he would have to lay his mom to rest. He had just hoped it wouldn't be so soon. She always seemed so full of life. She never complained about her aches and pains, even though he knew she had many.

The week following her death was filled with arrangements. When he learned that she wanted to be cremated, he wanted to punch the wall. The woman who held him in her arms as a baby would soon be no more than ash. It was a bizarre thought.

Jacque had been a godsend. She was taking care of all the things that he just couldn't. She would stop and ask him how he was doing and then give him grace when he couldn't answer. He wished he could answer, but for now, he didn't have the words.

His sister, Lisa, stood with a quiet strength. She and Jacque made quick work of his mom's things because that was something he just couldn't do. The day before the memorial service, she finally broke down and hugged him tightly. So many tears were being shed around him, but he couldn't shed even one.

Truth be told, he was angry. Angry that God would take the first woman who loved him. His mind told him that everyone dies, his heart asked, *why her?* Grace Bennett was the epitome of love, and the world was a darker place without her in it. He was reminded of this every time someone shared another story about her.

So many people came to honor her, and even though he was angry that God had taken her, David was also filled with pride to know that his mom had touched so many lives. Even Senator Gabriel Hawke showed up.

"David, can we have lunch tomorrow?" He asked.

Relieved for a welcome distraction, he answered, "Sure."

It was Maddie he worried about. She had such a strong relationship with her grandmother that David wasn't sure how long it would take for her to get over her death. *Maybe a trip to Atlanta wouldn't be such a bad thing,* he contemplated. Even though the idea of sending his daughter to a warzone was terrifying.

He and Tom had discussed the girls going to Atlanta with Jade. Maddie would be eighteen in three months. There would be conditions, of course. He and Tom would join them, and Tom would call in some reinforcements. Whether he liked it or not, she was going to live her life. He wanted to make sure she was ready.

When the attorney came by the house to read the will, David felt cold. He didn't want all the things she had left behind, he wanted her. But it was too late. *Why didn't I spend more time with her while I had the chance?*

"David, your mom left a letter for you. Would you like me to read it now, or would you prefer to do so in private?"

As he looked around the room, he could see the desire for each person to hear her last words. How can I keep this one thing from them? He thought.

"You can read the letter," he answered.

My Dearest David,

From the first moment I laid eyes on you, my heart swelled with pride. Why the good Lord entrusted me to partner with him to bring life into the world was beyond me. When I looked into your eyes, I could see his love, his heart and his joy staring back at me.

David, you, and your sister brought me the greatest joy. Watching you grow into the wise and strong man that you are today was a great honor. One that I pray you will enjoy as you watch your own.

Son, life is a gift and what I want to leave you with is this. It is also a whisper—here today and gone tomorrow. The legacy that I hope to leave as I take my last breath is for those that I love to know Jesus. My greatest prayer is that you know and love him as much as he loves you. This isn't something I can give you, Son, but something that he has already given. You only have to say yes.

David, the world will grow dark, but remember that Light shines in the darkness and the darkness has not and will not overcome it. The people of God will overcome the darkness because Jesus overcame. This is my great hope for you, Jacque, and my grandchildren.

Paul will share with you that I am leaving my house to you. It is fully paid off. George and I left your sister the money she needs to rebuild her home as she and Richie desires. It is my hope that the two adjoining properties will become a legacy for our family, cherished by generations to come.

I gave Maddie my precious sword. This is to be a reminder to her of her calling. David, God has a calling on her life greater than you or I could imagine, but she must say yes. She must lay down all fear to fully step into this call on her life. I want you to encourage her, Son.

I want you to know how very proud I am of Michael and his decision to walk away from the darkness and into the light. It has been an honor to see him find Jesus and Melissa. I pray many years of blessings over them both. I leave

*my wedding china and the quilt George gave to
me as our first wedding gift to them and pray
their marriage will be filled with joy and love.*

*Many years from now, when you and Jacque
join me in Heaven, I would like for Matthew to
inherit my house and the land it resides on. He
will be the one to carry it to the next generation.*

*Son, it's okay to let go. You have permission
to hold everything loosely, including me. Our
Father in Heaven has you and your family in his
perfect hands. Trust him and he will help you
with every detail. Promise.*

I love you, Son.
Until Heaven, Mom

There wasn't a dry eye in the room, including David's. After reading the letter, Paul read her last will and testament, which included expanded details concerning her property and her expectations for Matthew and Lisa, who would steward the two adjoining properties.

As Paul finished the reading, he looked at the family and said, "Grace Bennett was the finest woman I've known. My heart goes out to each of you in this hour. I will leave you alone to talk."

As the attorney softly closed the door on the office, the tears David held back came out like a flood. His mom always told him to hold everything loosely, or in other words, let go of control. *How has holding on to control worked for me lately?* He thought bitterly. *Maybe she's right, maybe it is time to let go.*

CHAPTER 21

Bad Vibes

Maddie had a song on her heart. Grateful that the dark cloud had finally lifted, she felt like doing a little dance. With an invisible mic, she belted out the lyric from "Living Hope" to her mirrored audience.

"Na-na-na-na! What are we celebrating?" Jade mimicked as she appeared in the doorway.

After straightening her clothes, she hugged her friend. "Hey, Girl!" Looking around her, she asked, "Where's Emma? She didn't kick you out already, did she?"

Suddenly serious, Jade looked in the mirror at her friend's reflection and said, "Emma and Rachel are coming in a bit, but I wanted to talk to you first."

As she sat on the bed and crossed her legs, Jade asked, "Why'd you stop singing? I haven't heard that song in a long time. It sounded good coming from your pipes."

Working through a knot in her hair, she grinned in relief when it finally broke free. "I wish I could sing the whole thing. I miss Spotify."

Distracted by an errant shoelace, Jade hummed the chorus to the song. When she reached the next verse, she frowned in agreement and said, "Yeah, me too."

It was obvious something was wrong with her friend as she watched her fight with her shoelaces. "So, what's up?" She asked cautiously.

"I don't know if I want to go to Momma Roseline's." Jade said.

Curious, Maddie asked, "Why?"

Irritated over the question, Jade stopped pacing to look at her friend, "I just get weird vibes from her and her son, alright?"

"Oh, Doc Walker is the best!" She exclaimed as she reasoned, *she just doesn't know them.* In an attempt to change her friend's mind, she added, "He let me patch people up after the flood. I am seriously considering working with him so I can learn about medicine."

After numerous times of trying to fix the distracting shoelace, Jade ripped it out of the shoe and said, "It's not that. I just feel like I know them from somewhere."

"What? Where? They're from Nashville." *How could she know them?* She wondered.

Shoving the shoelace in her pocket, she stood in frustration. Jade's height made her a giant in the small room, but she managed to pace it, even if only a few short steps. Looking away from her friend, she blurted out, "I don't know, like I said, it's just a bad vibe I get."

Grabbing her friend's shaky hand, Maddie encouraged her to sit down. "What are you afraid of?" She asked softly.

Jade flinched as she looked at her friend, "Oh, what do you know anyway?" Pulling away, she marched out of the room.

Confused over her friend's anger, Maddie stared at her rejected hand. The slam of the front door announced Jade's exit and Rachel's entrance. "Hey, what's up with Jade?" Rachel asked as she walked into her bedroom.

Shaking off the hurt, she walked past her friend toward the living room. "She doesn't want to go to Momma Roseline's."

Refusing to let the subject go, Rachel asked, "Why?"

Maddie shrugged, "She said something about bad vibes."

"That's not like Jade. She's never met a stranger."

"I know, right! Something's wrong, but I don't know

what." Tension filled her as she wondered what was up between her friend and the Walkers.

Suddenly, the front door opened again, and Emma walked in. "Hey, why is Jade talking to herself in the front yard?" She asked as she pointed behind her.

The girls looked out the front window to see Jade pacing and talking to the air. Her animated hands and attempts to punch at the air made it clear to anyone watching that she was angry.

"Let me talk to her," Rachel said as she opened the front door.

The slam of the screen door reverberated in the house. Everything was suddenly quiet as Emma and Maddie walked into the kitchen.

"Kinda quiet without Grammy, isn't it?" Emma asked.

The cloud that had dissipated that morning suddenly returned with all its fury. Clutching her midsection, Maddie fought the dark thoughts that threatened her peace.

Sensing her friend's pain, Emma changed the subject as she grabbed the coffee canister. "Have you had any issues with your power?"

The stiffness in Maddie's shoulders relaxed as she redirected her thoughts. "Naw, the solar panels Grammy had put in last year have been a godsend. We conserve energy at night, but during the day, we have no issues."

Measuring out the needed two tablespoons to place in the filter, Emma asked, "Our power has been flickering lately. I wish we had solar like you guys."

Pulling out a sealed container of oatmeal, she put water on to boil. "Are y'all still paying the electric company?"

"No, some guy worked out a deal with Dad to trade hydropower for labor."

"Hydro? You mean like from water?"

"Yeah, it's kinda cool. He takes the water from the river and runs it through a turbine that produces electricity. I'm not sure the dam was permitted, though."

"What do you mean?" Maddie asked.

Emma poured water into the coffeemaker and set it to brew. Grabbing a piece of paper and a pencil, she drew a simple drawing of a river, a turbine, and a dam. A cute little deer and rabbit made the drawing complete.

"You can't just dam up a river, Emma said. "You must permit it. I did some research on it last summer. An environmental report is required to make sure there's no impact on the wildlife or properties downstream."

"You don't think he did that?"

"I know he didn't. He just built it, without asking anybody. Then he went door to door to sell electricity to others. And it isn't cheap."

After the water began to boil, she poured oatmeal into the pot. "Do you want me to find out the name of the solar guy Grammy used?"

"I don't know if we can afford it, but yeah. I just don't want Dad to get into trouble, ya know. After what the PeaceKeepers did, there's no telling how the government will take revenge."

"Emma, do you think the government and the PeaceKeepers are connected?"

Gaping in disbelief, Emma asked, "Are you kidding me? Of course they are. They're in their back pocket."

"I just don't understand. Don't they know what they're doing?"

"It's all about control. My mom said that's how the antichrist works. Come up with a plan to save the world and then destroy it from within—counterfeit, right?"

"Yeah, that's what the PKO was like. Everything felt so fake."

"If y'all hadn't been rescued, what would have happened?"

Frowning over the dark thoughts she couldn't seem to shake, Maddie said, "Honestly, I don't want to even think about it."

Not wanting to let go of the subject, Emma prompted, "Were girls ever allowed to go home?"

Staring at the spoon as she stirred the oatmeal, Maddie

said, "For most of the girls, the PKO was home."

With pursed lips, her friend looked down sadly and whispered, "I can't imagine." A sudden look of horror crossed her face as she asked, "Do you think they'll try to take over the world?"

A figurine of a blue bird sat on a shelf just above the sink. *How have I never seen you?* She wondered. Realizing her friend was waiting for an answer, she looked at her solemnly and said, "It sounds like they already have."

"Maddie, can I ask you a personal question?"

"Sure." Her eyebrows drew together as she leaned over the counter. It was obvious that Emma was worried about something.

Opening her mouth, her friend paused a moment and then asked, "Are you going to Atlanta with Jade?"

"I'm thinking about it."

"Are you afraid?"

"A little bit, but Em, we can't hide. You've read Revelation."

"I know, but it feels safer here in Wild Rock than in the city."

"Safe is with the Lord, right? We serve a mountain-moving God." *Where did that come from?* She wondered.

"Yeah, I guess," Emma said apprehensively.

Courage, Maddie, she thought as she encouraged her friend and perhaps herself as well, "No, Emma, either you're safe or you aren't."

"Maddie?"

"Yeah?"

"You sounded a lot like Grammy just then." Emma rested her head on her friend's shoulder as she added, "But without the accent."

As they set the table, Rachel and Jade made their way into the house, just in time for breakfast. Maddie was relieved when Jade acted as if nothing had happened.

"Hey, Mads, this is pretty good," Jade said as she stuffed a spoonful of oatmeal into her mouth.

"Not as good as Grammy's, but it's getting there," She admitted sheepishly.

"I don't know. I like it better. Did you add butter?" Rachel asked.

Blushing, she said, "Yeah, Dad calls it the secret sauce."

"Hey, where is yer ole dad?" Jade asked.

"He and Mom went to have breakfast with somebody from Atlanta. He drove up for Grammy's service and asked to meet them today."

"There sure were a lot of people there."

"Yeah, she was loved."

"Because she loved," Emma said with a smile.

David and Jacque made their way down the mountain to meet Senator Hawke for breakfast. He was grateful for the distraction.

Jacque insisted that she join him because she was worried about him, but David wondered if perhaps she wanted to hear about Atlanta and her dad. She didn't talk much about Jack since they arrived in Wild Rock, but he knew that she worried about him.

Jade was right about Atlanta, but what she may not have known was that the destruction was in pockets. The PeaceKeepers didn't control the whole city, only the parts they were able to strongarm their way into. He was thankful for friends in high places who kept him informed.

David was encouraged by the show of strength, or the lack thereof, when the PeaceKeepers attempted to take over Wild Rock. They didn't seem to be very competent in the intelligence department. If it were his job, he would have found all the weak spots in the town and strong-armed them one by one, rather than exerting all their power in one place.

It was obvious the non-conformists were nothing more than discontent and rebellious bullies with little to no leadership.

As David drove into the parking lot of the same diner where he and Jacque spent their date nights, he saw the Camry with Georgia plates parked right near the front door.

"Is that the Senator?" Jacque asked.

"Considering it's the only car with Georgia plates…" David said with a smirk.

Frowning, Jacque said, "Don't be a jerk."

Holding the door open for his wife, he scanned the room to find the Senator. *In the back, as always.* Surprised to see him wearing a ballcap and a pair of sweats, he walked up and said, "Not on duty today, Senator?"

The Senator stood as Jacque sat across from him in the booth. "Everyone deserves a day off now and again, David, even public servants."

"You've met my wife. Jacque, this is Senator Gabriel Hawke."

"Hello Senator Hawke, I've heard a lot about you."

"Please, call me Gabe. I'm sure it was not all bad," he said with a wink.

Laughing at the Senator's quip, she said, "Only the good parts."

Gabe gave a hearty laugh as he looked at David. "David, your wife is charming. Be careful, I might steal her from you."

Raising a brow, David looked across the table and retorted, "You'd have to move this mountain first."

Nodding his head in agreement, he smiled as he said, "Touché." After giving their orders to the waitress, the Senator asked, "I assume you received my letter?"

"I did, thank you very much."

"Don't forget to get back to me with the details."

"I won't," David said as he glanced at his wife. This was not something he wanted her to know about.

As David, Jacque, and Gabe ate their breakfast, the conversation around the table was casual, with the occasional witty remark thrown in now and again. David was thankful for the lighthearted exchange.

After the waitress laid the bill next to his plate, Gabe's banter turned serious as he leaned in and looked at David with concern. "David, Jacque, I am so sorry for your loss. Grace was a good woman. My mom sends her condolences. She wanted to be here, but there was no way she could make the trip."

Nodding at the compassionate gesture, he said, "Of course, and thank you."

"Now that we've eaten, I'll get right to it. Atlanta is a mess. Since you left, Lucien Baldur and his minions have moved in and have practically taken over the legislature."

"Practically? I expected he would have all of it by now."

"Well, he doesn't have me," Gabe said sarcastically.

"How about the governor's office?"

"You would be proud of our governor, he is standing strong, but I'm not sure for how much longer. Truthfully, I think he is the only reason the whole city hasn't been taken."

"So, it's not all destroyed?" Jacque asked, a worried expression on her face.

Gabe looked at Jacque with compassion. He knew Jack Ruby and his daughter. Reaching to cover her hand, he shook his head and said, "No, Jacque, and your dad is well. In fact, he's making quite a ruckus himself."

Relieved to hear this news, she withdrew her hand and with a polite smile placed both hands in her lap.

David reached for his wife's folded hands and squeezed. "So, this Project Manna isn't saving the world after all, is it?"

Gabe rolled his eyes and let out a derisive snort, "What do you think?"

"What exactly is the problem, then?"

"Washington passed the bill to enact the Kindness Tax, but the PKO is having a little trouble getting certain states to comply. Georgia's governor is adamant that they would have to take him out before he would subject his state to their control."

"It's nice to finally see someone in authority with some common sense."

Ignoring the sarcastic jab, Gabe replied, "In Georgia. I wish I could say that around the nation." Rubbing at the back of his neck, he added, "Unfortunately, Lucien Baldur has the president, too many governors, and churches I might add, at his beck and call. He is a master manipulator; I'll give him that."

"Churches, what do you mean?"

"You haven't heard? Oh, pastors all over the country are spouting to their congregations that this man is being used by God to feed the world." He said sarcastically. "They're even donating their tithe to the cause."

"Wait, I thought that he was believed to be the antichrist? Shouldn't the church be against him?" David asked.

"The real church. Don't get me wrong, there are a handful of churches standing up and sharing the truth, but there's so much propaganda out there that if you're not a true believer, you're not going to understand."

"A true believer?"

The Senator paused as the waitress came by to top off their drinks. After she left, he lowered his voice and said, "Let me ask you a question, David. How often have you seen a nation fall because of a lack of discernment on behalf of its leaders?"

Following the Senator's lead, David looked out of the restaurant window and replied quietly, "Too many times to count."

"We've become too fat and sassy, to quote my dear Momma. This has lowered our ability to discern the truth, which has created a hotbed for someone to swoop in and deceive a weakened state. I'm afraid too many have been deceived. This Lucien Baldur... What do the kids say nowadays? He gives off a bad vibe. The true Church knows that Lucien Baldur is a false prophet and his boss, a counterfeit savior, but the rest of the world has been deceived by his promise to rid the world of hunger and food insecurity.

His manipulation shows all the signs of trying to fill the shoes that only One could fill."

"Who is that?" David asked.

Gabe paused as he looked at Jacque first and then David. A look of empathy crossed his face as he carefully considered what he would say next. "Look, David, I'm a Senator of the United States of America, but first I am a child of God. I'm not here to evangelize you, but I would be remiss if I didn't tell you the truth. I believe that your removal from the US Navy was intentional. I believe that Lucien Baldur wanted you out of the way from any organization that he wanted under his wings." Lifting his hands when David attempted to interject, he continued, "Look, I know all of this sounds crazy, but there is a war going on right now, a war for our eternal souls. The Church is called to feed the hungry and to care for the widow and orphan, yet we are ignoring this mandate from Jesus and allowing a system to fulfill that which we are called to. How has that worked for the nations you've seen fall?"

David was at a loss for words. This was all new territory for him, and he wasn't sure how to respond. Since his mom's death, a battle was waging for his heart. He had seen enough this year to know that Jesus was real; the question was whether he was going to follow him. When the woman from the plane refused to give in to the PKO demands, he thought she was crazy. *They were just words, right? But what if they weren't?*

"David, I'm sorry. I know you're grieving, and I didn't come here to add to your loss."

"Why did you come?" David asked.

"I'd like you to come to Atlanta. The governor is asking for anyone with first-hand knowledge of the PKO to convince the General Assembly to repeal the bill to enact the Kindness Tax."

He was proud of his wife, who sat quietly through the exchange. As he hesitated, looking at the cook behind the counter, she squeezed his hand. *Oh, to trade places,* he pondered. "To be honest, I'm beginning to feel like a pawn in this so-called war you speak of. I'm not sure the Governor knows what he's in for."

"David, you obviously don't know our governor."

CHAPTER 22

A Mountain Moved

The ride to Momma Rosaline's was a bit uncomfortable. Jade agreed to go, albeit begrudgingly. Maddie just couldn't understand what the problem was, she thought Doc Walker's mom was awesome.

"Come in, come in," Momma Rosaline said as the girls knocked on the door. Can I get ya somethin' to drink? We got lemonade, sweet tea."

"I'll take some sweet tea, please," Rachel said with a smile.

"Nothing for me, thank you," Jade said curtly.

Maddie and Emma joined Rachel in grabbing a glass of their own.

"Come, have a sit."

As she looked around at the small cabin, she loved the homey feel. The walls were covered in photos. Walking around the room, Maddie noticed a much younger Grace Bennett in several of the photos. "Momma Roseline, Grammy said that your husband was in the Navy with my Grandpa George?"

"Yes, ma'am."

"Is this them?" She asked, as she pointed to a group of young men in uniform.

"Why, yes, that'd be them. Ain't my Carl jes' fine in that uniform?"

Maddie smiled as she looked at the picture. The colors were muted, but she could see the handsome good looks of her Grandpa George. He sported black hair combed in a wave that looked very similar to her dad's and green eyes that seemed to twinkle with a knowing smile. Nostalgia pricked her heart as she remembered sitting at his feet while he played on his banjo.

"Did ya know 'im?" Momma Rosaline asked.

"He died when I was ten," she said. "He used to call me his Princess."

Momma Rosaline chuckled as she tilted her head to gaze at the photograph. "He was a good man, that one. He loved Grace more'n anybody could. I'll never ferget the look on his face when we met after they left the Navy. Yer Grammy was busier 'n a bee in a bonnet, always goin' off this way 'n that. Yer Grandpa would jes' look at her and smile. He knew she had everythin' under control."

"Was Grammy different when she was younger?" Maddie asked.

"Here, let's sit." Momma Rosaline pointed to the couch. Pulling a box from the table in front of her, she took the top off and began to pull photographs out.

"Now, I only knew yer Gram fer a short time, but she marked me. She loved greater'n anyone I know. When she said yes to Jesus, I saw a transformation in her that led me to say yes, too. She was diff'rent, but that fire, it never changed."

"What do you mean?"

"Grace Bennett had to control ever'thin. She wasna 'fraid to let ya know it. Whether it be a party, a weddin', or a church picnic, she had ever'body in check. When she met Jesus, I saw that woman soften. She turned from a woman in control to one in charge."

"What's the difference?" Emma asked.

"Well, a woman in control is doin' ever'thin' herself. She thinks she can fix ever' person, while she is dyin' on the inside from stress and worry. That's not the way our good Lord wants us to live. Yer Gram had to learn that lesson. I watched as Jesus unrolled that spirit of control from my friend and placed a mantle of intercession on her. Ya see, we all gotta choose whose gonna be in control. When the flesh is in control, it's us. When our spirit leads, we are informed by his Spirit. Now, he may put us in charge, but ultimately, we trust him to lead us, and instead of feelin' like we have to control it all, we're connectin' others to the One who does.

"Oh, lookee, here's a picture of yer dad playin' with my Carl Jr."

Suddenly, Jade was interested as Momma Roseline began to pull out pictures of the babies.

"You have another son?" Rachel asked.

A sadness crossed her eyes as Momma Roseline said, "Yes ma'am, he's not with us no more."

"What happened to him?" Jade asked.

Momma Roseline paused as she looked at Jade with a penetrating gaze. Maddie watched as the two stared at one another. *What is going on?* She wondered. Everyone just sat there in suspended silence, waiting for Momma Roseline to speak.

"I'm headed to the office, Momma. Doc Walker said as he walked into the room. The tension was broken as he walked over and kissed her on the cheek. "I'll see you later."

"Bye, Hon. Have a good day."

"He's an amazing doctor, Momma Roseline," Maddie said as the doctor left. "He took such good care of Benjamin and Kali. I didn't know that doctors could be veterinarians."

Momma Roseline looked at her and smiled. "He's got a heart the size of Texas. After my Carl left the Navy, he found another construction job in Nashville. He liked Virginia Beach but wanted to make roots away from the military. Carl Jr. was born a year after yer daddy was born, Maddie Ruth. A couple of years later, my Charlie came along. Yer Gram and I wrote letters back and forth in that season. I learned all 'bout yer dad as he played football and went into the Navy himself. I wish my Carl had signed up. Things might've been different," she added looking off into the distance.

"What happened?" Rachel asked.

Momma Roseline looked at the girls, gazing hard at Jade.

"Carl was hangin' with the wrong crowd—people who used him. He finished high school, barely, and then met an amazin' woman. I thought he had finally turned a corner. They fell head over heels in love and got married. She wanted to be a doctor and so she went off to school. That left my Carl alone to his own devices, which weren't good fer nobody."

"She left him to go to school, even though they were married?" Maddie asked.

"Yes ma'am. No differ'ent that my Carl leavin' me to go into the Navy. She was on a mission to save the world. We weren't gonna stand in her way. But, Carl Jr., he was lost. He did'na have the grades nor the desire to go back to school. So, he took on a job with his dad and worked construction. He worked hard. There were good days when he'd be happy with his life, but then thar were days when a darkness grabbed hold. It was like watchin' Dr. Jekyll and Mr. Hyde."

"What happened to his wife?" Rachel asked.

"She worked hard. She was on scholarship, but she still had to come up with livin' expenses. Ever' time the construction jobs dried up, she had to provide fer them both, but that girl was strong. Even when she got pregnant, she worked harder than anybody I did see."

Jade's eyes were wide as she sat frozen as if in a state of shock. "Hey, are you okay?" Maddie whispered.

Jade batted at her hand. "Did she have a girl or a boy?" She asked a bit defensively.

Momma Roseline tilted her head and leaned forward. "She had a girl." Her eyes gleamed as she paused to see how she would respond.

Jade looked away, shaking her head.

"Jade, do you want to hear the rest of the story?" Momma Roseline asked. "If ya don't, I'll understand."

Confused, Maddie looked at her friend, whose eyes were filled with tears. Jade nodded as Emma grabbed her hand. Rachel threw a knowing look for her to grab the other.

Momma Roseline looked at Jade as if speaking directly to her. "Carl Jr. tried. He really did. But the demons got the better of 'im. He wanted to give his little family the best life he could, but in his mind, he had to have a lot of money, prestige, and power to do it." A look of disgust crossed her face as she said, "The people he hung around with made empty promises, and he believed ever' one. One night, he went on a job that turned sour. He was shot. When we got the call, I could'na believe it. My boy was gone. I cried and cried. It was you, Jade, who consoled me that night. Yer Momma was at school, so I took care of you when she was away. I'll never ferget yer words, 'It's okay Mimi, it'll all be okay.' When I called Alisha and told her the news, she came and picked ya up. And I never saw you again."

The room was so quiet you could hear a pin drop. Maddie couldn't believe her ears; Momma Roseline was Jade's grandma? *God, what are you doing?*

After a few moments, Momma Roseline continued as Jade sat in shock. "I was in mourning. If it weren't fer Machaseh, I don't know where I would be today."

The familiar Name snapped Jade out of her daze. "What did you say?"

"Oh, you've probably never heard the name, Machaseh means…"

"Refuge," they said in unison.

"Or shelter. That's right! How did you know?" Momma Roseline asked.

Jade looked at each of her friends through the tears of someone with a revelation, "God is our refuge and strength, an ever-present help in trouble."

Momma Roseline hit her knee and proclaimed, "Well, I'll be!"

Rachel leaned in as she whispered, "Jade, he moved a mountain today, didn't he?"

The gentle reminder from their winter retreat to Woodlands was all it took. Jade could no longer hold back the tears she harbored over the loss of her dad. Each girl surrounded Jade in a big group hug as she wept.

After lunch, Momma Roseline proudly shared stories of

Grammy and Carl Jr. as if they were yesterday.

It was if a weight had lifted from Jade. She seemed almost giddy as she looked at pictures of her dad when he was younger. "He was handsome, wasn't he?" She asked her friends.

Maddie couldn't believe what they had learned today. Trying to connect all the dots, she sat in awe at the goodness of God.

As they made their way back to her place, Rachel voiced what she couldn't figure out. "Did y'all see what God did today?"

"Honestly, I'm still in shock. I'm not sure I can even say," Emma admitted.

"It was a miracle," Maddie blurted out. "A real miracle!" She couldn't help but feel a little giddy herself.

Rachel stopped in the driveway and took the key out of the ignition. "Well, to take a page out of Sonya's book, this'll cook your noodle," she teased.

Anticipating Rachel's next, they each leaned in closer to hear.

"Not only did God reunite you with your grandma, Jade, but he placed you in the same neighborhood with the granddaughter of the one who befriended her so you could. How is that for a cooked noodle?"

Jade clutched the photos Momma Roseline had given to her tightly to her chest. "I will never forget this day," she said. "Now, I just have to figure out how to tell Mom."

As she walked into the house, she heard her mom calling from the back of the house, "Is that you, Maddie?"

"Yes, Mom." The door to Grammy's bedroom was opened, as her mom sat on the floor.

"There are some things I wanted to show you."

Her senses heightened as she sat next to her mom. Her Gram's perfume, dresses hung neatly in the closet, her shoes perfectly ordered under her bed. Taking a deep breath, she closed her eyes and allowed herself to feel the moment.

"Are you okay?" Her mom asked. "If you're not ready, we can do this another time."

"No, it's okay, I just haven't walked in here since…"

"I know, Sweetie." Jacque sighed as she ran her fingertips across the embossed engraving on the box in front of her. "You know, she was a mother to me."

Placing her hands on her mom's, Maddie wanted to ease the heaviness she could see in her bowed shoulders. "She loved you very much, Mom."

"Yes, I know. Even from the first moment we met." Raising a brow, she added, "I was rude to her, you know."

A look of shock crossed her face as she asked, "What happened?"

"The night she came to visit David at school, we had a date. We were supposed to meet at his apartment because boys weren't allowed in my building. Anyway, I knocked on the door, and here was this little old lady whipping the door open like I was some kind of salesperson."

Maddie chuckled, she couldn't help herself, but she could see her Grammy in all her glory, ready to defend her son with all her 5'1" self.

Her mom couldn't help but giggle, and before they knew it, their laughter caught the attention of Matthew, who joined them.

The three spent the next hour telling stories of their beloved Gram. A warm glow filled the room as the sun made its descent. If she didn't know any better, she would think her Gram orchestrated this moment. *God's presence is all 'round, Maddie.*

The thick orange envelope had her name neatly written in cursive, "Maddie Ruth Bennett." When her mom handed it to her, she was filled with joy. One more conversation with

Gram. Part of her wanted to wait to open it, but at the same time, she yearned to hear her voice.

Deciding that she couldn't wait, she carefully opened the seal. The inside was filled with a letter and cards that were neatly banded together. Removing the rubber band, she flipped through the cards and read aloud from some of her Gram's favorite verses.

The last card was blank. Curious, she turned the card over. A message written in tiny writing at the bottom said, "And now it's your turn…" *What does that mean?* She wondered.

Opening the letter, she was thankful to see the handwriting in print, even if a little shakily written. While she loved to see her Gram's handwriting, reading a whole letter in her shaky cursive would have taken a lifetime.

Maddie Ruth,

It's a beautiful day, what with the sunshine flowing over the back deck like a quilt on a warm summer night. I can hear your Carolina Wren singing to his bride in the background. A gentle breeze is causing the sunflowers to wave at me from their beds.

I write this letter to you, my Love, to encourage you to keep your eyes on Jesus. When you receive this, I will be in his presence. I wonder if I'll jump in his arms or bow at his feet. Who knows, maybe I'll do a little jig. But know this, I will be in the very place that I prepared my whole life for!

I won't tell you not to be sad, I know you will be. But I encourage you with this: grieving is a gift. Allow the Lord to draw you into his presence—into his heart. He knows you better than anyone, Maddie Ruth, and he will heal your heart with his comfort, strength, and love. As you are healed in his presence, abide in his peace. Remember that song you and Emma wrote? The Lord gave you that song to remind you that his peace is your strength and rest. It will carry you through the fire into the promised future he has for you.

Now, let's talk about that future. Maddie Ruth, my time is done. Now, it's your turn. You are the little blessed one who'll be a companion to many. Never forget who you are and Whose you are. Always remember that you are on mission. Keep your eyes on Jesus and point others to him. Don't let anything or anyone else distract you from your calling. The Lord is with you and has a plan to give you hope and a future—Jesus is your hope and life and eternity with God is your future. Never forget this, Love! No matter what you face on this earth, these two remain true. Hold them close to your heart as you allow him to hold you. Until the day when you meet your Savior face to face, you are on mission. Now, this is very important. I want you to pray for God to lead you into the calling he has on your life. I've already told you what I think, but it's what he says that matters, so you listen to him. The Holy Spirit will show you the way.

And don't forget to put on your armor—every day, ya hear? Don't you walk out of your house without clothing yourself with the armor of God and the compassion of Christ. Take that blank card and write down the scripture that means most to you in this season. The Spirit will lead you as he writes his word on your heart.

Finally, yes, Jesus was the one walking with Shadrach, Meshach, and Abednigo in the fire. And Maddie Ruth, he will walk with you, too.

I love you, Maddie Ruth, and will see you again,
  Grammy

"You obviously don't know our governor." David couldn't shake the senator's last comment before they left the diner. Gabe made it seem as if the governor knew more about David than he would have liked him to.

"David, did you hear me?" Jacque said, breaking his concentration as he made his way up the mountain.

"I'm sorry, Jacque, what did you say?"

"Really, David, I don't want to go back to that place where I can't talk to you."

"I am sorry. Please repeat."

"I was just saying, I think we should take the Senator up on his offer. I'm sure Dad will be more than happy to have us stay with him. He hasn't seen the kids in over a year."

"Did Maddie tell you that she wanted to go back with her friend Jade?"

Stunned, Jacque paused before saying, "I think we should let her go."

"Are you sure? Do you understand the danger involved?"

"I understand that there isn't a lot that we can control, and I would much rather my daughter learn to fight than to hide."

David gave a knowing grin as he said, "I'm proud of you, Wife."

"What, why?" Jacque asked.

"It took a lot to move that mountain of fear."

Lifting a brow, Jacque asked, "For me or you?"

CHAPTER 23

The Master Plan

"We're actually going, I can't believe it!"

From the back seat of the cab of the truck, Emma yawned as she said, "We heard you for the tenth time."

The blue display on the center console reflected one a.m. Maddie had to agree with her friend as she yearned for sleep, even if she was a little excited.

"I'm happy, too," Rachel whispered.

Dad was adamant that they all pile in the car at midnight and make their way to Atlanta. He said they would have a better chance of making it to Atlanta without running into trouble.

"Do you girls remember Laura?" He asked.

Jade leaned forward, placing her forehead on the captain's chair before her. "Oh, Mean Mug Laura? Yeah!"

"What did she teach you?"

Crossing her arms, she sat back against her seat and replied, "That she's got a strong right punch."

David smiled, "What else did she teach you?"

"Be aware of your surroundings," Maddie answered.

"That's right. Atlanta is not the same, Girls. No matter your surroundings, you need to remember this. What else did she teach you?"

"Walk with purpose," Rachel said, "Walk with others."

"That's right. And if you think you're being followed?"

"Walk into a store or a coffee shop and ask for help."

Quiet filled the cab of the truck as Jade mumbled, "Not too many of those left."

"All the more reason to be careful where you go and who you're with," Dad said. "Wild Rock was a safe bubble. Atlanta is not so much. So, I want you girls to stay together and preferably have a trustworthy male with you."

"I'll protect them, Dad," Matthew said with a serious look on his face.

Maddie looked at her brother. He now stood taller than his dad after growing a whole foot over the last year. She believed that he believed that he could.

Her dad looked into the rearview mirror at her brother and said, "No lone ranger stuff, Matthew."

"Yes, Sir thar, Pilgrim," he said as he gave the worst John Wayne imitation while tipping an invisible hat.

ATLANTA, GEORGIA

"We're here!" Jade tapped each of the girls to wake them up. "Wake up, we're here!" She repeated.

Sitting up to stretch, Maddie checked their surroundings. "Are we at Grandpa Jack's?" She asked with a yawn.

"Yes," her mom turned around and smiled. "He'll be so happy to see you guys."

She hadn't seen her grandpa in a year and a half. Suddenly, she felt a bit emotional. He was the only grand she had left. Shaking off the lonely thought, she turned to wake a stubborn Emma and Matthew from their unconscious state.

As she exited the truck, she joined her brother to give Grandpa Jack a hug. "Grandpa!"

"Well, hey y'all, I wondered if you'd ever get here." Opening his arms wide, he had enough room for them both.

"You've lost weight," Maddie said, a touch of concern in her voice.

"Yeah, the Doc has me on a weight loss plan," he said as

he patted his belly and looked at her mom. "Too many donuts. I told him there was no such thing as too many, but he disagreed."

"Hey, Dad," Jacque said as she came up behind them for a hug.

"How's my girl?" He asked as he hugged her tightly. "I've missed you. I've missed all of you. Come on in, let's get you inside where it's warm."

"Warm? As in heat?" Rachel asked, suddenly wide awake.

"Yes, we've got heat," he said with a smile. "And a warm fireplace. Put your things upstairs, and you can grab some hot cocoa and sit in front of the fire."

"I don't know, Dad; it's been a long drive. We should probably just head up to bed."

Five voices groaned, "UGH!!"

"Come on, up to bed with you. Maddie, you and the girls take the room with the two queens, Matthew can have the bunkroom. Dad and I will take the room downstairs."

Everyone carried their bags upstairs, half asleep.

"Thank you, Dad. I appreciate it," She heard her mom say.

"You're welcome. Get some sleep."

The Atlanta sun wasn't giving the girls the grace to sleep in.

"Too early," Maddie groaned as she rolled over, hitting Rachel in the face. "Oops, sorry!"

"I expect brutality from Jade in the morning, but not you." Her friend teased.

"Speaking of Jade…" Soft snores sounded on the other side of the room. "How can she sleep with the sun in her face?"

"That girl can sleep anywhere," Rachel laughed. "Hey, do you need the shower? If not, I need one badly."

"No, you go ahead. I'm going to take my journal downstairs and spend some time in the quiet."

"Okay, go for it."

As Maddie walked downstairs, she felt a strong need to pray. She wasn't sure where it was coming from, maybe from her dad's warning the night before, but whatever was stirring, she knew just the perfect place. Well, maybe not as perfect as Grammy's, but perhaps her second favorite.

As she walked through the double doors, she was happy to see all the windows open to the spacious sunroom. White wicker furniture sported colorful pillows and the perfect chaise lounge for her to sit and journal away. Grabbing a fuzzy blanket, she covered her lap and sat in her favorite chair. It wasn't long before she noticed the happy chirping of the birds in his backyard. Where Grammy's backyard was one big vegetable and sunflower garden, Grandpa Jack's was a manicured lawn with perfectly trimmed rosebushes, expertly placed. *Emma will be in gardening heaven,* she thought.

Closing her eyes, she prayed and asked the Lord to meet her there. It wasn't long before she felt the prompting in her spirit to write. This had happened to her sparsely before Grammy went home to be with Jesus, but afterward, it happened daily. It was weird, but she was filled with words and just had to get them out.

Father,

Thank you for calling us back to Atlanta. I don't know what you want us to do here, but we're here. Please go before us and prepare us for what you would have us do. And Lord, please give Emma peace. I think she's a little afraid. In Jesus' Name, Amen

As she finished her writing, she looked out of one of the windows and noticed a pair of armed guards standing at the front of the drive. *Hmm, were they there last night?* She wondered.

Breakfast was served promptly at eight. Grandpa Jack had

a strict schedule that everyone in the household followed. If you weren't awake, you just didn't eat. Although, he would sneak in snacks throughout the day.

Jade's eyes were as big as saucers. "Ooohhh, look, cinnamon rolls!"

"There is a chocolate donut with my name on it!" Matthew said.

Maddie looked around the room. When she didn't see what she was looking for, she asked, "Grandpa, do you have any fruit?"

"You are every bit your Momma's daughter," he said with a chuckle. "Bananas are in the pantry. You'll find some strawberries in the frig."

Awe filled her at the amount of food in the commercial refrigerator. Their diet over the past year included oats, fruits, and veggies from the garden, eggs (lots of eggs), and freshly caught deer and rabbit. Occasionally, they would be surprised with pork. But this....

"Grandpa, is all of this food for you?" She asked.

"When your mom called and told me you were coming, I sent someone to Costco. It's been a while since I've had so many mouths to feed."

"Is Costco still open?" Jacque asked.

"Just the one in Dunwoody. It might as well be a fortress, as protected as it is. As much as they've tried, nobody has been able to take it down, yet."

"Grandpa, Jade said everything was destroyed."

"In most places, she's right. But there are a handful of places where the local people created their own safe haven. They refused to give in to the delinquents. This area is one such place."

"Delinquents? That's an interesting name for them," David said as he grabbed a donut.

"Well, that's what they are. No brains in any of 'em. But I expect that's exactly how Baldur likes it."

"Do you know him?"

Jack grunted. "We've had words."

"Does he know who you are?"

With chest puffed out, Grandpa Jack swelled with pride as he retorted, "Oh, he knows exactly who I am."

"I think Dad wants to know if he knows that you are our grandpa," Matthew asked wisely.

"If he knows, he hasn't said a word."

"It's probably better that it stays that way," David said. "Although I would be highly surprised if he didn't know. He seems to have it out for me."

"You just can't go anywhere without making an enemy, can you, Boy?" Grandpa Jack smirked.

"I could say the same of you," David countered.

Grandpa Jack bellowed at the subtle insult. "I guess you could say we're cut from the same cloth."

"I think that's the best compliment you've ever given me, Sir."

After breakfast, the girls wandered around the backyard. Maddie was right, Emma was in heaven.

"Look at these roses! There are so many of them!" She exclaimed. "In a month, these buds will mature into the most beautiful blooms. Each one is unique in her own right." Bending down to take a deep whiff of the flower's scent, she closed her eyes in bliss. Bending down to take a handful of soil, she said, "Someone takes very good care of this garden."

"It helps to have people working for you," Jade said.

"Does he?" Emma asked Maddie.

"Grandpa Jack works harder than anyone I know," she replied. "I can't imagine he would have the time to do any of this himself."

Suddenly, a little woman came up from behind them with a rose in her gloved hand. "Here Girl, I understand you wanted one of these."

Joyfully surprised, Emma clapped her hands and took the rose from the woman's hand. "Are you the gardener?" She asked.

"That would be me." Pulling off her gloves so she could shake Emma's hand, she added, "My name's Myrna, what's yours?"

"Oh, I'm Emma. I like to garden too."

"Do you, now? What's your favorite?"

"Oh, that's hard." Emma placed her finger on her chin as she looked up to the sky, "Let me see, I love daffodils. Irises make my heart sing. When I sit with the sunflowers, I feel like I'm at a party. Roses make me think of God working in the garden of my heart." Counting her fingers for each plant, she added, "Then there's tomatoes, corn, green beans. Oh, there are so many! I don't think I can pick just one!"

Myrna laughed at Emma's zeal. "No need to have a favorite. Come over here, let me show you something."

As they rounded the bend, Maddie gasped. A small waterfall surrounded by trees was tucked into a quiet corner of the yard. A simple wooden bench with a cushion sat in the middle of the intimate space with two rosebushes on either side. *A safe place*, she thought.

"Oh my, this is glorious! Girls, check out these willows, aren't they lovely?" Emma asked as she ran her fingers over the slender branches.

"This is my Eden," Myrna said. When I need to get away from the world, I come right here and kneel before my Father. He is my Shelter, my Refuge."

"Machaseh," Jade said quietly.

"What's that?" Myrna asked.

Jade's face lit up with excitement as she shared, "Machaseh, it means Refuge. God is our Refuge."

"Yes, that's right!" She said, clearly impressed. Turning to Maddie, Myrna asked, "You're Jack's granddaughter?"

"Yes ma'am, I'm Maddie."

"Good to meet you. I keep the grounds here. Jack saved me from the streets and brought me here. He allows me to live in the bunkhouse rent-free and lets me tend to the garden."

"Wait, so you have to take care of all of this, for free?" Jade asked.

"Oh no ma'am, not have to, I get to. It's Jack's way. He's taken in a lot of strays."

"You're not a stray," Rachel said. Her brows furrowed even as her voice softened with concern.

"Oh no, but I know where I came from, and I know who brought me here. All part of his master plan."

"Master plan?" Jade asked.

"Oh yes, God is working on that man's heart. I'm just a doorkeeper in his house."

"Wait, I thought you said you were the gardener?" She asked, confused.

Myrna laughed, "Have you never heard Psalm 84? 'For a day in your courts is better than a thousand anywhere else. I would rather stand as a doorkeeper at the threshold of the house of my God than to live at ease in the tents of wickedness.' When you are on mission for the Lord, you are a doorkeeper in his house. You have the highest honor of welcoming others into the kingdom. Jack Ruby may think he saved me, but all along the Lord Almighty is saving him!"

Rachel elbowed Maddie as she smiled at her friends. "This is going to be an awesome trip!" She whispered under her breath.

After an official tour around the garden, the girls left Myrna to her work.

"That's pretty cool about Grandpa Jack," Emma said as they walked up to the house.

"Yeah, I can't believe I didn't know he helped the homeless," Maddie said, troubled.

"You know now," Rachel said with a smile.

David sat with his father-in-law in the salon as the stench of a cigar filled the room. It had been a long time since he had to endure the odor.

"How's Wild Rock?" Jack asked.

"Quiet. Like a little taste of Mayberry in Tennessee."

Jack chuckled as he bit down on the cigar. "Hasn't changed a bit."

"Well, except for the flood. It took out quite a bit of land."

"Sounds like the town made their way."

"Barely. It was quite interesting. I've never seen so much neighborly bonding."

"And you probably won't see it again," Jack said as he puffed on the cigar. "Is any of it real, anyhow?" He asked.

David sat quietly. This is when his mother would tell Jack about the love of God.

"How about you and Jacque?" Jack asked. "How are you doing?"

"Jacque thrived in Wild Rock. You would have been proud of her. She headed up several of the town's projects and seemed to truly find her place."

"That's my girl. Always in control of something."

"Actually, Jack, she delegated quite a bit. I saw a change in her. She enjoyed allowing others to take the limelight."

"Hmm." Putting the cigar out, he seemed to be collecting his thoughts for the next quip. "So, how are you and Jacque…financially?" Jack asked.

"We're doing okay. I invested most of the money I received from Magnum Lock and Mom left us her house and a little nest egg."

Tilting his chin downward, Jack peered over his glasses as he asked, "Have you looked at your investments lately?"

The hard edge to his father-in-law's words set David on edge. "Not recently."

"You know that the stock market has taken a dive twice in the last six months."

"I expect it hasn't been all roses," David said. "But it always bounces back."

"I don't know, David. I think that Lucien Baldur's master plan is to change all that."

CHAPTER 24

Look for the Love

Time for the girls at Grandpa Jack's was short-lived. Maddie wished they could stay, but Jade was eager to get back to Underground.

"Pastor Chris will be expecting us. Oh, and I have a surprise for you!" She said excitedly.

Rachel gave her friend a knowing look. Keeping a surprise was nearly impossible for their Jade. The fact that she had kept it the whole time she was in Wild Rock meant that it was probably going to rock their world.

The black nondescript van gave Maddie the chills. It reminded her of faded green shag carpet and hooded head coverings. Hearing her dad's voice from behind shook her out of the moment of fear.

"Yes, stay close to them, but not too close. We don't want to alert anyone to your presence."

The two men talking to her dad nodded in agreement.

"UGH, do we have to have bodyguards?" Jade asked. "That's gonna make everyone feel weird."

"That was the only reason Dad allowed me to come," Rachel said. "Apparently, they're the same two that rescued Michael."

"Let me talk to Dad," Maddie said.

"Hey Dad, can we talk privately?" She asked. "Hey, like, I know that you and Rachel's dad want us to be safe and all, but are these guys gonna follow us around everywhere?"

Placing his hand on her shoulder, he said, "These guys are intel. We have to know what's going on down there. It's not that we don't trust Alisha, but we want to know that where you're going is safe. Once they give us the all clear, you can have your freedom."

"Okay, thanks Dad. I turn eighteen in a month, and you're going to have to let me go."

"I know, Ruthie, but I will always be your dad," he said with a wink.

The ride to Underground Atlanta was tense for everyone. Jade was right, Atlanta was a different town. Men with machine guns walked down the road as if it were wartime. Maddie saw a woman clutching a baby as she ran into an alley. Every building was covered in plywood. "NO ORDER, NO PEACE" was sprayed in big red letters everywhere.

"Do you ever get the impression that they want you to memorize their mantra?" Rachel asked.

"I told you guys, this is all indoctrination," Jade said. "Pastor Chris said it's all to inspire fear."

Staring out the windshield before them, Rachel's eyes glazed over as she added, "And control the people."

The first thing she noticed as they made their way to the Five Points neighborhood of downtown Atlanta was the heavy presence of armed guards. "What's with all of the armed guards?" She asked.

"We need them. I told you, Mads, we don't have luxurious gardens like y'all do in Wild Rock. I mean, don't get me wrong, I'm glad you do, but here, it's just not… Food is scarce, which means that thieves are everywhere." Jade trailed off as she looked sadly around her.

As she looked and listened to her friend's despair, concern gripped Maddie's heart. *It's as if we all have something we're struggling with, God. Please give us strength,* she prayed silently.

Look for the love.

The gentle voice encouraged her embattled heart. "Look for the love," she said.

"What did you say?" Emma asked.

A wave of courage filled her as she repeated, "Look for the love.

"Girls, we can all agree that everything has changed. So, now we have to make a new way. Remember Daniel and his friends? They were enslaved and made their way in a completely different world. Well, that's us. It's time to lay it all down and declare a new day!" *Where did that come from, God?* She wondered.

Rachel nodded in agreement. "You're right. So, how do we look for the love?"

Wondering if this was a test, she looked outside the window. She wasn't sure she could answer her friend's question. Everything looked so dark.

After the van stopped, the girls were told to wait. Jade's face lit up as she saw her mom run over to the van.

"Mom!" She yelled.

Alisha spoke to the men who opened the door to the van and motioned for the girls to exit.

As they disembarked, Jade ran to her mom and hugged her tightly.

"Well, there you go, that's love," Emma said with a smile.

"Yeah…" Maddie agreed.

"This place is amazing!" Rachel said as they walked down the metal stairs.

What used to be shops were now boarded-up homes for people to live. Alisha told them that the area was constructed during the city's post-Civil War Reconstruction Era.

"When I was a girl, these shops were booming with life," she said. "These streets were once at the same level as the city, until they raised the street level in the early 1900s," she said. "That was around the time of Prohibition, when these shops served as bars."

"How big is Underground?" Rachel asked.

"It's around twelve acres, I think," Alisha responded.

"How many people live down here?"

"A couple of thousand, I imagine. We have new people showing up every day. They go through a strict vetting process before they're allowed to live here."

"There are armed guards everywhere. Where do they come from?"

"Everybody who lives here has a job here to support the community. You can't come here and not work—well, there are exceptions, but most everyone here works. The armed guards are made up mostly of police officers who were forced out of the city's force by the PeaceKeepers."

"It's crazy to me how quickly society broke down," Rachel said to her friends. "I mean, just two years ago, everything was normal. Now, look at this place."

"Well, here we are!" Alisha pulled out a ring of keys and unlocked a metal door mounted in the center of a wall of cinder blocks.

"It looks like a hospital," Emma whispered.

Nodding as she walked into the small loft apartment, Maddie's mouth suddenly fell open in surprise as she looked at the huge mural covering the white walls before her. Machaseh was painted in bright blue with highlights of gold interwoven throughout. "Jade," she said with tears in her eyes.

"The Lord is my Refuge," she said proudly. "I need a daily reminder."

"Oh Jade, I love it!" Emma said. "Did you paint it?"

"No way, Girl! You know me, there ain't a drop of creativity in these hands," she exclaimed. "Mom knew a guy."

Rachel walked up to the mural, studying it intently. Tracing the gold threads peeking through each curve of the letters, she had a dreamy look on her face. "Jade?"

"Hmm?" Jade asked as she opened a dresser drawer.

"Is the thread the Holy Spirit?"

Placing her arm around her friend, Jade's head tilted as she watched her touch the wall's art. "God protected us at the PKO, ya know? I realized that God didn't make the bad things go away, he walked with us through them."

"Yeah. Oh, Jade, I'm with Emma, I love this so much. I love you so much." Rachel grabbed her friend in a hug.

"Why are you crying?" Jade asked.

"I guess I'm looking at love," she said as she looked at Maddie. "You girls have no idea how long I've prayed for you to know Jesus. Not to just know about him, but to KNOW him! Watching you grab hold of your faith; it really grows mine."

The next week brought with it a flurry of activity. On day two, they walked to Hurt Park, where Jade introduced them to Pastor Chris, leader of the WTL movement. Maddie was out of breath as they reached the park entrance. She forgot how long Jade's legs were. Keeping pace with her friend was quite the challenge.

"Pastor Chris, these are my friends, Rachel, Maddie, and Emma. Girls, this is Pastor Chris. All these amazing peeps are the WTL," Jade waved her hand around the small park.

Rachel was in heaven as she looked at the volunteers all serving one another. People of all colors and ages were working in some capacity. An old silver tub sat next to the fountain.

"What is the WTL?" Rachel asked.

"Jesus is the Way, Truth, and Life." Pastor Chris said, "We have chosen to walk in his way."

"Check it out, cherry blossoms!" Emma exclaimed as she ran to the green spindly trees. "I'll bet these are beautiful in the spring."

"Yes, beautiful," Pastor Chris said. "In my culture, the cherry blossom represents life and death, beauty and violence. As spring begins, we know that new life is right around the corner."

"Are you Japanese?" Rachel asked curiously.

"Why yes, I am. Third generation immigrant," he said proudly.

"That means…"

"Yes, my grandparents lived in the internment camps of San Francisco."

"Wait, what?" Maddie asked.

"Come on, Girl, have you forgotten your history? Pearl Harbor?" Jade asked.

"Don't be snarky, I just didn't do the math, is all."

"How did you end up in Atlanta, Pastor Chris?" Rachel asked.

"After the internment camps were disbanded, our people left California for a better life. My grandparents moved to Arkansas first, and then to Georgia. Our family has been here ever since. My mom is over there," Pastor Chris said as he pointed to a beautiful woman crocheting under one of the cherry blossom trees. She smiled and waved when they waved at her.

"So, the cherry blossom tree is very important to us. They remind us that Jesus is the vine, and we are the branches, and we are to remain in him. Life may be uncertain, but he never is." Pastor Chris poured water from a five-gallon water cooler. Filling up five reusable cups, he brought them over. "Water?" He asked.

"Oh, thank you, I'm parched!" Maddie exclaimed. "Jade practically raced to get us here."

"I walk with purpose," Jade said defensively.

"More like you're running to a fire," Rachel laughed.

Rolling her eyes at her friends, she walked over to a group of people preparing lunch.

"So, when did y'all get here?" Pastor Chris asked.

"A couple of days ago," Maddie said. "We're staying with Jade."

"She's a pretty amazing young woman. She jumped right in from day one. I'll never forget the first time she led someone to Christ. She walked right up to them, asked their name, and if they knew Jesus. It typically takes people weeks to get comfortable with sharing the Gospel, but your friend here was on it her second day. Bold as a lion that one!"

She always knew her friend was bold. It was pretty cool to hear a stranger echo this truth.

"Pastor Chris, we were wondering if we could hang out over the next couple of days," Rachel said. "Do you have any jobs that we can do?"

"Oh, there's always work to do," he replied.

And that was only the beginning. The girls flourished in the WTL. On the Saturday after they arrived, they experienced their first service. People from all over flooded the little park. Rachel and Jade both worked together to share the Gospel with newcomers, while Emma helped the hospitality crew. Pastor Chris took Maddie under his wing and allowed her to shadow him.

It didn't take long for him to recognize her spiritual gift. "You're an intercessor, aren't you?" He asked.

"Do I have a sign on my forehead?" She asked with a laugh.

"Maddie, you show the gifts of faith, exhortation, and mercy. These are prevalent spiritual gifts in the heart of an intercessor. Your friend, Jade, is an evangelist. She has a unique ability to share the Gospel. So, her gifts are likely to be evangelist, faith, and mercy."

This is wild, she thought to herself. "But, how do you know?"

"I watch people. The bible tells us to be quick to listen and slow to speak. This allows us to pay attention to people and connect with them through the Holy Spirit. He tells us what we need to know. When you're connected to the Spirit, his fruit is evident. 'It is by their fruit that you will know them.'"

"Do you mean fruit of the Spirit?" She asked.

"That's right, so you know about them?" He asked.

"My mentor told me about them, and my Grammy said that love is a fruit."

"That's right. Think of fruit as anything that grows—good or bad. Jesus is the vine, and we are the branches. He is the life giver, and when we are connected to him, his Spirit pours out the good fruit of love that we, in turn, pour into others."

"And what is bad fruit?"

"Well, the enemy has fruit too. If God gives the fruit of love, the enemy gives the fruit of fear. If God gives the fruit of joy, the enemy gives the fruit of misery or dissension. The opposite of peace would be division or conflict. Every fruit, whether good or bad, can be seen. As intercessors, we become very sensitive to the fruits and pray into them."

"So, you're an intercessor too?" She asked.

"Yes, ma'am, I am. It is a great honor to be a Watchman on the wall of my God."

"I don't know if I'm a Watchman," she said as she remembered the PeaceKeepers fiasco.

"Why would you say that?" He asked.

"Oh, I heard about something and told my dad, and while it saved the town, I got in trouble for disobeying him. Kind of irresponsible."

"Maddie, you're human and you made a mistake. Did you repent for it?"

"Repent?" She asked.

"Yes. Repent means to change your mind and turn away from your sin. When you disobeyed your dad, did you tell him and ask for forgiveness?"

"Yes, Sir."

"And did you choose not to do it again?"

Trying to remember if she said the words aloud, she answered, "Yes."

"Then, you repented. That is what we are called to—turn away from sin and turn to Jesus, who is transforming us daily into his likeness. This is a lifelong change, not something that happens overnight. Don't let shame keep you from stepping into God's calling on your life. That's the enemy's MO. He will isolate you under a mantle of shame until you think you're no longer good enough to do God's work. That is not of the Lord. You rebuke that lie, receive the forgiveness Jesus freely gave at the cross, and turn to him, moving forward in the strength that you have."

A wave of relief covered Maddie in that moment. She didn't realize the heaviness she was carrying over that one bad choice. The way Pastor Chris explained it helped her to see that was the very reason Jesus came—to set us free from sin and death. She didn't have to be stuck under the shame of her sin.

That night as she debriefed the day, she thanked God for Pastor Chris and all the people he had placed in her life, for the love that he gave her through his Spirit, and the opportunity to share it with others. She just knew something big was about to happen. She couldn't put her finger on it, but there was an expectation that left her weeping. "I don't know why you chose me," she prayed, "but I'm grateful."

The week after they arrived in Atlanta, David was called to meet with Senator Hawke and Governor Mitchell. Jerry Mitchell was a two-time governor who was a favorite of his constituents. He was a man known for his no-nonsense approach and ability to tell it like it was, qualities David voted for in the last election.

"Governor Mitchell, it's good to meet you," he said as he shook the governor's hand.

"David Bennett, I've heard a lot about you," Governor Mitchell said as he sat in his high -backed leather chair. "Have a seat."

David sat and looked around the sparsely populated room.

"It's quite empty, isn't it?" The governor said.

"I was wondering if a bomb went off," he said, half-jokingly.

The governor laughed at his attempt at humor. "I like him," he said to the Senator.

"I told you that you would," Senator Hawke said.

"Let's get down to brass tacks, Commander Bennett. We have a problem. This PKO and their hooded crazies have ruined this town. They might as well be Sherman for all the damage they've done. I know this Lucien Baldur has had the carpet rolled out in other states, but not this one. Not while I'm Governor. We've got people who've been hoodwinked in our state legislature by his Pollyanna lies. It's time to set 'em straight. Are you the man for the job?"

Stunned by the brashness of the governor of Georgia, he collected his thoughts before saying something he might regret. "Are you offering me a job?" He asked.

"As much as I would love to, there's no money in the budget for that. The PKO has sucked us dry." Governor Mitchell sat back in his chair with his hands folded together, his index fingers tapping in unison. "You're a smart man, Mr. Bennett, and I need a smart man by my side. I'll give you three months. You help me convince the General Assembly to repeal this blasted bill and I'll move heaven to keep you on."

"Three months," David said as he shook the Governor's hand.

"Good, that's good."

As they walked out of the office building and made their way to their trucks, Gabe turned to David and said, "I appreciate your service, David. It means a lot that you are willing to stand with the Governor like this."

David looked around to confirm there weren't any listening ears. "Senator, there is something you should know," he said softly.

The Senator tilted his head curiously.

"The drawings you sent me. They will be used in a hard shutdown."

"Hard shutdown? What do you mean?"

"We're taking out the PKO's communications."

CHAPTER 25

To Die is to Live

The Atlanta July sun beat down unmercifully, but Maddie didn't care. She and her girls worked on the streets of Atlanta, serving food to the homeless.

Watching her friends serve, she thought about how far they had come. Jade and Rachel led people to Jesus while Emma built urban gardens with WTL. Maddie served with the prayer team by interceding for those in need.

The girls spent their weekends helping Pastor Chris and his team with church services. The only standing church building in Atlanta had been turned into a PKO center, so they were left to hold church in the park. This church was so different from the ones of her past. Rachel's church was where Jesus stirred her heart. Grammy's church was where Jesus taught her to stand. And now, WTL Freedom Church—well, WTL was her church. *Who cares that we aren't in a building?* She thought. *The church is the people!*

The PeaceKeepers left the WTL alone for the most part. A few scary guys had walked by, shooting menacing looks toward the group. When they saw her dad's bodyguards, they promptly left. Maddie was thankful for Wes and Mark. They were former seals who worked with Rachel's dad, Tom. One day, she asked why they stayed around.

"Don't you have families?" She asked.

Wes' chiseled features reflected a brief glimpse of sadness as he said, "They're all gone." That was it. There were no details; they're just gone.

Mark chimed in, "California fires."

Mr. Tom's bodyguards were men of few words but loyal to a fault. They reminded her of the Warriors of the Way. It was as if God was drawing all these men together to fight for his people.

The water in the cooler looked amazing for someone who had been praying nonstop for three hours. Maddie walked over and grabbed a cup. Wiping her brow with her arm, she looked around at everyone who served so valiantly. She was grateful for each one. Ruby and Emma, and their hospitality team. Jade and Rachel, and their evangelical team. Rob and Matthew, and their resource team. Pastor Chris and his team of intercessors, of which she was grateful to be a small part.

Glancing around the park, her eye caught sight of an older gentleman standing by himself under the trees. *Who is he?* She wondered, thinking how strange he looked among the group of worshippers. His skin was weathered, and his hair long and gray. He seemed very interested in what was happening in the park but didn't appear to pose any threat. After taking a sip of water, she hid behind her cup, hoping he wouldn't catch her watching him. *Come on, Maddie, stop being paranoid,* she thought, making a note to walk over and introduce herself.

As she finished the cup of water, the man disappeared as a picture suddenly crossed her field of vision—a sea of people entered the park, looking for food. Standing perfectly still, she tried to capture every detail in her mind's eye.

Emma walked over to grab a cup of water. Concerned over the look on her friend's face, she asked, "Hey, Girl, what's wrong?"

Shaking her head, hoping not to forget the vision, she said, "I just had a vision."

Excited over her friend's revelation, Emma asked, "You did?"

"Yeah, thousands of people were coming toward us. They looked dead—like zombies," Maddie took another sip of water and frowned. I just want to understand, she thought.

"Zombies? You don't think…" Emma trailed off, a look of worry crossing her face.

I will not be afraid, Maddie reflected as she turned to comfort her friend. "No, I don't think it's anything like that. I don't know what it means. I need to pray about it."

"You're getting a lot of these lately, aren't you?" Emma asked.

"Yeah. Remember the sunflower dreams? God was leading me to him the whole time. I just wish I could figure these out when they happen. All I know to do is write them down and pray over them."

Emma grabbed her hand and smiled, "That sounds like the best plan. Can we pray now?"

After the girls prayed, Pastor Chris walked up to them with a clipboard in his hand. "Ladies!" He exclaimed. "Check this out!"

"Thirty names!" Maddie counted excitedly. Wondering if the older man was one of them, she looked toward the trees and noticed he was gone. "Hey, what happened to the man?" She asked.

"What man?" Emma asked, looking toward the trees.

Maddie shook her head. *Maybe I imagined him,* she thought.

The following Saturday, they went to the Chattahoochee River with the WTL. Pastor Chris negotiated a deal with a bus driver to take a group for open water baptism.

Once upon a time, this spot was a recreation area for family and friends to gather. Since the PeaceKeepers took over, that was all gone. Every commercial public space around town was shut down. The PKO made it clear that they were the family, and people had to do things their way. So, to hold a private event at a place like this was quite dangerous.

Maddie was a bit anxious as they drove through the city. A sadness washed over her as she thought about the lost in their city. Perhaps it was time to take territory for the Lord here in Atlanta.

"Remember when we were there?" Jade asked one day as they were talking about how much everything had changed. "There was no life in that place. Why? Because Jesus wasn't there."

"We were there," Rachel said. "So, Jesus must've been there."

Snorting, Jade retorted, "Don't be salty. If you follow the way of the PKO, you're dead. Following the PKO is following the Beast."

Maddie still didn't understand all the beast/antichrist talk. According to Rachel, that Helel guy was the antichrist who claimed to be the world's savior, and Lucien Baldur was his prophet. And then there was this beast. "Was the beast a person?" She wondered aloud.

"No," Jade said, "It's a system. The PKO is a system. You are sucked in with no way out—well, except for Jesus."

"Don't get tripped up in the weeds." Pastor Chris would say. *"Keep your eyes on Jesus."* And so, she resolved to take Pastor Chris's advice and just focus on Jesus instead.

As they drove to the river, she thought about the second group of people who lived in a community: groups like WTL and Wild Rock. I wonder how many more there are, she wondered. Rachel told her once that they were blessed despite everything that happened to them. "Blessed" was a funny word. To be blessed in the PKO's eyes was to have everything you ever wanted. But to be blessed in God's eyes was to have everything you ever needed. They were complete opposites. *Perhaps that is what Matthew meant when he said we are living in an upside-down world.*

When the bus stopped, she and Emma got off first. They were responsible for checking everyone off and make sure they knew where to go.

As Pastor Chris put on his boots and Fly-fishing waders, he said, "It's going to be a long day, we need to stay dry and hydrated."

After they checked everyone in, they walked over to the water. Green like the trees around it, some spots looked deep and murky, but then there were areas where the sun reflected straight to the bottom like little beams of light.

"Check it out. I wonder how long it is," Emma asked.

"Pastor Chris said the river is a little over four hundred miles," Maddie said. It starts at the south end of the Appalachian Mountains."

"No way! Awe, I miss Wild Rock," Emma said sadly.

Encouraged by the scenery, she agreed with her friend and said, "Yeah, me too. But look, there's a diving rock and a trail.

"Do you think we can come back sometime?" Emma asked.

"Sure, I would love that." Realizing their need for towels, she ran back to the bus and grabbed them from the back. Making her way back to the riverbank, she took inventory and decided that everything was ready. *This is so exciting!* She thought as she shot her friend an excited smile.

Pastor Chris and a helper stepped into the water and said a prayer. Reaching out his arm, he motioned to Maddie to send in the first person. She watched as a woman walked into the water and shivered. She looks nervous. "God, please meet her here and tell her it will be okay."

As she watched from the riverbank, the pastor spoke to the woman privately and then said a prayer. After lowering her into the water, he lifted her. It was in that moment that everything about the woman changed. Smiling from ear to ear, she stood and lifted her arms in the air joyfully. There wasn't a dry eye around as everyone watched her move from death to life.

Pastor Chris said to the crowd, "Today, she shed her grave clothes. Before we meet Jesus, we carry baggage we aren't designed to carry. When we meet him, he takes off our old self and gives us new life. The greatest exchange you'll ever make!"

Maddie cheered and clapped with everyone in attendance.

She knew exactly what he meant. *Jesus shed her fear and gave her faith.*

As she gave a towel to the woman exiting the river, she couldn't help but share in her excitement. After an emotional hug, the woman joined others to watch the next person be baptized.

This continued through the end of the morning. A sudden touch on her elbow broke her concentration. "Water?"

"Thanks, Rach. I didn't realize I was thirsty."

"It's beautiful, isn't it?" Rachel asked.

"Oh, my goodness. I've never seen anything like this!"

Pointing toward the people waiting to be baptized, Rachel asked, "Hey, have you looked at the line?"

Confused, she looked at the checked-off names. There should have been only five left, but there were at least another thirty waiting to be baptized. "Wait, where did they come from?"

"They drove in. Look at the parking lot."

Peering around her friend, she saw a line of cars parking. "There are more!" Curiosity filled her as she noticed the older man she saw at the park standing by the entrance. She started to ask Rachel if she knew him, but her excitement over all the people was palpable, and the thought left her mind as quickly as it entered.

"I know, right?! Maddie, do you know what this means?" Rachel asked.

Shaking her head, she asked, "What?"

"We're at a real revival!"

At the end of the day, Maddie couldn't believe her eyes as she looked over the sign-up sheets. Feeling especially happy to see the names Wes Malone and Mark Jacobs (their bodyguards), she quietly thanked God for his goodness. Over two hundred people went from death to life that day.

When Pastor Chris realized there were more people than

they came with, he called Jade and Rachel to grab the extra suits he brought so they could help. "This is just how it is," he said, beaming. "I hope you girls are up for more. I expect this to continue over the coming weeks."

Thinking back over the day, she was grateful to be even a small part. As Pastor Chris, Jade, and Rachel baptized, Maddie, Emma, and the rest of the prayer team served by praying over the day and helping those baptized. It seemed the longer it went, the more powerful it felt, but also the stranger it got. People would come in angry, fearful, and crying that they needed help. Then they would leave the waters happy, joyful, like everything had changed. *Death to life*, she pondered.

As she shared the phenomenon with her friend, Emma looked at her and whispered, "Dry bones?"

"Huh?" Maddie asked.

"Your vision. You had a vision of zombies walking into the park. That's what we saw today, wasn't it? Remember the story of Ezekiel and the valley of Dry Bones? God breathed on them, and they came alive again."

"Oh, my goodness, I can't believe it!" Maddie exclaimed as she realized that was exactly what she had witnessed that day.

As they traveled back to Underground, she shared her vision with Pastor Chris. He smiled and said, "To die is to live, Maddie. The things and people in our dreams can be symbols, but sometimes our dreams just expound on what we're feeling inside. I expect the zombies in your vision symbolized people who are tired of empty, powerless lives. They're tired of empty promises, and they want more. You've been feeling some of that, haven't you? We all have! The truth is, when we are baptized in Christ, we die to the old self and rise to new life in him. Perhaps what you saw today was a response to his invitation."

This was all so much. Overwhelmed by the idea that God was doing something, she was also confused about how people were drawn to the gathering. "But how did they know we were here?" She asked.

He looked at her and asked, "How did you know?"

Trying to remember the moment she realized she needed Jesus, she said, "Rachel invited me."

"That's right, it always starts with an invitation and God does the rest."

Trudging into Jade's little apartment, Jade looked at her exhausted friends and said, "Y'all need a shower. You stink!"

Rachel gave her friend a little shove and said, "Ditto! So, get to it!"

After taking turns, they huddled up with a cup of hot tea and reminisced over the day. Emma shared Maddie's vision with the girls. When Rachel heard it, she looked at her friend in awe.

Wanting to take the focus off her, Maddie shook her shoulders and said, "I still can't believe that Wes and Mark went to the water. I wonder what Dad will think?" She couldn't say it aloud, but she hoped he wouldn't mock them for getting baptized.

"Watching little Pastor Chris dunk the two brawny bodyguards made my day," Jade exclaimed. "Didn't I tell you girls? What's happening here is nothing short of amazing!"

Tired and a bit emotional, Rachel said, "I can't believe what God has called us to! Jade, thank you for inviting us here."

"What is God calling us to?" Jade asked. "I still can't figure it all out."

"Maybe we aren't meant to figure it out, but just to experience it," Emma said.

"Hey, I had a thought today," Maddie said. "What do you guys think about doing a prayer walk around the city, like we did in Wild Rock?"

You would've thought it was Christmas morning as Rachel shouted, "Yes!"

"Atlanta's really big," Jade said.

"That's okay, we'll focus on the Underground, right?" Emma asked, "We're taking territory for God's kingdom!" After picking up a pad to note local streets, she glanced at her watch. A look of horror crossed her face as she said, "Maddie, it's your birthday!"

"No way! Oh, my goodness, I can't believe we forgot!" Rachel shouted.

Smiling, she shook her head. "Girls, this was the best birthday ever. I wouldn't change a thing."

"Wait, wait, I know what to do!" Jade jumped up and went into the little galley kitchen. After opening a few drawers and grabbing something out of the refrigerator, she said, "Close your eyes, Maddie."

"Hey, you don't have to do anything!" Maddie said.

Jade lifted an eyebrow and said, "Did I mumble? Close your eyes!"

Her heart was racing; she loved her friends so much.

"Okay, you can open them."

The room was suddenly very dark. A short and obviously used candle adorned a chocolate chip cookie, threatening to cover the top with melted wax. Maddie's heart filled with joy as she looked at her friends. Rachel was right, she was very blessed. She wouldn't have it any other way, cutting the cookie into four bites, she gave one to each of her friends. After their elaborate birthday cookie, they went to work figuring out the areas they were going to declare for Jesus.

David massaged his tight neck muscles to stop a threatening headache. "That was a big waste of time," he mumbled angrily.

"No, David, that's politics. We speak and they counter. They speak and we counter. And after we've volleyed a couple of times, we compromise with a vote."

David hesitated as he considered the collateral damage he

had left behind from his testimony. "I didn't see any compromise in that room."

"Now you can respect the governor's pain."

"It sounds exhausting. How does anyone get anything done?" David said.

"The Senator forced a laugh as he replied, "We show up. Speaking of showing up, what's the status on Project Shutdown?"

David suddenly stopped to pull out his vibrating phone. "Fancy you ask," he said as he answered Mordy's call.

"Mordy, good to hear your voice," David said. "Yes, I'm just standing here with Senator Hawke. No, no need to call back. What did you find out?" Mordy's angry voice elevated loudly enough for the Senator to hear. "Well, that's unfortunate. I guess we're on our own. No, I can handle it. Let me talk to my guy, and I'll get back to you."

"Nobody is willing to help, huh?"

"Sounds like it. I need to talk to my guy and see if he can push out the update internationally."

"David, this is going to be painful."

"Well, if the governor can endure the pain, then I guess we're in it with him. This is no different than any other case I've worked."

"Except this time, you're going against the system."

CHAPTER 26

Surprise!

Floating on the high of Saturday's revival, the girls found themselves overwhelmed by worship on Sunday. The most natural thing in the world was to worship and give thanks to the One who made it all happen. Looking around the park, Maddie realized the church had doubled in size. "We're going to need a new park, Lord," she prayed.

After the service, Jade grabbed her arm and said, "Remember the surprise I said I had for you? Follow me!"

To be honest, she had forgotten all about it. An excited flutter grew in her belly as she and her friends followed Jade toward the cherry blossom trees at the side of the park.

Maddie suddenly stopped in her tracks and let go of her friend's hands. The man she had seen twice before stood looking at them from the sidewalk next to the road. *Who is this guy?* She wondered. Normally, she would feel cringe over the thought of some guy watching them, but there was something about him... "Maddie, what are you waiting for? Come on!" Jade yelled.

Suddenly, Rachel yelped when she saw Sonya.

"Sonya!" Maddie squealed. The moment was gone. She couldn't believe her mentor was here!

"I told you she was working at the hospital. I just didn't tell you she's working with my mom."

Giddy, she grabbed Jade's arm as she watched Rachel ugly cry again over their mentor.

"She sure is doing that a lot lately," Jade whispered as she nodded to their friend.

"She's happy," Maddie smiled, wiping away a tear of her own. She understood the joy of weeping. *Wasn't there a verse about that somewhere?*

"Well, hello, Girls. I have missed you." Sonya gave them each a hug.

Turning to Jade, Emma's eyebrows lifted in delight as she said, "I can't believe you kept this secret!"

Sonya laughed at the exchange. "So, what are you girls up to?"

They spent the next minute talking over each other as they tried to catch Sonya up.

"Whoa, whoa, whoa, one at a time. Emma, you go first."

Emma looked like she was going to hyperventilate as she started to share. "When we were in Wild Rock, I worked with a team to build gardens for the community. When we arrived in Atlanta, I had the opportunity to help WTL do the same. It's been straight fire!"

"Wow, that's awesome. God is good! Rachel, how about you?"

"I never would've thought I could live without so many of the comforts we grew up with, but it wasn't so bad. I'll never forget how the community came together to help each other. I hope to be able to pay it forward someday."

With a grin, Sonya said, "I expect there's a non-profit somewhere in your future."

As her friend looked off into the distance, Maddie wondered what she was thinking—*a non-profit? It had been a hot minute since she had pondered their future. I wonder where we will all end up?*

As Sonya turned to her, Maddie said the first thing she could think of, "Grammy passed away a couple of months ago."

Placing a hand on Maddie's shoulder, Sonya said, "Oh Maddie, your grandmother was a wonderful woman. A true kingdom warrior. She will be missed on this earth. I am so sorry for your loss, sweet Girl."

Not gonna cry, not gonna cry, she pleaded with herself as she swallowed the lump in her throat. "It's okay. She told me that she had run her race and now it's time that I run mine."

Sonya nodded and said, "Yes, ma'am, and run it you shall. It's obvious you girls have experienced a lot of change. Where did you see God move over the last year?"

Suddenly excited over all the things she wanted to share, she exclaimed, "Oh, Sonya, I got to help deliver a horse! It was a red bag and everything!"

Confused, Sonya asked, "Wait, what? A red bag? What's that?"

"Oh, sorry, I thought you would know. It's when the foal's placenta detaches from the horse's uterus before it's born. It falls out in this red bag thingie." Placing her hands in front of her to demonstrate the size, she added, "If you don't open it up, the foal will die."

Visibly impressed by the story, Sonya did a double-take at her mentee. "Wow, you helped with that?"

"Well, I prayed," she said sheepishly.

The corners of Sonya's lips twitched as she appeared to hold back a laugh. "Well, there you go. You helped with that."

"Oh, and we got to help the town when the flood came through," Maddie added, waving her hand toward all her friends. "We performed triage on several who came in injured. One guy was impaled!"

Sonya's eyes widened. "A flood, too? Boy, you girls went through a lot!"

"Oh, and Sonya, Rachel, and Jade have been leading people to Christ! Even when the PeaceKeepers came and tried to bully them!"

"Oh, that's nothing." Jade interjected. "Maddie here fought the PeaceKeepers and her Grammy stood up and gave them…"

Suddenly nervous over the direction the conversation was taking, she interrupted Jade, "No, I didn't fight them. The warriors of the way rescued us; otherwise, I would probably be back at the PKO."

Sonya leaned forward and placed her hands on both Jade's and Rachel's shoulders as she looked around at them all. "I am stunned, Ladies! The fact that you are standing in front of me, healthy and happy is a clear sign that the Lord is with you. So, one of you tell me what you have learned through this past season."

The girls looked around at each other, uncertain who should go first.

Rachel looked at her friends and said, "You, Maddie. Tell her what we've learned."

She paused. There was so much. She didn't know how she could boil it down to just one thing. Remembering their time at Overlook, she began, "Grammy took us to this place called Wild Rock Overlook. It is this big boulder sticking out of the side of the mountain that overlooks the valley below. We would sit on that boulder and spend hours talking, reading, and praying. In every season, the valley looked different. Spring would bring flowers of all colors. Winter would bring snow. Summer would bring trees as green as the greenest grass, and fall would bring reds, browns, and golds that were so beautiful. Grammy said that the valley was sure to change with the seasons, but our God would never change. She encouraged us to seek him first, to watch and pray, knowing that he was with us no matter where we went. She prayed Psalm 91 over us every time we went and taught us how to intercede for others. I guess we learned just that, partnering with God in intercession." Pausing to make sure she didn't forget anything, she asked, "Would y'all agree?"

Each girl looked at their friend and nodded. Rachel nodded her head once again, overwhelmed with emotion. "Yes, that's it."

"Girl, what is wrong with you?" Jade asked in pure Jade fashion. "You've been crying more than a baby who needs a diaper change."

Throwing a wadded-up napkin at her friend, Maddie

placed her head on Rachel's shoulder in solidarity. She could empathize with Rachel's response. She, too, was filled with joy over all God was doing.

"Well, it sounds to me as if God is moving through each of you," Sonya said, ignoring Jade's insult. "You are all mighty warriors. Speaking of mighty warriors, Ladies, meet my son, Isaiah, and his friend, Marvin. Isaiah, Marvin, this is Rachel, Maddie, Emma, and Jade."

Emma's eyes grew big as saucers as she said, "Marvin!"

After Emma released him from her bear hug, he asked, "Where have you been? I looked everywhere after the fires."

"Oh, we went to Wild Rock," she said as she blushed.

Happy over the surprise reunion, Maddie watched as Jade's countenance suddenly changed. Straightening her shoulders so she could reach her full height, Jade was several inches shorter than Sonya's son, Isaiah. A giggle bubbled up inside as her friend stared at him, rubbing her hand self-consciously through her short hair.

Isaiah seemed to have eyes for their friend, too. He had to break free from staring long enough to shake each of their hands. His handshake was quite strong.

Sonya broke the tension by asking, "Isaiah, would you please grab that box for me and give it to Ms. Ruby?"

He nodded as he answered most deliberately, "Yes, ma'am."

As he turned away, Rachel burst out laughing.

Sonya lifted an eyebrow and joined her.

"That's rude. He might hear you!" Jade said, crossing her arms in feigned anger.

"Jade, if you could see your face right now!" Rachel said as she covered her mouth.

"Don't look at me, look at Emma!" She said as Marvin walked away with his friend.

Sonya looked at Jade and Emma with a wink and said, "Just don't break their hearts."

Afterward, the girls split up so they could set up for lunch. Concerned over Rachel's earlier response to her sharing Wild

Rock with Sonya, Maddie walked over to Rachel.

"Hey, can we talk?"

"Sure," she said, walking around the table to join her friend.

Are you okay?" Maddie asked as she hopped onto the knee wall. "Jade's right, you have been emotional lately."

Sitting next to her friend, Rachel said, "I'm just so proud of you, all of you. Who would've thought we would be here, now?"

Wanting to know for sure that her friend was okay, she looked at Rachel and asked, "So, you're not sad?"

Rachel's face broke into a wide grin as she bumped shoulders with her friend. "Maddie, remember what Grammy said? We've got bottles in Heaven, so it's okay to cry. Don't let anyone take that away from you."

As she debriefed the night, Maddie found herself suddenly without words. When she didn't have the words, she found that drawing stirred her thoughts. Opening her journal, she sketched a river with trees, a rock overlook, and her favorite Carolina Wren. She smiled as she heard the very words she yearned for.

Father,

I don't know what to say. I am in awe of the miracles you have blessed us with this year. Life hasn't been easy, but you have been there every step of the way. Grammy always said that if we wanted to see you, to just look up. Your glory is all around us, and she was right. Thank you for the baptisms and for allowing us to see Sonya. Thank you for Pastor Chris and all the WTL is inviting us into. Thank you for the honor of

*serving you and watching you move. Thank you
for my friends who have taught me that it's
okay to feel.*

*God, I don't know what tomorrow will bring, but
I pray for your strength for all of us. As Grammy
always prayed, please go before us, and
prepare the way you have for us to go with your
loving eye upon us.*

*And when you see Grammy, please give her a
hug from me. I sure do miss her.*

I trust you, Lord, Amen

Sitting at the desk loaned to him by his father-in-law, David had the drawings of the PKO laid out before him. As he made a list of all the locations and their respective coordinates, his phone buzzed on the desk.

Annoyed by the interruption, he tapped the phone and said, "David Bennett here."

"Mr. Bennett, my name is Representative Michael Keel. I was present for your testimony before the Georgia General Assembly."

Confused over the call, David put his pen down and leaned back in the office chair. "What can I do for you, Representative Keel?"

"I was moved by your testimony and wanted to thank You and your family for sacrificing much for this nation. I want to know how I can help."

Sitting up straight in the chair, David made a fist in elated surprise. Only, he wasn't sure how to answer the representative. "Well, Sir, I believe the Governor made clear his desire. Repeal the Kindness Tax bill and give the city back their freedom."

"I'm sorry, Mr. Bennett, but I cannot do that. I can; however…"

"Why?!" David interrupted, pounding his fist on the desk.

"Mr. Bennett, please understand. There's more here than meets the eye."

Calm, David, he told his racing heart. Suddenly realizing the man's first name, David asked, "Representative Keel, may I call you Michael?"

"Of course."

"My son's name is Michael. You know, he was a hostage to Lucien Baldur. He was lied to and coerced into a cult that trafficks the vulnerable for selfish gain."

"I am so sorry, Mr. Bennett."

David could hear the compassion in the man's voice, but his thoughts were clouded by frustration. He couldn't understand why people didn't get that this man was pure evil! "Do you have children, Michael?" He asked.

Michael sighed as he said, "I do, I have a daughter."

Good, let him feel the helplessness! David thought. A deep desire for retaliation burned in his chest. "How old is your daughter, Michael?"

"She's sixteen."

Two years younger than Maddie. *Careful, David.* "My daughter was fifteen when she was kidnapped by Lucien Baldur's PeaceKeepers." He responded sarcastically. "Do you want to know how, Representative Keel?"

"How-how?" He asked timidly.

Guilt tore at David's heart. Running his hand through his hair, he leaned back and closed his eyes. The last thing he wanted to do was manipulate this man into doing his bidding. *That was Lucien Baldur's MO, not his.* Taking a deep breath, he said, "I'm sorry, Representative Keel, that was wrong of me. You asked how you can help. The General Assembly is meeting next week to repeal this bill. The governor asked me to share my story, which I have done. I don't need to go into specifics with you. You can look them up if you so choose.

They are public record. But I will leave you with this. For every parent who sits on the assembly, they too are in danger of finding themselves in Lucien Baldur's crosshairs. The last three years have been filled with suffering for my family, but they've also been filled with something else."

"What's that?" Michael asked.

Suddenly noticing a picture of his family set on the corner of the desk, he picked up the frame and said, "Joy." The truth of the matter hit him square in the chest. "We've learned to trust one another and to trust God as we face the evil of the PKO. We don't have to be afraid of Lucien Baldur or the PeaceKeepers, and Michael, neither do you. God has us all in the palm of his hand." As he hung up the phone, a weight seemed to lift as he looked closely at the drawings in front of him. Folding them up, he knew what he had to do.

Worship in the Storm

On the next Saturday, the girls showed up at the park early. After prayer walking the five blocks around the park, they set up for WTL Freedom Days. At first, adrenaline surged through Maddie over the thought that they were taking Atlanta back for God, but then the humidity set in. Pulling at the collar of her t-shirt for the hundredth time, she attempted to cool off so she could get her mind off the stickiness and focus on preparing for the people. Fanning her face, she looked at her friends, who appeared to be just as miserable.

Suddenly, Emma broke out with a big grin and began to sing. Worship was Emma's love language. From the first moment Maddie had watched her lead worship at church, she knew. What took her a hot minute was learning that it was hers, too.

When Maddie first learned to worship, she felt very self-conscious. Everyone at Rachel's church would lift their hands and look up to the ceiling. *Why?* She would wonder as she tried to figure out what they were looking at. When Grammy took them to Wild Rock Overlook, she would watch her Gram yell, pace, and sing to the Lord. "Ya wanna be a woman after God's own heart?" She would ask. "Worship like David." Then she would read the words of David in Psalm 63:1-5:

"Because your love is better than life, my

lips will glorify you. I will praise you as long
as I live, and in your name I will lift up my
hands. I will be fully satisfied as with the
richest of foods; with singing lips my mouth
will praise you."

God's love was better than life. As she joined in her
friend's worship, she couldn't help but smile. Suddenly, the
damp tendrils sticking to her neck weren't such a burden, and
as she looked up to Heaven, she was grateful for this honor
to worship her King. A gentle breeze caressed her cheek as
she closed her eyes to take in the moment. Opening them,
she noticed the leaves on the cherry blossoms swaying. She
was growing accustomed to these little blessings from the
Lord.

As she helped Emma place daisies on the tables, she
asked, "Emma, do you miss your parents?"

With a sigh, Emma said, "Yes."

"Do you see yourself going back to Wild Rock?"

Looking longingly at the newly planted garden on the
backside of the park, her friend said, "Honestly, I'm torn. As
much as I want to go back, I feel like I'm needed here."

"Yeah, me too," she said as she straightened the
tablecloth.

"Hey, did I hear that Sonya offered you a job?" Emma
asked.

Maddie brightened up as she said, "Yes! She asked if I
wanted to help her and Jade's mom at Atlanta Memorial
Hospital."

"Wow, that's amazing! What would you be doing?" Emma
asked.

"All I know is patient care. Sonya was impressed when I
talked about the guy who was impaled," she said as she shook
her head. "I never thought I would get a job based on helping
to set a guy's leg and deliver a horse."

"You have a talent."

"What do you mean?"

"Mercy—it's one of your gifts. Mercy builds compassion, which gives you a heart to serve others even in the worst situations. The intercession you extend through Jesus makes it even greater."

"Whoa, I never thought about it like that."

"Yeah, all the gifts God gives us build on each other to strengthen us for the calling he has on our lives. We just have to say yes."

"Em?"

"Yeah?"

"What are your gifts?"

"Hmm, well, my momma says I have the gift of exhortation."

"What is that again? Pastor Chris said I have that, too."

"Encouragement."

Smiling in agreement, she smiled, "Oh yeah, you've got lots of that!"

"I've also been told that I have the gift of helps, which I think everybody has, and the gift of mercy."

"What about the gift of faith?" Maddie asked.

Emma paused as she pulled a dead leaf off the plant in front of her. "I like to think I have the gift of faith; I mean, I believe and all."

Curious over her friend's doubt, she asked, "Why would you think you didn't?"

"Every believer has faith. I mean, if you believe in God and follow him, you have faith in his salvation. But Momma told me once that the gift of faith is special. She said that it's used to encourage God's children."

"What do you mean?"

"How do I explain it?" Emma looked around for something to help her put her thoughts into words. "Do you remember when we were helping the search parties after the flood?"

"Yeah."

"Remember Duke, who led us to Clyde?"

Overwhelmed by the memory, she said, "Oh yeah, that

Great Dane's nose saved Clyde's life. Crazy."

"Maddie, something happened to *you* that day. Do you remember how we met?"

"Oh, please, don't make me," she said with a nervous laugh.

"Come on, now, you know you love me! No, really, though. Ashley was a bully; it was three against one. Maddie, you were covered in fear. On the day we found Clyde, you just weren't. I'll never forget your words."

"What words?" She asked her friend. If truth be known, she barely remembered the details of that day.

"Give me eyes to see. Maddie, you had no idea what we would find, and you prayed for God to give you his eyes to see like him. That is the gift of faith. You showed me that no matter what, God would help us. And here I was, worried about having to rebuild the community garden."

Walking over to her friend, she gave her a side hug. Looking down at the now young woman who had always encouraged her when she was down, she realized it was her turn. "Emma, you have a heart bigger than anyone here. I can't tell you how many times your trust and quiet strength have helped me. If that isn't the gift of faith, then I don't know what is."

"Oh, Maddie!" Emma cried in gratitude.

As the day wore on, the humidity seemed to get worse. Pulling her t-shirt from her sweaty back, Maddie tried to find relief.

Normally, Pastor Chris only taught on Sundays, but after the mass baptism at the Chattahoochee, he was fired up for God to move in the city. About fifty people from the WTL sat on blankets in the grass surrounding them. Crafting a paper fan from a piece of paper on the table, she and her friends took turns fanning each other off.

"What would you do?" He asked. "Shadrach, Meshach,

and Abednigo had been given an edict: Bow down and worship the image of gold or die." Pastor Chris leaned against the short wall behind him as he let the people chew on his words.

"We would fight!" Someone shouted from the crowd.

"Fight, how? You have a king who is the greatest king of all. He has more gold than all of us here will have in our lifetimes. He has more power and subjects who will overpower you in a New York minute."

"We could pray," a woman from behind them said.

"Okay, Lori, that's good. Prayer is always our first response. Let's read what our boys did next."

As Pastor Chris read from Daniel three, Maddie was reminded of her Grammy's words to the PeaceKeepers.

"Could you say those words?" Pastor Chris asked. "We do not need to defend ourselves. Who can tell me why?" He asked.

"Because God is their Defender!" Jade shouted.

"Yes! God is their Defender, and so what did they do?"

Maddie knew the answer to that question. "They said that they would not serve the gods or worship the image the king set up."

"Yes, and what is that, Maddie?"

"A stand. They took a stand for God."

"That's right. What do you think they sacrificed by doing so?"

A boy in the front who didn't look much older than Maddie and her friends said, "They could have lost their lives."

"Last week, we watched as many of you were willing to lay down your old life for the new life you have in Christ through baptism. When we choose to follow Jesus, we don't do so lightly. There will be sacrifice. But watch what happens next to our boys."

As Pastor Chris read, his tempo increased until he shouted, "Look! I see four men walking around in the fire, unbound and unharmed, and the fourth looks like a son of the gods!"

"Jade, tell me who was with our boys in the furnace."

"Jesus!" She exclaimed.

"That's right—Jesus. Friends, we are going to walk through the fire. It's not if, but when. Shadrach, Meshach, and Abednigo chose to walk through the fire because they knew their Defender was with them. Listen to these words again, 'If we are thrown into the blazing furnace, the God we serve is able to deliver us from it, and he will deliver us from Your Majesty's hand. But even if he does not…' Shadrach, Meshach, and Abednigo chose that day whom they would serve. They knew Jesus would be with them even if it meant death. Can you say those words? Are you willing to lay down your life for Jesus? When you are asked to bow down to the system, will you be able to stand?"

The crowd was quiet as Maddie pondered her Gram's last words to her, *"There isn't any room for fear. You've got to be ready. Carry the shield of faith and the sword of the Spirit, knowing that it's yours to carry. God gave it to you to use in the battle and know that Jesus will be with you, just like he was with them."* It's not if, but when.

As Pastor Chris prayed, people came forward. Maddie slipped out to pray over those who wanted a fresh encounter with Jesus. She loved these moments. Connecting a person in pain to the One who would heal and deliver them was one of the greatest honors of her life.

As the number of people standing in line dwindled, murmurings arose in the crowd as a convoy of trucks passed by. Men all in black were carrying guns and looking straight at them.

Maddie shivered as she saw the dreaded black flag with an upside-down cross overlaid by a bolt of lightning. "Don't stop, don't stop, don't stop," she whispered, but to no avail. She watched as they stopped in front of the park and hopped out.

It happened so quickly. One moment they were praying, the next, a circle of men surrounded the little church and their people. The men began tapping their feet in unison,

"NO ORDER, NO PEACE, NO ORDER, NO PEACE." The mantra started as a whisper and grew to a shrill pitch until they stopped. Suddenly, the group parted to allow none other than Carissa Blackwell through.

"Good afternoon, Pastor. It's been a while since we've taken up a collection. We thought it was time to pay a friendly visit."

"What is she doing here?" Jade asked, fuming.

Maddie looked at her friend. Rachel shook her head when Jade attempted to move.

"Does anyone find it ironic that we were just talking about this?" Rachel whispered.

Carissa walked to the front. Turning to the people, she asked, "What, no collection plate? Tsk, tsk, tsk. You just don't care about the people who are suffering, do you? So much for giving to the widow and the orphan." Turning to Pastor Chris, she said, "What kind of church are you running here, Pastor?"

Everyone stayed perfectly still as she walked through the crowd. Maddie got the impression they had been through this before.

"You, what's your name?" Carissa asked.

"John, my name is John," he stuttered.

"Say the words, John."

John looked around the church. The pleading in his eyes broke her heart. Shaking her head, she whispered, "Don't do it, John. Don't do it."

As John noticed her movement, he looked at her and gave a weak smile. She had just prayed for strength for him when he came forward, not even fifteen minutes ago. "Please, God, give him strength." She whispered under her breath again.

Noticing John's weak smile sent her way, Carissa searched the crowd to see who he was looking at. When she locked eyes with her, Maddie's heart sank.

To take out the PKO's communications would be a monumental feat. There was no way he could do it alone. Picking up the phone to call Mordecai, he hoped his friend would answer.

"Shalom, David! I was hoping to hear from you today." Mordy sounded a little too giddy for David's liking.

"Is everything okay?" David asked. The background noise coming through the phone was unnerving.

"Everything is happening just as Yeshua said. We just need to stand in this hour and worship through the storm."

"Have Helel and Lucien Baldur taken control of the city?" David asked.

"They think they have, but Yeshua is coming. Have you procured a copy of the blueprints we discussed?"

"I did."

"Good, and so Project Shutdown begins. It will be Adonai who will end the enemy's reign of terror, but we can help slow the enemy down a bit."

David smiled at his friend's weak attempt at humor.

"I spoke to my buddy at Magnum Lock. He was able to get me the names of the ISPs serving the PKO facilities around the world."

"How many are there?" Mordy asked.

"Three, and thankfully, there is only one command center."

"What, no redundancy? And I thought Mr. Baldur was resourceful." Mordy said ironically. "Where is this command center?"

"You won't believe it," David said with a pause.

"Let me guess. Jerusalem."

"Yes, it appears he's setting up his command in your city."

Mordecai laughed. "David, did I not tell you? Helel wants the world to believe he is the Mashiach. Of course, he would set up his command here. So, when are you coming?"

"I need to make some arrangements. I will call you soon."

"Excellent, my Friend. Be blessed in the Lord, Shalom."

CHAPTER 28

The Fiery Furnace

An evil look of delight crossed Carissa's face as she left John and walked toward her. "Well, well, well, Ms. Bennett, We meet again. Everyone, please welcome my friend, Maddie Bennett!"

Raucous applause erupted from the PeaceKeepers as they stood in perfect circular formation. Then the booming sound abruptly stopped.

Rachel and Emma each grabbed a hand and squeezed.

"Oh, and look, her friends are here, too. Jade, let me look at those hands."

Jade immediately curled her fingertips into her hand.

"No? You don't want me to look at your precious fingernails? Tsk, tsk, tsk. Not very neighborly, are we?"

Turning to Maddie, Carissa stared with her green cat-like eyes. If they were lasers, she would have a hole through her right now.

As she stared into the calculated smile of the woman responsible for her PKO kidnapping, she wondered if this woman had anything to do with Lucien Baldur. The way she heard her dad talk about him, she expected so.

"This little woman and her friends thought they had outsmarted us, Men! Here we sheltered them and provided for their every need, and they just left without a word. That was so rude, Maddie!"

"Boooo!" The PeaceKeepers shouted.

"Don't you girls know that the PKO is for the people? We will provide for your needs!"

As she and her friends held to one another tightly, Carissa looked down at their clasped hands with a look of disgust.

"I think it's time for you Ladies to bow. You had your chance to be part of our mission, but you decided you wanted your Jesus instead. Well, today you will choose whom you will serve. Say the words, Maddie!"

Carissa laughed with contempt as she and her friends stood perfectly still. The PeaceKeepers jeered and laughed in agreement with their leader.

Shouts of "Say it! Say it!" rang in Maddie's ear.

Suddenly serious, Carissa motioned for quiet. Looking around the group of churchgoers with slanted eyes, she said, "Where is he? Where is this Jesus you worship? I don't see him! Do you, Men?"

"NOOOOOO!" They shouted.

Carissa walked back to the girls and stood directly in front of her.

Maddie tried to focus on an errant hair hanging near Carissa's ear. Suddenly, she looked into her eyes and realized this woman was lost.

"Jesus is right here, Carissa, and he loves you, too."

Carissa's eyes winced in pain. Then her face became a block of stone as she yelled, "Will your Jesus save you now?"

The dream she had months ago suddenly crossed her mind. Continuing to glare into Carissa's green uncompromising eyes, she tried to remember the details. There was something she had to do. *Didn't I sneeze? What does that have to do with anything?* She prayed silently. The soft, gentle voice spoke inside her mind.

Bless her, Maddie.

Surely, she heard wrong. Trying not to show the shock she

felt inside, the voice once more whispered:

Bless your enemy.

Confused over the command, she suddenly had a picture of her Grammy standing in front of the church. *What was it she said? Oh, yes!*

"Carissa Blackwell, my name is Maddie Ruth Bennett, and I want you to look at me. I am a servant of El Shaddai, Almighty God. My Lord and King is Jesus Christ, and there is nobody on this earth who will change that. My allegiance is to him. Now that we've gotten that out of the way, I would like to bless you. May the Lord bless you and keep you. May he make his face to shine upon you and be gracious to you. May he turn his face to you and give you, his peace."

With that, she stood quiet and still. She was shaking so hard, she had to bite her tongue to keep her teeth from chattering. Determined not to show fear, she continued to stare into Carissa's eyes as she saw something change. Her face seemed to soften for a moment. Maddie could have sworn she saw something akin to compassion cross her face, and then she heard it.

"Those who dwell in the shelter of the Most High will rest in the shadow of the Almighty. I will say of the Lord my God, you are my Refuge and my Fortress, my God in whom I trust."

As Rachel and her friends recited Psalm 91, the others joined in. Carissa suddenly looked nervous as she looked around at the faces turned up to Heaven. "Shut up!" She yelled. But the chorus of worship just grew louder and louder until they broke into song.

Even the PeaceKeepers were caught off guard. They didn't know what to do with these people who were holding hands and worshiping the God of Heaven.

Then, it happened. The rainclouds that had threatened all day let loose their rain in a powerful deluge. It was obvious to the church that this was not planned as the PeaceKeepers suddenly broke formation and ran toward their trucks. While the church continued to sing, Maddie looked around. She could see Jesus on the faces of each person as water poured down each face. It was glorious. *This is worship*. She thought.

A tug on her sleeve broke the moment as Pastor Chris said. "We need to leave, Maddie." As he pointed to the sky, she could see a dark raincloud swirling above them.

Everyone worked double time to pack everything in the van. As they jumped in and shut the doors, the rain started.

"Whew, that was close!" Jade said. "Maddie, THAT was straight Fire! Grammy would be so proud!"

It didn't take long before the rain was coming down in buckets. Maddie's weak smile was followed up by her stomach doing somersaults as hail started to fall on the van. As the wind picked up, the girls watched as trees on either side of the street bent in unnatural positions. Everything seemed to be coming at them from all directions.

Pastor Chris drove up to the opening to Underground and said, "Quick, Girls, I want you to run carefully down to the apartment."

"What do you mean, what's wrong?" Emma asked.

"Just do it, okay? I'll park the van and be right behind you."

Emma's face was pale as she asked, "Do you promise?"

"Go!" He yelled.

As they jumped out of the van and ran to the stairs, the slicing rain was coming down so hard that they couldn't see five feet in front of them. Hail pelted them like hard little snowballs. Carefully descending the stairs, the girls turned the corner and found shelter. With shaky hands, Jade pulled out her keys and attempted to unlock her door. Dropping the keys, she began to cry as they heard the sound. It was like a freight train so loud that Emma had to cover her ears. Rachel grabbed Jade's keys and unlocked the door. Pushing everyone in, she shut the door and locked the deadbolt behind them.

"Find a pillow and get in the bathroom," she said as she grabbed one herself.

The girls each grabbed a pillow and piled into the small bathroom. Jade and Emma crouched into the tub while Rachel and Maddie sat next to the commode and closed the door. Suddenly, the lights went out as everything went deathly still.

"What's happening?" Emma asked.

"It's a tornado," Rachel said nervously. "Maddie, can you please pray?"

Shaking, she realized this was her first tornado. Honestly, she wasn't sure what to say. She had heard about them on the news but...

"Maddie, please pray!" Rachel repeated.

Father God,

We need you. Please, God, send your angels to protect Pastor Chris and the church. Please protect us, Lord, as we sit in this tiny bathroom. We don't know what to do, Lord, but our eyes are on you.

As she prayed, the others joined in with their own whispered prayers. Emma rocked as she began to sing the song she wrote from the Lord's Prayer.

After repeating the song, a time or two, she and her friends joined in. There was just something about worship that seemed to calm even the storm in their hearts. They just sang the song over and over until everything quieted. The lights flickered on for a moment and then went back off.

"Is it over?" Jade asked.

"I think so," Rachel said. "Maddie, open the bathroom door, slowly. Be careful. Y'all, remember what Ms. Laura said, situational awareness, look around at your surroundings."

As she slowly opened the door, she peered into the dark living space. Her anxious thoughts were going haywire, but she was determined to keep moving forward. Thankful for the encouraging message in fluorescent paint on the concrete wall, she squinted to look around the apartment.

"Well, that's helpful," Rachel said as she noticed the paint.

"Yeah, apparently, it's a thing when you live underground. I haven't had to use it until now," Jade added as she bit her lower lip.

As the girls walked into the apartment, Jade breathed a sigh of relief. "We made it," she said.

"Yeah, but what's outside that door?" Emma asked.

The girls looked at each other, unsure if they wanted to know.

"Come on, let's pray again," Rachel said as she prayed over them and for those outside of the apartment. As Rachel finished praying, a heavy knock on the door caused each of them to jump.

"Jade, Girls, are you alright?" The knock turned to pounding as Pastor Chris called their names from outside.

Jade opened the door to see Pastor Chris, soaked, blood trickling down his forehead.

"Are you okay?" Rachel asked as she pulled him into the apartment.

"I'm okay," he said, "but there are others."

"Here, let me get that for you," Maddie said as she grabbed a washcloth and some water and put pressure on his forehead.

"Ouch!" He yelped.

"Sorry. Just hold it, I'll get some peroxide. Jade, you do have peroxide?"

"What's that?" Jade asked.

"Your mom is a nurse, and you don't know?"

Jade shrugged her shoulders as she looked blankly at her friend. "If I have it, I'm sure Mom put it in the medicine cabinet."

Rustling through the cabinets in the bathroom, she sighed with relief as she found what she was looking for. "Yes!" A bottle of hydrogen peroxide, a bag of cotton balls, and a first aid kit later, she went back into the living space to clean Pastor Chris' forehead.

After placing a Band-Aid on his head, she put two fingers in front of his eyes and asked how many she was holding.

"Twelve," he said with a puny laugh.

"That's not funny, Pastor," she said authoritatively. "How many?"

"Two," he said with a snort.

Feeling his forehead for contusions, she said, "Okay, I don't feel any bumps, does this hurt?"

"Ouch!"

"Okay, it hurts. Jade, can you please get me a bag of vegetables or something?"

"Vegetables, really?" Jade asked.

"Ice, do you have ice?"

"Ice, I have."

"Okay, get a couple of cubes of ice and put them in a small plastic bag. Crunch them up into small pieces."

"Do I crunch up the ice before or after I put it in the bag?"

"After?" Maddie said sharply.

"Hey, you don't have to be snarky. I'm just trying to help!"

"Do you have a headache, Pastor Chris?" She asked.

"No more than normal," he said with a grin.

Giving him her best mom look, she said, "You are not a very nice patient," as she looked at his ears and nose. "How about dizziness? Ringing in the ears?"

"Nope, the only ringing in these ears is the sound of Def Leppard being played in my neighbor's apartment at all hours of the night."

"I would say you're fine, but if you start to get dizzy or if your headache gets worse, we need to get help, okay?"

"Yes, ma'am!" He said with a salute.

"Wow, you did good, Maddie. You're going to do great at the hospital," Rachel said.

"Pastor Chris, should we go outside or stay in here?" Jade asked. "I'm kinda worried about my mom. Can I go check to see if she's home?"

"Yes, but let's go together. Do you have a flashlight?"

"That, I do. Under the kitchen sink," she said.

"Okay, Girls, put on a jacket with a hood. Maddie, bring the first aid kit and grab some baggies and a cooler of ice in case we need it."

"I don't have a cooler, but I have a big water cup. "Will that work?"

"That'll do. If you have two, fill them both with ice."

"Okay."

As the five ventured into the hallway, everything looked normal. Those who were sheltered in their apartments emerged to check on one another.

As they made it to Ms. Alisha's apartment, Jade did not look well. Knocking on the door timidly, her lips and chin were trembling as she looked at her friends helplessly. Knocking a second time, this time louder, she began to jump up and down nervously as she did when she was afraid.

"It's okay, Jade. She's okay, I know it," Emma said confidently.

Suddenly, the door opened wide, and Alisha grabbed her daughter and cried, "I was so worried," she said.

Maddie breathed a sigh of relief as the two wept together.

"Girls, we need to make some rounds. Who wants to come with?" Pastor Chris asked.

"I'll go!" She said as she raised her hand.

"Me, I'll go," Rachel said.

"Let me grab my bag and my glasses," Ms. Alisha said as she went back into the apartment.

Giving Ms. Alisha a look, he said, "Grab a jacket, it's pretty rough outside."

As they ascended the stairs, Maddie couldn't believe her eyes. There was metal everywhere. Power lines covered the streets while trees had been pulled completely out of the ground by the roots. Thoughts of her family crossed her mind. There was no way she could get to them.

"This is terrible," Jade said.

As they walked up the street, worry turned to dread as they saw so much destruction.

Emma grabbed her hand as she said, "Give us eyes to see, God."

David was angry. His plans were falling apart. "Where is Maddie?" He asked for the hundredth time. "I thought they were at the park!"

Wes stood stock still before him, looking completely defeated. "I think she's back at the apartment, Sir."

"Why aren't you with her?" David asked.

"We left during their worship service, Sir. We were coming right back."

"You were coming right back, and now they are where?"

"We went back to the park, and everything was gone. They must've gone back to the apartment before the storm rolled in."

"Okay, okay, I'm sorry, Wes. Thank you both. I know you're doing the best you can do. Do you think we can drive to Underground?"

"Honestly, I'm not sure, but we can try."

"Okay, let's do it."

C H A P T E R   29

My Source of Strength

Maddie couldn't believe her eyes. The destruction in Wild Rock was small compared to what they saw as they walked around the Underground compound. Pastor Chris was insistent on going first, warning them not to step on any downed power lines. Trees had either been completely uprooted or snapped in two. Debris in the form of glass, bricks, wood, and metal had been thrown around like toys in a playroom. Cars had been flipped over like matchbox cars.

"Pastor Chris, there's a car on fire!" Jade yelled as they turned to make their way up Martin Luther.

"Okay," he said as he turned back.

"Should we put it out?" She asked desperately.

"Jade, Hon, we don't have anything to put it out with," Her mom said as she tried to calm her daughter.

"Girls, we need to look for people. Focus."

It was obvious that he was taking them in a circle around the compound, and now she could see why. The plaza on Central Avenue behind Underground was full of people who had made their way to a public space.

"Come on," he yelled behind him as he started to run.

"I'm not sure the ice is going to make it," Jade said to Rachel.

As Maddie looked at all the people, panic began to set in. "There are too many," she said to Ms. Alisha.

"One at a time, Maddie. That's all we can do. Focus on

289

one at a time. Look for surface injuries. If you see someone struggling to breathe or gushing blood, have one of the girls come get me." Walking forward to find the first injured person, Alisha began to perform triage. As she bent down to help, Ms. Alisha said, "No, Maddie, go find someone else." Turning to the patient, she asked their name and opened her bag. Realizing her charge was not leaving, she repeated. "Go. You can do it," she said with an encouraging smile.

"Come on, Maddie. We'll do this together," Jade encouraged.

The girls split into groups of two. Rachel and Emma walked around writing down names with physical characteristics, address, phone number, and location. Maddie and Jade worked together to triage the person in front of them. As Maddie assessed the person in front of her, Jade began crushing ice into baggies, just as she did for Pastor Chris. They worked together to clean up any wounds and determine if they needed to tell Jade's mom about any life-threatening injuries.

Minutes turned to hours as they worked. Thankfully, they weren't the only ones. Sonya, Isaiah, Marvin, and a doctor friend were also helping those in their path.

When her dad showed up, she thought she would collapse. "Daddy!" She said as she ran into his arms.

"Ruthie, I've been looking for you everywhere. Are you okay?"

"Yes, Sir, we're just helping people who are injured."

Her dad looked around. *He looks tired, too,* she thought.

"Who's in charge here?" He asked.

"Sonya and Ms. Alisha are over there," she pointed. "Pastor Chris is over…" Looking around, she saw him crouched down, praying over a man who was lying on the grass. "He is over there."

"I'll talk to your pastor," he said, his stern expression firm and unyielding. "Keep helping these people, and I'll see you in a bit."

Worry over her family overwhelmed her. She didn't want

to ask, but felt she had to. "Hey Dad, is everybody okay?"

He nodded with a smile that didn't quite reach his eyes. "Yes, Grandpa Jack's house was spared. Everything around it is a mess, though. This is going to take weeks to clean up." He kissed her briefly on her forehead and went to talk to Pastor Chris.

Looking at the old woman in front of her, she sat on the grass in front of her and gave a weak smile, asking her name. "Why, my name is Grace, little Girl. And what's yours?"

Tilting her head, she realized this woman could be her Gram. Strength, she didn't know she had, rose from within. Grabbing a handful of cotton balls and the bottle of peroxide, she said, "My name is Maddie." Pouring peroxide on her hand, she couldn't help but chuckle under her breath. "My Grammy's name was Grace, too," she said.

"You don't say. Well, somebody tole me once that grace means favor or blessin'. You're Grammy must've been quite a blessin' to ya."

As she pushed the woman's hair away to assess the laceration on her head, she said, "Yes, ma'am, she was."

Maddie was encouraged by the people who sat in the park looking for help. Everyone was so nice and those uninjured were helpful to those who were. *It's like Wild Rock,* she thought.

As the day became evening, Sonya walked over with Ms. Alisha and asked her, "Tired?"

"Exhausted," she answered honestly.

"There's a group of men from the compound who've been working to clean up debris. One of the guys checked the wires on the ground with a voltage tester. It looks like the power has been shut off at the source. Alisha and I are going to the hospital. Do you have the strength for round two?" Sonya asked.

She had never felt so tired before, but this wasn't a time to give in to the weariness. Encouraged by Jade's nod, she said, "Sure, let's do it. Are you going too, Jade?"

"Yeah, we'll snag Rach and Emma too."

"Okay."

◆◆◆

What did I get myself into? Maddie asked herself as she looked at the hospital gurneys crowding the hallway. Atlanta Memorial Hospital was a huge hospital, with almost a thousand beds, according to Ms. Alisha. She wasn't sure that any hospital had enough beds to help all these people.

"Remember, one at a time," Ms. Alisha said when she saw her face. "Here, eat this," she said as she gave her a sandwich and a juice box. "You're going to need your strength. And here, this time we wear gloves," she added as she handed her a gown and a pair of gloves.

Embarrassment filled her when she realized she had not worn any as she helped those in the plaza.

"Ya gotta do, what ya gotta do," Ms. Alisha said, reading her thoughts. "Go eat and we'll meet up here."

After gulping down the sandwich and the juice box, she felt better. Taking a deep breath, she walked into the bathroom. Looking into the mirror, she realized she was a hot mess. After re-adjusting her ponytail into a bun, she took some towels to wipe down her neck and face, and then washed her hands. Afterward, she made her way into the hallway and inhaled deeply. Antiseptic, mixed with what Maddie thought could only be death, teased her nostrils, which motivated her to jump into action. She wondered if it always smelled like this in the hospital. "Is this really where you want me, God?" She prayed as she looked down the hallway. The soft gentle voice that always encouraged her in moments like this said:

Look for the love, Maddie.

She nodded as she resolved to do just that. It wouldn't be long before she found it. A young nurse, not much older than she, was helping a little boy. His mom was looking worriedly at her son as the boy looked up in admiration at the nurse. The nurse chatted as if this little boy were the only person in her world.

The girls worked with Alisha and Sonya well into the night. Maddie took mental notes of each patient as she prayed for them. She wanted to remember each moment. She didn't know if she would have the chance to write about them all in her journal, but she hoped she would have the opportunity.

The next morning, as the sun peeked through the windows, Sonya said, "You girls need to go home."

"What about you guys?" Rachel asked with a yawn.

"Our shift will end in a bit. Go home, eat some breakfast, take a shower, and you can come back tonight."

Confused, the girls looked at one another.

Emma took charge and asked what everyone else was thinking. "Um, how do we get there?"

"Pastor Chris is waiting in the hallway. He'll take you home."

Relieved, they made their way to the pastor.

Heaviness filled the van as they made their way to Jade's apartment. The organized chaos of the hospital seemed so far away as they gazed at the destruction on the streets.

"Pastor Chris, were you here when the PeaceKeepers burned everything down?" She asked.

"I was," he said.

With bloodshot eyes, she looked at him and mumbled, "Did it look this bad?"

Pastor Chris placed his hand on her shoulder and said, "Yeah, it was bad. But remember—God is in it. He makes all things for the good of those who love him."

"How did he make the fires good?" Jade asked bitterly.

"You're here, aren't you?" He answered with a smile.

After their showers, the girls dropped into bed. Maddie fell asleep with those words on her tongue.

Moments later, or so it seemed, Rachel was urging them awake.

The next night was another chaotic mess. They had the opportunity to take a break midway, for which Maddie was thankful. As she sat with Sonya sipping on a lukewarm cup of burned coffee, she asked, "Sonya, how are you so strong for others when so many hard things are going on around you?"

"I go to the Source," Sonya said.

Confused over her mentor's answer, she asked, "What do you mean, the Source?"

"I am a vessel for my God—as long as I stay connected to him and allow his Spirit to pour into me, well, I have all I need to pour out to those in front of me."

But what are you pouring out?" Maddie asked.

Sonya looked seriously into her eyes as she said, "'Whoever believes in me, as Scripture has said, rivers of living water will flow from within them.' The living Water is God's Spirit—out of his Spirit comes fruit. The more you receive God's Spirit and the fruit he pours out, the greater the harvest of fruit." Pointing to the water once more, she said, "See the water as love. As you receive, love overflows out of you. As you give it away, God's Spirit pours out more."

"Wow, that's pretty cool."

"Yeah. Maddie, I'm not gonna lie, I am not strong on my own power. Only with God's help can I do anything, but through Christ I can do all things he calls me into."

Maddie nodded. She knew Sonya was right. The truth was, she had been thinking a lot about Jacob lately. She hated to even think about it, but guilt still plagued her. She wasn't sure she could pour out anything. Unfortunately, she couldn't talk to Rachel, and she didn't feel like Emma or Jade would understand. And there was no way she could tell her mom. She wished she had told Grammy before... Shaking her head as she tried to take her thoughts captive, she realized Sonya was the only one she could confide in. What a mess, she thought. "Hey, Sonya?"

"Yeah."

"There's something kinda personal I was wanting to ask."

Looking at her curiously, Sonya took a sip of coffee as she awaited her question.

After taking a deep breath to calm her nerves, Maddie just spit it out. "What does God say about kissing boys?"

Choking on her coffee, Sonya stuttered as she regained composure. "You girls and your questions." After clearing her throat, she said, "Well, the Bible encourages purity and discourages intimacy that leads to sexual immorality."

Shame covered Maddie as she swallowed the lump in her throat that was threatening. "Sexual immorality? Like making out?"

Sonya chuckled quietly and then thought better of it as she covered her mouth. Resting her hand on Maddie's, she asked, "What is this about?"

"Well, I kissed Jacob, but it wasn't just kissing." Looking down at her lap, she added, "There were a lot of...hands."

Sonya lowered her face so Maddie could look her in the eye. "Did you give him permission to kiss you?"

"I did, but I didn't know it would be like that," she said quickly. Humiliated, she clasped her hands as she looked toward the kitchen refrigerator.

"Maddie, look at me. Do you feel guilty over what happened?" Sonya asked.

Nodding, she clasped her hands even tighter.

"Sweet Girl, this is a safe place, got it?"

Maddie nodded again, doing everything she could to hold back tears.

"God created man and woman and drew them together; the Word says that he made them one flesh—marriage. This union is sacred, intimacy is sacred. Culture may say otherwise, but it is God's way that matters. Maddie, when you choose to wait until marriage, you are saving this intimate act for your husband."

Maddie's voice cracked as tears began to fall. "I didn't." Shaking her head, she hung her head as she repeated, "Sonya, I didn't wait."

Sonya reached across the table to grab Maddie's hand. "Oh, Sweetie, do you know how much Jesus loves you? He knows you better than you know yourself."

"But I want to follow him, and I've messed everything up! How can he ever pour anything into me?" Quiet sobs racked Maddie's body as she sat in shame. *What have I done?*

Sonya sat still as she squeezed her hand. Waving someone away who walked in on their conversation, she quietly sat as Maddie calmed. "Maddie, look at me. There is not one perfect human being on the earth. We will all make choices both knowingly and unknowingly that will lead to guilt. But God does not want us to sit in a place of condemnation. Jesus specifically said that he did not come to condemn the world but that the world would be saved. Do you know what that means?"

"That Jesus came to save us?" A hiccup followed the whispered answer.

"Yes. His sacrifice on the cross set us free from all condemnation, but we have to receive it. When we receive his free gift of grace, he pours into us everything we need to live the life he has called us to. Again, we receive. Do you know how to receive?"

Placing her hands in an open position in front of her, Maddie said, "Surrender?"

A smile brightened Sonya's face as she looked at her charge with empathy. "Yes, we surrender everything we're holding. You know this, we've talked about this before. Not just our pain, but our guilt and our shame. We lay it all down and give it to him. His grace is sufficient, Maddie, do you believe that?"

Nodding, she said, "Yes, I do. He's done so much for me, Sonya. That's why I was so worried I had made him mad, or something."

Tears filled Sonya's eyes as she shook her head. "Girl, I

don't believe God is mad at you. I just think he wants you to come home. To say, I'm tired of following other people and I want to follow you, Jesus. Are you ready to say that?"

"Yes." Nodding her head, she repeated, "Yes, I need him. I'm so tired of being confused and worried and afraid of what other people think."

"Okay, well, let's tell him."

After they prayed, Maddie went back to helping the people who looked at her helplessly, but now, she felt a bolt of renewed purpose. Suddenly, the words of the song she and Emma wrote popped into her head:

God you are faithful.
My source of strength.
Father, I thank you,
For giving me peace.

Giggling at the reminder, she looked at the person in front of her and said, "It all comes around full circle, doesn't it?"

"Huh?" He asked as he looked at her quizzically.

David was on a mission as he and his men helped in the cleanup effort around the city. Everything he planned was falling apart. Or was it?

Disappointment filled him as he considered the plans that he and Mordecai had made to shut down communications between PKO locations might not come to fruition.

It was the perfect plan. Find someone willing to write a program that would re-route communications. It was the perfect virus that would take months to uncover. The echo of his prideful words, "I'm the gatekeeper now," haunted him as he labored to pick up a piece of metal debris.

Apparently, someone higher up had a different plan. As he looked up at the clear blue sky above him, he found it ironic that all the destruction before him was undertaken in less than an hour, fifteen minutes even. It was as if the hand of God had swooped down and carried out locally what would take a month for someone to write in code.

"Ironic," he said as he shook his head.

The only problem—all communications were knocked out. The F3 tornado left a path of destruction in Atlanta and the surrounding counties that would take at least a week to clean up. If there was a silver lining in the dark cloud that had covered the city, it would have to be the pain the PKO was experiencing due to the loss of data operations from a server farm that was destroyed. Lucien Baldur was beating down his father-in-law's door to return the church they had seized to normal operations, but there was no redundancy in the system, and a rebuild of the farm would take months, if not a year, due to material shortages across the nation. "You're powerful, I'll give you that, but couldn't we have narrowed down the pressure points just a bit?" He mumbled under his breath. He just hoped God was listening.

Taking a moment to wipe his brow, he took the cup of water from Wes and thanked him.

"Commander, do you want us to go to the hospital?" Wes asked.

David had told Wes he could drop the formalities, but old habits die hard. "No, if there's anywhere that Maddie's safe, it should be the hospital," David said confidently.

"10-4. By the way, we were able to get through to Tom."

"Really? How did you manage that?"

"We started up the ham radios. It was tricky getting the antennas set up properly, but we were finally able to do so. It helps to know which satellites are active so you can jump on the correct frequency."

"There isn't any chance of the PeaceKeepers listening in, is there?"

"Only if they know the source," Wes said with a laugh.

"Source?" David asked.

"Yeah, you know Tom, if the enemy's listening, he'll make sure he knows who he's listening to."

David chuckled. He knew Tom, it had to be something outrageous. "I'm not sure I want to know."

"Good call," Wes said with a laugh.

"So, what did Tom say?" David asked.

"He was insistent on making his way to Atlanta. I tried to talk him out of it, but you know him."

"Yeah. Logistically, can he make it?"

"He'll find a way."

CHAPTER 30

Rebellion's Curse

A week after the tornado blew into Atlanta, there were still so many people filtering into the hospital. The pace was beginning to wear on Maddie.

As she finished replacing the sheet on a gurney, she heard a voice say, "Hey Girl, there's someone out here asking for you."

"Okay, be right there." After taking a moment to tighten her hair band, she walked toward the intake room. As she turned the corner, she stopped in her tracks as her eyes landed on none other than Jacob Sullivan.

"Hey, Maddie," Jacob said.

The deep Tennessee drawl caused her heart to leap. Absently checking her messy bun again to make sure it was still in place, she looked into his eyes and said, "Hi, Jacob. What are you doing here?"

"Well, I heard you were workin' here and wanted to see ya."

Suddenly, every limb in her body felt heavy. She knew she had a hundred things to do, but only one seemed necessary.

"Aren't you going to school for the army?" She asked. "How did you end up here?"

Placing his hands in his pockets, Jacob shifted his weight as he looked around the room.

She didn't know whether to be embarrassed or giddy over his visible nervousness. After giving the eye to a couple of nosy eavesdroppers listening in, she led him to a private corner.

"I'm on a pass," he said as he followed her.

"Oh, well, I'm kinda working," Maddie said. "Will you still be on a pass later?"

"What time?" He asked.

Looking up at the clock overhead, she said, "Sixish? We'll be going home then."

"Alrighty then, I'll be back." As he prepared to leave, he turned around and said, "Maddie…"

The look on Jacob's face tore at her heart. There was something wrong, but she couldn't put her finger on it. "Yes, Jacob?"

"Never you mind. I'll see ya at six." And with that, Jacob walked out of the hospital.

"What was that all about?" Jade asked.

Looking toward the door, Maddie rubbed her arms in worry. "I don't know, but something feels weird."

"Yeah, I felt it too," Emma said.

After the hospital rooms were tidied, she stood in for the front office clerk so she could take the rest of the afternoon off to be with her son.

At four o'clock, she found herself staring at the clock.

"Ma'am?"

Her thoughts were in a million different places. Deaf to the woman's plea in front of her, she finally broke out of her trance and mumbled, "Huh?"

"Here is my paperwork," the woman said as she handed her the clipboard.

"Oh, um, thank you so much." She smiled at the woman briefly and pointed to the waiting room. "Take a seat, and someone will be with you shortly." The mantra she had repeated numerous times that day was not very fun. She much preferred to be in the back where the action was.

Glancing at the clock again, she groaned inside as she realized that six o'clock was still a whole two hours away.

At six o'clock on the dot, Pastor Chris pulled up to the curb to pick up Maddie and her friends. Standing outside, leaning against the wall, was Jacob, shaving an apple with his pocketknife.

"Maddie, do you want us to go with you?" Rachel asked. A wrinkle in her brow signified her worry.

Maddie shook her head no, embarrassed by her friend's audacious ask.

"Are you sure?" Jade asked. "If he tries anything, I'll karate chop 'im!"

Shaking her head, she said, "Y'all go wait in the van. I'll be right there."

As her friends walked away, she suddenly felt all alone. *Her friends were right there. They were right there!* She encouraged herself. *God, why am I so nervous?*

"Hey Jacob, I only have a minute. My ride is here."

"Oh, okay," he said as he stood up. Walking up to her, he started to put his hand up to move a lock of hair out of her face.

Goosebumps slid along the back of her neck as butterflies in her stomach began to flutter. She took a step back and immediately felt guilty. *Why do I feel this way?* She wondered. "Jacob, are you okay?" She asked.

Lowering his gaze, he took the apple he was peeling and placed it in his pocket. Pretending to follow suit with his other hand, Jacob suddenly lunged and said, "Maddie, I'm so sorry, but I have no choice," as he grabbed her.

"What are you doing?" Time suddenly stood still. She could hear her friends screaming from behind, even as Jacob grabbed and held her close. Fight or flight suddenly kicked in as she drew up her knee and punched Jacob in the belly.

Jacob yelped as he bent over in pain.

Her instincts took over as she turned and ran toward the van. Before she knew it, two men all in black grabbed her by the arms, one of them placing her over their shoulders. As much as she tried to fight, she suddenly went slack as she realized she was quite dizzy. Slumping over the shoulder of the man carrying her, every sense was lost except her hearing the thump of his boots hitting pavement. And then she was out.

Maddie awoke with a huge headache. The cold, hard chair she was sitting in was quite rickety. Shutting her eyes tight, she hoped to wake up from this dream. Deciding to open her eyes, she looked around. "Where is Rachel? God?" She said aloud.

"Well, well, Ms. Bennett. We meet again."

Maddie blinked, trying to wipe away the vision of Carissa Blackwell standing in front of her.

"What do you want?" She asked as she tried to break free from her bonds. Carissa's laugh sent chills down her spine.

"Don't worry, your friends aren't far away. You'll be reunited very soon. First, we need to have a chat, woman to woman." Carissa pulled a chair forward and sat directly in front of her.

Father, give me strength, she prayed as she sat perfectly still. A memory of the look on Carissa's face when she blessed her crossed her mind.

"Maddie, my Dear, I've waited patiently for this day. You and your dad thought you outsmarted us, with that little stunt you pulled in Baldersville. Didn't you? Two long years I had to wait before I could see your pretty little face." With a click of her tongue, she lifted Maddie's chin with her perfectly manicured hand and then released it, as if it were something distasteful. "Well, who's the one in control now?"

She was shaking inside but wasn't going to let this woman get the better of her——not this time. She sat perfectly still as she said, "What do you want, Carissa?"

"Oh, to be young again." She cackled. "I'll bet you believe that you will be rescued by your brave little daddy. Oh, no! Better yet, I'll bet you think you'll be rescued by your Jesus, don't you?"

A wave of compassion covered her. She didn't understand

where it was coming from. "Who hurt you?" She asked.

Carissa jerked back as if a jolt of electricity ran through her body. "What did you say?"

"Who hurt you?" Maddie repeated. "I can see it in your eyes." *And she could, it was the strangest thing.*

"Nobody hurt me, silly Girl. I am a strong independent woman. Unlike you and your spineless dad, stuck in your little Podunk fantasy land."

"Look, you guys killed my friend!" She yelled defiantly, seething in anger. Suddenly, she heard the words *slow to anger,* encouraging her. With a sigh, she whispered, "You killed her, and you just left her to die."

Carissa shrugged her shoulders and looked at her perfectly manicured fingernails. "To live is to die. Live it up while you have it, Girlie, because that's all there is."

"No, Carissa, to die is to live," she said softly.

Laughter floated around the small room as Carissa got up and looked at a small painting hanging from the wall. Maddie didn't know what to do. Looking up, she thought, *God, tell me what to say.* Suddenly, her Aunt Lisa's words popped into her mind, *"David is askin' God to give 'im eyes to see so he's not stuck in the weeds of his problem."* She realized what Aunt Lisa meant when she said this was a dangerous prayer. *Father, give me eyes to see Carissa and this situation, just like you did for David when Saul tried to kill him. Please show me.* A vision of a video she saw once of a chained-up dog being kicked around, unloved, suddenly crossed her mind.

As she tilted her head, she breathed deeply, watching Carissa return to her menacing position in front of her chair. "Carissa, you think I'm your enemy, but Jesus tells us to love our enemy. He loves you. Now, what is it that you want from my family?" She asked again.

The silence was deafening. Carissa leaned over the chair in front of her and searched Maddie's eyes for anything she could mock. But she just sat there with love in her eyes for a woman lost in the system—a woman Jesus wanted to save. "Lucien wants what he has already requested, complete submission. He will save the world, with or without your dad. Now, excuse me," Carissa turned around and left.

As Carissa walked out of the room, the air Maddie held on to exhaled in a whoosh. "God, what are you doing?" She prayed.

Suddenly, the door opened, and a man said, "Maddie, come with me."

As she stood, the man abruptly cut the bonds holding her hands together and motioned for her to follow. Rubbing her wrists to ease the ache, she wondered where he was taking her. *Please, God, no hoods,* she pleaded.

As she looked around, she realized she was in a church— an old church. The stained-glass windows were beautiful, with colors that were bright and cheery. As she passed one of the pieces of stained glass, she saw a picture of Jesus with the word 'HOPE' above it. She looked up at the ceiling and smiled. The man stopped and opened a door. He motioned for her to go in, half pushing her in when she stepped forward.

"Maddie!"

Suddenly pulled into a group hug, she sighed with relief, "I am so glad to see you guys!"

"Not as glad as we are to see you," Rachel said. "What happened to Jacob? What did he say to you?" She asked.

With all the Carissa business, she had forgotten all about him. "Nothing," she said. "All he said was 'okay' when I told him I only had a minute, and then he mumbled being sorry."

With her hand on her hips, Jade exclaimed, "Girl, when you kicked him, I've never been prouder!"

With a giggle, she said, "Honestly, I don't know where it came from. I just knew I had to get away. A lot of good it did me. Maybe you guys wouldn't be sitting here if I had just let him take me."

"No! We're in this together," Rachel said.

"Ahem." Maddie looked around the girls to see where the male voice came from.

"Pastor Chris! They got you, too?"

"It comes with the territory," he said.

Surprised over her pastor's shrug, Jade asked, "Wait, so you've been kidnapped before?"

"This is my first time," he said ironically. "Thankfully, the Lord isn't done with me yet. Some of my friends, however, were taken, never to be seen again." A sad look crossed his face as he proceeded to tell them how, from the first moment he started WTL, the PeaceKeepers were constantly persecuting and taking those who preached the Name of Jesus. "First, it was bullying, then they sent a mob to scare us. Oh, and then there was the time they tried to arrest me. That was interesting," he added with a laugh.

"But why? What have you ever done?" Emma asked.

Leaning forward, Jade had a gleam in her eye as she interjected, "I want to hear about the arrest!"

Pastor Chris looked at Jade and then Emma, "Rebellion has a curse on it, and they know it." Pounding his chest, he proclaimed, "I'm a warrior for Jesus. When I said yes to him, a target appeared on my back, but more importantly, a seal graced my forehead. As the Lord's, I wear my helmet of salvation into battle knowing that he has won the victory over sin and death, and so I too have won the victory." Waving his hand around the room, he laughed and said, "They may take my mortal body, but they can't have my soul."

"What do you mean rebellion has a curse?" Rachel asked.

"When Adam and Eve sinned, their disobedience wasn't the only catalyst for the curse on humanity, the serpent had a curse on him as well."

"What was it?" She asked.

"The serpent was cursed to crawl on its belly and eat dust—this signified hardship and suffering for Satan. Then God declared he would put enmity between the serpent and the woman. Man would crush his head, and the serpent would strike man's heel. In other words, the enemy and man would forever be in conflict, but man would crush the enemy's head. Do you know how?"

Rachel smiled, "Jesus."

"That's right—Jesus crushed the enemy's head through his death and resurrection, and he gave us the authority to do the same. So, the enemy may come after us, but ultimately, we are victorious in Christ." Pointing up to the ceiling, he added, "I'm happy to be persecuted if it means others come to Jesus and find the victory they have in him."

"I'm sorry, but that makes no sense," Jade said.

"Jade, Jesus said, 'Blessed are those who are persecuted because of righteousness, for theirs is the kingdom of heaven.' The early church in Acts took this to heart as they willingly walked into blazing furnaces. Even Paul wrote to the Corinthians that we are treasures in jars of clay that show the all-surpassing power is from God and not from us. 'We are hard pressed, but not in despair; persecuted, but not abandoned; struck down, but not destroyed.' Paul went on to say that we who are alive are given over to death for Jesus' sake, so that his life may be revealed in our mortal body." Looking at Maddie, he said, "Remember, death to life. They can try to take our bodies, but they can't take our soul."

Thinking back to her reading in Daniel, Maddie said, "This is our blazing furnace, isn't it?"

"What's that?" He asked, cupping his ear toward her.

Embarrassed as she realized her thoughts came out of her mouth, she said, "You know, the message you gave Saturday about Shadrach, Meshach, and Abednigo. Just like them, this is our fiery furnace."

Leaning forward, he placed his elbows on his knees and took an even, serious tone. "Maddie, can I ask you a question? Do you remember what Jesus said when he hung on the Cross?"

As she looked around at her friends, her eyes landed on Rachel, who shook her head toward the pastor. She's no help, she thought jokingly. As he patiently waited for her response, she looked at the walls, hoping for some kind of clue. *Lord, I need you,* she pleaded quietly.

"It's okay, Maddie, I'll take the pressure off. But listen, you must know the Word. The Sword of the Spirit is our only

offensive weapon. If you allow the Lord to write his word on your heart, the Text says that you will not sin against him."
He looked at her closely and nodded, and then he said, "Jesus said 'Tetelestai,' which is Hebrew for 'It is finished.' Do you know what this means?"

Shaking her head, she waited for him to tell her.

"It means he has declared victory, yesterday, today, and tomorrow. Our mission is to receive this victory through our surrender to him and declare it for ourselves by choosing not to allow the enemy a foothold in our hearts. Then we pass it on to others. While we are facing a fiery furnace, yes, we are not alone because he is right here with us. This is what he wants us to focus on, not the furnace.

Hesitating for a moment as the girls processed the encouraging word, Pastor Chris asked, "Do you remember when we talked about your spiritual gifts?"

"Yes, Sir."

"The gifts the Lord pours into us are for a purpose—his purpose. Think about it like this. Sonya invited you to work at the hospital because she recognized certain skills in you that were needed. The spiritual gifts God placed in you are skills written into your DNA. Once you know you have them, you allow him to mold and shape them for his purpose. It doesn't matter what situation you find yourself in, they have purpose. So, do you remember yours?"

"Faith, mercy, and exh… What's that word, Em?"

"Exhortation or encouragement."

"Yeah, that one."

"Good. So, how do you think God would use faith, mercy, and exhortation in this circumstance?"

Maddie looked around her, thinking through his question. "He would have me love my enemy." Pausing to look at her friends, she added, "He would have me remind each of you that he is with us all in the fire."

Raising his eyebrows, he offered a questioning gaze and asked, "And?"

Hesitating as she considered what else was left, a thought

suddenly popped into her head. She smiled and said, "He would have me declare victory."

"Tom, good to see you, Man!" David clapped his friend on the back and, after hugging Olivia, invited his friends into the house. "I just got back from working in the city. Perfect timing!"

"Sorry it took so long to get here. It's a mess out there."

"Tell me about it. You should try cleaning it up." Happy to have his friend with him, David led them into the kitchen for a drink.

"Commander, we have a problem." Wes Malone stood in the doorway of the kitchen. The look on his face told David everything he needed to know.

"Where is she?" He asked.

Jacque chose that inopportune moment to walk into the kitchen, "Olivia! Oh, it is so good to see you!" She completely missed the tension in the room as she embraced her friend.

Wes hesitated, uncertain if he should share his news in front of everyone.

"It's okay, they will find out anyway. Where is Maddie?" David asked again.

"She's been taken. She and her friends were kidnapped in front of the hospital. In broad daylight. It was the PeaceKeepers."

"Nooooo!!!!" Jacque cried. A look of shock crossed her face as she turned to her husband. "David, you were supposed to protect her!"

"It's okay, Jacque, she can't have gotten far," David said.

Clearing his throat, Wes added, "Oh, and you should know Commander. She put up quite the fight."

David smiled, "That's my Girl."

CHAPTER 31

The Power of Love

When Maddie and Rachel saw their dads through the glass, they couldn't be happier.

Indifferent to their presence, Jade muttered, "You realize this means that we are bait."

Waving to her friend to be quiet, Maddie whispered, "Hush!" Muffled sounds among a word or two were all she could hear as she leaned in.

"Can you hear what they're saying?" Rachel asked.

"I just heard the word communications," she said.

Emma, who was talking to Pastor Chris, suddenly said, "Hey, I have an idea." Raising her eyebrows, she rubbed her hands together and asked, "What if we worship?"

"What? You mean sing?" Jade asked.

"Yeah, just like at the park! If we are in a fiery furnace, we have Jesus with us, right?" Energized by the idea, she said, "They need to see him! Let's worship!"

Pastor Chris laughed. "Very bold," he said. "In my country, you girls would be called daitan." Standing up, he clasped hands with each of the girls as they circled up.

Following Emma's lead, they kept singing a worship song over and over, lifting their voices to Heaven.

For Maddie, it was exhilarating. Just as she learned when she sang Peace for the same time, worship did something within her that wrung out every ounce of fear and built-up courage within. And when they were together, it just seemed

310

to make them stronger.

Suddenly, the door swung open, and a voice yelled, "Shut up! That's quite enough!"

That just led them to go higher. Catching a glimpse of her dad with a wide smirk on his face was all she needed to take it up a notch. As her friends were singing, she began to speak Psalm 91. She could almost hear her Gram's voice as she spoke the words. *Those who dwell in the Shelter of the Most High....*

As the man rushed into the room to force them to stop, they kept their gaze focused on one another and refused to let go. With hands clasped, their chorus lifted into the ceiling and around the room like a symphony. There was nothing their captors could do to stop them.

The clicking of high heels sounded and then stopped at the door's opening. "Let them go," Carissa spoke authoritatively.

The man looked at her with confusion. "What? I thought..."

"I said, let them go! We aren't going to get what we want from them anyway." Crossing her arms, she sneered at Maddie as she said, "Come get your daughter, Mr. Bennett, she's caused enough trouble for today."

Maddie looked at her friends and smiled. "Oh, my goodness, it worked!" She whispered.

"Just like in Daniel," Pastor Chris said. "That is the power of love."

Her heart pounding in relief, she responded, "And victory."

Before their captors could change their minds, they hurried out of the room and into the arms of their dads.

"Mr. Bennett," Pastor Chris said as he shook his hand.

"Let's bust out of here," Maddie's dad said as he held his daughter. Turning to Carissa, David said, "Ms. Blackwell, tell your Boss I will see him on the battlefield."

A snort signified her disgust.

Rachel, in tears, couldn't let go of her dad. "When did you

get here?" She asked.

"Actually, just this morning," he said. "I'm starting to wonder if I need to keep a tracking device on you."

"Naw." Pointing to her forehead, she added, "We've got the Holy Spirit's seal."

David couldn't have been prouder of his daughter. For the first time, he recognized that warfare didn't require an earthly weapon. He wondered if today's events were the spiritual warfare his mom always talked about.

Once the girls were safely in bed at his father-in-law's house, he and Tom sat in the backyard listening to the crickets serenade the Atlanta night.

"What did I see today?" David asked his friend.

"That, my friend, was Daniel three."

Remembering his reading of Daniel, he asked, "Not the furnace."

"The very one."

"But how…"

"David, God loves you and he loves your family. There is nowhere you can go that he won't be. Do you know that?"

David shook his head, "I've seen too much."

"Hey, me too," Tom said. "Remember Sudar?"

"Yes, I remember. But I was in control then." Throwing his hands up in the air, he added, "I have no control over whatever this is."

"And you think that I do? David, it is God who has the power, the glory, and the control. He gave the girls the freedom and courage they needed to face their furnace today. Maddie will not always have you around, but God will always be with her. It's time you start recognizing that. You would do a lot better to surrender her into his hands and trust him with the outcome."

David sat quietly, thinking on his friend's words. *Why am I fighting this?* He wondered. His daughter was more a warrior than most men he fought alongside on the battlefield.

"What do you think this means for the girls?" He asked his friend as he gestured toward their room.

"Honestly, I think they will face even greater warfare than in the last forty-eight hours. Remember, the antichrist has been given control over the earth for three and a half years. Considering he stepped foot on the holy place a year and a half ago, we know we've got at least two years. And if this weekend was any sign, the enemy sees them as a threat. Which means…"

"That we have to prepare them."

"David, no." Tom leaned over and looked closely at his friend. "God must prepare them. Remember, they are fighting with his weapons."

"What weapons, Tom?"

"Well, the belt of truth for one. God's truth holds everything together. The breastplate of righteousness is the righteousness of Christ we receive when we say yes to him. Then there are the shoes that carry the Gospel of peace. When we step out to share the good news of Jesus, we step out in his shoes. The helmet of salvation—our salvation is secure in him. The shield of faith snuffs the enemy's arrows; and the sword of the Spirit is the word of God."

"I don't understand. How do these weapons work?" David asked, frustrated.

Tom suddenly laughed as he had a revelation. "David, what happened to your plan to knock out PKO communications?"

Confused over the change in subject, David waved his hand in the air and said, "I only have to fly to Israel. Unfortunately, every plane is grounded currently."

With a smirk, Tom asked, "The tornado put quite a kink in your plans, didn't it?"

"Yes, but it's not over."

"Obviously, like your mom said, Jesus hasn't come yet."

Annoyed, David asked, "Where are you going with this, Tom?"

Sitting back with his elbows on the arms of the chair, Tom thought carefully about how to say what he had to say. "David, have you ever thought that perhaps God took out their communications on your behalf?"

David chuckled, "The thought did cross my mind. Eh, but I would've done it differently."

"That's right!" Tom exclaimed as he pointed at his friend. "God's ways are not your ways, and your ways are not God's. But what if God's ways are better?"

"Better than taking out communications globally?" David asked.

"Look, I'm not going to speak for Jesus, but what if he has a plan greater than your own? Our enemy is not the PeaceKeepers, it's Satan, who has been defeated. When we use the armor of God, we are working under the authority of Christ, who defeated the enemy. When we go into battle with his weapons, we too will defeat the enemy."

David rubbed his head in frustration. *All this God talk!*

Let it go, son.

Looking up, David asked, "What'd you say?"

With his brow lifted, Tom lifted his hand and said, "I didn't say anything."

"That was weird, I thought I heard…"

"Heard what?" Tom asked.

David shook his head, "You'll think I'm crazy."

"No, I won't, what did you hear?"

"'Let it go, Son.' I know, it's crazy," he said as he placed his forehead in his hands.

Tom smiled and leaned forward. "Not crazy at all. David, do you want to let it go?"

The weight he had been carrying was so heavy. David was ready to let it all go. With a frustrated sigh, he asked, "Tom, can I ask you something?"

"Of course."

"Can I trust him?"

Compassion filled Tom's heart. If there was anyone on earth who knew the pain that David Bennett carried, it would be Tom. Even Jacque didn't know half of the things that David had seen. But Tom knew, and better yet, Jesus knew. "Yes, my friend. Jesus is greater than a brother. He is the best friend you will ever have, and he offers you the right to call your Creator Father. He purchased with his blood that right, and he covered your sin, past, present, and future, so you could dwell with him always. There is no fiery furnace that will ever take that away from those who say yes to him."

"Is that all I need to do, say yes? It seems like a flimsy plan—for eternity's sake, that is."

Tom laughed at his friend's tactical thinking. "The truth is that Jesus said, 'God so loved the world that he gave his One and only Son that whosoever believes will not perish but have everlasting life. It's an eternal relationship with your Creator, not a transaction."

"What's plan B?" David asked.

Tom laughed at his weak attempt at a joke. "David, our human brains don't work like the Lord's. Jesus is the only way."

"So, what happens if I do say yes to Jesus?"

"He will give you his Spirit, who will go to work transforming your heart to be more like his. He will walk with you and give you strength.

"What's this transformation like? I've experienced enough transformation in the last three years to last a lifetime."

"Honestly, I don't know that I can explain it. Sometimes it's painful when he reveals the things he wants to break off you, but then there are these times when his joy is greater than any high you could ever experience on this earth. His joy is our strength. He walks us through sorrow, pain, depression, weariness, and gives us the strength to endure, but more so the strength to go forward in him.

"When you go into battle, you go forward knowing someone is going with you, right?"

"Hopefully. There are a couple of times...."

"Alright, I get it. But David, when you go into battle with an army, you're not alone. You know the power of the team you have behind you. Now, imagine the power of God going with you into battle. The one who created the universe. The one who formed you and knew every day before even one came to be. Imagine he goes to battle with you, before you, beside you, behind you."

Gritting his teeth in angst, David pleaded, "But Tom, people still die."

"Yes, they do, and where do they go? David, Jesus died so we could be with him forever. If you die today, do you know where you will go?"

David slumped as he realized, "No, I don't."

Tom could see the battle in his friend's heart. He wanted to release his friend from his self-imposed prison, but there was only One who could do that. Realizing there was no time like the present, Tom asked, "Would you like to? We can do it right now. We don't need anything more than what we have right here." Holding out his hands, he encouraged his friend to do the same.

A tear fell down David's cheek as he opened his hands. Years of hard work had aged his hands at least ten years, but he knew he could trust these hands. He knew what they were capable of. But he also knew that one day they wouldn't work. Whether he liked it or not, he would have to surrender to death. He couldn't control anything on this earth except himself, and he had learned that the hard way. Perhaps Tom was right. Perhaps God did have a better way. If he could find this joy that Tom spoke about, perhaps that would make all the difference.

"I saw this painting once," David whispered. "The painting was of Jesus hanging on a cross, nails in his wrists and feet. A crown of thorns on his head. Blood pouring out of wounds, impossible to see. The painting had something written at the bottom that always intrigued me, 'Hope is revealed, His Name is Jesus.'" Weary eyes looked up at his friend, "What does that mean?"

Tom took his friend's hand and said, "It means that he will take everything you are holding in this hand, and he will give you his yoke that is light. It means that he will exchange your sin for his righteousness. It means that he will give you the right to be called a child of God. That's the hope that we have in him. That, my friend, is the power of love."

Turning his hands over so his palms faced up, David looked up and said, "Yes, I want to know Jesus."

Pick Up Your Sword

Maddie sat at the little desk in the guest room of Grandpa Jack's house with her bible and journal before her. Candlelight gave her just enough light to debrief the day, but oh, how she missed her room, Carolina Wren, and Wild Rock.

It had been a week since they lost power. Dad said it wouldn't be long before the city restored it. While she didn't mind so much, she couldn't help but wonder: *how much more? How much more change could they take?*

Rachel told her once to expect change. *"Don't be afraid, Maddie. Be patient and endure. The only thing we can depend on is God,"* she said. *"He will never leave us."*

He will never leave us. These words kept her strong as she worshiped with her friends today. She still couldn't believe how the day ended or how it had begun.

"What a mess," she thought as she drew circles at the top of the page.

She was grateful for Jesus, who gave them the strength to stand, but if she were honest, her heart was broken for Jacob. God, what is wrong with him? She wrote. Placing her chin on her palm, she remembered her brother's wedding. A Harvest Moon Hootenanny, Grammy called it. Goodness, it seemed so long ago, but it had only been ten months. The moon was so bright that Jacob's eyes almost glowed. When he took her hand to dance, she knew only one thing: she never wanted the night to end. That was the night they sat in the back of the truck, and he loaned her his jacket. He told her about the army and asked her to go with him to Kalispell. *I'll never get it back, will I, God?* That night was all she had, and it was forever marked by a shadow that she couldn't remove. *Did he ever really like me?* She wondered. *Or was he part of the PeaceKeepers this whole time?* Remembering the kiss that filled her with shame, she placed her head on her forearms and wept. *How stupid I was to follow him.* Shaking her head to clear the bitter thoughts, she immediately replaced them with thoughts of who she was—a daughter of the King. She couldn't go back to that dark place. She could only follow the Lord, from now on.

"Maddie, are you okay?" Emma asked.

Giving her friend a puny response, she wiped tears from both her face and the paper in front of her. A few words into her prayer, and she heard the gentle whisper:

Look for the Love.

> *Father,*
>
> *Where is the love? I don't know anymore. Grammy's gone. Jacob betrayed me. My dad and my friends are all I have.*

I am with you always, even to the end of the age.

> *Yes, Lord, I have Jesus. How can I ever forget? Thank you. Thank you for being with us in that room today. I will never forget standing there with my friends and singing to you. It was just like Paul, in Acts, wasn't it? And you changed Carissa's heart, didn't you? God, can you change Jacob's heart, too? I don't want him to be lost like so many at the PKO.*

With God, all things are possible.

The scripture she had heard so many times popped into her head. She opened her bible to Matthew 19:26,

"Jesus looked at them and said, "With man this is impossible, but with God all things are possible."

And that's it, isn't it, God? Okay, I get it. I place Jacob in your hand and ask that you do what only you can do.

I trust you. In Jesus' name, Amen.

After closing her journal, she extended her hands and laid everything down. She wanted an authentic and genuine relationship with the One who created her. "God, I surrender fear, worry, anxious thoughts, and my need to follow others. I need You, Lord. Jesus, please show me how to live Your way." With her amen, she rested her head on the desk and fell asleep.

Rows upon rows of white lilies stood before her. Walking down the first row, she couldn't help herself as she knelt and breathed deeply of the sweet scent. The knees of her jeans were now a lovely mess. Looking at her hands, they weren't much better.

As she caressed the strong stem of the flower, she suddenly heard a man's voice. Looking up, she shielded her eyes from the bright sun. All she could see was a silhouette that seemed to glow. The glare was blinding as she wiped her hands on her jeans and stood. Suddenly, the brown-eyed man from dreams past stood before her.

"Hello Maddie," he smiled warmly. Bending down to pick one of the beautiful flowers, he lifted it to his nose and closed his eyes. *"Aren't they beautiful?"* He asked. *"Consider the lilies of the field, how they grow; they toil not, neither do they spin: yet I say that even Solomon in all his glory was not arrayed like one of these."* Handing the flower to her to smell, he said, *"I've always loved lilies."*

Peace flowed from each word and surrounded her like a blanket. As she took the flower from his hand, she realized the One who created this lily was placing it in her hand. She didn't know what to say.

He smiled at her and said,

"Maddie, it's time to pick up your Sword."

Pausing to find her voice, she asked, "The one that Grammy gave me?"

"My Sword—the Sword of my Spirit."

Suddenly, her bible was in her hand. She didn't even think twice about how it got there. She knew that it was supposed to be there.

"This lily represents resurrection and new life. I have called you for such a time as this. Everything you have walked through has prepared you for this very moment. And like this lily, you will blossom with new life before me. As the rain and the snow come down

from heaven, and do not return to it without watering the earth and making it bud and flourish, so that it yields seed for the Sower and bread for the eater, so is my word that goes out from my mouth: It will not return to me empty, but will accomplish what I desire and achieve the purpose for which I sent it. You will go out in joy and be led forth in peace; the mountains and hills will burst into song before you, and all the trees of the field will clap their hands." The man looked at her and asked, *"Do you understand?"*

"Grammy said that everything you send out will return to you."

"That's correct, Maddie—in time, you will return to me. Until then, you have a purpose. Pick up your sword, follow me, and remember that I am with you always."

The dream abruptly ended as Maddie felt a soft tap on her shoulder.

"Maddie, wake up. Your dad wants to talk to you," Emma said quietly.

"What? Dad?" She asked, wiping the drool from her mouth. It was still dark out, and the house was quiet. *What time is it?* She thought, still in a sleepy daze.

Disappointed that the dream was over, she made a note to write it down later.

"Yeah, your dad is at the door. He said to wake you, it was important."

Her dream was now a memory. She stood up and opened the door to find her dad standing on the other side. "Dad, is everything okay?" She asked. His face looked withdrawn, the skin under his eyes dark and tired. *He looks exhausted,* she thought.

"More than okay, can you come downstairs?"

As she walked downstairs, she realized the September night might be a little chilly for shorts and a t-shirt. Grabbing one of her grandpa's coats from the coat closet, she put it on and walked outside behind him. Surprised to see Mr. Tom sitting at the patio table, she looked at them both and asked, "Am I in trouble?"

Her dad laughed and said, "No, Ruthie, sit down. I would like to have a chat if that's okay."

Sitting down between her dad and Mr. Tom, she placed her hands under her legs in hopes of keeping them from shaking.

As David looked at his daughter, he suddenly felt extremely vulnerable. This was a new feeling for him. *The walls Tom talked about, am I ready for them to come down?* David watched a myriad of emotions cross his daughter's face as she waited expectantly for him to tell her why he called her downstairs.

"Maddie, I wanted you to be the first to know."

Her feet were tapping on the patio. Her arms were shaking in unison. Lifting a brow, she asked, "Know what?"

His hesitation was filling him with guilt. *What are you waiting for, David? Just tell her.* "Ruthie, when communications are back and flights are running again, I will be going to Israel."

Her heart sank. "Israel?"

"Yes, and I will be gone for a while."

Looking at her best friend's dad, she asked, "Is Mr. Tom going too?"

"No, he'll stay here and keep an eye on you guys, along with Wes and Mark. And Maddie, if you want to go back to Wild Rock, you can."

While the thought of returning to Wild Rock was comforting, she needed to be here.

"Thank you, Dad, but Sonya offered me a job at the hospital. But I can go up on the weekends, right?"

"Well, that's a long drive, Ruthie. Perhaps a week at a time. I'm going to send your mom and brother back. We got word from Michael that Melissa is pregnant, so your mom wants to be there when the baby is born."

"Are you kidding me? That's great!" *She was going to be an aunt! Suddenly, the idea of going back had merit.*

Okay, David, out with it now, he thought. "Ruthie, there's something else. I want to tell you something important—something that has changed my life." David hesitated as he looked at Tom. Encouraged by his friend's nod, he said, "Tonight, I decided to give my life to Jesus."

"Daddy!" She stood up and grabbed his neck. "Oh, Daddy, you have no idea how happy this makes me. Her eyes suddenly widened as she yelled, "I prayed for this!" Looking up to the sky, she exclaimed, "Thank you, Jesus!"

David looked at his friend, who shrugged over her unintelligible prayer and said, "I may need an interpreter."

Tom laughed as he watched his best friend and his daughter's best friend share the best news ever. Only God could do something like this.

As Maddie returned to the chair, she looked as if she would fly out of it. Placing his hand on her arm, he said, "It's okay. I'm okay."

"I know, I just… Dad, you have no idea how much I've prayed for this!" Maddie bowed her head as she started to cry."

"Hey, what's wrong?" He asked.

"Oh, these are happy tears." She said as she fanned her face. "It's just been so crazy all the miracles God has given us. Even in all the bad stuff. It's almost like the worse things get, the better they get."

David chuckled at his daughter's brutal honesty. Nodding in agreement, he lifted his hands to his chest and said, "Yes, and can I say my chest already feels lighter?"

Tilting her head in confusion, she asked, "Lighter?"

"Ruthie, I have carried too much for far too long, and I have done a disservice to this family. I don't want you and your brothers to suffer like your mom and I have. So, we make a pact tonight to lay it down, get it off our chest, and lay it at Jesus' feet."

Lifting her hand in agreement, she asked, "Pinkie promise?"

David looked down and smiled. The gesture he began with his daughter when she was a toddler was coming around full circle. "Pinkie promise. Now, what's this about a sword?" He asked.

Epilogue

January 3
Israel

Today was the day. After three long months away from his family, David had the code ready to execute. Rubbing his hand over the full-grown beard he sported, he looked out of the dirty galley window and then secured his laptop in the nondescript bag. Something was nagging at him, yet he couldn't figure out what it was.

As he glanced at the well-worn bible on the bedside table, he smiled. His mother had written so many notes on the edges that he felt as if he had walked through God's Word with her. She had told him once that this Bible gave her the strength she needed to keep going after his dad died. It was doing the same for him now. Long nights writing code, combined with the loneliness of a Christmas season away from his family, was hard. But for the first time in his life, he was finding joy in the hard.

David had missed holidays before, but this one was different—he was different. Never had being with his family for the celebration of Christ's birth been more important, but as Mordecai said, they were fighting a war of epic proportions.

It had been a long time since he was the one responsible for writing and executing code, but there was too much at stake to trust anyone else with this task. Since the vote to repeal The Kindness Tax failed in the General Assembly, he felt even more strongly about moving forward. The plan he and

Mordecai derived was brilliant, but dangerous. The destruction to the server farm in Atlanta revealed a weakness in the communications of the PKO, a weakness they could perfectly exploit. He was confident in their plan to disrupt global communications in Lucien Baldur's organization, except...

After grabbing his wallet and keys, he pulled the black hoodie over his head and proceeded to walk out of his room. "Good day," the woman at the front desk said as he walked by. Nodding, he walked through the double doors and into the waiting nondescript black car.

"Good morning, Mr. Bennett," the driver said as he handed a note through the glass window separating them. *My name is Michael. I am stepping in for Levi today.*

"Morning, Michael," he replied. As he opened the note, he recognized Mordecai's handwriting immediately, yet confusion filled him as he read the words, *"This is not the way."*

Curious over the message, he asked, "Michael, where did you get this note?"

The note was forgotten as he looked out of the window and noticed they were going in the opposite direction from the warehouse where he was to deploy the program. "Where are you taking me?" He asked calmly. Strangely, he didn't feel as if he was in danger, yet it was obvious to him that the plan was being diverted. "Michael?"

The man named Michael looked in the mirror and nodded. After a long pause, he answered, "David, do not be afraid. Those who are wise will shine like the brightness of the heavens, and those who lead many to righteousness, like the stars forever and ever."

The strange response caught David off guard. As he tried to remember where he had heard that before, Michael added, "Summer is near."

Sometime in October – Three months earlier . . .
Wild Rock, Tennessee

Maddie was so happy to be back in Wild Rock. After the

trauma of the tornado and then the kidnapping, her dad convinced her to wait a month before starting at the hospital full time so she could rest and visit her brother and sister-in-law. Considering her mom and Matthew were going up anyway, she took him up on the opportunity. Since it was October and the planting season was over, Rachel and Emma decided to join her.

As she unpacked her things, she smiled, remembering Jade's surprise at joining them. "But only for a week," she said. "There's business in Atlanta to attend to. These people need Jesus!"

The real surprise came when Jade's mom decided to join them. She was never so happy as when she heard that Ms. Alisha wanted to see Momma Roseline again. *Oh Father, there is nothing impossible for you,* she thought as she looked out the bedroom window.

The song of Mr. Carolina Wren delighted her as he perched on his little limb. She would never forget the first time they met. It was a little over three years ago when she looked out of this very window super annoyed at his song. "I have changed, Mr. Carolina Wren," she said. "You inspire me to be better," she said as the bird serenaded her through the window.

Feeling the inspiration to write, she opened her journal and spent the next hour writing down all the things they had experienced over the last year.

Her dad's question about a sword allowed her to share Grammy's sword and the Sword of the Spirit. One of the gifts Grammy left to her was her bible. As much as she wanted to keep it for herself, she felt Grammy would have wanted her dad to have it, for now. So, she gave it to him and asked him to read it when he went to Israel. As she wrote of the conversation with her dad, she couldn't help but get teary. The fire they faced in the past few years was overwhelming, but God had moved mightily this year—the most incredible move of his hand in and through her dad. She completely understood the joy Amy Jayne felt when her dad found Jesus, despite the destruction surrounding them.

Writing was cathartic. She was so grateful to Grammy and Mr. C, who challenged her to write. This rhythm was one of the ways she knew she could get everything out so the Lord could heal her wounded heart and remind her of the good things that needed to be remembered.

Oh, how she missed her Grammy. Her heart ached as she thought of all the conversations missed. Pulling out a well-worn piece of paper from the back of her journal, she re-read her last words of encouragement.

"Maddie Ruth, my time is done. Now, it's your turn. You are the little blessed one who'll be a companion to many. Never forget who you are and Whose you are. Always remember that you are on mission. Keep your eyes on Jesus and point others to him. Don't let anything or anyone else distract you from your calling. The Lord is with you."

Drawing a heart with tears falling from it, she wished more than anything that she could hear her voice even one more time. Pulling out the banded stack of cards her Gram left to her, she read 1 Peter 1:6-7. Running her thumb over the indentation of the asterisk in the top corner, she assumed this meant that her Gram wanted her to remember this one specifically.

> *"In all this you greatly rejoice, though now for a little while you may have had to suffer grief in all kinds of trials. These have come so that the proven genuineness of your faith—of greater worth than gold, which perishes even though refined by fire—may result in praise, glory, and honor when Jesus Christ is revealed."*

This scripture described Maddie's life over the last three years to a T. It was as if her Gram spoke this as an encouraging last word. Grabbing her bible, she opened to the chapter in Peter. The passage spoke of a living hope, an inheritance, salvation, and the word of the Lord that endures forever. *This was why Grammy gave me the sword, she thought. She knew the trials I would face and wanted me to know that my hope would be found in Jesus.*

After pulling the blank card from the stack that Grammy left her, she copied the verse written in her Gram's perfect print. Turning the card over, she wrote "MEMORIZE" on the other side. "Thank you," she whispered as she held the cards close to her chest. She only wished she could say it in person.

"Maddie, what are you writing?" Matthew asked from the open doorway.

Wiping away a stray tear, she placed the card in her pocket and said, "I'm writing a verse." Turning to look at him, she added, "What's up?"

"Oh, I'm going to see Uncle Tom, but I wondered if you wouldn't mind if we went to Wild Rock Overlook?" He asked.

Relieved to break free from the heaviness in her room, she exclaimed, "Yes!" It had been a long time since she had been to the rock. "Let me grab my coat."

As they made their way to the trail, she was surprised by the overgrowth that covered the path they had walked so many times. Kicking through a heavy layer of dead leaves with her boots, she sighed.

Her brother must've been thinking similarly, as he said, "I think Wild Rock misses Grammy," he said sadly.

"Yeah." An idea popped into her head. *How cool would it be if we cleared the area and made it our own?* "You know, we can cut back these weeds and branches while I'm in Wild Rock. Would you like to do that together?"

Matthew was never more excited than when he was asked to work with his hands. "Yes! Can I ask James, too?"

"Of course. I'll invite the girls, and we'll make it a group project. Grammy would be proud of us, don't you think?"

Grabbing a limb so his sister could pass, he nodded and asked, "Hey, Maddie, are you going to go back to Atlanta?"

Always thinking of others, she smiled. "Thanks, Bro, Yes, I am."

"I'm glad," he said. "I'll miss you, though."

Tousling the hair of her now much taller brother, she said, "I'll be back."

His eyes widened in joy as he asked, "For my birthday? I'll be fourteen!" He exclaimed.

Smiling, she said, "Yes, I would be honored."

His countenance changed as he glanced down at his sister, a worried crease between his brows. "Hey, what about Kali and Hope? Won't you miss them?" He asked.

"I'm going to see them tomorrow," she said with a smile. "Do you want to come?"

"Yeah, that would be cool. I can't wait to see James, I have so much to tell him!"

Maddie felt the same about Amy Jayne. *I wonder how she and Mr. Don are getting along.*

"What about Jacob and Rory?" Matthew asked. "Will they be back?"

Unsure if she could talk about it, she walked quietly along the path. Matthew patiently waited. He was always so patient. *Oh, how she loved her brother.*

After a few moments, he said, "Maddie?"

"Yes, Matthew."

"I'm sorry I wasn't there to protect you. I know I made you a promise," he said sadly.

Stopping to look at her brother, she said, "Oh, Matthew, you have always been the best brother." Pointing to an off-the-beaten trail, she added, "Sometimes people take the wrong direction. We have an enemy who comes to steal, kill, and destroy. If we aren't careful, we'll get caught in his web. That's why we must keep our eyes on God."

After grabbing a leaf from a nearby branch, he nodded in agreement. "And be a man after God's own heart?"

She watched as he tore the leaf into four squares. Raising a brow as he tried to match the squares perfectly, she said, "That's right, but even if we get it wrong, he will always bring us back. We don't have to be perfect."

A look of relief flashed across his face as he smiled.

"Look, I still have the boomerang," he said happily as he pulled it from his back pocket.

Taking his prized possession from him, she ran her fingers along the engraved words as she spoke them aloud, *Man after God's own heart.* "Seek him first, little Brother, and you always will be," she said.

"Just like David?"

"Perhaps even greater," she said.

"Whoa…" The concerned look on his face told her that he wouldn't let the subject go. "I have been wanting to ask, do you miss Jacob?"

She wasn't sure how to answer her brother's innocent question. There were so many feelings swirling around in her heart. The familiar grief stung when she thought of her naivety toward Jacob. Any other feelings were swept aside as she attempted to divert her brother's attention. "I do, and I think Rachel misses Rory."

"Did Rory join the PeaceKeepers too?" He asked, his voice laced with alarm.

"No, he's still in the army. Rachel just received a letter from him." As they made their way to the rock she loved so dearly, she shivered, a feeling of nostalgia overwhelming her. She could almost feel Grammy with them. Sitting on the rock, she laid her chin on her knees and looked at her brother, who waited expectantly for her to tell him the letter's contents.

"Jacob left the Army," she said sadly. "Rory wrote that he wasn't happy with the lack of support to the community and wanted to do something about it. So, he joined the PeaceKeepers," she shrugged. Looking at her brother, she grinned, remembering the good news in the letter, "I expect Rory will be home for Christmas, and you'll get to see him!"

"That's cool, I liked Rory, too."

"Me, too," Maddie agreed.

"Hey, when do you think Dad will come back?" Matthew asked, a look of worry on his face. He wasn't talking much about Dad's departure to Israel. She had been a little worried that he was angry.

"Honestly, I don't know. Dad wasn't sure how long his project would take, but he promised to be home as soon as he could."

Tilting his head, he drew his eyebrows together in concern as he asked, "Tell me straight. Is Dad in danger?"

She had made a pact with her little brother to always tell it to him straight. She never wanted him to fall into the wrong hands because he was naïve. Looking out over the valley, she wondered how Grammy would answer his question. *Father, please give me the right words,* she prayed silently.

"You and I both know that God has kept him safe to now, right?" She asked. "We have to believe that he will continue to hold him in his hand, and even if something happens to him on earth, God will still have him in his hand."

Matthew nodded, satisfied with her answer, for the moment. As Matthew whittled, she sketched the landscape below. Reds, greens, oranges, browns, and yellows painted a beautiful palette of color greater than any painted landscape—God's palette. *Grammy would love this view,* she thought to herself. *Oh, but she has an even greater view, she's in Heaven!* She giggled quietly.

Laying her journal down, she suddenly had an idea. "Hey, Matthew, can I pray over you?" She asked softly.

Matthew, who was slumped over his piece of wood, suddenly darted up and sat up good and straight. He looked at his sister with such love. "Could you?" He asked.

Father,

> *Thank you for bringing us here. Thank you for going before us and preparing the way you have for us to go. Thank you for having a plan for us, to give us hope and a future. Lord, I thank you for my little brother, who is so wise and strong. Thank you for making him a man after your own heart. Lord, I pray that you will go before*

Matthew and prepare the way You have for him to go. Please draw him near and teach him the great love of your heart. Allow him to see himself through your eyes, just as you have done for me.

And Lord, I pray that you will protect him, guide and direct him in the way he should go with your loving eye upon him. He is a son of the King, may he always stand on the Name of Jesus, knowing that NO WEAPON formed against him will prevail!

And may he step into your promise, knowing that you are with him and for him. May he take up the shield of faith and the sword of the Spirit, that is, the word of God. Thank you, Lord, for my little brother. I pray that he will be a mighty warrior in your kingdom and that many will come to know the Name of Jesus through the work of his heart and his hands. I pray that you will bless him and keep him. Make your face shine upon him and be gracious to him. Turn your face to him and give him your perfect peace. In Jesus' Name, Amen

And don't you know that he will?

APPENDIX

Appalachian Dictionary

Grammy was born in Appalachia. The Appalachian vocabulary is very colorful. While this isn't a comprehensive list, you may find several of these colorful sayings sprinkled through the book.

'bout = about	
'Cause = because	
'Cept = except	
'em = Them	
'er = her	
'ere = here	
'fraid = afraid	
'im = him	
'Magine = imagine	
'Mater = tomato	
'maters = tomatoes	
'Nother = another	
'Nough = enough	
'Spect = expect	
'Splain = explain	
S'posed = supposed	
'Tater = potato	
A' = of	
A'course = of course	
Acrost = across	
Acrost the waters = from overseas	
Afeared = afraid	
A'fore = before	
Aggin = against	
A'growin' = growing	
Aimin' = have been going to	
Ain't = is not	

Ain't got a dog in that fight = It's none of my business
Ain't no hill fer a climber = Not a big deal for someone with experience
Anxi'ty = anxiety also Jim Jams = Anxiety (Appalachian)
Any word with "g" on the end is abbreviated with an apostrophe at the end
App-a-LATCH-un = Appalachian
Appa-latch-uh = Appalachia
As the twig is bent so shall the tree grow = The direction you point something/someone in is the direction it/they will go
Back in the day = years ago
Bad off = very sick
Bad turn = someone ill-tempered
Barking up the wrong tree = you're wrong
Bat = quick blink of the eye
Be a-waitin' on 'em at the house = I'll be waiting for them at the house
Beauty never made the kettle sing
Bein' ugly = being hateful, rude, cross, cruel
Beside Oneself = confused or worried
Better git on = need to leave
A bird in the hand is worth two in the bush = It's better to have the certainty of what you do have that the possibility of what you might have
Bite yer tongue = be quiet, don't say it
Black dark = night time
Blackberry winter = time when there is cool weather at the same time as the blooming of wild blackberry shrubs in May
Bless yer pea-pickin' lil heart = you poor, unfortunate soul
Blind house = windowless cabin
Blinked milk = sour milk

Bobble = mistake
Britches = pants
Brung up = raised, as in from childhood
Bugger = frightful (wooly bugger = anyone who is frightful looking)
Buggy = shopping cart
Bumfuzzle = confused or puzzled
C'mon = come on
Cain't = Can't
Cain't tell nobody nothin' that ain't ever been nowhere! = They think they know more than they do
Cain't think of nothin' right off = Can't think of anything at the moment
Cake a' soap = bar of soap
Call on = to visit someone
Care = will do something, don't mind to do something
Carry on = to misbehave
Catawampus = askew, awry
Cause = because
Cheer = chair
Chewed up and spit out = feeling poorly
Chil'ens = children
Chock Full = full to running over
Clean fergot = I forgot
Commode = toilet
Conniption = a mad fit
Could'na = could not
Courtin' = dating
Crayun = crayon
Crick = creek
Crooked as a dog's hind leg = a person who is crooked or deceitful
Cut on the light = turn on the light
Cuttin' up = acting a fool
D'ya = Do you

Dab = cooking measurement – small amount
Dahlin' = darling
Dawg = dog
Did'na = did not
Differ'nt = different
Diggin' his own grave = messing up
Do what? = What did you just say?
Dodge = to avoid
Don't go gittin' yer gussie up = don't get upset
Done = finished
Don't you blare yer eyes at me = don't give me a dirty look
Dope = soda water - coca-cola
Dorter = daughter
Drawers = underwear
Dreckly = directly
Druthers = things one would rather do over anything else
Duns = bills
Ears are burnin' = someone is saying bad things behind your back.
Eat up = consumed. "I'm eat up with love."
Eh law = Oh well
Ever'body = everyone
Ever'time = every time
Ever'where = everywhere
Ever'thin'll be fine, good Lord willin' and the creek don't rise = something should happen unless
Fair to midlin' = I'm okay
Fair up = when rainy weather clears up
Far = fire
Farboard = fire place mantle
Faster than a hot knife through butter – fast and easy
Fatback = fatty meat from the back of a hog that is salt cured

Favor = to resemble
Feisty = spunky, lively
Fer = for
Ferget = Forget
Fetch = to get or bring
Finer 'n frog hair = Things are going well.
Fisticuff = a fist fight
Fit = suitable, ready to use
Fit as a fiddle = fine
Fit ta be tied = angry
Fitified = frozen with fear
Fixin' = fixing to or a side dish
Flatter'n a flitter = something is pretty flat
Fler = flour
Flares = flowers (I chose to substitute flow'rs instead)
Foller = follow
Foller = follow
Follerin' = follow
Foretole = foretold
Fotch = fetch
Frail = old, feeble, sickly
Fret = to worry
Friz = frozen
Fuss at = to scold
Gall = nerve
Galoot = an older man who acts like a fool
Gander = look, stare
Garden sass = greens-turnip, mustard, lettuce
Garntee = guarantee
Father up = to assemble; to collect
Gimme some sugar = Give me a kiss
Gittin' = leaving
Gob = a large amount of something
Gom = make a mess or stop up something
Gonna = going to

Go on = talk at length
Good turn = someone with a pleasant personality
Got that straight = You are correct
Gotta = Have to
Gotta = must or got to
Grinnin' like a possum eatin' a sweet tater = someone who is a mite too pleased with themselves.
Hand = worker or hired hand
Hanker = want or crave
Hard feeling = animosity between people
Harder'n a one-eyed man doin' push-ups = Doing something really hard- with all your strength.
Haul off = to take action
He 'bout skeered me outta my house shoes = he scared me.
He ain't got no sense a-tall = He doesn't make any sense
He ain't no count a-tall = of any account
He gets my goose = irritated
He's as crooked as a dog's hind leg = he's a thief
He's as happy as if he had good sense = Happy and that's a good thing
He's crooked as a jay bird = a thief
He's lower 'n a snake's belly in a wagon rut = bad character
He's mad as a mule chewin' on bumblebees! = He's really angry
He's probably just laying off drunk somewheres = drunk and passed out
Heap o' = a lot of
Hear tell = to be informed or learn of
Heared = heard
Hep = help
Hesh up = be quiet
Hissy fit = tantrum

Hold yer horses = wait
Holler = valley
A holler is a place where ya can let yer young'uns run loose cause ya know ya got plenty a time a'fore it gets dark.
Holp = help
Hootenanny = a part with fold music and dancing
Hotter 'n blue blazes = really hot
Hunker = to work in a determined manner
I better git on = I have to leave
I don't chew my cabbage twice = I'm not going to repeat myself
I feel like I've been chewed up and spit out = Yelled at and criticized
I knowed = I knew
I reckon = I guess
I'm just loaferin' today = I'm just hanging out
Ideal = idea
Iffen = if and
Ill = hateful, angry, combative, always ill-tempered.
If I had my druthers = If I had my way
Infare = wedding
In a great while = a long period of time
In under = beneath, underneath or below
Is all = that's all
It's blowin' up a storm = really windy
It's rainin' cats and dogs = it's raining hard
It's never to late to mend = It's never too late to forgive
It's ver' airish = a little bit chilly outside
I've a mind to = of a particular inclination
It doesn't amount to a hill of beans = something that has little of no value
Jack = bust, tear, steal
Jasper = a bad person, a dishonest person

Jaw = talk
Jerk = pulled
Jim jams = to be restless or feel anxiety; nervous
Jes' = Just
Jist =Just
Job = poke
Jump the broom = get married
Jumped out of the fryin' pan an' into the fire = someone went from one bad situation right into another
Keer = care
Kilt = past tense of killed
Kin = family
Kinda = kind of
Kindly = kind of, somewhat, rather
Knee-high to a grasshopper = someone or something is short
Knee-deep = a bull frog
Knock a tater in the head = Let's go eat
Knows'll = knows will
Knowed = past tense of know
Laid up = sick, hurt, bedridden
Latch = lock, close
Lay down = to give up or surrender
Leastways = at least, at any rate
Leave things in the floor = leave things on the floor
Lemme' = let me
Lessen = unless
Let on = pretend
Lie down with dogs and you'll get up with fleas = bad pals will rub off on you
Like it or lump it = deal with it
Lil' = little
Lipping full = filled to capacity
A little birdie tole me = Juicy gossip that you don't

want to share who told
Lookie = look
Lookie here = Look here
Lookin' like the hind wheels o' destruction = You look terrible
Looks to me like = I agree
Lotta = lot of
Ma = my
Makin' a mountain outta molehill = exaggerating
Mayhap = perhaps and maybe
Meaner 'n a wet hen = making someone really mean or meaner.
On the Mend = to improve in health
Mess = enough food for your family
Might could = it's a possibility
Mighty = very, especially, exceedingly
Mill over = to study or ponder
Mind = to watch or attend
Mite = little
Mizzle = fine misty rain
Mock = imitate
More'n = more than
Mushmelon = cantaloupe
N'er = never
Nary = none, not one
Naw = no
Near about = nearly
Never get yer horse in a place where ya cain't turn 'round = don't do something you'll regret later
Never mind = makes no difference
No bigger 'n a minnow in a fishin' pond = not very important.
No count = of little value
No how = in any case
Not shore = not sure or Shore = sure

Notion = inclination
Now that's the pot callin' the kettle black = don't criticize someone for something you do
Now y'all don't be bad-mouthin' her = Don't talk about her in a mean way.
Of a mind to = to decide to do something
Offer = To try
Offish = quiet, unfriendly, hard to get to know
Ole = familiar with somethin', an attachment.
Oh, my country alive = an expression of unbelief
Old as methusaleh's housecat = pretty old
Oodlins = a large amount
Ornery = hard to deal with or get along with
Outlander = a stranger; outsider
Paper Poke = a bag to carry groceries
Pick = to play a stringed instrument
Pick'n' grin'n = A party with stringed instruments
Piddlin' = dawdling, wasting time doing something
Pig in a poke = not having all the information about what's about to happen
Pinch = small amount in cooking
Pitch a fit = to become uncontrollably upset
Plumb foolish = stupid (Plumb added to a word = completely)
Plumb give out = exhausted
Plumb tickled = pleased to hear
Plumb wore out = tired
Point blank = exact; precise
Pot callin' the kettle black = accusing someone of something you're guilt of
Pole cat = skunk
Pray'r = prayer
Prouda = proud
Puny = sick or sickly feeling
Quit piddlin' around and get ta work

R'call = recall
R'member = remember (In a command, you always say r'member)
Racket = a noisy fight, a sudden loud occurrence
Ragler = regular
Rare up = to raise up
Reach me a = hand me a
Recollect = remember to do something
Reckon = suppose
Rern = ruin. Past tense: rernt
Resternt = restaurant
Right quick = quickly
Right smart = pretty good amount
Righter'n rain = You did that correctly
Rightly = correctly
Riled up = angry
Ruckus = a commotion
Ruination = total destruction
Run together = spend time together
Salat = salad
Ser'ous = serious
Settin's cheaper'n standin' = sit down and rest yourself
She's as pretty as a peach = she's pretty and sweet
Shine = to like
Shiny britches = dress pants
Shivaree = a loud noisy celebration occurring after a wedding
Sight = a large amount
Sigogglin = not built correctly, skewed or out of balance
Silly ole' me = I should have known better
Sit with me a spell = sit with another typically for conversation
Skedaddle = leave immediately

Skeered = scared
Skift = A dusting of snow
Sleep tight, don't let the bed bug's bite = can lids filled with oil were placed under each bed post to discourage "bed bugs" – this was a hint that it was time to leave.
Slew = a large amount
Slip off = ran away and got married
Slower than a Sunday afternoon = slow
Smack = to chew loudly on food
Smidgen = small amount in cooking
Sorry = worthless
Stout = physical strong
Stove up = hurt, arthritis
Sweet milk = regular milk (as opposed to buttermilk)
Sweet on = you like someone
Swipe off = to wipe off
T'know = to know
Ta = to
Take after = to inherit qualities from someone
Talkingest = talkative
Tell a man what fer = tell him off
Thar' = there
Thar's a fox in the hen house = someone is somewhere they don't need to be
That dog don't hunt = the story doesn't add up
That possum's on the stump = that's as good as it gets
Thataway = that way
Them polecats are from my neck of the woods =
Thick = dense, numerous, plentiful
Thick as fleas on a dog's back = Where there is a lot of something- such as a crowd
Til the cows come home
Toboggan = snug wool cap- like a beanie

Tole' = told	
Too big fer his britches = conceited, self-important	
Tore up about it = upset	
Torn up = something is broken	
Tote it in the house = carry it in the house	
Upscuddle = A quarrel	
Ustocould = past tense of could	
Varmint = a wild animal	
Ver' = very	
Wanna = Want to	
Want'cha = want you	
Warsh = wash	
Warshed = washed	
Was you born in a barn? = shut the door or you don't have manners.	
Ways = a distance	
Worter = water	
We just live right 'round the bend = we live around the corner	
Weddin' without courtin' is like vittles without salt = salt seasons food just as courting prepares for and seasons a marriage.	
Well, I'll be = surprise or astonishment	
Well, it's six of one, half dozen of the other = no difference between two choices	
Whaddya' = What do you.	
What can't be cured must be endured = Be patient and endure	
Give someone what fer = Going to tell them just what you think	
What's got yer bee in a bonnet = someone who is agitated about something	
Whatch'all = what are y'all	
Whatcha' = What are you	
Where thar's bees thar's honey = something

attractive to a person or group
Whoo-wee = astonished
Whoo-wee doggee = astonished
Whoop and a holler = a short distance
Winder = window
Windshaken = a crack or twisted grain in timber, produced by high wind
Woulda = would have
Ya = You
Y'all = You all
Y'all come back now, ya hear? = Come back soon
Yassir = yes sir
Yer = Your
Yer not from 'round these parts are ya? = You're not from around here, are you?
Yer slower than molasses = slow
Yonder = Over there
You favor yer Momma = You look like your mom
You'ns = You all
You'ns ain't seen me in a coon's age = You haven't seen me in a long while
Young'un(s) = One or Multiple young people
Younger'n = younger than

<u>Many thanks to:</u>

Backroads Living
Blind Pig & the Acorn
Directory of Smoky Mountain English
Dancing on Mountaintops
These Storied Mountains – John Parris
Three Ladies and their Babies
And many more who lovingly share the beautiful Appalachian culture.

<h1 style="text-align:center">Acknowledgments</h1>

Thank you to my Heavenly Father for pouring Your Word into me and giving me a deep desire to serve you. May You be glorified by this work.

To my amazing husband, Tony. When the Lord laid this daunting task on my heart, I had no idea where to begin. You encouraged me through your excitement. You led me to people and places that would help me on my journey. I am so grateful for your support my Love!

Mom, thank you for loving us always. I am eternally grateful for the life you gave and the love you taught. Thank you for sharing with us your love of reading.

To my Grandmomma and Granny, thank you both for being my Grammy! Your love and consistent faith have helped me on my journey. I am forever grateful for your prayers over my life.

To my sisters, Jennifer, Patricia, Amanda, and Beth, thank you for helping me to become a better sister.

Thank you, Lauren, for helping me to sort out my jumbled thoughts and make them legible. Thank you for being a prayer warrior and an encouragement master. You never let me quit and for that, I am eternally grateful. Now go write that story!

Thank you, Natalie, for dotting my I's and crossing my T's. You make me better.

Derik, you unlocked the zeal for God's Word within me that I never knew I had. You had no idea that as you taught my girls, you were teaching me. God has changed my life through His word. I thank you for allowing Him to work through you.

Dave, thank you for leading students so well. Your intentionality makes others feel seen. We are eternally blessed through your shepherding heart.

To my Flourish girls, thank you for saying yes. You have forever marked me with your love for the Lord. Thank you for allowing me to be part of your journey.

To every young woman who has allowed me the honor of walking alongside you, thank you. You have blessed me in your journey. Keep the faith, Beautiful, and run your race knowing that God is with you always.

Nelum, thank you for your yes to Jesus! I am so thankful for your servant's heart and for all that God does through you. It is an honor to serve alongside you, my sister!

To the Merchants, thank you for your selfless service to our community. I am so grateful for your love for Jesus and how well you love those He places in your path. It is an honor to walk alongside you on this journey my friends!

Olha, thank you for your beautiful photography! You have a beautiful eye for God's creation- may the Lord bless you and keep you always. You can find Olha and her journey at @life.by.olia on Instagram and YouTube.

Rachel, you are a world changer, my friend! Thank you for shining the light of Jesus everywhere you go.

Thank you to my launch team! You have inspired me more than you know.

Thank you to the many who publicly share the life and speech of our Appalachian neighbors. And a special thank you to @CelebratingAppalachia for sharing the love of your culture so well. Your heritage is rich and beautiful my friends!

Thank you to the people in the Western North Carolina and Tennessee regions who showed so much strength and love for community after Hurricane Helene. I am forever encouraged by your love for one another and the character you exemplified as you navigated your own fiery furnace.

Thank you to King Radios for radio jargon.

Thank you to Morse Code Converter and Morsecode.world for teaching the world morse code.

Thank you to Lil' Troyer Farm @liltroyerfarm for sharing your beautiful story of Breeze and Jitterbug.

Thank you to every reader who joined me on this journey. I hope you loved it as much as I did. If so, please take a moment to post a review and tell a friend.

Thank you to Creative Fabrica and designer genesislabstudio for the beautiful Malibu Script Font used under license for the book and chapter titles.

I love feedback! You can submit feedback and suggestions directly to me on my website at https://evemharrell.com.

<u>**Additional works from Eve M. Harrell**</u>

Confessions:
A Mom's Journey from Hovering to Hope

Hello Beautiful:
See Yourself Through the Father's Eyes

Hello Beautiful:
Companion Journal

Running with Zebras:
A Daughter's Journey Through the Fire

Revealed Book Series™
Book 1 – Revealed Truth: A Journey from Fear to Faith
Book 2 – Revealed Mercy: A Journey to the Tower of Trust
Book 3 – Revealed Courage: A Journey Forged Through Fire
Book 4 – Revealed Hope: A Journey For Such a Time as This

Revealed: A Journey Through Prayer Journal
Revealed Pocket Journal
Living Revealed: A Discipleship Journey

IN ADDITION TO ALL THIS, TAKE UP THE
SHIELD OF FAITH, WITH WHICH YOU CAN
EXTINGUISH ALL THE FLAMING ARROWS OF
THE EVIL ONE. TAKE THE HELMET OF
SALVATION AND THE SWORD OF THE SPIRIT,
WHICH IS THE WORD OF GOD.
EPHESIANS 6:16-17

About The Author

Eve Harrell and her husband, Tony serve their local church as Small Group Leaders to some amazing future leaders. In addition to serving students and their leaders, Eve encourages women of all ages to rest in the love of their Heavenly Father.

Singing, blogging, speaking, writing, spending time in nature, and watching others find freedom in Christ are some of Eve's favorite things.

Eve's passion includes encouraging the next generation to recognize the great value, purpose, and strength they have been given while finding the Father's little gifts along the way.

You can connect with her at https://evemharrell.com.